# The Collected Supernatural and Weird Fiction of Rhoda Broughton

# The Collected Supernatural and Weird Fiction of Rhoda Broughton

Twelve Short Stories of the Strange and Unusual Including 'The Man with the Nose', 'Across the Threshold', 'Betty's Visions', 'Was She Mad?', 'Mrs. Smith of Longmains', and 'His Serene Highness'

Rhoda Broughton

LEONAUR

*The Collected*
*Supernatural and Weird*
*Fiction of*
*Rhoda Broughton*
*Twelve Short Stories of the Strange and Unusual Including 'The Man with the Nose',*
*'Across the Threshold', 'Betty's Visions', 'Was She Mad?', 'Mrs. Smith of Longmains',*
*and 'His Serene Highness'*
by Rhoda Broughton

Leonaur is an imprint of Oakpast Ltd

Copyright in this form © 2025 Oakpast Ltd

ISBN: 978-1-971666-40-4 (hardcover)
ISBN: 978-1-971666-41-1 (softcover)

**http://www.leonaur.com**

# Contents

# Across the Threshold

"We have not seen anything of the Bells for a long time." This remark was addressed by Mrs. —— to her daughter—an only one—at the breakfast table on a winter morning not a great many years ago. Mrs. —— was, and indeed is, the wife of the great mad doctor, Dr. ——, which illustrious functionary sat facing her behind a couple of hot breakfast dishes. The only reason why her observation was not addressed to him in preference to the girl was that she knew, by a quarter of a century's experience, that—excellent husband in all other respects—he never answered, or ever heard, any speech made to him while his bald head was between the sheets of his morning's paper. Miss ——'s mind being more disengaged, she answered at once: —

"Not for ages."

"Considering what intimate friends we are, we meet very rarely."

"Very."

"I do not even know whether they are back from Scotland yet."

"Well, on that point I can enlighten you; when I was in D—— yesterday, I passed down King-Street, and their house looked all alive; if it had not been so late, I should have gone in." Mrs. ——'s eyes rested thoughtfully on the private garden of the doctor's house, a very nicely laid out and roomy plat, from which when the trees were bare, there was not at all a bad view of the lunatics' asphalt tennis court immediately contiguous to it. The hour was too early for any lunatics to be as yet engaged in that healthy exercise, and Mrs. ——'s look returned to her child.

"I would ask the girls to luncheon on Wednesday, only that it would be pitch dark before they could get home again. You may call it eight miles, but I always think it the longest eight-and-a-half I know, from here to D——."

"Pooh!" (disrespectfully) "if it were dark what would they care? That little old pony of theirs knows every step of the way, and could find it blindfold."

"It turns so bitterly cold as soon as the sun is set."

"They never feel the cold, they are as hard as nails."

"As hard as nails! What a pretty expression to apply to young ladies!"

"Well, there can't be anything harder than nails, can there?" (Laughter).

"I should scarcely like to propose it. If they caught a chill Mrs. Bell would lay the blame on us. And fond as I am of her, I must own I do not know a fussier woman about her children's health."

"They will not catch a chill; father, will Peggy and Caroline Bell die of it if they drive over to luncheon here on Wednesday?"

"It is not the least use your asking him! he does not hear a word you say."

"He shall hear me," with the half petulant, humorous tyranny of an only child; "father!" raising her voice, "I am asking you for a professional opinion, will it do Peggy and Caroline Bell any harm to drive over here to luncheon?"

Thus, authoritatively adjured, and further aroused by his daughter's hand jogging his elbow, the doctor suddenly dropped his *pince-nez* from his nose; and answered:—

"Do them any harm? what harm should mischief do to them if they wrap up a little, they are as hard——"

"As nails," interrupted Miss ——, finishing her parent's sentence, then with a glance of triumph at her mother: "You see where I get my metaphor from. Will you write to them, or shall I?"

The acceptation of the invitation when sent was accompanied with much less hesitation than the invitation itself had been. The Misses Bell, two lively athletic girls of the normal British type, always glad of an excuse for an outing of any size or shape, and in this case really pleased at the prospect of a renewal of intercourse with one of their most favourite families of friends, set out in their little yellow cart on the appointed day, and with their good pony new clipped and full of beans, did the distance in forty minutes—a circumstance which added to the elasticity of spirits that marked their arrival.

The pleasure of the friends in meeting again after an interval of some months was reciprocal and the general cheerfulness was heightened by the entrance of the doctor himself, with whom both the young ladies had long professed themselves to be deeply in love. It is true that that entrance did not take place till luncheon was almost half over, and that at first the host did not seem to be up to his usual mark in spirits. But the joint influence of a couple of glasses of his own excellent sherry and of the sprightly looks and challenging jests of his young visitors, soon brought up his conversation to its wonted level of cheerful persiflage, and the buzz of talk was so loud and the topics so gaily absorbing that it was not till the servants had brought in coffee that the little assembly became conscious by the difficulty of seeing the lumps of sugar in the small silver basin, of what an unusual darkness for the time of day had overspread the sky.

"This *is* Blind Man's holiday!" exclaimed the elder Miss Bell, pouring the cream—she was misguided enough to drink cream with black coffee—into her saucer instead of her cup.

"Turn on the electric light," ordered the doctor.

"This is really past a joke," cried the doctor's wife," it is only ten minutes to three! One might as well be in London—ah!" looking towards the garden, "there comes the snow."

"I thought something odd was going to happen," added the daughter, her eye following the direction of her mother's, "the recording barometer has taken such a jump down since last night."

"It is beginning with a will," said the host, walking towards the now obscured window; "we are in for a heavy fall."

"And the ground is so hard that it will lie." They had all risen and followed the master of the house, and now stood staring out in silence at the furious flurry of flakes that occupied the whole air, which had grown so dark, that it was only by reason of the snow's whiteness that it was seen at all. It was one of those occasions when the elements had thoroughly got the better of the man. The sight—if that could be called a sight which was scarcely visible—was so phenomenal that for some moments it occupied the whole attention of the party; but after a few minutes the voice of the younger and least valiant of the guests was raised in lamentable appeal to her sister.

"How shall we get home?"

"We had better set off at once, as soon as the pony can be put in," replied the more decided senior.

"Mrs. —— may I ring and tell them to bring the cart round?"

But the proposal (which in the face of the weather was indeed almost maniacal enough to have issued from the walls of the adjoining institution) was negatived so decisively by the whole family, and most authoritatively of all by its head, that its author was compelled to modify it by a consent to wait half an hour, on the chance of an improvement in the aspect of affairs. At the end of the half hour no such improvement had taken place; and at the end of a second half hour not only had the storm greatly increased in violence, a strong wind having uprisen, but the abnormal darkness had been deepened and intensified by the natural waning of the light. Under these circumstances a family, much less hospitable than that of the mad doctor's, would have changed their request to the visitors to delay their departure into an urgent invitation to spend the night under the safe shelter of their roof, instead of braving the rage of a tempest as fierce as that which broke over King Lear's dishonoured head.

And in point of fact, nothing could be heartier and more warmly urged than the entreaties of father, mother, and daughter. Upon the younger of the Misses Bell these entreaties were far from being without effect. She would willingly have yielded to them had not her sister offered a resistance as obstinate as it was apparently senseless to the hospitable tenders made her, parrying each objection with a resolved and almost fevered brevity of refusal.

"You have no lamp?"

"I can borrow some from your stable."

"They would not be of the slightest use; in the snow you could not see them half a yard off."

"Puck knows every inch of the way; he could find it blindfold. And——" catching eagerly at what on the first blush might seem a sounder reason, for her headstrong determination—"my mother will be so nervous about us if we do not get home in good time."

"If you set off now you will probably never get home at all, and as to your mother you know we have a telegraph office in the asylum, and I can send her a wire at once, to tell her that we are keeping you."

Silenced but not convinced the girl stood still, looking out upon the winter night now fully fallen, though the afternoon was yet young; her objections all met and answered, but with her mysterious repugnance to adopting the one rational course evidently not in the least abated.

"Why will not you say yes?" asked Mrs. ——, who is a kind motherly soul, "we are quite hurt that you are so loth to give us a few more hours of your company, and yet we are not half talked out yet."

"I believe," exclaimed Miss ——, "that the truth is she is afraid to spend a night in a mad-house! Ah!"—crying out as one that had made a discovery; since something in Miss Bell's face told her that she had hit the right nail on the head—"that is it!"

"Is that really possible?" asked the doctor, in a tone of grave surprise. "My dear Miss Peggy, I have too good an opinion of your sense to credit such an accusation."

"Indeed, you need not be afraid of them," added his wife, eagerly. "This house is quite shut off from them. We never even hear a sound of them, and as to their getting at you——"

"Even from your point of view, you would be safer here than anywhere else just now," said Miss —— seriously, "for it happens one of them escaped last night, and——" she stopped abruptly, arrested in the indiscreet confidence by a displeased glance from her father.

"One of them escaped!," repeated Miss Bell, slowly, and with blanching lips, and though it soon became clear that she would get no further information on the subject from any member of the doctor's family, the idea of an enfranchised maniac lurking possibly behind snowy hedge or blind wall to pounce out upon her and her sister on their lonely homeward drive did what the prayers and reasonings of her friends had been powerless to effect. Without any further resistance she consented to submit to the exigencies of fate and weather and remain at the Lunatic Asylum till the next morning.

The evening passed pleasantly enough, the banging of the tempest outside against the well-shuttered windows serving only to emphasise the contrast of the warm luxury within. The doctor—a fact which his family pointed out to the guests as an unwonted compliment to them—spent the whole evening in the little circle, enlivening them with his easy cheerfulness, and now and again interesting them by brief excursions into more serious themes, connected in some degree with the experiences of his professional life.

Once or twice, it is true, he was interrupted in the middle of an anecdote or a phrase by a summons to speak with some person or persons unknown, whose names were communicated in an undertone to his master alone by the butler; and on all these occasions the visitors saw or fancied a slight cloud on his brow when he returned. The hour of bedtime—a moderately early one—had arrived, and Mrs. —— volunteered to show her two young visitors to their room. It was their first introduction to it, as at the hour of dinner it had still been in course of preparation for them, and they had made such brief toilet as their want of a change of raiment allowed in Miss ——'s sleeping chamber.

As she bid her friends goodnight the elder Miss Bell took occasion to ask her, in a nervous whisper, whether it were really true that one of the patients had lately escaped? Miss ——, casting a hasty glance behind her, to assure herself that her father was not within hearing, nodded a reluctant assent, adding eagerly, "I am sure it is not due to any neglect; they are most carefully looked after, but you have no notion how cunning they are. This one squeezed himself through a hole where you would not have thought there was room for a starved cat to pass."

"And he has not been recaptured? He is still at large?"

Again, the daughter of the head of the asylum made a sound of unwilling assent, immediately followed by the eager assurance:—

"They are sure to find him; father has sent out warders in every direction, and the police are scouring the country besides; it was the inspector whom father went out to speak to just now."

Then as the visitors still looked uncomfortable, she added, with emphasis—

"He is certain to be brought back in the course of a day or two; they all are; very likely he will come back of his own accord. Poor wretch; I am sure I hope so. What he must be suffering, exposed to such weather as this!" as the hurricane, in a fresh access of ungovernable fury, made even the substantially built walls rock.

"Is he a young man or an old one?"

"Not young! That is what made his activity so doubly astonishing, but"—with a rallying laugh—"it is quite a revelation to me that you are such a coward. I thought you were a paladin of valour. Is not it true that you once knocked down a cabman in Paris who was impertinent to you?"

"I am not afraid of anything I can knock down, but one could not knock down a lunatic. They are so frightfully strong. Well, there, I can't help it, and it is no use arguing about it, but I am inexpressibly afraid of anyone who has lost their wits."

This colloquy, not very satisfactory to either party, was ended by Mrs. —— calling to her daughter to stop chattering, and let her friends go to bed. The friends in question bid the young girl thereupon a hasty goodnight, and followed their hostess. To their not altogether pleasant surprise, they found their guide turning away from that part of the house occupied by the family, and passing through a swing door, which gave access to a long passage with doors on each side of it.

"We are not going to be near you, then?" said Caroline Bell, in a rather faltering voice.

"Not very."

"Do any of the—the patients sleep in those rooms?" indicating the doors before mentioned.

"Oh, dear no," with a shade of impatience. "As we assured you before, we are entirely shut off and separated from the asylum—as completely as you could be at D——"

"Then"—hesitating—"does anyone sleep in those rooms?"

"They are almost all spare rooms. My husband's predecessor had a large family, and built this wing for nurseries and schoolrooms; but as we are such a small party, we keep it for friends." Nothing could be plainer or with less of the alarming or mysterious than this explanation. It would have savoured of ill breeding to try the hostess' patience by any further enquiries; and so, after replying suitably to her hospitable hope that they would sleep well and ask for anything they wanted, they saw her depart. No sooner was her back turned than both—the escaped lunatic being, despite all reassurances, a good deal on their minds—began an exhaustive examination of the apartment.

"It is rather a mockery to bid us ask for anything we want when there is no bell," said Peggy, reconnoitring the wall.

"Ah! There was evidently one of the old-fashioned bell-pulls, and it has come down and not been replaced."

"What is far worse than there being no bell there are no matches," ejaculated Caroline, coming back to the fire from an excursion round the hastily, and as now appeared carelessly, prepared apartment.

"And what is worst of all," cried Peggy, from the door whose handle she was distractedly rattling; "there is no bolt and the lock is out of order!"

"How truly awful," said Caroline, now fully infected with her sister's terrors; "and there is no earthly reason why that unfortunate escaped madman may not be hiding in one of those empty rooms."

"And we have absolutely no means of keeping him out!"

They looked at one another, the eyes of each large with apprehension. Peggy, being always the most fertile in resource, was the first to recover the use of her common sense. Her looks wandering round in search of weapons against their joint peril alit upon an old-fashioned box-couch, the seat of which when raised, disclosed a receptacle where some former maid or matron of the family had kept her clothes. It was a heavy, solid, well-stuffed old piece of furniture, and the idea instantly flashed upon Miss Bell's mind that it might be used as a barricade. This notion was at once imparted to her sister, and without any delay both girls employed their muscles, hardened by continual use of oars and tennis bats, in rolling the ponderous mahogany settle up against the otherwise undefended door. The effort which it cost them to effect this gave them the consolation of knowing that at least so serious an obstacle to entrance would not be mastered without their being awakened in time to be made aware of the fact.

"As to there being no matches," Peggy said, when they had completed their defence, "we must make up as good a fire as we can—at least there is plenty of coal—and stack it up with small coal and hot ashes, and whichever of us wakes first in the night—no doubt" (gloomily) "we shall both wake often enough, must replenish it."

Having made these dispositions, they were preparing to get into bed, when the younger sister asked in a cautiously lowered voice—

"Have you looked under the bed? Do you remember that terrible story by Dickens', of the maniac who came out from under the bed, covered with hair and clinking chains?"

"For heaven's sake, do not remind me of it now?" cried the elder precipitately, and then they both dropped on their knees and explored the recesses under the large double bed, extending their scrutiny afterwards impartially to every possible and impossible article of furniture. But no lunatic lurked even in one of the little drawers of the washhanstand; and so, with a couple of sighs of comparative relief, they at length really did retire for the night, and their youth, the pinching cold of the night, and their morning drive through the cold air, prevailing even over their terrors, they soon fell asleep. Both were awakened at the same instant, with the same start, and by the same noise.

"What is that?" asked Caroline, in a voice betwixt sleep and wake.

"It is only the chiming clock of the Asylum Chapel. Someone, who had a mad husband here, gave it to them; it plays a tune once every three hours! Listen! it is '*Home, Sweet Home.*'"

"I am sure I wish we were at '*Home, Sweet Home,*'" rejoined Caroline, reassured and half-laughing. "What a fright it gave me! How my heart is beating! Is not yours?"

"What time is that striking? One, two, three, four, five, six, seven, eight, nine, ten, eleven, twelve! Dear me! only twelve! I should have thought it had been much later, though, to be sure, one might have told by the fire being so good still that it was not."

These words were scarcely out of Peggy's mouth when her sister broke into her speech with an alarmed whisper.

"Hush! What was that? Did you hear another noise—quite a different one?"

Both listen.

"It was only your imagination," irritably. "I wish you would not be so fanci——."

The word broke off in the middle, for the speaker's ear had caught the same sound as had her sister's. It was a very trifling sound but there was no doubt about it. It sprang apparently from a footfall at the far end of the passage outside their door. It was not the step of a person walking along naturally on some confessed and open errand; as indeed, what should bring anyone to that isolated part of the house at night?

To the ears of the listeners, it seemed beyond doubt that it was a stealthy step that sought not to be overheard; with something slow, and strange, and shuffling about it. Slow as it was it came nearer and nearer. It had, judging from the sound, reached their door.

"He has stopped!" said one of the suffocated girls to the other, in a strangled whisper.

On neither of their minds did there rest the shadow of a doubt that this surreptitious visitor was the runaway patient, who had concealed himself in one of the empty bedrooms opening on the passage; and now re-assured by the stillness of the slumbering house had issued forth. It was quite true he had stopped; not only stopped but was trying the door. By the firelight they could see the handle turn.

Apparently baffled by the resistance offered by the barricading box-sofa, their unseen assailant paused, no doubt to pull himself together for that thrust whose maniacal strength would send the obstacle so futilely built up by them flying into the middle of the room, leaving them an absolutely defenceless prey to his insane rage, irritated probably to frenzy by the opposition. Both had sat up in bed, and with eyes starting out of their heads and ears strained almost to bursting, waited in a dreadful silence, broken after a moment or two by an exchange of anguished whispers.

"What shall we do?"

"Shall we hide under the bed?"

"He would pull us out."

"Can we get out of the window?"

"It is shuttered."

"Shall we try to get hold of the fireirons?"

"No, no, the least noise would rouse him!"

The words were scarcely out of Miss Bell's mouth, when instead of the expected thrust against the door, a voice—a thin, husky voice—

was heard piping through the keyhole. Both girls were listening so intently that—faint as the utterance was—not a syllable was lost upon them.

"I—cannot—lie—there! I—must—lie here! I—am—dead! I—am—buried!"

Then silence, perfect silence. The listeners even then were incapable of exchanging even a whisper. In the excess of their terror at the obvious confirmation of the lunacy of their visitor contained in the words they had overheard, petrified by fear, expecting every moment to see their defences give way, yielding to a momentary expected push, they sat for what seemed to them to be hours, but what they learnt to have been only a quarter of an hour, by the stroke of the clock that had originally awaked them, and had announced the first fifteen minutes after midnight. The sound had scarcely died away, when again the ghostly piping voice outside became audible.

"I—cannot—lie—there! I—must—lie here! I—am—dead! I—am—buried!"

The words were identical with those before uttered, but in this case they were followed by an inarticulate sound, which might be a sigh or a groan; and by the noise as of some heavy object falling or throwing itself on the floor. There could be no doubt that the madman had stretched himself across their threshold. What would be his next move? It seemed incredible that he would make no further effort to effect an entrance. And yet, as the time went on, as the leaden footed minutes stole one by one past the paralysed watchers, cramped with keeping one position so long, yet not daring to move, stole past bringing no tidings of fresh speech or movement from outside, the idea occurred to the trembling girls that the madman might have fallen asleep.

That his slumber might be prolonged till morning could bring help and rescue to them was their passionate prayer; a prayer that as the talkative chapel clock told them of the march past the eerie hours of the night, seemed more and more likely to be granted. At length—oh, what a long length that seemed!—at about six o'clock, to their inexpressible relief, they heard the sound of the swing door opening, of several feet coming down the passage, and of two or three voices talking in subdued tones.

"It must be the warders who have traced him here!" said Peggy, finding voice, for the first time for several hours, and speaking with a quivering accent as of one reprieved at the gallow's foot.

"Oh, I hope there are plenty of them! He is sure to resist desperately."

"I have a good mind to peep out; shall I?"

"Oh, do not, do not; he might spring upon us before they could stop him."

Again, they listened. The voices and feet had obviously, like the lunatic, paused outside their door. Exclamations of a smothered sort, and expressions of what the listeners could not exactly determine were audible, but to the surprise of the two girls no tones at all resembling the uncanny ones they had heard at midnight could be distinguished.

"He is evidently letting them take him quite quietly without making any resistance."

"Do you think it possible he could have stolen away without our hearing him?"

"Quite out of the question. Why, what odd noises they are making! What can they be doing with him? They must be carrying him off! And how is it that he does not utter a sound? Do you think they can have gagged him?"

"I cannot imagine. Their tread does sound strangely heavy. Well, thank God! we are safe now. What a dreadful night, and how tired I am!" flinging herself on her pillow. A couple of hours later a housemaid, tired of knocking and pushing, at length succeeded in waking the exhausted guests, and induced them to drag themselves out of bed, and remove their no longer needed bulwark from the door. The maidservant looked white and flurried.

"Whatever did you do that for, miss?" she enquired, with an astonished glance at the piece of furniture thus diverted from its natural use. Her tone was so reproachful that the elder Miss Bell replied hastily that it was in consequence of there being no lock on the door; but the girl for some reason seemed to think the explanation an insufficient one, and continued to regard them, as they felt, with a pale and upset air while arranging their baths. The family's breakfast hour was nine, and as the guests knew that the doctor was the soul of punctuality they hastened over their toilets, despite the temptation which their feeling of fatigue and the desire to talk over their adventure held out to them to dawdle.

But, on the other hand, the eager wish to tell of their perils and to hear the explanation of their rescue gave a more than usual alacrity to their movements; so that, with only one glance of curiosity, that was still a trembling one, at the door mat across which their visitor had been extended, and one at the doors of the corridor, to see, by its being ajar, which was the one that had given egress to him, they hurried into the breakfast room before the last stroke of the hour had chimed upon the frosty air. It was empty, and although in a few moments the butler, who had caught his master's virtue, brought in the breakfast, yet the kettle had been spitting and blowing over its spirit lamp, and the hot dishes sitting with their hats on for a good quarter of an hour before the family appeared.

"They cannot all be putting on the strait waistcoat!" said Caroline, in a low voice to her sister.

"Mrs —— and Lily have never anything to do with the patients. What can have become of *them?*"

The ladies alluded to answered their expressions of wonder by entering at that moment, and the doctor followed hard upon them. But was it the doctor? Was it the doctor's wife. Was it the doctor's daughter of yesterday?

Preoccupied as were the Misses Bell by their experiences of the past night, and bursting into eagerness to impart them, they could not fail to perceive the change that had come over their hosts since they had parted from them on the previous evening. An unmistakable cloud of gloom rested on each and all of the habitually cheerful faces of the ———— family; and the doctor met them without the smallest approach to that friendly jesting which usually marked his greeting. They were so taken aback by this unexpected metamorphosis that— full as they were of their own adventure, they felt at once that for some mysterious reason it was impossible, for the moment, to introduce the subject.

They all sat down to the table in constrained silence; the host with mechanical hospitality offering his visitors the contents of the dishes before him, and then absently helping himself, Mrs. —— had by a motion of the head intimated the uselessness of offering *her* anything. The daughter ate her breakfast with a rather furtive air, as if ashamed of having any appetite! The meal had proceeded for some time in this gloomy fashion when Peggy Bell, unable any longer to bear the oppression of the unexplained dullness that had fallen upon the party; and considering that it had probably no connection with the incidents of the night, resolved to break the spell of silence by a narrative of her own and her sister's alarms, and began rather abruptly.

"We had such an adventure last night."

Nobody made any comment upon this opening; somewhat to the

narrator's surprise; and she proceeded.

"Someone came to our door at twelve o'clock and tried to get in."

Still—how odd—no comment, but a sort of rustling movement from behind the tea kettle showed that the communication had made the hostess give a sort of start.

"Whoever it was, turned the handle of the door, but could not get in, because we had dragged the sofa up against the door, as it would not lock."

"Yes?" The doctor's voice unquestionably sounded oddly, and he had put on his *pince-nez,* the better to see the speaker. Miss Lily had dropped her bit of toast.

"When he found he could not get in, he said something through the keyhole, in such a queer voice, as if—with a hesitation, born of fear of giving offence—he was not in his right mind."

"Oh, he was as mad as a hatter," put in Caroline, eagerly. "That was what terrified us so. There was no sense in what he said. We heard it quite distinctly. What where the exact words, Peggy?"

"I cannot lie there; I must lie here; I am dead! I am buried!" replied the elder sister, endeavouring to give as nearly as possible the quavering piping quality of the utterance.

"He said it twice," added Caroline, "with just a quarter of an hour between, and after the last time he gave a sort of grunt and seemed to throw himself or fall down right across the threshold, and we heard no more of him; but oh, how fright——" She stopped abruptly with the half-finished word upon her lips, for Mrs. —— had risen suddenly from the table; and with a scarcely stifled sob had hurried out of the room. Her daughter hastened after her and the doctor, with a smothered ejaculation of concern followed them. The guests were left staring at each other in consternation.

"What has come to them all?" asked the elder, in a tone of blank dismay.

"Something dreadful has evidently happened," replied the other.

"Perhaps he murdered somebody before he came to us—a warder, probably?"

"Or perhaps he has escaped again?"

They had time to indulge in many other conjectures, with less or more of probability about them, as for a considerable period they remained in undisturbed possession of the breakfast room and the cooling viands. Uncertain whether to leave the room or wait the return of the family, they sat in a state of thorough discomfort of mind; but at length the door, greatly to their relief, opened, and gave an admittance to their host. A cloud still lay on his brow, but he came up to them with more of the heartiness of his usual manner than before.

"My dear girls," he said, taking a hand of each, "I do not know what you will think of us; we owe you a thousand apologies; but I am sure your kind hearts will forgive us when I tell you of the very painful event that has happened."

He paused; but seeing the eager expectation in the eyes of his two auditors proceeded.

"You no doubt did not know—for it was a subject that there was no reason for speaking of—that my wife's father, who has long been in a state of imbecility—he was 82 years old—has lived here for many years, and has occupied some of the rooms in that corridor out of which yours opened."

The doctor paused, as if approaching a disagreeable theme.

"Last night, I grieve to say, the nurse in charge of him, a person in whom I had the most absolute confidence, got helplessly drunk, and the poor old man, in the absence of all control, got out of bed and rambled—we had no idea that he would have been capable of such an exertion—to your door."

The two girls, who had been listening breathlessly, with their mouths open, here gave utterance to an exclamation of horror, but their host, making a sign to them not to interrupt him, went on:—

"The reason why he chose that door in particular, was that 20 years ago his wife, to whom he was passionately attached, died in your room, and in his weakened state of intellect, which, however, never impaired his memory of her, he imagined he should still find her there, where he had last seen her."

Again, the doctor halted, but this time he had no need to enjoin silence on his hearers. Dumbfounded and aghast at the entire upsetting of their preconceived theory, struck with horror at the consequences of their own cowardice, they awaited the denouncement with dilated eyes and blanched cheeks.

"The effort must have exhausted the little vitality left in him, for after he had given utterance to the sentence you overheard, he must have fallen down in a state of insensibility; the groan which frightened you so much"—(here a horrid reminiscence flashed across Caroline that she had characterised it as a grunt)—must have been his last sigh. He must have been dead some hours—he was quite cold when he was found at six o'clock this morning."

20

The story was ended. But not for some time was there any comment upon it forthcoming. Then one of the hearers said, almost in a whisper:—

"It was not the escaped lunatic then, not the runaway patient?"

"God bless you, no," returned the doctor with a burst of ill humour which seemed to do him good. "How the plague could it have been when he was brought back five minutes after you had left the drawing room? If you had not had that unlucky idea so firmly wedged in your mind, things might have terminated differently, the poor old gentleman might——"

He interrupted himself, remembering that however foolish their conduct had been, it was not quite kind to tell his young friends that they had been directly instrumental in his father-in-law's death. But though he did not finish his sentence they were very well able to do it for him in their own minds; and not long afterwards, without having been admitted to any farewell from their hostess, or her daughter, they set off, much crestfallen, for their home.

★★★★★★★★★★★★★★★★

Although it was represented to her by her husband, that her conduct was both irrational and unchristian, Mrs. —— could never be persuaded to invite the Misses Bell to luncheon at the Lunatic Asylum again.

# Behold, it was a Dream!

## CHAPTER 1

Yesterday morning I received the following letter:

> Weston House, Caulfield ——shire.
>
> My Dear Dinah—You must come: I scorn all your excuses, and see through their flimsiness. I have no doubt that you are much better amused in Dublin, frolicking round ball rooms with a succession of horse-soldiers, and watching Her Majesty's household troops play Polo in the Phoenix Park, but no matter—you *must* come. We have no particular inducements to hold out. We lead an exclusively bucolic, cow-milking, pig-fattening, roast-mutton-eating and to-bed-at-ten-o'clock-going life; but no matter—you *must* come. I want you to see how happy two dull elderly people may be, with no special brightness in their lot to make them so. My old man—he is surprisingly ugly at the first glance, but grows upon one afterwards—sends you his respects, and bids me say that he will meet you at any station on any day at any hour of the day or night. If you succeed in evading our persistence this time, you will be a cleverer woman than I take you for.
>
> Ever yours affectionately.
>
> Jane Watson.
>
> *August 15th.*
>
> P.S.—We will invite our little scarlet-headed curate to dinner to meet you, so as to soften *your fall from* the Society of the Plungers.

This is my answer:

> My Dear Jane,—Kill the fat calf in all haste, and put the bake meats into the oven, for I will come. Do not, however, imagine that I am moved thereunto by the prospect of the bright-

headed curate. Believe me, my dear, I am as yet at a distance of ten long good years from an addiction to the minor clergy. If I survive the crossing of that seething, heaving, tumbling abomination, St. George's Channel, you may expect me on Tuesday next. I have been groping for hours in 'Bradshaw's' darkness that may be felt, and I have arrived at length at this twilight result, that I may arrive at your station at 6.55 p.m. But the ways of 'Bradshaw' are not our ways, and I *may* either rush violently past or never attain it. If I do, and if on my arrival I see some rustic vehicle, guided by a startlingly ugly gentleman, awaiting me, I shall know from your wifely description that it is your 'old man.' Till Tuesday, then.

> Affectionately yours.

> Dinah Bellairs.

*August 17th.*

I am as good as my word; on Tuesday I set off. For four mortal hours and a half I am disastrously, hideously, diabolically sick. For four hours and a half I curse the day on which I was born, the day on which Jane Watson was born, the day on which her old man was born, and lastly—but oh! not, *not* leastly—the day and the dock on which and in which the *Leinster's* plunging, curtseying, throbbing body was born.

On arriving at Holyhead, feeling convinced from my sensations that, as the French say, I touch my last hour, I indistinctly request to be allowed to stay on board and *die*, then and there; but as the stewardess and my maid take a different view of my situation, and insist upon forcing my cloak and bonnet on my dying body and limp head, I at length succeed in staggering on deck and off the accursed boat.

I am then well shaken up for two or three hours in the Irish mail, and after crawling along a slow by-line for two or three hours more, am at length, at 6:55, landed, battered, tired, dust-blacked and qualmish, at the little roadside station of Caulfield. My maid and I are the only passengers who descend. The train snorts its slow way onwards, and I am left gazing at the calm crimson death of the August sun, and smelling the sweet peas in the station-master's garden border.

I look round in search of Jane's promised tax-cart, and steel my nerves for the contemplation of her old man's unlovely features. But the only vehicle which I see is a tiny two-wheeled pony carriage, drawn by a small and tub-shaped bay pony and driven by a lady in a hat, whose face is turned expectantly towards me. I go up and recognise my friend, whom I have not seen for two years—not since before she fell in with her old man and espoused him.

"I thought it safest, after all, to come myself," she says with a bright laugh. "My old man looked so handsome this morning, that I thought you would never recognise him from my description. Get in, dear, and let us trot home as quickly as we can."

I comply, and for the next half hour sit (while the cool evening wind is blowing the dust off my hot and jaded face) stealing amazed glances at my companion's cheery features. *Cheery!* That is the very last word that, excepting in an ironical sense, anyone would have applied to my friend Jane two years ago. Two years ago, Jane was thirty-five, the elderly eldest daughter of a large family, hustled into obscurity, jostled, shelved, by half a dozen younger, fresher sisters; an elderly girl addicted to lachrymose verse about the gone and the dead and the for-ever-lost.

Apparently the gone has come back, the dead resuscitated, the for-ever-lost been found again. The peaky sour virgin is transformed into a gracious matron with a kindly, comely face, pleasure making and pleasure feeling. Oh, Happiness, what powder, or paste, or milk of roses, can make old cheeks young again in the cunning way that you do? If you would but bide steadily with us, we might live for ever, always young and always handsome.

My musings on Jane's metamorphosis, combined with a tired headache, make me somewhat silent, and indeed there is mostly a slackness of conversation between the two dearest allies on first meeting after absence—a sort of hesitating shiver before plunging into the sea of talk that both know to lie in readiness for them.

"Have you got your harvest in yet?" I ask, more for the sake of not utterly holding my tongue than from any profound interest in the subject, as we jog briskly along between the yellow cornfields, where the dry bound sheaves are standing in golden rows in the red sunset light.

"Not yet," answers Jane; "we have only just begun to cut some of it. However, thank God, the weather looks as settled as possible; there is not a streak of watery lilac in the west."

My headache is almost gone and I am beginning to think kindly of dinner—a subject from which all day until now my mind has hastily turned with a sensation of hideous inward revolt—by the time that the fat pony pulls up before the old-world dark porch of a modest little house, which has bashfully hidden its original face under a veil of crowded clematis flowers and stalwart ivy. Set as in a picture-frame by the large drooped ivy-leaves, I see a tall and moderately hard-featured gentleman of middle age, perhaps, of the two, rather inclining towards elderly, smiling at us a little shyly.

"This is my old man," cries Jane, stepping gaily out, and giving him a friendly introductory pat on the shoulder. "Old man, this is Dinah."

Having thus been made known to each other we shake hands, but neither of us can arrive at anything pretty to say. Then I follow Jane into her little house, the little house for which she has so happily exchanged her tenth part of the large and noisy paternal mansion. It is an old house, and everything about it has the moderate shabbiness of old age and long and careful wear. Little thick-walled rooms, dark and cool, with flowers and flower scents lying in wait for you every-where—a silent, fragrant, childless house. To me, who have had oily locomotives snorting and racing through my head all day, its dumb sweetness seems like heaven.

"And now that we have, secured you, we do not mean to let you go in a hurry," says Jane hospitably that night at bedtime, lighting the candles on my dressing-table.

"You are determined to make my mouth water, I see," say I, inter-rupting a yawn to laugh. "Lone, lorn me, who have neither old man, nor dear little house, nor any prospect of ultimately attaining either."

"But if you honestly are not bored you will stay with us a good bit?" she says, laying her hand with kind entreaty on my sleeve.

"St. George's Channel is not lightly to be faced again."

"Perhaps I shall stay until you are obliged to go away yourselves to get rid of me," return I, smiling. "Such things have happened. Yes, without joking, I will stay a month. Then, by the end of a month, if you have not found me out thoroughly, I think I may pass among men for a more amiable woman than I have ever yet had the reputation of."

A quarter of an hour later I am laying down my head among soft and snow-white pillows, and saying to myself that this delicious sensation of utter drowsy repose, of soft darkness and odorous quiet, is cheaply purchased even by the ridiculous anguish which my own sufferings and—hardly less than my own sufferings—the demoniac sights and sounds afforded by my fellow passengers, caused me on board the accursed *Leinster*—

*Built in the eclipse, and rigged with curses dark.*

CHAPTER 2

"Well, I cannot say that you look much rested," says Jane next morning, coming in to greet me, smiling and fresh—(yes, sceptic of eighteen, even a woman of thirty-seven may look fresh in a print gown on an August morning, when she has a well of lasting quiet happiness inside her,)—coming in with a bunch of creamy *gloire de Dijons* in her hand for the breakfast table. "You look infinitely more fagged than you did when I left you last night!"

"Do I?" say I rather faintly.

"I am afraid you did not sleep much?" suggests Jane, a little crestfallen at the insult to her feather beds implied by my wakefulness. "Some people never can sleep the first night in a strange bed, and I stupidly forgot to ask whether you liked the feather bed or mattress at the top."

"Yes, I did sleep," I answer gloomily. "I wish to heaven I had not."

"Wish—to—heaven—you—had—not?" repeats Jane slowly, with a slight astonished pause between each word. "My dear child, for what other purpose did you go to bed?"

"I—I—had bad dreams," say I, shuddering a little and then taking her hand, roses and all, in mine. "Dear Jane, do not think me quite run mad, but—but—have you got a 'Bradshaw' in the house?"

"A 'Bradshaw?' What on earth do you want with 'Bradshaw?'" says my hostess, her face lengthening considerably and a slight tincture of natural coldness coming into her tone.

"I know it seems rude—insultingly rude," say I, still holding her hand and speaking almost lachrymosely; "but do you know, my dear, I really am afraid that—that—I shall have to leave you—today?"

"To leave us?" repeats she, withdrawing her hand and growing angrily red. "What! when not twenty-four hours ago you settled to stay *a month* with us? What have we done between then and now to disgust you with us?"

"Nothing—nothing," cry I eagerly; "how can you suggest such a thing? I never had a kinder welcome nor ever saw a place that charmed me more; but—but—"

"But what?" asks June, her colour subsiding and looking a little mollified.

"It is best to tell the truth, I suppose," say I sighing, "even though I know that you will laugh at me—will call me vapourish—sottishly superstitious; but I had an awful and hideous dream last night."

"Is that all?" she says, looking relieved, and beginning to arrange

27

her roses in an old china bowl. "And do you think that all dreams are confined to this house? I never heard before of their affecting any one special place more than another. Perhaps no sooner are you back in Dublin, in your own room and your own bed, than you will have a still worse and uglier one."

I shake my head. "But it was about this house—about *you*."

"About *me?*" she says, with an accent of a little aroused interest.

"About you and your husband," I answer earnestly. "Shall I tell it you? Whether you say 'Yes' or 'No' I must. Perhaps it came as a warning; such things have happened. Yes, say what you will, I cannot believe that any vision so consistent—so tangibly real and utterly free from the jumbled incongruities and unlikelinesses of ordinary dreams—could have meant nothing. Shall I begin?"

"By all means," answers Mrs. Watson, sitting down in an arm-chair and smiling easily. "I am quite prepared to listen—and *dis*believe."

"You know," say I, narratively, coming and standing close before her, "how utterly tired out I was when you left me last night. I could hardly answer your questions for yawning. I do not think that I was ten minutes in getting into bed, and it seemed like heaven when I laid my head down on the pillow. I felt as if I should sleep till the Day of Judgment. Well, you know, when one is asleep one has of course no measure of time, and I have no idea what hour it was *really*; but at some time, in the blackest and darkest of the night, I seemed to wake. It appeared as if a noise had woke me—a noise which at first neither frightened nor surprised me in the least, but which seemed quite natural, and which I accounted for in the muddled drowsy way in which one does account for things when half asleep.

"But as I gradually grew to fuller consciousness I found out, with a cold shudder, that the noise I heard was not one that belonged to the night; nothing that one could lay on wind in the chimney, or mice behind the wainscot, or ill-fitting boards. It was a sound of muffled struggling, and once I heard a sort of choked strangled cry. I sat up in bed, perfectly numbed with fright, and for a moment could hear nothing for the singing of the blood in my head and the loud battering of my heart against my side.

"Then I thought that if it were anything bad—if I were going to be murdered—I had at least rather be in the light than the dark, and see in what sort of shape my fate was coming, so I slid out of bed and threw my dressing-gown over my shoulders.

"I had stupidly forgotten, in my weariness overnight, to put the

28

matches by the bedside, and could not for the life of me recollect where they were. Also, my knowledge of the geography of the room was so small that in the utter blackness, without even the palest, greyest ray from the window to help me, I was by no means sure in which direction the door lay. I can feel *now* the pain of the blow I gave this right side against the sharp corner of the table in passing; I was quite surprised this morning not to find the mark of a bruise there.

"At last, in my groping I came upon the handle and turned the key in the lock. It gave a little squeak, and again I stopped for a moment, overcome by ungovernable fear. Then I silently opened the door and looked out. You know that your door is exactly opposite mine. By the line of red light underneath it, I could see that at all events someone was awake and astir within, for the light was brighter than that given by a night-light.

"By the broader band of red light on the right side of it I could also perceive that the door was ajar. I stood stock still and listened. The two sounds of struggling and chokedly crying had both ceased. All the noise that remained was that as of some person quietly moving about on unbooted feet. 'Perhaps Jane's dog Smut is ill and she is sitting up with it; she was saying last night, I remember, that she was afraid it was beginning with the distemper. Perhaps either she or her old man have been taken with some trifling temporary sickness. Perhaps the noise of crying out that I certainly heard was one of them fighting with a nightmare.' Trying, by such like suggestions, to hearten myself up, I stole across the passage and peeped in——"

I pause in my narrative.

"Well?" says Jane, a little impatiently.

She has dropped her flowers. They lie in odorous dewy confusion in her lap. She is listening rather eagerly. I cover my face with my hands. "Oh! My dear," I cry, "I do not think I can go on. It was *too* dreadful! Now that I am telling it I seem to be doing and hearing it over again——"

"I do not call it very kind to keep me on the rack," she says, with a rather forced laugh. "Probably I am imagining something much worse than the reality. For heaven's sake speak up! What *did* you see?"

I take hold of her hand and continue "You know that in your room the bed exactly faces the door. Well, when I looked in, looked in with eyes blinking at first, and dazzled by the long darkness they had been in, it seemed to me as if that bed were only one horrible sheet of crimson; but as my sight grew clearer, I saw what it was that caused that frightful impression of universal red——" again I pause with a gasp and feeling of oppressed breathing.

"Go on! go on!" cries my companion, leaning forward, and speaking with some petulance. "Are you never going to get to the point?"

"Jane," say I solemnly, "do not laugh at me, nor poohpooh me, for it is God's truth—as clearly and vividly as I see you now, strong, flourishing, and alive, so clearly, so vividly, with no more of dream haziness nor of contradiction in details than there is in the view I now have of this room and of you—I saw you *both*—you and your husband, lying *dead*—*murdered*—drowned in your own blood!"

"What, both of us?" she says, trying to laugh, but her healthy cheek has rather paled.

"Both of you," I answer, with growing excitement. "You, Jane, had evidently been the one first attacked—taken off in your sleep—for you were lying just as you would have lain in slumber, only that across your throat from there to there" (touching first one ear and then the other), "there was a huge and yawning gash."

"Pleasant," replies she, with a slight shiver.

"I never saw anyone dead," continue I earnestly, "never until last night. I had not the faintest idea how dead people looked, even people who died quietly, nor has any picture ever given me at all a clear conception of death's dread look. How then could I have *imagined* the hideous contraction and distortion of feature, the staring starting open eyes—glazed yet agonised—the tightly clenched teeth that go to make up the picture, that is *now, this very minute* standing out in ugly vividness before my mind's eye?" I stop, but she does not avail herself of the pause to make any remark, neither does she look any longer at all laughingly inclined.

"And yet," continue I, with a voice shaken by emotion, "it was *you, very* you, not partly you and partly someone else, as is mostly the case in dreams, but as much *you*, as the *you* I am touching now" laying my finger on her arm as I speak.

"And my old man, Robin," says poor Jane, rather tearfully, after a moment's silence, "what about him? Did you see him? Was he dead too?"

"It was evidently he whom I had heard struggling and crying," I answer with a strong shudder, which I cannot keep down, "for it was clear that he had fought for his life. He was lying half on the bed and half on the floor, and one clenched hand was grasping a great piece of the sheet; he was lying head downwards, as if, after his last struggle, he had fallen forwards. All his grey hair was reddened and stained, and I could see that the rift in his throat was as deep as that in yours."

"I wish you would stop," cries Jane, pale as ashes, and speaking with an accent of unwilling, terror; "you are making me quite sick!"

"I *must* finish," I answer earnestly, "since it has come in time, I am sure it has come for some purpose. Listen to me till the end; it is very near." She does not speak, and I take her silence for assent. "I was staring at you both in a stony way," I go on, "feeling—if I felt at all—that I was turning idiotic with horror—standing in exactly the same spot, with my neck craned to look round the door, and my eyes unable to stir from that hideous scarlet bed, when a slight noise, as of someone cautiously stepping on the carpet, turned my stony terror into a living quivering agony. I looked and saw a man with his back towards me walking across the room from the bed to the dressing-table. He was dressed in the dirty fustian of an ordinary workman, and in his hand, he held a red wet sickle.

"When he reached the dressing-table he laid it down on the floor beside him, and began to collect all the rings, open the cases of the bracelets, and hurry the trinkets of all sorts into his pockets. While he was thus busy, I caught a full view of the reflection of the face in the glass——" I stop for breath, my heart is panting almost as hardly as it seemed to pant during the awful moments I am describing.

"What was he like—what was he like?" cries Jane, greatly excited. "Did you see him distinctly enough to recollect his features again? Would you know him again if you saw him?"

"Should I know my own face if I saw it in the glass?" I ask scornfully. "I see every line of it *now* more clearly than I do yours, though that is before my eyes, and the other only before my memory——"

"Well, what was he like?—be quick, for heaven's sake."

"The first moment that I caught sight of him," continue I, speaking quickly, "I felt certain that he was Irish; to no other nationality could such a type of face have belonged. His wild rough hair fell down over his forehead, reaching his shagged and overhanging brows. He had the wide grinning slit of a mouth—the long nose, the cunningly twinkling eyes—that one so often sees, in combination with a shambling gait and ragged tail-coat, at the railway stations or in the harvest fields at this time of year." A pause.

"I do not know how it came to me," I go on presently; "but I felt as convinced as if I had been told—as if I had known it for a positive fact—that he was one of your own labourers—one of your own harvest men. Have you any Irishmen working for you?"

"Of course we have," answers Jane, rather sharply, "but that proves nothing. Do not they, as you observed just now, come over in droves at this time of year for the harvest?"

"I am sorry," say I, sighing. "I wish you had not. Well, let me finish; I have just done—I had been holding the door-handle mechanically in my hand; I suppose I pulled it unconsciously towards me, for the door hinge creaked a little, but quite audibly. To my unspeakable horror the man turned round and saw me. Good God! he would cut my throat too with that red, *red* reaping hook! I tried to get into the passage and lock the door, but the key was on the inside.

"I tried to scream, I tried to run; but voice and legs disobeyed me. The bed and room and man began to dance before me; a black earthquake seemed to swallow me up, and I suppose I fell down in a swoon. When I awoke *really* the blessed morning had come, and a robin was singing outside my window on an apple bough. There—you have it all, and now let me look for a 'Bradshaw,' for I am so frightened and unhinged that go I must."

## Chapter 3

"I must own that it has taken away appetite," I say, with rather a sickly smile, as we sit round the breakfast table. "I assure you that I mean no insult to your fresh eggs and bread-and-butter, but I simply *cannot* eat."

"It certainly was an exceptionally dreadful dream," says Jane, whose colour has returned, and who is a good deal fortified and reassured by the influences of breakfast and of her husband's scepticism; for a condensed and shortened version of my dream has been told to him, and he has easily laughed it to scorn. "Exceptionally dreadful, chiefly from its extreme consistency and precision of detail. But still, you know, dear, one has had hideous dreams oneself times out of mind and they never came, to anything.

"I remember once I dreamt that all my teeth came out in my mouth at once—double ones and all; but that was ten years ago, and they still keep their situations, nor did I about that time lose any friend, which they say such a dream is a sign of."

"You say that some unaccountable instinct told you that the hero of your dream was one of my own men," says Robin, turning towards me with a covert smile of benevolent contempt for my superstitiousness; "did not I understand you to say so?"

"Yes," reply I, not in the least shaken by his hardly-veiled disbelief.

"I do not know how it came to me, but I was as much persuaded of that, and am so still, as I am of my own identity."

"I will tell you of a plan then to prove the truth of your vision," returns he, smiling. "I will take you through the fields this morning and you shall see all my men at work, both the ordinary staff and the harvest casuals, Irish and all. If amongst them you find the counterpart of Jane's and my murderer (a smile) I will promise *then*—no, not even *then* can I promise to believe you, for there is such a family likeness between all Irishmen, at all events between all the Irishmen that one sees *out* of Ireland."

"Take me," I say eagerly, jumping up; "now, this *minute!* You cannot be more anxious nor half so anxious to prove me a false prophet as I am to be proved one."

"I am quite at your service," he answers, "as soon as you please. Jenny, get your hat and come too."

"And if we do *not* find him," says Jane, smiling playfully—"I think I am growing pretty easy on that head—you will promise to eat a great deal of luncheon and never *mention* 'Bradshaw' again?"

"I promise," reply I gravely. "And if, on the other hand, we *do* find him, you will promise to put no more obstacles in the way of my going, but will let me depart in peace without taking any offence thereat?"

"It is a bargain," she says gaily. "Witness, Robin."

So, we set off in the bright dewiness of the morning; on our walk over Robin's farm. It is a grand harvest day, and the whitened sheaves are everywhere, drying, drying in the genial sun. We have been walking for an hour and both Jane and I are rather tired. The sun beats with all his late-summer strength on our heads and takes the force and spring out of our hot limbs.

"The hour of triumph is approaching," says Robin, with a quiet smile, as we draw near an open gate through which a loaded wain, shedding, ripe wheat ears from its abundance as it crawls along, is passing. "And time for it too; it is a quarter past twelve and you have been on your legs for fully an hour. Miss Bellairs, you must make haste and find the murderer, for there is only one more field to do it in."

"Is not there?" I cry eagerly. "Oh, I *am* glad! Thank God, I begin to breathe again."

We pass through the open gate and begin to tread across the stubble for almost the last load has gone.

"We must get nearer the hedge," says Robin, "or you will not see their faces; they are all at dinner."

We do as he suggests. In the shadow of the hedge, we walk close in front of the row of heated labourers, who, sitting or lying on the hedge bank, are eating unattractive looking dinners. I scan one face after another—honest bovine English faces. I have seen a hundred thousand faces *like* each one of the faces now before me—very like but the exact counterpart of none. We are getting to the end of the row, I beginning to feel rather ashamed, though infinitely relieved, and to smile at my own expense. I look again, and my heart suddenly stands still and turns to stone within me. He is *there!*—not a handsbreadth from me!

Great God! how well I have remembered his face, even to the unsightly smallpox seams, the shagged locks, the grinning slit mouth, the little sly base eyes. He is employed in no murderous occupation *now*; he is harmlessly cutting hunks of coarse bread and fat cold bacon with a clasp knife; but yet I have no more doubt that it is *he*—he whom I saw with the crimsoned sickle in his stained hand—than I have that it is I who am stonily, shiveringly, staring at him.

"Well, Miss Bellairs, who was right?" asks Robin's cheery voice at my elbow. "Perish Bradshaw and all his labyrinths! Are you satisfied now? Good heavens!" (catching a sudden sight of my face) "How white you are! Do you mean to say that you have found him at last? Impossible!"

"Yes, I have found him," I answer in a low and unsteady tone. "I knew I should. Look, there he is!—close to us, the third from the end."

I turn away my head, unable to bear the hideous recollections and associations that the sight of the man calls up, and I suppose that they both look.

"Are you sure that you are not letting your imagination carry you away?" asks he presently, in a tone of gentle kindly remonstrance. "As I said before, these fellows are all so much alike, they have all the same look of debased squalid cunning. Oblige me by looking once again, so as to be quite sure."

I obey. Reluctantly I look at him once again. Apparently becoming aware that he is the object of our notice, he lifts his small dull eyes and looks back at me. It is the same face—they are the same eyes that turned from the plundered dressing-table to catch sight of me last night.

"There is no mistake," I answer, shuddering from head to foot.

"Take me away, please—as quick as you can—out of the field—home!"

They comply, and over the hot fields and through the hot noon air we step silently homewards. As we reach the cool and ivied porch of the house I speak for the first time. "You believe me *now?*"

He hesitates. "I was staggered for a moment, I will own," he answers, with candid gravity; "but I have been thinking it over and on reflection I have come to the conclusion that the highly excited state of your imagination is answerable for the heightening of the resemblance which exists between all the Irish of that class into an identity with the particular Irishman you dreamed of, and whose face (by your own showing) you only saw dimly reflected in the glass."

"*Not* dimly," repeat I, emphatically, "unless I now see that Sun dimly" (pointing to him as he gloriously, blindingly, blazes from the sky). You will not be warned by me, then?" I continue passionately, after an interval. "You will run the risk of my dream coming true—you will stay on here in spite of it? Oh, if I could persuade you to go from home—anywhere—anywhere—for a time, until the danger was past!"

"And leave the harvest to itself?" answers he, with a smile of quiet sarcasm; "be a loser of two hundred or three hundred pounds, probably, and a laughing-stock to my acquaintance into the bargain, and all for—what? A dream a fancy—a nightmare!"

"But do you know anything of the man?—of his antecedents?—of his character?" I persist eagerly.

He shrugs he shoulders.

"Nothing whatever; nothing to his disadvantage, certainly. He came over with a lot of others a fortnight ago, and I engaged him for the harvesting. For anything I have heard to the contrary, he is a simple inoffensive fellow enough."

I am silenced, but not convinced. I turn to Jane. "You remember your promise: you will now put no more hindrances in the way of my going?"

"You do not mean to say that you are going, really?" says Jane, who is looking rather awed by what she calls the surprising coincidence but is still a good deal heartened up by her husband's want of faith.

"I do," reply I, emphatically. "I should go stark staring mad if I were to sleep another night in that room. I shall go to Chester tonight, and cross tomorrow from Holyhead."

I do as I say. I make my maid, to her extreme surprise, repack my just unpacked wardrobe and take an afternoon train to Chester. As I drive away with bag and baggage down the leafy lane, I look back and

35

see my two friends standing at their gate. Jane is leaning her head on her old man's shoulder, and looking rather wistfully after me: an expression of mingled regret for my departure and vexation at my folly clouding their kind and happy faces. At least my last living recollection of them is a pleasant one.

## CHAPTER 4

The joy with which my family welcome my return is largely mingled with surprise, but still more largely with curiosity, as to the cause of my so sudden reappearance. But I keep my own counsel. I have a reluctance to give the real reason, and possess no inventive faculty in the way of lying, so I give none. I say, "I am back: is not that enough for you? Set your minds at rest, for that is as much as you will ever know about the matter."

For one thing, I am occasionally rather ashamed of my conduct. It is not that the impression produced by my dream is *effaced*, but that absence and distance from the scene and the persons of it have produced their natural weakening effect. Once or twice during the voyage, when writhing in laughable torments in the ladies' cabin of the steam-boat, I said to myself, "Most likely you are a fool!" I therefore continually ward off the cross-questionings of my family with what defensive armour of silence and evasion I may.

"I feel convinced it was the husband," says one of my sisters, after a long catechism, which, as usual, has resulted in nothing. "You are too loyal to your friend to own it, but I always felt sure that any man who could take compassion on that poor peevish old Jane must be some wonderful freak of nature. Come, confess. Is not he a cross between an orang-outang and a Methodist parson?"

"He is nothing of the kind," reply I, in some heat, recalling the libelled Robin's clean fresh-coloured *human* face. "You will be very lucky if you ever secure anyone half so kind, pleasant, and gentleman-like."

Three days after my return, I receive a letter from Jane:

Weston House, Caulfield.
My Dear Dinah—I hope you are safe home again, and that you have made up your mind that two crossings of St. George's Channel within forty-eight hours are almost as bad as having your throat cut, according to the programme you laid out for us. I have good news for you. Our murderer elect is *gone*. After hearing of the connection that there was to lie between *us*,

36

Robin naturally was rather interested in him, and found out his name, which is the melodious one of Watty Doolan

After asking his name he asked other things about him, and finding that he never did a stroke of work and was inclined to be tipsy and quarrelsome he paid and packed him off at once. He is now on his way back to his native shores, and if he murders anybody it will be *you* my dear. Goodbye, Dinah. Hardly yet have I forgiven you for the way in which you frightened me with your graphic description of poor Robin and me, with our heads loose and waggling.

> Ever yours affectionately.
>
> Jane Watson.

I fold up this note with a feeling of exceeding relief, and a thorough faith that I have been a superstitious hysterical fool. More resolved than ever am I to keep the reason for my return profoundly secret from my family. The next morning but one we are all in the breakfast-room after breakfast, hanging about, and looking at the papers. My sister has just thrown down the *Times*, with a pettish exclamation that there is nothing in it and that it really is not worthwhile paying threepence a day to see nothing but advertisements and police reports. I pick it up as she throws it down, and look listlessly over its tall columns from top to bottom. Suddenly my listlessness vanishes. What is this that I am reading?—this in staring capitals?

## SHOCKING TRAGEDY AT CAULFIELD.
## DOUBLE MURDER.

I am in the middle of the paragraph before I realise what it is.

> From an early hour of the morning this village has been the scene of deep and painful excitement in consequence of the discovery of the atrocious murder of Mr. and Mrs. Watson, of Weston House, two of its most respected inhabitants. It appears that the deceased had retired to rest on Tuesday night at their usual hour, and in their usual health and spirits. The housemaid, on going to call them at the accustomed hour on Wednesday morning, received no answer, in spite of repeated knocking. She therefore at length opened the door and entered.
> The rest of the servants, attracted by her cries, rushed to the spot, and found the unfortunate gentleman and lady lying on the bed with their throats cut from ear to ear. Life must have

been extinct for some hours, as they were both perfectly cold. The room presented a hideous spectacle, being literally swimming in blood. A reaping hook, evidently the instrument with which the crime was perpetrated, was picked up near the door. An Irish labourer of the name of Watty Doolan, discharged by the lamented gentleman a few days ago on account of misconduct, has already been arrested on strong suspicion, as at an early hour on Wednesday morning he was seen by a farm labourer, who was going to his work, washing his waistcoat at a retired spot in the stream which flows through the meadows below the scene of the murder.

On being apprehended and searched, several small articles of jewellery, identified as having belonged to Mr. Watson, were discovered in his possession.

I drop the paper and sink into a chair, feeling deadly sick.

So, you see that my dream came true, after all.

The facts narrated in the above story occurred in Ireland. The only liberty I have taken with them is in transplanting them to England.

# His Serene Highness

"It must be true, for His Serene Highness told me so himself."

His Serene Highness!

We were all a little awed. An unfledged and rustic band, in the case of most of us but lately freed from educational trammels, the idea of one of ourselves having had intimate communications made to them by a crowned head, or, at the very least, a crowned head's second cousin, filled us with a pleasing stupefaction, and stemmed our usually voluble utterance, His Serene Highness!

"I forget whether I mentioned" (we had not forgotten) "that when I was in London last week, I met Prince Waldemar of Saxe Thür, at dinner." Our narrator, to do her justice, had tried to make her voice as colourless and matter of fact as possible; but the glory of the related fact blazed through it.

"Yes?" in several keys of acute interest.

"Of course, I was not near him at dinner" (with a slight disclaiming laugh); "but in the evening he asked that I might be presented to him."

"What fun for you!"

"And the story? How did it come about?"

"Someone was relating an odd incident, and the prince said, 'I had a very curious experience once.'"

"Does he speak English?"

"OF course he does!" (almost indignantly); "as well as, if not better than, you or I, only that he rolls his r's as they all do."

"As all who do? Do all royalties roll their r's?"

"Oh! I do not know. At all events, all Germans roll their r's."

"Well?"

"Oh, then of course our hostess asked him whether he would be so kind as to relate the experience he spoke of."

"And he did?"

"Oh yes, at once; he did not make the least difficulty; he was so good-natured about it."

"I daresay, like the rest of us, he enjoyed talking about himself."

"He began by saying, 'You must remember that I am rather credulous about the supernatural,' and then he laughed. He has such beautiful teeth!"

"That was not a bad sentence for showing off his r's."

"He went on to say, 'My sisters ridicule me for it.'"

"He has sisters, then?"

"Yes; I looked them out in the *Almanach de Gotha*: there are three— Olga, Amalia, and Walpurga; but I think Walpurga died when she was a baby."

"Yes?"

"'My sisters ridicule me for it; they are *esprits forts*.'"

"*Esprits forts!* All of them?"

"There are only two: don't I tell you that Walpurga died when she was a baby?"

"Well?"

"I was so afraid that he would be prevented from finishing it, because people kept coming in and expecting to be presented to him. Lady —— said she was only going to have 'a small tail,' but it ended by being a crush."

"Did not he get out of patience?"

"Not in the least! Royalties never get out of patience; it is part of their education; he took the story up every time just where he had left off; only once his memory failed him for a moment, and then *I* came to the rescue."

"You?"

"Yes, I. And thenceforward he—unless it was my fancy—addressed himself specially to me. I suppose he saw that I was more genuinely interested than any of his other listeners; he must have seen that they listened out of politeness, I because I was really impressed by the story; I should have been equally so if it had been told me by a tinker."

"Well?"

"Twenty years ago, Prince Waldemar was in the army."

"Twenty years! Then he cannot be in his first youth?"

"He was in an *Uhlan* regiment, and had been in the service a year or two— I think he must have joined in '70, just before the declaration of war—when his regiment was ordered to a remote village in Bavaria."

"Yes?"

"It was not a place where troops were generally quartered; his *Uh-*

*lans* and a regiment, or detachment of a regiment, of infantry were sent there because there either had been some rioting, or there was an apprehension of likely disturbance—I did not quite make out which—in the neighbourhood. There were no barracks, and the soldiers had to be billeted on the inhabitants. Of course, the local *Gast Höfe* were not nearly big enough to contain them, so every private house—they were mostly very humble ones—was saddled with two or three."

"And was the prince billeted, too?"

"Well, no; not exactly. Of course, though he was supposed to be serving on precisely the same terms as any of his brother officers, yet no doubt his colonel was anxious that he should have a few little extra luxuries. He did not tell me so, but I gathered it."

"I daresay that he thought a little roughing it rather fun than otherwise?"

"Perhaps so. German life is always much simpler than ours; even, I fancy, in royal circles. But still he owned that his heart sank a little on the very raw spring evening when he rode up to his quarters; and he could not help exclaiming to his equerry, in German of course, 'What a God-forsaken hole!'"

"What is 'God-forsaken' in German?"

"I have not the least idea, and what does that matter? The equerry answered, 'That it is, sir; but it is the best which, under the circumstances, could be procured for Your Highness.'"

"Well?"

"So, then Prince Waldemar just shrugged his shoulders, as he did in telling me, and said, 'Then we must make the best of it.' As he explained, 'I saw there was no use in grumbling; and I am a philosopher; I never grumble when there is no use.'"

"Did he describe it—the house, I mean?"

"Yes, he said it was a newish house, not more than ten years old at most, yet already falling into decay; the plaster was tumbling off the front, and there were livid green patches of damp here and there; some of the outside shutters were broken off and swinging loose."

"I should personally have much preferred to be billeted."

"It had evidently been intended to form one of a row, as the projecting brick ends at one side showed; but the rest of the row had remained unbuilt; and there it stood, forlorn and alone."

"Were there houses opposite it?"

"No, it was on a waste piece of ground covered with rubbish heaps; where the neighbours were evidently in the habit of shooting their old tin kettles and broken crockery, and tufts of rank grass and nettles grew between."

"They might have pulled up the nettles, and mended his shutters for him!"

"So, one would have thought; but you see the whole thing happened quite suddenly, the troops were sent to the village at a moment's notice, having been telegraphed for by the civil authorities of the district."

"And did the inside match the outside?"

"Very nearly. Some hasty attempts had been made to give it a habitable look; a few chairs and tables sent in, and a carpet or two put down, and the windows had evidently been newly glazed here and there, which showed, as indeed the prince soon learned upon inquiry, that the house had stood empty and desolate for several months."

One of the audience shrugged her shoulders. "'For my part I should have taken French leave."

"Well, he did not. He got off his horse, and followed by his equerry, entered the house I have described."

"Well?"

"His own confidential valet had of course been sent on beforehand, but the whole thing had happened so suddenly that he had arrived scarcely more than an hour before his master, and had not had time to get the loutish country servants, who had been hastily sent in, into any serviceable shape; and though big fires were burning all over the house, the whole place struck as chill as a vault on entering. 'You know,' Prince Waldemar said, 'I have already told you that I am terribly superstitious; and it appeared to me as if a breath from the grave met me on the threshold.'"

"Ugh!"

"The blazing fires had been too lately lit to be able to overcome the penetrating feeling of intense and long-established damp, and though the March wind outside was shrewish and keen, it seemed warm and amiable compared to the temperature inside."

"I should have swallowed my dignity and joined the troopers at the pot-house."

"I suppose he could not well do that; at all events he did not."

"Was it a large house or a small one?"

"Oh, small; but though small, it had none of the snugness which people associate with a cottage; but that was in great part due, no doubt, to its having been uninhabited through what had been a severe winter; and after all it was only for a very short time that it was to be occupied by him. He said all this to his equerry; and they both grew quite cheerful in laughing over the shifts they were driven to, and recalling to each other's memory to what far worse hardships they had often to submit in their conquering march through wintry France.

"But it is a truism that great woes and privations are very much more easily borne with dignity than small ones; and he acknowledged that when he returned at night to his dismal abode, after having dined at mess with his brother officers in an uncomfortable shed, ill adapted for the purpose to which it was forced, he was, as he told me, 'in what you call a devil of a temper'; he made the confession with such an angelic smile that one felt it could not possibly be true. 'Poor Von Hammerstein!' he added, beginning to laugh, 'you had better ask him what sort of a memory he has of our first night at ——.'"

"Was Von Hammerstein at the party too?"

"Oh no: I imagine he is dead!"

"He can't be dead if the prince advised you to ask him a question!"

"No more he can. Well, anyhow, he was not there."

"No?"

"So, the prince went to bed grumbling a good deal; went to bed rather early, as there was certainly nothing to tempt him to stay up late."

A laugh. "According to your description of his surroundings, certainly not."

"The house was three storeys high; and there were three rooms on each floor; so, you see, there were twelve in all, besides the basement. The prince's bedroom—of course they had given him the best one—was the front one on the second floor; his equerry slept next door to him, the rooms opening out of each other; and the valet in the third; the other servants were above, the sitting-rooms below; and on the ground floor, in addition to two dining-rooms—front and back—was a small, dingy room, quite unfurnished, scarcely more than a closet, which had probably, when the house was occupied, been used as a passage to the weed-and-brickbat-grown back yard, which might once have done duty as a garden.

"This last room had a glass door, opening out on the forlorn plot of ground. It was not till the next day that Prince Waldemar became aware of the existence of the empty room, or rather, as I have said, closet, by seeing its door—not the outer glass one, but the one that opened inwards into the house—left accidentally ajar. He passed through it by the glass door into the garden, and, looking up at the dismal, sordid exterior of the building, fell to wondering over his cigar, as he told me, upon the problem of how life could ever have been endured by any inhabitant of such a spot."

"That was next morning, you say. Then" (in a tone of slight disappointment) "nothing at all happened that first night?"

"Have I ever said that anything happened any night?"

"Well?"

"The prince is, I imagine, never a very good sleeper; and though he looks so robust and muscular, has—he told us so—a highly-strung nerve system, and on this particular night he did not sleep at all. The odd thing was that there was no apparent cause for his wakefulness, no great discomfort, no noise. The house stood on the outskirts of the village, and even had it been in the middle of it, the little place's sounds were hushed by midnight, all the soldiers, who earlier had given it unwonted life, having betaken themselves to their billets; but yet he could not close an eye until very near morning, and he seemed scarcely to have lost consciousness before it was sharply summoned back again by the bugles from the little village Platz blowing the '*Reveillé*,' or whatever is the German equivalent to it.

"He woke quite unrefreshed, and with a heavy feeling of inertness and want of spring. This went off in the course of the morning, or he forgot to think about it as he was riding about all day with his troop, who were sent to awe by their presence, or, if need were, to coerce into submission those outlying hamlets, where the inclination to riot, the bent towards burning ricks and breaking windows had been most pronounced.

"Happily the mere presence of the clattering *Uhlans* had sufficed for the repression, at least momentary, of the revolutionary spirit; and Prince Waldemar and his troop returned at evening to their Dorf, without having been obliged to oppose anything but the sight of their swords to the pitchfork-bearing peasants, against whom they had been sent: But though quite bloodless, the day's ride had been a long and tiring one, covering a very considerable mileage, and occupying many hours; and, after his previous wakeful night, the prince felt quite ready to turn in at an even earlier hour than he had done the evening before; and he felt, up to the moment of going to bed, so heavy with sleep that the idea, as he said, never once struck him that he would not fall at once into a profound slumber, out of which even the unwelcome 'Reveillé' would be powerless to rouse him."

"I foresee that he is not going to get a wink of sleep."

"Then you are wrong. He did fall asleep the moment he was be-tween the sheets; but only to find his eyes wide open again, after what seemed a very short interval. He looked at his watch—he always has a light burning in his room—and found that he had slept just three-quarters of an hour. However, short as that allowance of sleep was, he was obliged to content himself with it, since, beyond a few dozes each of five or ten minutes duration, he got no more. He was very much puzzled, and rather annoyed; tossed about impatiently enough, smoked a cigar, read a page or two, took several turns about the room, held his hands for several minutes in a basin of cold water, which he had heard of as a remedy for wakefulness; but all in vain.

"On this occasion the bugles had not the trouble of waking him, for he was broad awake already. He compared notes with Von Ham-merstein, and also with his valet, as to the way in which they had passed the night, and from both of them elicited the acknowledgment of having slept ill and disturbedly, but not of the absolute wakefulness he himself had suffered from. He felt the effect of his unwilling vigil all through the day, which was again one of hard riding and fatigue; and when it was followed by a third night, if possible, more sleepless than its predecessors, he began to feel quite ill, feverish with loss of appetite."

"Royalties generally have good appetites!"

"With loss of appetite and heaviness in the limbs; he felt as if he could barely drag himself on to his horse."

"No doubt Von Hammerstein and the valet felt quite as bad, only they said nothing."

"He said, 'I am afr-raid I am always rather highly str-rung, and you will laugh at me, but my nerves were in r-ribbons.' To add to his discomfort, he found on this third morning that his favourite charger, Porthos—he had christened him after one of the '*Trois Mousquetaires*,' as, though he is a German, he adores Dumas—had fallen seriously ill with inflammation of the lungs."

"Poor Porthos! I hope he did not die like the murdered Athos of that arch-devilish long-distance ride?"

"I do not think he did."

"Well?"

"As the day went on the prince felt so increasingly ill that the colonel, noticing his pale looks, and no doubt nervous about so great a personage, ordered him, or requested him—I do not know which form of speech a colonel would employ to a royal subordinate—back to his quarters, and begged him to go to bed and send for the doctor."

"If he is as nervous as you say, I daresay he did not need much persuading."

"He took half the colonel's advice; he did not go back to bed, as his three *nuits blanches* had given him a horror of it, but he sent for the doctor."

"The regimental one, of course?"

"No; for some reason which he did not explain to me, it was not the regimental doctor; it was a local practitioner, who, on first arriving, was so overwhelmed with the honour of prescribing for a prince, that for a few moments he was incapable of articulating, but presently, reassured by Prince Waldemar's charm of manner——"

"Did Prince Waldemar say so?"

"Of course not; but I read it between the lines. He has a great charm of manner—the sincerity which comes from a really good heart; and no doubt the poor apothecary soon found it out, and plucked up courage to take His Serene Highness' temperature, and go through the usual little medical manoeuvres. He was able to assure the prince that there was not much the matter with him; and after prescribing bromide to quiet his nerves, and one or two other simple medicines, was awkwardly going to take leave, trying to back out of the room, and tumbling over his own obsequious legs in the attempt, when the prince called him back. 'Do not be in such a hurry, Herr Doktor, unless you are hastening away to some very urgent case. I should be glad to ask you a few questions about this house, where perhaps I may be compelled to make a longer stay than I at first supposed, as' (laughing) 'from their manners towards us your peasants do not seem in any hurry to let us go.'

"Indeed, the mutinous spirit in the district showed as yet no sign of calming down. 'The doctor came back at once, and stood as nervously awaiting the queries about to be put to him as if they referred to his own complicity in some crime. 'I want you to be so good as to tell me, Herr Doktor, what you know about this house, which seems to me, and also to Herr Von Hammerstein, to have something very odd and *unheimlich* about it.'

"'Indeed, Your Serene Highness, I know very little about the house; I should be delighted to give Your Serene Highness any information in my power, but I am but a newcomer in the village; I know nothing of the house, except that ever since I have lived here it has stood empty.'

"'H'm! Do you know any reason why it should have remained unoccupied, since it is the best house as to size in the place?'

"No reason whatever, Your Serene Highness—that is to say, no rational reason—but, as Your Serene Highness knows far better than I do, no doubt there is an immense mass of degrading superstition still lurking in remote country places such as this is; and I have reason to believe that the real cause of this excellent residence having remained uninhabited is that our poor benighted people have a prejudice against it because it is built on the site of a disused churchyard.'

"The prince says that he knows that here he gave a start: you see he had not yet taken the bromide, and his nerves were still jumpy. 'A disused churchyard!' he cried; 'but surely, surely that must be very unhealthy! The sanitary arrangements—the drains——'

"I think that Your Serene Highness need have no alarm on that score; the burial-ground had been disused for over three centuries, and the ground had lain waste and idle, only a tradition remaining that it had once been consecrated.'

"It has certainly not proved a *Fried Hof* to me!" interjected the prince, making a rather rueful pun on the German name for churchyard.

"The doctor laughed nervously; then checked himself suddenly, as if not quite sure how far it was etiquette to show amusement at a royal jest. 'About four or five years ago the civil authorities of the district, who were very energetic persons, penetrated with the spirit of the age, thought it a pity that the site should be wasted; and as at the time there was some idea of developing the resources of the place by running a new line of railway through it,—an idea which never came to anything—they projected a street where this house now stands; but the public feeling—this benighted superstition of which I spoke just now to Your Serene Highness—was so strongly against the plan, that it had to be given up, and only this one solitary dwelling came into existence.'

"What form does the superstition take?' asked the prince, not feeling quite that contempt for the villagers' weakness which was expected of him. The doctor shrugged his shoulders.

"I am afraid that Your Serene Highness' opinion of our poor people's intelligence will not be raised when I tell you that they have a belief—which I have in vain tried to combat—that the churchyard claims a yearly tribute of a life from any family which dares to inhabit this sacrilegious dwelling.' He laughed contemptuously while he spoke; but the prince, as he told me, was quite unable to echo his mirth.

"It has always stood empty then?' he asked, with rather a sinking heart.

"Oh, dear no, sir; if I have conveyed that idea to Your Serene Highness, I have expressed myself very clumsily; it has indeed been vacant for some little time, but during the first years after it was built—indeed, until just before my own arrival, and I am but a newcomer—it was continuously, or almost continuously, inhabited.'

"'And was there—did there ever happen any—any accident—any—any event to justify or confirm the villagers' prejudice against it?'

"The doctor hesitated. 'Not to *justify* it certainly, sir,' he answered, rather warmly; 'but to give it a slight colour possibly. As ill luck would have it, the first tenant was found dead in his bed only ten days or so after his taking possession; there got about some rumour of foul play, because there were black marks on the man's throat; but they were quite without foundation: he was an apoplectic subject, his death attributable to purely natural causes, and the whole unlucky accident a pure coincidence.'

"'Not a very pleasant coincidence!' the prince replied; 'but still, no doubt as you say, it was only that, which of course was proved by no repetition of it happening?'

"The doctor was silent

"'Did not people's alarm begin to subside when they found that no death occurred in the second year?' inquired the prince, wilily.

"The visitor fell into the trap.

"'Well, sir, unfortunately there did happen another death in the second year; but it was one which might just as well have occurred in any other house in the place: such culpable carelessness must have had the same result wherever it existed, In the second year, a stupid servant girl upset a lighted paraffin lamp over her own clothes, and was so badly burnt that she died of her injuries,'

"The prince smiled rather grimly. 'No. 2!' he said, checking the catastrophes off on his fingers. 'But that was all? were there no more *coincidences*?' (with a slight ironical accent): 'the third year's character was quite clear?'

"Again, a hesitation was apparent before the person addressed responded. 'In the third year, I must own to Your Serene Highness, that there was an accident, but it was as clearly due to gross carelessness as the death of the servant girl: a woman standing at an open window on the third floor with a baby in her arms let it fall on to the roadway beneath, and of course the poor infant was picked up stone dead; but, as Your Serene Highness will allow, there could be no possible connection between——'

"'And since then, it has stood empty?' broke in the prince, with less than his usual courtesy. 'You do not answer; but I see by your manner that such has been the case.'

"'At least, sir, there have been no more deaths in it; I can vouch for that,' returned the other, jesuitically.

"'Well, Herr Doktor, I must not detain you any longer from your patients,' the prince said, and so the visitor bowed himself out with some alacrity, leaving his patient feeling very uncomfortable. You must remember that it was his nerves that chiefly ailed, and what he had heard had not tended to improve their condition. He told Von Hammerstein the story, and tried to jest with him as to the obviously impending fate of one or other of them, proposing a dismal bet as to which it would be; but Von Hammerstein was a little superstitious too, and his answering mirth did not ring very genuine. To do him justice, the prince, rather ashamed of the impression made upon him, tried his best to shake it off, and was fairly successful all day, but when night came it returned on him, do what he would, with redoubled force.

"The yearly tribute exacted by the churchyard, by those vengeful three-hundred-year-old dead who were lying beneath him, haunted his imagination with an unaccountable power of producing terror. It was doubtless he whom they would claim. He, no other than he! Had not he under their baleful influence already become aware of a diminution of vital force, of a sickly languor? His evil star had sent him to this charnel-house where it was only a matter of time how soon he should join his fellow-victims—the throttled man, burnt woman, and mangled child!

"After hours of these agreeable musings, the bromide at last took effect; and he fell into a sound sleep, from which he awoke so much refreshed that he felt quite cheerful, and rather ashamed of the completeness with which his supernatural fears had got the better of him over night. After having drunk his morning coffee he felt so well, that he dressed and got on his horse—not poor Porthos, who was still *hors de combat*—he said the idea struck him that perhaps the tribute need not be a human one, and that Porthos might be the doomed victim.

"The prince served all day with his troop; the work was light, as the district was evidently beginning to realise the futility of its struggle against the armed hand of law and order; and was riding home in very good spirits at the thought that his further stay at his charnel-house, as he now always called it, would be brief, when, at the entrance of the little *Platz*, he saw a very handsome young man in a naval uniform—there were, of course, no sailors among the troops stationed at the village—saluting, and looking, meanwhile, with a pleasant smile of recognition, at his own equerry.

"'Who is your friend?' he asked.

"'He is my brother, sir,' Von Hammerstein answered. 'He has just returned from the South African station, and not knowing that we had left Munich, went thither, thinking to find me, and, hearing that we had been ordered here, followed us. We have not met since before the war,' he added, in explanation of this fraternal eagerness.

"'He is a very good-looking fellow,' the prince said.

"'He is not a bad boy,' Von Hammerstein answered; then beginning to laugh, 'I think he has already repented of the impulse that brought him here, for the place is so crammed that he cannot find a hole or a corner to sleep in: he must bivouac under a haystack; a sailor is accustomed to hardships.'

"'So!' replied the prince, with that long-drawn German monosyllable, which is as comprehensive as our 'Oh!' Then a good-natured thought struck him.

'Why should not he come to us? That room on the ground floor, the one with the glass door into the garden, is vacant: why should he not occupy it? Nothing would be easier than to rig up a bed or a sofa there for him.'

"'It is extremely kind of Your Serene Highness,' Von Hammerstein answered, looking pleased.

"'Call him, and tell him so.'

"The equerry gladly complied, and the young sailor approached, and, being offered the proposed hospitality by the prince, thanked him with much propriety and modesty, and with blushes that so heightened his good looks that His Serene Highness expressed himself to the youth's brother as quite prepossessed in his favour. He invited him to join the regiment at mess that night, and, after it, returned to the 'Charnel-house,' feeling almost cured of his temporary illness, in high good-humour at the thought of a speedy return to the pleasures of Munich, and laughing with the two Von Hammersteins at his own superstitious fears of the previous night. 'I bid defiance to the churchyard and all its inhabitants!' he cried gaily, as he bade a kindly goodnight to his young guest.

"'*Kam je ein Todter aus der Gruft gestiegen?*'

"He jumped into bed; and, feeling that bromide or any other calming potions were superfluous, fell instantly and soundly asleep. He says he does not think that even the Last Trump would have awoke him, so ample were the arrears of slumber that he had to make up. Nor does he believe that he ever stirred—lying like a log through the whole night in the position in which he had first placed himself.

"It was broad daylight when he at length sprang into consciousness. I say sprang, for even when he did awake, it was not spontaneously, but he was violently dragged back to life and motion by the noise of the door of his room being burst open."

"I thought he said that the Last Trump would not have awoke him?"

"Possibly it would not; but, anyhow, the door did, and, when he had collected his sleep-scattered wits, he thought that he must still be in the land of visions, so strangely unexpected and unaccountable was the sight that met his eyes."

"What was it?"

"His colonel, usually a stolid, buckrammed German officer, was kneeling by his bedside, kissing his hand, and crying, 'Oh, thank God! Thank God!'

"The spectacle was such an astonishing one that it roused the sleeper effectually.

"'My dear colonel! Is it possible? What has happened?'

"But the colonel could only reiterate, 'Thank God! 'Thank God you are safe!'

"'Why should not I be safe?' inquired the prince, hopelessly puzzled. 'I have been enjoying the best sleep I ever had in my life, from which, but for your most unexpected help, I do not know when I should have roused myself; there is nothing very dangerous in that!'

"'Thank God! thank God!' his superior officer repeated once again, in a key of the most intense relief; then collecting himself, 'You know, sir, that I am not superstitious—no believer in dreams and omens. Well, last night I had the most astonishingly vivid dream that I saw you—I felt that it must be you, though I could not see your face—that I saw a dead man, covered with a bloody sheet, being carried out of the door of this house.' (The prince was wide awake enough by this time, and had sprung up into a sitting position.)

"'It was repeated three times, the last time with such an extraordinary reality of presentment that I woke up all in a cold sweat, and, unable to bear the impression made upon me, threw on my clothes and rushed here at once to convince myself that I had been fooled by a devilish vision. Imagine my horror when on nearing your door I saw just such a procession as I had dreamed of—the prostrate figure covered with a bloody sheet—being carried out by two or three of your servants!'

"'Dear God!' cried out the prince, horrified: 'who was it?'

"'I could not ask them,' answered the colonel, again almost mastered by his emotion, to the intensity of which his livid complexion sufficiently testified; 'but I tore the sheet off the face and saw, thank God, not Your Highness' features, but——'

"'But whose? But whose?'

"But those of Von Hammerstein's poor young brother, Albrecht, to whom you so kindly offered your hospitality last night.'

"'Dead' shouted the prince, in the extremity of his horror and amazement. 'How? where?'

"'It seems,' returned the other, now beginning to grow able to tell his tale more connectedly, 'that the unhappy lad had been subject from childhood to epileptic fits. He must have felt one coming on soon after he went to bed last night, have risen and tried to find the door; but in the dark and his ignorance of the room must have made for the glass door into the garden instead. The fit must have seized him just as he reached it, for he had fallen right through it, severing an artery in his throat, by which—since no one was near to come to his help—he bled to death, and was found perfectly cold this morning.'

"'Good God!' gasped the prince; nor for the moment could he bring out anything but this ejaculation.

"'Your people, as I arrived, were in the act of carrying him to the mortuary, as they were anxious to have all trace of the catastrophe removed before Your Highness awoke; but I hope you will pardon me, sir; I could not rest until I had assured myself, by the sight of my own eyes, that you were safe; and so intruded; upon you in a manner which, you will believe, I never should have permitted myself under any less urgent circumstances.'

"'So, you see,' the prince said in conclusion, 'the churchyard claimed its victim after all.'"

**★★★★★★★★★★★★★★★★**

There was a short silence; then, "I call it a detestable story!" said

52

one.

"But it is true."

"Truth is often detestable."

# Poor Pretty Bobby

### CHAPTER 1

"Yes, my dear, you may not believe me, but I can assure you that you cannot dislike old women more, nor think them more contemptible supernumeraries, than I did when I was your age."

This is what old Mrs. Wentworth says—the old lady so incredibly tenacious of life (incredibly as it seems to me at eighteen) as to have buried a husband and five strong sons, and yet still to eat her dinner with hearty relish, and laugh at any such jokes as are spoken loudly enough to reach her dulled ears. This is what she says, shaking the while her head, which—poor old soul—is already shaking a good deal involuntarily. I am sitting close beside her armchair, and have been reading aloud to her; but as I cannot succeed in pitching my voice so as to make her hear satisfactorily, by mutual consent the book has been dropped in my lap, and we have betaken ourselves to conversation.

"I never said I disliked old women, did I?" reply I evasively, being too truthful altogether to deny the soft impeachment. "What makes you think I do? They are infinitely preferable to old men; I do distinctly dislike *them!*"

"A fat, bald, deaf old woman," continues she, not heeding me, and speaking with slow emphasis, while she raises one trembling hand to mark each unpleasant adjective; "if in the year '2 anyone had told me that I should have lived to be that, I think I should have killed them or *myself!* and yet now I am all three."

"You are not *very* deaf," say I politely—(the fatness and baldness admit of no civilities consistent with veracity)—but I raise my voice to pay the compliment.

"In the year '2 I was seventeen," she says, wandering off into memory. "Yes, my dear, I am just fifteen years older than the century and *it* is getting into its dotage, is not it? The year '2—ah! that was just about the time that I first saw my poor Bobby! Poor pretty Bobby."

"And who *was* Bobby?" ask I, pricking up my ears, and scenting, with the keen nose of youth, a dead-love idyll; an idyll of which this poor old hill of unsteady flesh was the heroine.

"I must have told you the tale a hundred times, have not I?" she asks, turning her old dim eyes towards me. "A curious tale, say what you will, and explain it how you will. I think I *must* have told you; but indeed I forgot to whom I tell my old stories and to whom I do not. Well, my love, you must promise to stop me if you have heard it before, but to me, you know, these old things are so much clearer than the things of yesterday."

"You never told me, Mrs. Hamilton," I say, and say truthfully; for being a new acquaintance I really have not been made acquainted with Bobby's history. "Would you mind telling it me now, if you are sure that it would not bore you?"

"Bobby," she repeats softly to herself, "Bobby. I daresay you do not think it a very pretty name?"

"N—not particularly," reply I honestly. "To tell you the truth, it rather reminds me of a policeman."

"I daresay," she answers quietly; "and yet in the year '2 I grew to think it the handsomest, dearest name on earth. Well, if you like, I will begin at the beginning and tell you how that came about"

"Do," say I, drawing a stocking out of my pocket, and thriftily beginning to knit to assist me in the process of listening.

"In the year '2 we were at war with France—you know that, of course. It seemed then as if war were our normal state; I could hardly remember a time when Europe had been at peace. In these days of stagnant quiet it appears as if people's kith and kin always lived out their full time and died in their beds. *Then* there was hardly a house where there was not one dead, either in battle, or of his wounds after battle, or of some dysentery or ugly parching fever.

"As for us, we had always been a soldier family—always; there was not one of us that had ever worn a black gown or sat upon a high stool with a pen behind his ear. I had lost uncles and cousins by the half-dozen and dozen, but, for my part, I did not much mind, as I knew very little about them, and black was more becoming wear to a person with my bright colour than anything else."

At the mention of her bright colour, I unintentionally lift my eyes from my knitting, and contemplate the yellow bagginess of the poor old cheek nearest me. Oh, Time! Time! what absurd and dirty turns you play us! What do you do with all our fair and goodly things when you have stolen them from us? In what far and hidden treasure-house do you store them?

"But I did care very much—very exceedingly—for my dear old father—not so old either—younger than my eldest boy was when he went; he would have been forty-two if he had lived three days longer. Well, well, child, you must not let me wander; you must keep me to it He was not a soldier, was not my father; he was a sailor, a post-captain in His Majesty's navy and commanded the ship *Thunderer* in the Channel fleet

"I had struck seventeen in the year '2, as I said before, and had just come home from being finished at a boarding-school of repute in those days, where I had learnt to talk the prettiest *ancien régime* French and to hate Bonaparte with unchristian violence from a little ruined *émigré maréchal;* had also, with infinite expenditure of time, labour, and Berlin wool, wrought out 'Abraham's Sacrifice of Isaac' and 'Jacob's First Kiss to Rachel,' in finest cross-stitch.

"Now I had bidden *adieu* to learning; had inly resolved never to disinter *Télémaque* and Thompson's *Seasons* from the bottom of my trunk; had taken a holiday from all my accomplishments with the exception of cross-stitch, to which I still faithfully adhered—and indeed, on the day I am going to mention, I recollect that I was hard at work on Judas Iscariot's face in Leonardo da Vinci's 'Last Supper'—hard at work at it, sitting in the morning sunshine, on a straight-backed chair. We had flatter backs in those days; our shoulders were not made round by lolling in easy-chairs; indeed, no *then* upholsterer made a chair that it was possible to loll in.

"My father rented a house near Plymouth at that time, an in-and-out nooky kind of old house—no doubt it has fallen to pieces long years ago—a house all set round with unnumbered flowers, and about which the rooks clamoured all together from the windy elm tops. I was labouring in flesh-coloured wool on Judas's left cheek, when the door opened and my mother entered. She looked as if something had freshly pleased her, and her eyes were smiling. In her hand she held an open and evidently just-read letter.

"'A messenger has come from Plymouth,' she says, advancing quickly and joyfully towards me. 'Your father will be here this afternoon.'

"'*This afternoon!*' cry I, at the top of my voice, pushing away my heavy work-frame. 'How delightful! But how?—how can that happen?'

"'They have had a brush with a French privateer,' she answers, sitting down on another straight-backed chair, and looking again over the large square letter, destitute of envelope, for such things were not in those days, 'and then they succeeded in taking her. Yet they were a good deal knocked about in the process, and have had to put into Plymouth to refit, so he will be here this afternoon for a few hours.'

"'Hurrah!' cry I, rising, holding out my scanty skirts, and beginning to dance.

"'Bobby Gerard is coming with him,' continues my mother, again glancing at her despatch. 'Poor boy, he has had a shot through his right arm, which has broken the bone, so your father is bringing him here for us to nurse him well again.'

"I stop in my dancing.

"'Hurrah again!' I say brutally. 'I do not mean about his arm; of course I am very sorry for that; but at all events, I shall see him at last I shall see whether he is like his picture, and whether it is not as egregiously flattered as I have always suspected.'

"There were no photographs you know in those days—not even hazy daguerreotypes—it was fifty good years too soon for them. The picture to which I allude is a miniature, at which I had stolen many a deeply longingly admiring glance in its velvet case. It is almost impossible for a miniature not to flatter. To the most coarse-skinned and mealy-potato-faced people it cannot help giving cheeks of the texture of a rose-leaf and brows of the grain of finest marble.

"'Yes,' replies my mother, absently, 'so you will. Well, I must be going to give orders about his room. He would like one looking on the garden best, do not you think, Phoebe?—one where he could smell the flowers and hear the birds?'

"Mother goes, and I fall into a meditation. Bobby Gerard is an orphan. A few years ago his mother, who was an old friend of my father's—who knows! perhaps an old love—feeling her end drawing nigh, had sent for father, and had asked him, with eager dying tears, to take as much care of her pretty forlorn boy as he could, and to shield him a little in his tender years from the evils of this wicked world, and to be to him a wise and kindly guardian, in the place of those natural ones that God had taken. And father had promised, and when he promised there was small fear of his not keeping his word.

"This was some years ago, and yet I had never seen him nor he me; he had been almost always at sea and I at school. I had heard plenty about him—about his sayings, his waggeries, his mischievousness, his soft-heartedness, and his great and unusual comeliness; but his outward man, save as represented in that stealthily peeped-at miniature, had I never seen. They were, to arrive in the afternoon; but long before the hour at which they were due I was waiting with expectant impatience to receive them. I had changed my dress, and had (though rather ashamed of myself) put on everything of most becoming that my wardrobe afforded.

"If you were to see me as I stood before the glass on that summer afternoon you would not be able to contain your laughter; the little boys in the street would run after me throwing stones and hooting; but *then*—according to the *then* fashion and standard of gentility— I was all that was most elegant and *comme il faut*. Lately it has been the mode to puff oneself out with unnatural and improbable protuberances; then one's great life-object was to make oneself appear as scrimping as possible—to make oneself look as flat as if one had been ironed. Many people *damped* their clothes to make them stick more closely to them, and to make them define more distinctly the outline of form and limbs.

"One's waist was under one's arms; the sole object of which seemed to be to outrage nature by pushing one's bust up into one's chin, and one's legs were revealed through one's scanty drapery with startling candour as one walked or sat I remember once standing with my back to a bright fire in our long drawing-room, and seeing myself reflected in a big mirror at the other end. I was so thinly clad that I was transparent, and could see through myself. Well, in the afternoon in question I was dressed quite an hour and a half too soon.

"I had a narrow little white gown, which clung successfully tight and close to my figure, and which was of so moderate a length as to leave visible my ankles and my neatly-shod and cross-sandled feet I had long mittens on my arms, black, and embroidered on the backs in coloured silks; and above my hair, which at the back was scratched up to the top of my crown, towered a tremendous tortoise-shell comb; while on each side of my face modestly drooped a bunch of curls, nearly meeting over my nose.

"My figure was full—ah! my dear, I have always had a tendency to fat, and you see what it has come to—and my pink cheeks were more deeply brightly rosy than usual. I had looked out at every upper window, so as to have the furthest possible view of the road.

"I had walked in my thin shoes half way down the drive, so as to command a turn, which, from the house, impeded my vision, when, at last, after many tantalising false alarms, and just five minutes later than the time mentioned in the letter, the high-swung, yellow-bodied, post-chaise hove in sight, dragged—briskly jingling—along by a pair of galloping horses. Then, suddenly, shyness overcame me—much as I loved my father, it was more as my personification of all knightly and noble qualities than from much personal acquaintance with him—and I fled.

"I remained in my room until I thought I had given them ample time to get through the first greetings and settle down into quiet talk. Then, having for one last time run my fingers through each ringlet of my two curl bunches, I stole diffidently downstairs.

"There was a noise of loud and gay voices issuing from the parlour, but, as I entered, they all stopped talking and turned to look at me.

"'And so, this is Phoebe!' cries my father's jovial voice, as he comes towards me, and heartily kisses me. 'Good Lord, how time flies! It does not seem more than three months since I saw the child, and yet then she was a bit of a brat in trousers, and long bare legs!'

"At this allusion to my late mode of attire, I laugh, but I also feel myself growing scarlet.

"'Here, Bobby!' continues my father, taking me by the hand, and leading me towards a sofa on which a young man is sitting beside my mother; 'this is my little lass that you have so often heard of. Not such a very little one, after all, is she? Do not be shy, my boy; you will not see such a pretty girl every day of your life—give her a kiss.'

"My eyes are on the ground, but I am aware that the young man rises, advances (not unwillingly, as it seems to me), and bestows a kiss, somewhere or other on my face. I am not quite clear *where*, as I think the curls impede him a good deal.

"Thus, before ever I saw Bobby, before ever I knew what manner of man he was, I was kissed by him. That was a good beginning, was not it?

"After these salutations are over, we subside again into conversation—I sitting beside my father, with his arm round my waist, sitting modestly silent, and peeping every now and then under my eyes, as often as I think I may do so safely unobserved, at the young fellow opposite me. I am instituting an inward comparison between Nature and Art: between the real live man and the miniature that undertakes to represent him. The first result of this inspection is disappointment, for where are the lovely smooth roses and lilies that I have been wont to connect with Bobby Gerard's name?

"There are no roses in his cheek, certainly; they are palish—from his wound, as I conjecture; but even before that accident, if there were roses at all, they must have been mahogany-coloured ones, for the salt sea winds and the high summer sun have tanned his fair face to a rich reddish, brownish, copperish hue. But in some things the picture lied not There is the brow more broad than high; the straight fine nose; the brave and joyful blue eyes, and the mouth with its pretty curling smile. On the whole, perhaps, I am not disappointed.

"By-and-by father rises, and steps out into the verandah, where the canary birds hung out in their cages are noisily praising God after their manner. Mother follows him. I should like to do the same; but a sense of good manners, and a conjecture that possibly my parents may have some subjects to discuss, on which they would prefer to be without the help of my advice, restrain me. I therefore remain, and so does the invalid.

## Chapter 2

"For some moments the silence threatens to remain unbroken between us; for some moments the subdued sound of father's and mother's talk from among the rose-beds and the piercing clamour of the canaries—fishwives among birds—are the only noises that salute our ears. Noise we make none ourselves. My eyes are reading the muddled pattern of the Turkey carpet; I do not know what his are doing. Small knowledge have I had of men saving the dancing-master at our school; a beautiful new youth is almost as great a novelty to me as to Miranda, and I am a good deal gawkier than she was under the new experience. I think he must have made a vow that he would not speak first I feel myself swelling to double my normal size with confusion and heat; at last, in desperation, I look up, and say sententiously, 'You have been wounded, I believe?'

"'Yes, I have.'

"He might have helped me by answering more at large, might not he? But now that I am having a good look at him, I see that he is rather red too. Perhaps he also feels gawky and swollen; the idea encourages me.

"'Did it hurt very badly?'

"'N—not so very much.'

"'I should have thought that you ought to have been in bed,' say I, with a motherly air of solicitude.

"'Should you, why?'

"'I thought that when people broke their limbs, they had to stay in bed till they were mended again.'

"'But mine was broken a week ago,' he answers, smiling and showing his straight white teeth—ah, the miniature was silent about them! 'You would not have had me stay in bed a whole week like an old woman?'

"'I expected to have seen you much *iller*,' say I, beginning to feel more at my ease, and with a sensible diminution of that unpleasant swelling sensation. 'Father said in his note that we were to nurse you well again; that sounded as if you were *quite* ill.'

"'Your father always takes a great deal too much care of me,' he says, with a slight frown and darkening of his whole bright face. 'I might be sugar or salt.'

"'And very kind of him, too,' I cry, firing up. 'What motive beside your own good can he have for looking after you? I call you rather ungrateful.'

"'Do you?' he says calmly, and without apparent resentment 'But you are mistaken. I am not ungrateful. However, naturally, you do not understand.'

"'Oh', indeed!' reply I, speaking rather shortly, and feeling a little offended, 'I dare say not.'

"Our talk is taking a somewhat hostile tone; to what further amenities we might have proceeded is unknown; for at this point father and mother reappear through the window, and the necessity of conversing with each other at all ceases.

"Father staid till evening, and we all supped together, and I was called upon to sit by Bobby, and cut up his food for him, as he was disabled from doing it for himself. Then, later still, when the sun had set, and all his evening reds and purples had followed him, when the night flowers were scenting all the garden, and the shadows lay about, enormously long in the summer moonlight, father got into the post-chaise again, and drove away through the black shadows and the faint clear shine, and Bobby stood at the hall door watching him, with his arm in a sling and a wistful smile on lips and eyes.

"'Well, we are not left *quite* desolate this time,' says mother, turning with rather tearful laughter to the young man. 'You wish that we were, do not you, Bobby?'

"'You would not believe me, if I answered "No," would you?' he asks, with the same still smile.

"'He is not very polite to us, is he, Phoebe?'

"'You would not wish me to be polite in such a case,' he replies, flushing. 'You would not wish me to be *glad* at missing the chance of seeing any of the fun?'

"But Mr. Gerard's eagerness to be back at his post delays the probability of his being able to return thither. The next day he has a feverish attack, the day after he is worse; the day after that worse still, and in fine, it is between a fortnight and three weeks before he also is able to get into a post-chaise and drive away to Plymouth. And meanwhile mother and I nurse him and cosset him, and make him odd and cool drinks out of herbs and field-flowers, whose uses are now disdained or forgotten.

"I do not mean any offence to you, my dear, but I think that young girls in those days were less squeamish and more truly delicate than they are nowadays. I remember once I read *Humphrey Clinker* aloud to my father, and we both highly relished and laughed over its jokes; but I should not have understood one of the darkly unclean allusions in that French book your brother left here one day. *You* would think it very unseemly to enter the bedroom of a strange young man, sick or well; but as for me, I spent whole nights in Bobby's, watching him and tending him with as little false shame as if he had been my brother. I can hear now, more plainly than the song you sang me an hour ago, the slumberous buzzing of the great brown-coated summer bees in his still room, as I sat by his bedside watching his sleeping face, as he dreamt unquietly, and clenched, and again unclenched, his nervous hands.

"I think he was back in the *Thunderer*, I can see now the little close curls of his sunshiny hair straggling over the white pillow. And then there came a good and blessed day, when he was out of danger, and then another, a little further on, when he was up and dressed, and he and I walked forth into the hayfield beyond the garden—reversing the order of things—*he*, leaning on *my* arm; and a good plump solid arm it was. We walked out under the heavy-leaved horse-chestnut trees, and the old and rough-barked elms. The sun was shining all this time, as it seems to me.

"I do not believe that in those old days there were the same cold unseasonable rains as now; there were soft showers enough to keep the grass green and the flowers undrooped; but I have no association of overcast skies and untimely deluges with those long and azure days. We sat under a haycock, on the shady side, and indolently watched the hot hay-makers—the shirt-sleeved men, and burnt and bare-armed women, tossing and raking; while we breathed the blessed country air, full of adorable scents, and crowded with little happy and pretty-winged insects.

"'In three days,' says Bobby, leaning his elbow in the hay, and speaking with an eager smile, 'three days at the furthest, I may go back again; may not I, Phoebe?'

"'Without doubt,' reply I, stiffly, pulling a dry and faded ox-eye flower out of the odorous mound beside me; 'for my part, I do not see why you should not go tomorrow, or indeed—if we could send into Plymouth for a chaise—this afternoon; you are so thin that you look all mouth and eyes, and you can hardly stand, without assistance, but these, of course, are trifling drawbacks, and I daresay would be rather an advantage on board ship than otherwise.'

"'You are angry!' he says, with a sort of laugh in his deep eyes. 'You look even prettier when you are angry than when you are pleased.'

"'It is no question of my looks,' I say, still in some heat, though mollified by the irrelevant compliment.

"'For the second time you are thinking me ungrateful,' he says, gravely; 'you do not tell me so in so many words, because it is towards yourself that my ingratitude is shown; the first time you told me of it it was almost the first thing that you ever said to me.'

"'So, it was,' I answer quickly; 'and if the occasion were to come over again, I should say it again. I daresay you did not mean it, but it sounded exactly as if you were complaining of my father for being too careful of you.'

"'He *is* too careful of me!' cries the young man, with a hot flushing of cheek and brow. 'I cannot help it if it makes you angry again; I *must* say it, he is more careful of me than he would be of his own son, if he had one.'

"'Did not he promise your mother that he would look after you?' ask I eagerly. 'When people make promises to people on their death-beds they are in no hurry to break them; at least, such people as father are not.'

"'You do not understand,' he says, a little impatiently, while that hot flush still dwells on his pale cheek; 'my mother was the last person in the world to wish him to take care of my body at the expense of my honour.'

"'What are you talking about?' I say, looking at him with a lurking suspicion that, despite the steady light of reason in his blue eyes, he is still labouring under some form of delirium.

"'Unless I tell you all my grievance, I see that you will never comprehend,' he says sighing. 'Well, listen to me and you shall hear it, and if you do not agree with me, when I have done, you are not the kind of girl I take you for.'

"'Then I am sure I am not the kind of girl you take me for,' reply I, with a laugh; 'for I am fully determined to disagree with you entirely.'

"'You know,' he says, raising himself a little from his hay couch and speaking with clear rapidity, 'that whenever we take a French prize a lot of the French sailors are ironed, and the vessel is sent into port, in the charge of one officer and several men; there is some slight risk attending it—for my part, I think *very* slight—but I suppose that your father looks at it differently, for—*I have never been sent.*'

"'It is accident,' say I, reassuringly; 'your turn will come in good time.'

"'It is *not* accident!' he answers, firmly. 'Boys younger than I am—much less trustworthy, and of whom he has not half the opinion that he has of me—have been sent, but I, *never,* I bore it as well as I could for a long time, but now I can bear it no longer; it is not, I assure you, my fancy; but I can see that my brother officers, knowing how partial your father is to me—what influence I have with him in many things—conclude that my not being sent is my own choice; is short, that I am—*afraid.*' (His voice sinks with a disgusted and shamed intonation at the last word.) 'Now—I have told you the sober facts—look me in the face' (putting his hand with boyish familiarity under my chin, and turning round my curls, my features, and the front view of my big comb towards him), 'and tell me whether you agree with me, as I said you would, or not—whether it is not cruel kindness on his part to make me keep a whole skin on such terms?'

"I look him in the face for a moment, trying to say that I do not agree with him, but it is more than I can manage. 'You were right,' I say, turning my head away, 'I *do* agree with you; I wish to heaven that I could honestly say that I did not.'

"'Since you do then,' he cries excitedly—'Phoebe! I knew you would, I knew you better than you knew yourself—I have a favour to ask of you, a *great* favour, and one that will keep me all my life in debt to you.'

"'What is it?' ask I, with a sinking heart.

"'Your father is very fond of you——'

"'I know it,' I answer curtly.

"'Anything that you asked, and that was within the bounds of possibility, he would do,' he continues, with eager gravity. 'Well, this is what I ask of you: to write him a line, and let me take it, when I go, asking him to send me home in the next prize.'

"Silence for a moment, only the hay-makers laughing over their rakes. 'And if,' say I, with a trembling voice, 'you lose your life in this service, you will have to thank me for it; I shall have your death on my head all through my life.'

"'The danger is infinitesimal, as I told you before,' he says, impatiently; 'and even if it were greater than it is—well, life is a good thing, very good, but there are better things, and even if I come to grief, which is most unlikely, there are plenty of men as good as—better than—I, to step into my place.'

"'It will be small consolation to the people who are fond of you that someone better than you is alive, though you are dead,' I say, tearfully.

"'But I do not mean to be dead,' he says, with a cheery laugh. 'Why are you so determined on killing me? I mean to live to be an admiral. Why should not I?'

"'Why indeed?' say I, with a feeble echo of his cheerful mirth, and feeling rather ashamed of my tears.

"'And meanwhile you will write?' he says, with an eager return to the charge; 'and soon? Do not look angry and pouting, as you did just now, but I *must* go! What is there to hinder me? I am getting up my strength as fast as it is possible for any human creature to do, and just think how I should feel if they were to come in for something really good while I am away.'

"So, I wrote."

## CHAPTER 3

"I often wished afterwards that my right hand had been cut off before its fingers had held the pen that wrote that letter. You wonder to see me moved at what happened so long ago—before your parents were born—and certainly it makes not much difference now; for even if he had prospered then, and come happily home to me, yet, in the course of nature he would have gone long before now. I should not have been so cruel as to have wished him to have lasted to be as I am. I did not mean to hint at the end of my story before I have reached the middle. Well—and so he went, with the letter in his pocket, and I felt something like the king in the tale, who sent a messenger with a letter, and wrote in the letter, 'Slay the bearer of this as soon as he arrives!'

"But before he went—the evening before, as we walked in the garden after supper, with our monstrously long shadows stretching before us in the moonlight—I do not think he said in so many words, 'Will you marry me?' but somehow, by some signs or words on both our parts, it became clear to us that, by-and-by, if God left him alive, and if the war ever came to an end, he and I should belong to one another. And so, having understood this, when he went, he kissed me, as he had done when he came, only this time no one bade him; he did it of his own accord, and a hundred times instead of one; and for my part, this time, instead of standing passive like a log or a post, I kissed him back again, most lovingly, with many tears.

"Ah! parting in those days, when the last kiss to one's beloved ones was not unlikely to be an *adieu* until the great Day of Judgment, was a different thing to the listless, unemotional goodbyes of these stagnant times of peace!

"And so, Bobby also got into a post-chaise and drove away, and we watched him too, till he turned the corner out of our sight, as we had watched father; and then I hid my face among the jessamine flowers that clothed the wall of the house, and wept as one that would not be comforted. However, one cannot weep for ever, or, if one does, it makes one blind and blear, and I did not wish Bobby to have a wife with such defects; so, in process of time I dried my tears.

"And the days passed by, and nature went slowly and evenly through her lovely changes. The hay was gathered in, and the fine new grass and clover sprang up among the stalks of the grass that had gone; and the wild roses struggled into odorous bloom, and crowned the hedges, and then *their* time came, and they shook down their faint petals, and went.

"And now the corn harvest had come, and we had heard once or twice from our beloveds, but not often. And the sun still shone with broad power, and kept the rain in subjection. And all morning I sat at my big frame, and toiled on at the '*Last Supper.*' I had finished Judas Iscariot's face and the other Apostles.

"I was engaged now upon the table-cloth, which was not interesting and required not much exercise of thought. And mother sat near me, either working too or reading a good book, and taking snuff—every lady snuffed in those days: at least in trifles, if not in great things, the world mends. And at night, when ten o'clock struck, I covered up my frame and stole listlessly upstairs to my room. There, I knelt at the open window, facing Plymouth and the sea, and asked God to take good care of father and Bobby. I do not know that I asked for any spiritual blessings for them, I only begged that they might be alive.

"One night, one hot night, having prayed even more heartily and tearfully than my wont for them both, I had lain down to sleep. The windows were left open, and the blinds up, that all possible air might reach me from the still and scented garden below. Thinking of Bobby, I had fallen asleep, and he is still mistily in my head, when I seem to wake. The room is full of clear light, but it is not morning: it is only the moon looking right in and flooding every object. I can see my own ghostly figure sitting up in bed, reflected in the looking-glass opposite. I listen: surely, I heard some noise:—yes—certainly, there can be no doubt of it—someone is knocking loudly and perseveringly at the hall-door.

"At first, I fall into a deadly fear; then my reason comes to my aid. If it were a robber, or person with any evil intent, would he knock so openly and clamorously as to arouse the inmates? Would not he rather go stealthily to work, to force a *silent* entrance for himself? At worst it is some drunken sailor from Plymouth; at best, it is a messenger with news of our dear ones. At this thought I instantly spring out of bed, and hurrying on my stockings and shoes and whatever garments come most quickly to hand—with my hair spread all over my back, and utterly forgetful of my big comb, I open my door, and fly down the passages, into which the moon is looking with her ghostly smile, and down the broad and shallow stairs.

"As I near the hall-door I meet our old butler, also rather dishevelled, and evidently on the same errand as myself.

"'Who *can* it be, Stephens?' I ask, trembling with excitement and fear.

"'Indeed, ma'am, I cannot tell you,' replies the old man, shaking his head, 'it is a very odd time of night to choose for making such a noise. We will ask them their business, whoever they are, before we unchain the door.'

"It seems to me as if the endless bolts would never be drawn—the key never be turned in the stiff lock; but at last, the door opens slowly and cautiously, only to the width of a few inches, as it is still confined by the strong chain. I peep out eagerly, expecting I know not what.

"Good heavens! What do I see? No drunken sailor, no messenger, but, oh joy! oh blessedness! my Bobby himself—my beautiful boy-lover! Even now, even after all these weary years, even after the long bitterness that followed, I cannot forget the unutterable happiness of that moment.

"'Open the door, Stephens, quick!' I cry, stammering with eagerness. 'Draw the chain; it is Mr. Gerard; do not keep him waiting.'

"The chain rattles down, the door opens wide, and there he stands before me. At once, ere anyone has said anything, ere anything has happened, a feeling of cold disappointment steals unaccountably over me—a nameless sensation, whose nearest kin is chilly awe. He makes no movement towards me; he does not catch me in his arms, nor even hold out his right hand to me. He stands there still and silent, and though the night is dry, equally free from rain and dew, I see that he is dripping wet; the water is running down from his clothes, from his drenched hair, and even from his eyelashes, on to the dry ground at his feet.

"'What has happened?' I cry, hurriedly, 'How wet you are!' and as I speak, I stretch out my hand and lay it on his coat sleeve. But even as I do it a sensation of intense cold runs up my fingers and my arm, even to the elbow. How is it that he is so chilled to the marrow of his bones on this sultry, breathless, August night? To my extreme surprise he does not answer; he still stands there, dumb and dripping. 'Where have you come from?' I ask, with that sense of awe deepening. 'Have you fallen into the river? How is it that you are so wet?'

"'It was cold,' he says, shivering, and speaking in a slow and strangely altered voice, 'bitter cold. I could not stay there.'

"'Stay where?' I say, looking in amazement at his face, which, whether owing to the ghastly effect of moonlight or not, seems to me ash white. "Where have you been? What is it you are talking about?'

"But he does not reply.

"'He is really ill, I am afraid, Stephens,' I say, turning with a forlorn feeling towards the old butler. 'He does not seem to hear what I say to him. I am afraid he has had a thorough chill. What water can he have fallen into? You had better help him up to bed, and get him warm between the blankets. His room is quite ready for him, you know—come in,' I say, stretching out my hand to him, 'you will be better after a night's rest.'

"He does not take my offered hand, but he follows me across the threshold and across the hall. I hear the water drops falling drip, drip, on the echoing stone floor as he passes; then upstairs, and along the gallery to the door of his room, where I leave him with Stephens. Then everything becomes blank and nil to me.

"I am awoke as usual in the morning by the entrance of my maid with hot water.

"'Well, how is Mr. Gerard this morning?' I ask, springing into a sitting posture.

"She puts down the hot water tin and stares at her leisure at me.

"'My dear Miss Phoebe, how should *I* know? Please God he is in good health and safe, and that we shall have good news of him before long.'

"'Have not you asked how he is?' I ask impatiently. 'He did not seem quite himself last night; there was something odd about him. I was afraid he was in for another touch of fever.'

"'Last night—fever,' repeats she, slowly and disconnectedly echoing some of my words. 'I beg your pardon, ma'am, I am sure, but I have not the least idea in life what you are talking about'

"'How stupid you are!' I say, quite at the end of my patience. 'Did not Mr. Gerard come back unexpectedly last night, and did not I hear him knocking, and run down to open the door, and did not Stephens come too, and afterwards take him up to bed?'

"The stare of bewilderment gives way to a laugh.

"'You have been dreaming, ma'am. Of course I cannot answer for what you did last night, but I am sure that Stephens knows no more of the young gentleman than I do, for only just now, at breakfast, he was saying that he thought it was about time for us to have some tidings of him and master.'

"'A dream!' cry I indignantly. 'Impossible! I was no more dreaming then than I am now.'

"But time convinces me that I am mistaken, and that during all the time that I thought I was standing at the open hall-door, talking to my beloved, in reality I was lying on my bed in the depths of sleep, with no other company than the scent of the flowers and the light of the moon. At this discovery a great and terrible depression falls on me. I go to my mother to tell her of my vision, and at the end of my narrative I say:

"'Mother, I know well that Bobby is dead, and that I shall never see him anymore. I feel assured that he died last night, and that he came himself to tell me of his going. I am sure that there is nothing left for me now but to go too.'

"I speak thus far with great calmness, but when I have done, I break out into loud and violent weeping. Mother rebukes me gently, telling me that there is nothing more natural than that I should dream of a person who constantly occupies my waking thoughts, nor that, considering the gloomy nature of my apprehensions about him, my dream should be of a sad and ominous kind; but that, above all dreams and omens, God is good, that He has preserved him hitherto, and that, for her part, no devil-sent apparition shall shake her confidence in His continued clemency. I go away a little comforted, though not very much, and still every night I kneel at the open window facing Plymouth and the sea, and pray for my sailor boy. But it seems to me, despite all my self-reasonings, despite all that mother says, that my prayers for him are prayers for the dead.

"Three more weeks pass away; the harvest is garnered, and the pears are growing soft and mellow. Mother's and my outward life goes on in its silent regularity, nor do we talk much to each other of the tumult that rages—of the heartache that burns, within each of us. At the end of the three weeks, as we are sitting as usual, quietly employed, and buried each in our own thoughts, in the parlour, towards evening we hear wheels approaching the hall-door. We both run out as in my dream I had run to the door, and arrive in time to receive my father as he steps out of the carriage that has brought him. Well! at least *one* of our wanderers has come home, but where is the other?

"Almost before he has heartily kissed us both—wife and child—father cries out, 'But where is Bobby?'

"'That is just what I was going to ask you,' replies mother quickly.

"'Is not he *here* with you?' returns he anxiously.

"'Not he,' answers mother, 'we have neither seen nor heard anything of him for more than six weeks.'

"'Great God!' exclaims he, while his face assumes an expression of the deepest concern, 'what *can* have become of him? what *can* have happened to the poor fellow?'

"'Has not he been with you, then?—has not he been in the *Thunderer*?' asks mother, running her words into one another in her eagerness to get them out.

"'I sent him home three weeks ago in a prize, with a letter to you, and told him to stay with you till I came home, and what can have become of him since, God only knows!' he answers with a look of the profoundest sorrow and anxiety.

"There is a moment of forlorn and dreary silence; then I speak. I have been standing dumbly by, listening, and my heart growing colder and colder at every dismal word.

"'It is all my doing!' I cry passionately, flinging myself down in an agony of tears on the straight-backed old settle in the hall. 'It is my fault—no one else's! The very last time that I saw him, I told him that he would have to thank me for his death, and he laughed at me, but it has come true. If I had not written *you*, father, that accursed letter, we should have had him here *now*, this *minute*, safe and sound, standing in the middle of us—as we never, *never*, shall have him again!'

"I stop, literally suffocated with emotion.

"Father comes over, and lays his kind brown hand on my bent prone head. 'My child,' he says, 'my dear child,' (and tears are dimming the clear grey of his own eyes), 'you are wrong to make up your mind to what is the worst at once. I do not disguise from you that there is cause for grave anxiety about the dear fellow, but still God is good; He has kept both him and me hitherto; into His hands we must trust our boy.'

"I sit up, and shake away my tears.

"'It is no use,' I say. 'Why should I hope? There is no hope! I know it for a certainty! He is *dead*' (looking round at them both with a sort of calmness); 'he died on the night that I had *that* dream—mother, I told you so at the time. Oh, my Bobby! I knew that you could not leave me forever without coming to tell me!'

"And so, speaking, I fall into strong hysterics and am carried up-stairs to bed. And so, three or four more lagging days crawl by, and still we hear nothing, and remain in the same state of doubt and un-certainty; which to me, however, is hardly uncertainty; so, convinced am I, in my own mind that my fair-haired lover is away in the land whence never letter or messenger comes—that he has reached the Great Silence. So, I sit at my frame, working my heart's agony into the tapestry, and feebly trying to say to God that He has done well, but I cannot.

"On the contrary, it seems to me, as my life trails on through the mellow mist of the autumn mornings, through the shortened autumn evenings, that, whoever has done it, it is most evilly done. One night we are sitting round the little crackling wood fire that one does not need for warmth, but that gives a cheerfulness to the room and the furniture, when the butler Stephens enters, and going over to father, whispers to him. I seem to understand in a moment what the purport of his whisper is.

"'Why does he whisper?' I cry, irritably. 'Why does not he speak out loud? Why should you try to keep it from me? I know that it is something about Bobby.'

"Father has already risen, and is walking towards the door.

"'I will not let you go until you tell me,' I cry wildly, flying after him.

"'A sailor has come over from Plymouth,' he answers hurriedly; 'he says he has news. My darling, I will not keep you in suspense a moment longer than I can help, and meanwhile pray—both of you pray for him!'

"I sit rigidly still, with my cold hands tightly clasped; during the moments that next elapse. Then father returns. His eyes are full of tears, and there is small need to ask for his message; it is most plainly written on his features—death, and not life.

"'You were right, Phoebe,' he says, brokenly, taking hold of my icy hands; 'you knew best. He is gone! God has taken him.'

"My heart dies. I had thought that I had no hope, but I was wrong. 'I knew it!' I say, in a dry stiff voice. 'Did not I tell you so? But you would not believe me—go on!—tell me how it was—do not think I cannot bear it—make haste!'

"And so, he tells me all that there is now left for me to know—after what manner, and on what day, my darling took his leave of this pretty and cruel world. He had had his wish, as I already knew, and had set off blithely home in the last prize they had captured. Father had taken the precaution of having a larger proportion than usual of the Frenchmen ironed, and had also sent a greater number of Englishmen. But to what purpose? They were nearing port, sailing prosperously along on a smooth blue sea, with a fair strong wind, thinking of no evil, when a great and terrible misfortune overtook them.

"Some of the Frenchmen who were not ironed got the sailors below and drugged their grog; ironed them, and freed their countrymen. Then one of the officers rushed on deck, and holding a pistol to my Bobby's head bade him surrender the vessel or die. Need I tell you which he chose? I think not—well" (with a sigh) "and so they shot my boy—ah me! how many years ago—and threw him overboard! Yes—threw him overboard—it makes me angry and grieved even now to think of it—into the great and greedy sea, and the vessel escaped to France."

There is a silence between us: I will own to you that I am crying, but the old lady's eyes are dry.

"Well," she says, after a pause, with a sort of triumph in her tone, "they never could say again that Bobby Gerard was *afraid!*

"The tears were running down my father's cheeks, as he told me," she resumes presently, "but at the end he wiped them and said, 'It is well! He was as pleasant in God's sight as he was in ours, and so He has taken him.'

"And for me, I was glad that he had gone to God—none gladder. But you will not wonder that, for myself, I was past speaking sorry. And so, the years went by, and, as you know, I married Mr. Hamilton, and lived with him forty years, and was happy in the main, as happiness goes; and when he died, I wept much and long, and so I did for each of my sons when in turn they went. But looking back on all my long life, the event that I think stands out most clearly from it is my dream and my boy-lover's death day. It was an odd dream, was not it?"

# The Man with the Nose

*(The details of this little story are of course imaginary, but the main incidents are, to the best of my belief, facts. They happened twenty, or more than twenty years ago.)*

## CHAPTER 1

"Let us get a map and see what places look pleasantest?" says she.

"As for that," reply I, "on a map most places look equally pleasant"

"Never mind; get one!"

I obey.

"Do you like the seaside?" asks Elizabeth, lifting her little brown head and her small happy white face from the English sea-coast along which her forefinger is slowly travelling.

"Since you ask me, distinctly *no*," reply I, for once venturing to have a decided opinion of my own, which during the last few weeks of imbecility I can be hardly said to have had. "I broke my last wooden spade five and twenty years ago. I have but a poor opinion of cockles—sandy red-nosed things, are not they? and the air always makes me bilious."

"Then we certainly will not go there," says Elizabeth, laughing. "A bilious bridegroom! alliterative but horrible! None of our friends show the least eagerness to lend us their country house."

"Oh, that God would put it into the hearts of men to take their wives straight home, as their fathers did," say I, with a cross groan.

"It is evident, therefore, that we must go somewhere," returns she, not heeding the aspiration contained in my last speech, making her forefinger resume its employment, and reaching Torquay.

"I suppose so," say I, with a sort of sigh; "for once in our lives we must resign ourselves to having the finger of derision pointed at us by waiters and landlords."

"You shall leave your new portmanteau at home, and I will leave all my best clothes, and nobody will guess that we are bride and bridegroom; they will think that we have been married—oh, ever since the world began" (opening her eyes very wide).

I shake my head. "With an old portmanteau and in rags we shall still have the mark of the beast upon us."

"Do you mind much? do you hate being ridiculous?" asks Elizabeth, meekly, rather depressed by my view of the case; "because if so, let us go somewhere out of the way, where there will be very few people to laugh at us."

"On the contrary," return I, stoutly, "we will betake ourselves to some spot where such as we do chiefly congregate—where we shall be swallowed up and lost in the multitude of our fellow-sinners." A pause devoted to reflection. "What do you say to Killarney?" say I, cheerfully.

"There are a great many fleas there, I believe," replies Elizabeth, slowly; "flea-bites make large lumps on me; you would not like me if I were covered with large lumps."

At the hideous ideal picture thus presented to me by my little beloved I relapse into inarticulate idiocy; emerging from which by-and-by, I suggest "The Lakes?" My arm is round her, and I feel her supple body shiver though it is mid July, and the bees are booming about in the still and sleepy noon garden outside.

"Oh—no—no—not *there!*"

"Why such emphasis?" I ask gaily; "more fleas? At this rate, and with this *sine quâ non*, our choice will grow limited."

"Something dreadful happened to me there," she says, with another shudder. "But indeed, I did not think there was any harm in it—I never thought anything would come of it."

"What the devil was it?" cry I, in a jealous heat and hurry; "what mischief *did* you do, and why have not you told me about it before?"

"I did not *do* much," she answers meekly, seeking for my hand, and when found kissing it in timid deprecation of my wrath; "but I was ill—very ill—there; I had a nervous fever. I was in a bed hung with a chintz with a red and green fern-leaf pattern on it. I have always hated red and green fern-leaf chintzes ever since."

"It would be possible to avoid the obnoxious bed, would not it?" say I, laughing a little. "Where does it lie? Windermere? Ulleswater? Wastwater? Where?"

"We were at Ulleswater," she says, speaking rapidly, while a hot colour grows on her small white cheeks—"Papa, mamma, and I; and there came a mesmeriser to Penrith, and we went to see him—everybody did—and he asked leave to mesmerise me—he said I should be such a good medium—and—and—I did not know what it was like. I thought it would be quite good fun—and—and—I let him."

She is trembling exceedingly; even the loving pressure of my arms cannot abate her shivering.

"Well?"

"And after that I do not remember anything—I believe I did all sorts of extraordinary things that he told me—sang and danced, and made a fool of myself—but when I came home I was very ill, very—I lay in bed for five whole weeks, and—and was off my head, and said odd and wicked things that you would not have expected me to say—that dreadful bed! shall I ever forget it?"

"We will *not* go to the Lakes," I say, decisively, "and we will not talk any more about mesmerism."

"That is right," she says, with a sigh of relief, "I try to think about it as little as possible; but sometimes, in the dead black of the night, when God seems a long way off, and the devil near, it comes back to me so strongly—I feel, do not you know, as if he were there—somewhere in the room, and I must get up and follow him."

"Why should not we go abroad?" suggest I, abruptly turning the conversation.

"Why, indeed?" cries Elizabeth, recovering her gaiety, while her pretty blue eyes begin to dance. "How stupid of us not to have thought of it before; only *abroad* is a big word. *What* abroad?"

"We must be content with something short of Central Africa," I say, gravely, "as I think our one hundred and fifty pounds would hardly take us that far."

"Wherever we go, we must buy a dialogue book," suggests my little bride elect, "and I will learn some phrases before we start"

"As for that, the Anglo-Saxon tongue takes one pretty well round the world," reply I, with a feeling of complacent British swagger, putting my hands in my breeches pockets.

"Do you fancy the Rhine?" says Elizabeth, with a rather timid suggestion; "I know it is the fashion to run it down nowadays, and call it a cocktail river; but—but—after all it cannot be so very contemptible, or Byron could not have said such noble things about it."

"*The castled crag of Drachenfels*
*Frowns o'er the wide and winding Rhine,*
*Whose breast of waters broadly swells*

77

*Between the banks which bear the vine."*

Say I, spouting. "After all, that proves nothing, for Byron could have made a silk purse out of a sow's ear."

"The Rhine will not do then?" says she, resignedly, suppressing a sigh.

"On the contrary, it will do admirably: it is a cocktail river, and I do not care who says it is not," reply I, with illiberal positiveness; "but everybody should be able to say so from their own experience, and not from hearsay: the Rhine let it be, by all means."

So, the Rhine it is.

## Chapter 2

I have got over it; we have both got over it tolerably, creditably; but after all, it is a much severer ordeal for a man than a woman, who, with a bouquet to occupy her hands, and a veil to gently shroud her features, need merely be prettily passive. I am alluding, I need hardly say, to the religious ceremony of marriage, which I flatter myself I have gone through with a stiff sheepishness not unworthy of my country. It is a three-days-old event now, and we are getting used to belonging to one another, though Elizabeth still takes off her ring twenty times a day to admire its bright thickness; still laughs when she hears herself called "*Madame*."

Three days ago, we kissed all our friends, and left them to make themselves ill on our cake, and criticise our bridal behaviour, and now we are at Brussels, she and I, feeling oddly, joyfully free from any chaperone. We have been mildly sightseeing—very mildly, most people would say, but we have resolved not to take our pleasure with the railway speed of Americans, or the hasty sadness of our fellow Britons. Slowly and gaily, we have been taking ours. Today we have been to visit Wiertz's pictures. Have you ever seen them, oh reader?

They are known to comparatively few people, but if you have a taste for the unearthly terrible—if you wish to sup full of horrors, hasten thither. We have been peering through the appointed peephole at the horrible cholera picture—the man buried alive by mistake, pushing up the lid of his coffin, and stretching a ghastly face and livid hands out of his winding sheet towards you, while awful grey-blue coffins are piled around, and noisome toads and giant spiders crawl damply about. On first seeing it, I have reproached myself for bringing one of so nervous a temperament as Elizabeth to see so haunting and hideous a spectacle; but she is less impressed than I expected—less impressed than I myself am.

"He is very lucky to be able to get his lid up," she says, with a half-laugh;"we should find it hard work to burst our brass nails, should not we? When you bury me, dear, fasten me down very slightly, in case there may be some mistake."

And now all the long and quiet July evening we have been prowling together about the streets. Brussels is the town of towns for *flânering*—have been flattening our noses against the shop windows, and making each other imaginary presents. Elizabeth has not confined herself to imagination, however; she has made me buy her a little bonnet with feathers—"in order to look married," as she says, and the result is such a delicious picture of a child playing at being grown up, having practised a theft on its mother's wardrobe, that for the last two hours I have been in a foolish ecstasy of love and laughter over her and it. We are at the "*Bellevue*," and have a fine suite of rooms, *au premier*, evidently specially devoted to the English, to the gratification of whose well-known loyalty the Prince and Princess of Wales are simpering from the walls.

Is there anyone in the three kingdoms who knows his own face as well as he knows the faces of Albert Victor and Alexandra? The long evening has at last slidden into night—night far advanced—night melting into earliest day. All Brussels is asleep. One moment ago, I also was asleep, soundly as any log. What is it that has made me take this sudden, headlong plunge out of sleep into wakefulness? Who is it that is clutching at and calling upon me? What is it that is making me struggle mistily up into a sitting posture, and try to revive my sleep-numbed senses?

A summer night is never wholly dark; by the half-light that steals through the closed *persiennes* and open windows I see my wife standing beside my bed; the extremity of terror on her face, and her fingers digging themselves with painful tenacity into my arm.

"Tighter, tighter!" she is crying, wildly. "What are you thinking of? You are letting me go!"

"Good heavens!" say I, rubbing my eyes, while my muddy brain grows a trifle clearer. 'What is it? What has happened? Have you had a nightmare?"

"You saw him," she says, with a sort of sobbing breathlessness; "you know you did! You saw him as well as I."

"I!" cry I, incredulously—"not I. Till this second, I have been fast asleep. *I* saw nothing."

"You did!" she cries, passionately. "You know you did. Why do you deny it? You were as frightened as I?"

"As I live," I answer, solemnly, "I know no more than the dead what you are talking about; till you woke me by calling me and catching hold of me, I was as sound asleep as the seven sleepers."

"Is it possible that it can have been a *dream?*" she says, with a long sigh, for a moment loosing my arm, and covering her face with her hands. "But no—in a dream I should have been, somewhere else, but I was here—*here*—on that bed, and he stood *there*," pointing with her forefinger, "just *there*, between the foot of it and the window!"

She stops, panting.

"It is all that brute Wiertz," say I, in a fury. "I wish I had been buried alive myself, before I had been fool enough to take you to see his beastly daubs."

"Light a candle," she says, in the same breathless way, her teeth chattering with fright. "Let us make sure that he is not hidden somewhere in the room."

"How could he be?" say I, striking a match; "the door is locked."

"He might have got in by the balcony," she answers, still trembling violently.

"He would have had to have cut a very large hole in the *persiennes*," say I, half-mockingly. "See, they are intact and well fastened on the inside."

She sinks into an armchair, and pushes her loose soft hair from her white face.

"It *was* a dream then, I suppose?"

She is silent for a moment or two, while I bring her a glass of water, and throw a dressing-gown round her cold and shrinking form.

"Now tell me, my little one," I say, coaxingly, sitting down at her feet, "what it was—what you thought you saw?"

"*Thought* I saw!" echoes she, with indignant emphasis, sitting upright, while her eyes sparkle feverishly. "I am as certain that I saw him standing there as I am that I see that candle burning—that I see this chair—that I see you."

"*Him!* but who is *him?*"

She falls forward on my neck, and buries her face in my shoulder.

"That—dreadful—man!" she says, while her whole body is one tremor.

"What dreadful man?" cry I, impatiently.

She is silent.

"Who was he?"

"I do not know."

"Did you ever see him before?"

"Oh, no—no, never! I hope to God I may never see him again!"

"What was he like?"

"Come closer to me," she says, laying hold of my hand with her small and chilly fingers; "stay *quite* near me, and I will tell you,"—after a pause—"he had a *nose!*"

"My dear soul," cry I, bursting out with a loud laugh in the silence of the night, "do not most people have noses? Would not he have been much more dreadful if he had had *none?*"

"But it was *such* a nose!" she says, with perfect trembling gravity.

"A bottle nose?" suggest I, still cackling.

"For heaven's sake, don't laugh!" she says, nervously; "if you had seen his face, you would have been as little disposed to laugh as I."

"But his nose?" return I, suppressing my merriment; "what kind of nose was it? See, I am as grave as a judge."

"It was very prominent," she answers, in a sort of awe-struck half-whisper, "and very sharply chiselled; the nostrils very much cut out." A little pause. "His eyebrows were one straight black line across his face, and under them his eyes burnt like dull coals of fire, that shone and yet did not shine; they looked like dead eyes, sunken, half extinguished, and yet sinister."

"And what did he do?" ask I, impressed, despite myself, by her passionate earnestness; "when did you first see him?"

"I was asleep," she said—"at least I thought so—and suddenly I opened my eyes, and he was *there—there*"—pointing again with trembling finger—"between the window and the bed."

"What was he doing? Was he walking about?"

"He was standing as still as stone—I never saw any live thing so still—*looking* at me; he never called or beckoned, or moved a finger, but his eyes *commanded* me to come to him, as the eyes of the mesmeriser at Penrith did." She stops, breathing heavily. I can hear her heart's loud and rapid beats.

"And you?" I say, pressing her more closely to my side, and smoothing her troubled hair.

"I *hated* it," she cries, excitedly; "I loathed it—abhorred it. I was ice-cold with fear and horror, but—I *felt* myself going to him."

"Yes?"

"And then I shrieked out to you, and you came running, and

caught fast hold of me, and held me tight at first—quite tight—but presently I felt your hold slacken—slacken—and though I *longed* to stay with you, though I *was* mad with fright, yet I felt myself pulling strongly away from you—going to him; and he—he stood there always looking—looking—and then I gave one last loud shriek, and I suppose I awoke—and it was a dream!"

"I never heard of a clearer case of nightmare," say I, stoutly; "that vile Wiertz! I should like to see his whole *Musée* burnt by the hands of the hangman tomorrow."

She shakes her head. "It had nothing to say to Wiertz; what it meant I do not know, but——"

"It meant nothing," I answer, reassuringly, "except that for the future we will go and see none but good and pleasant sights, and steer clear of charnel-house fancies."

## Chapter 3

Elizabeth is now in a position to decide whether the Rhine is a cocktail river or no, for she is on it, and so am I. We are sitting, with an awning over our heads, and little wooden stools under our feet. Elizabeth has a small sailor's hat and blue ribbon on her head. The river breeze has blown it rather awry; has tangled her plenteous hair; has made a faint pink stain on her pale cheeks. It is some *fête* day, and the boat is crowded. Tables, countless camp-stools, volumes of black smoke pouring from the funnel, as we steam along.

"Nothing to the Caledonian Canal!" cries a burly Scotchman in leggings, speaking with loud authority, and surveying with an air of contempt the eternal vine-clad slopes, that sound so well, and look so *sticky* in reality. "Cannot hold a candle to it!" A rival bride and bridegroom opposite, sitting together like lovebirds under an umbrella, looking into each other's eyes instead of at the Rhine scenery.

"They might as well have stayed at home, might not they?" says my wife, with a little air of superiority. "Come, we are not so bad as that, are we?"

A storm comes on: hailstones beat slantwise and reach us—stone and sting us right under our awning. Everybody rushes down below, and takes the opportunity to feed ravenously. There are few actions more disgusting than eating can be made. A handsome girl close to us—her immaturity evidenced by the two long tails of black hair down her back—is thrusting her knife half way down her throat.

"Come on deck again," says Elizabeth, disgusted and frightened at this last sight. "The hail was much better than this!"

So, we return to our camp-stools, and sit alone under one mackintosh in the lashing storm, with happy hearts and empty stomachs.

"Is not this better than any luncheon?" asks Elizabeth, triumphantly, while the raindrops hang on her long and curled lashes.

"Infinitely better," reply I, madly struggling with the umbrella to prevent its being blown inside out, and gallantly ignoring a species of gnawing sensation at my entrails.

The squall clears off by and by, and we go steaming, steaming on past the unnumbered little villages by the water's edge with church spires and pointed roof, past the countless rocks with their little pert castles perched on the top of them, past the tall, stiff poplar rows. The church bells are ringing gaily as we go by. A nightingale is singing from a wood. The black eagle of Prussia droops on the stream behind us, *swish-swish* through the dull green water. A fat woman who is interested in it, leans over the back of the boat, and by some happy effect of crinoline, displays to her fellow-passengers two yards of thick white cotton legs. She is, fortunately for herself, unconscious of her generosity.

The day steals on; at every stopping place more people come on. There is hardly elbow room; and, what is worse, almost everybody is drunk. Rocks, castles, villages, poplars, slide by, while the paddles churn always the water, and the evening draws greyly on. At Bingen a party of big blue Prussian soldiers, very drunk, "glorious" as Tam o' Shanter, come and establish themselves close to us. They call for Lager Beer; talk at the tip-top of their strong voices; two of them begin to spar; all seem inclined to sing. Elizabeth is frightened.

We are two hours late in arriving at Biebrich. It is half an hour more before we can get ourselves and our luggage into a carriage and set off along the winding road to Wiesbaden. "The night is chilly, but not dark." There is only a little shabby bit of a moon, but it shines as hard as it can. Elizabeth is quite worn out, her tired head droops in uneasy sleep on my shoulder. Once she wakes up with a start.

"Are you sure that it meant nothing?" she asks, looking me eagerly in my face; "do people often have such dreams?"

"Often, often," I answer, reassuringly.

"I am always afraid of falling asleep now," she says, trying to sit upright and keep her heavy eyes open, "for fear of seeing him standing there again. Tell me, do you think I shall? Is there any chance, any probability of it?"

"None, none!"

We reached Wiesbaden at last, and drive up to the *Hôtel des Quatre Saisons*. By this time, it is full midnight. Two or three men are standing about the door. Morris, the maid, has got out—so have I, and I am holding out my hand to Elizabeth, when I hear her give one piercing scream, and see her with ash-white face and starting eyes point with her forefinger—

"There he is!—there!—there!"

I look in the direction indicated, and just catch a glimpse of a tall figure, standing half in the shadow of the night, half in the gaslight from the hotel. I have not time for more than one cursory glance, as I am interrupted by a cry from the bystanders, and turning quickly round, am just in time to catch my wife, who falls in utter insensibility into my arms. We carry her into a room on the ground floor; it is small, noisy, and hot, but it is the nearest at hand. In about an hour, she re-opens her eyes. A strong shudder makes her quiver from head to foot.

"Where is he?" she says, in a terrified whisper, as her senses come slowly back. "He is somewhere about—somewhere near. I feel that he is!"

"My dearest child, there is no one here but Morris and me," I answer, soothingly. "Look for yourself. See."

I take one of the candles and light up each corner of the room in succession.

"You saw him!" she says, in trembling hurry, sitting up and clenching her hands together. "I know you did—I pointed him out to you—you cannot say that it was a dream *this* time."

"I saw two or three ordinary looking men as we drove up," I answer, in a commonplace, matter-of-fact tone. "I did not notice anything remarkable about any of them; you know the fact is, darling, that you have had nothing to eat all day, nothing but a biscuit, and you are overwrought, and fancy things."

"Fancy!" echoes she, with strong irritation. "How you talk! Was I ever one to fancy things? I tell you that as sure as I sit here—as sure as you stand there—I saw him—*him*—the man I saw in my dream, if it was a dream. There was not a hair's breadth of difference between them—and he was looking at me—looking——"

She breaks off into hysterical sobbing.

"My dear child!" say I, thoroughly alarmed, and yet half angry, "for God's sake do not work yourself up into a fever: wait till tomorrow, and we will find out who he is, and all about him; you yourself will laugh when we discover that he is some harmless bagman."

"Why not *now?*" she says, nervously; "why cannot you find out *now*—this *minute?*"

"Impossible! Everybody is in bed! Wait till tomorrow, and all will be cleared up."

The morrow comes, and I go about the hotel, inquiring. The house is so full, and the data I have to go upon are so small, that for some time I have great difficulty in making it understood to whom I am alluding. At length one waiter seems to comprehend.

"A tall and dark gentleman, with a pronounced and very peculiar nose? Yes; there has been such a one, certainly, in the hotel, but he left at '*grand matin*' this morning; he remained only one night."

"And his name?"

The *garçon* shakes his head. "That is unknown, *monsieur*; he did not inscribe it in the visitor's book."

"What countryman was he?"

Another shake of the head. "He spoke German, but it was with a foreign accent."

"Whither did he go?"

That also is unknown. Nor can I arrive at any more facts about him.

## Chapter 4

A fortnight has passed; we have been hither and thither; now we are at Lucerne. Peopled with better inhabitants, Lucerne might well do for Heaven. It is drawing towards eventide, and Elizabeth and I are sitting hand in hand on a quiet bench, under the shady linden trees, on a high hill up above the lake. There is nobody to see us, so we sit peaceably hand in hand.

Up by the still and solemn monastery we came, with its small and narrow windows, calculated to hinder the holy fathers from promenading curious eyes on the world, the flesh, and the devil, tripping past them in blue gauze veils: below us grass and green trees, houses with high-pitched roofs, little dormer-windows, and shutters yet greener than the grass; below us the lake in its rippleless peace, calm, quiet, motionless as Bethesda's pool before the coming of the troubling angel.

"I said it was too good to last," say I, doggedly, "did not I, only yesterday? Perfect peace, perfect sympathy, perfect freedom from nagging worries—when did such a state of things last more than two days?"

Elizabeth's eyes are idly fixed on a little steamer, with a stripe of red along its side, and a tiny puff of smoke from its funnel, gliding along and cutting a narrow white track on Lucerne's sleepy surface.

"This is the fifth false alarm of the gout having gone to his stomach within the last two years," continue I, resentfully. "I declare to Heaven, that if it has not really gone there this time, I'll cut the whole concern."

Let no one cast up their eyes in horror, imagining that it is my father to whom I am thus alluding; it is only a great uncle by marriage, in consideration of whose wealth and vague promises I have dawdled professionless through twenty-eight years of my life.

"You *must* not go," says Elizabeth, giving my hand an imploring squeeze. "The man in the Bible said, 'I have married a wife, and therefore I cannot come;' why should it be a less valid excuse nowadays?"

"If I recollect rightly, it was considered rather a poor one even then," reply I, dryly.

Elizabeth is unable to contradict this, she therefore only lifts two pouted lips (Monsieur Taine objects to the redness of English women's mouths, but I do not) to be kissed, and says, "Stay." I am good enough to comply with her unspoken request, though I remain firm with regard to her spoken one.

"My dearest child," I say, with an air of worldly experience and superior wisdom, "kisses are very good things—in fact there are few better—but one cannot live upon them."

"Let us try," she says, coaxingly.

"I wonder which would get tired first?" I say, laughing. But she only goes on pleading, "Stay, stay."

"How can I stay?" I cry, impatiently; "you talk as if I wanted to go! Do you think it is any pleasanter to me to leave you than to you to be left? But you know his disposition, his rancorous resentment of fancied neglects. For the sake of two days' indulgence, must I throw away what will keep us in ease and plenty to the end of our days?"

"I do not care for plenty," she says, with a little petulant gesture. "I do not see that rich people are any happier than poor ones. Look at the St. Clairs; they have £40,000 a-year, and she is a miserable woman, perfectly miserable, because her face gets red after dinner."

"There will be no fear of *our* faces getting red after dinner," say I, grimly, "for we shall have no dinner for them to get red after."

A pause. My eyes stray away to the mountains. Pilatus on the right, with his jagged peak and slender snow-chains about his harsh neck; hill after hill rising silent, eternal, like guardian spirits standing hand in hand around their child, the lake.

As I look, suddenly they have all flushed, as at some noblest thought, and over all their sullen faces streams an ineffable rosy joy—a solemn and wonderful effulgence, such as Israel saw reflected from the features of the Eternal in their prophet's transfigured eyes. The unutterable peace and stainless beauty of earth and sky seem to lie softly on my soul. "Would God I could Stay! Would God all life could be like this!" I say, devoutly, and the aspiration has the reverent earnestness of a prayer.

"Why do you say, '*Would God!*'" she cries, passionately, "when it lies with yourself? Oh, my dear love," gently sliding her hand through my arm, and lifting wetly-beseeching eyes to my face, "I do not know why I insist upon it so much—I cannot tell you myself—I dare say I seem selfish and unreasonable—but I feel as if your going now would be the end of all things—as if——." She breaks off suddenly.

"My child," say I, thoroughly distressed, but still determined to have my own way, "you talk as if I were going for ever and a day; in a week, at the outside, I shall be back, and then you will thank me for the very thing for which you now think me so hard and disobliging."

"Shall I?" she answers, mournfully. "Well, I hope so."

"You will not be alone, either; you will have Morris."

"Yes."

"And every day you will write me a long letter, telling me every single thing that you do, say, and think."

"Yes."

She answers me gently and obediently; but I can see that she is still utterly unreconciled to the idea of my absence.

"What is it that you are afraid of?" I ask, becoming rather irritated. "What do you suppose will happen to you?"

She does not answer; only a large tear falls on my hand, which she hastily wipes away with her pocket handkerchief, as if afraid of exciting my wrath.

"Can you give me any good reason why I should stay?" I ask, dictatorially.

"None—none—only—stay—stay!"

But I am resolved *not* to stay. Early the next morning I set off.

## CHAPTER 5

This time it is not a false alarm; this time it really has gone to his stomach, and, declining to be dislodged thence, kills him. My return is therefore retarded until after the funeral and the reading of the will. The latter is so satisfactory, and my time is so fully occupied with a multiplicity of attendant business, that I have no leisure to regret the delay. I write to Elizabeth, but receive no letters from her. This surprises and makes me rather angry, but does not alarm me. "If she had been ill, if anything had happened, Morris would have written. She never was great at writing, poor little soul. What dear little babyish notes she used to send me during our engagement; perhaps she wishes to punish me for my disobedience to her wishes. Well, now she will see who was in the right."

I am drawing near her now; I am walking up from the railway station at Lucerne. I am very joyful as I march along under an umbrella, in the grand broad shining of the summer afternoon. I think with pensive passion of the last glimpse I had of my beloved—her small and wistful face looking out from among the thick fair fleece of her long hair—winking away her tears and blowing kisses to me. It is a new sensation to me to have anyone looking tearfully wistful over my departure. I draw near the great glaring *Schweizerhof*, with its colonnaded, tourist-crowded porch; here are all the pomegranates as I left them, in their green tubs, with their scarlet blossoms, and the dusty oleanders in a row.

I look up at our windows; nobody is looking out from them; they are open, and the curtains are alternately swelled out and drawn in by the softly-playful wind. I run quickly upstairs and burst noisily into the sitting-room. Empty, perfectly empty! I open the adjoining door into the bedroom, crying "Elizabeth! Elizabeth!" but I receive no answer. Empty too. A feeling of indignation creeps over me as I think, "Knowing the time of my return, she might have managed to be indoors." I have returned to the silent sitting-room, where the only noise is the wind still playing hide-and-seek with the curtains.

As I look vacantly round my eye catches sight of a letter lying on the table. I pick it up mechanically and look at the address. Good heavens! what can this mean? It is my own, that I sent her two days ago, unopened, with the seal unbroken. Does she carry her resentment so far as not even to open my letters? I spring at the bell and violently ring it. It is answered by the waiter who has always specially attended us.

"Is *madame* gone out?"

The man opens his mouth and stares at me.

"*Madame!* Is *monsieur* then not aware that *madame* is no longer at the hotel?"

"*What?*"

"On the same day as *monsieur*, *madame* departed."

"*Departed!* Good God! what are you talking about?"

"A few hours after *monsieur's* departure—I will not be positive as to the exact time, but it must have been between one and two o'clock as the midday *table d'hôte* was in progress—a gentleman came and asked for *madame*——"

"Yes—be quick."

"I demanded whether I should take up his card, but he said 'No,' that was unnecessary, as he was perfectly well known to *madame*; and, in fact, a short time afterwards, without saying anything to anyone, she departed with him."

"And did not return in the evening?"

"No, *monsieur; madame* has not returned since that day."

I clench my hands in an agony of rage and grief. "So, this is it! With that pure child-face, with that divine ignorance—only three weeks married—this is the trick she has played me!" I am recalled to myself by a compassionate suggestion from the *garçon*.

"Perhaps it was the brother of *madame*."

Elizabeth has no brother, but the remark brings back to me the necessity of self-command. "Very probably," I answer, speaking with infinite difficulty. "What sort of looking gentleman was he?"

"He was a very tall and dark gentleman with a most peculiar nose—not quite like any nose that I ever saw before—and most singular eyes. Never have I seen a gentleman who at all resembled him."

I sink into a chair, while a cold shudder creeps over me as I think of my poor child's dream—of her fainting fit at Wiesbaden—of her unconquerable dread of and aversion from my departure. And this happened twelve days ago! I catch up my hat, and prepare to rush like a madman in pursuit

"How did they go?" I ask incoherently; "by train?—driving?—walking?"

"They went in a carriage."

"What direction did they take? Whither did they go?"

He shakes his head. "It is not known."

"It *must* be known," I cry, driven to frenzy by every second's delay. "Of course, the driver could tell; where is he?—where can I find him?"

"He did not belong to Lucerne, neither did the carriage; the gentleman brought them with him."

"But *madame's* maid," say I, a gleam of hope flashing across my mind; "did she go with her?"

"No, *monsieur*, she is still here; she was as much surprised as *monsieur* at *madame's* departure."

"Send her at once," I cry eagerly; but when she comes, I find that she can throw no light on the matter. She weeps noisily and says many irrelevant things, but I can obtain no information from her beyond the fact that she was unaware of her mistress's departure until long after it had taken place, when, surprised at not being rung for at the usual time, she had gone to her room and found it empty, and on inquiring in the hotel, had heard of her sudden departure; that, expecting her to return at night, she had sat up waiting for her till two o'clock in the morning, but that, as I knew, she had not returned, neither had anything since been heard of her.

Not all my inquiries, not all my cross-questionings of the whole staff of the hotel, of the visitors, of the railway officials, of nearly all the inhabitants of Lucerne and its environs, procure me a jot more knowledge. On the next few weeks, I look back as on a hellish and insane dream. I can neither eat nor sleep; I am unable to remain one moment quiet; my whole existence, my nights and my days, are spent in seeking, seeking. Everything that human despair and frenzied love can do is done by me. I advertise, I communicate with the police, I employ detectives; but that fatal twelve days' start for ever baffles me.

Only on one occasion do I obtain one tittle of information. In a village a few miles from Lucerne the peasants, on the day in question, saw a carriage driving rapidly through their little street. It was closed, but through the windows they could see the occupants—a dark gentleman, with the peculiar physiognomy which has been so often described, and on the opposite seat a lady lying apparently in a state of utter insensibility. But even this leads to nothing.

Oh, reader, these things happened twenty years ago; since then I have searched sea and land, but never have I seen my little Elizabeth again.

# The Truth, the Whole Truth, and Nothing but the Truth

**Mrs De Wynt to Mrs Montresor.**

18, Eccleston Square,
May 5th.

My dearest Cecilia,

Talk of the friendships of Orestes and Pylades, of Julie and Claire, what are they to ours? Did Pylades ever go *ventre à terre*, half over London on a day more broiling than any but an *âme damnée* could even imagine, in order that Orestes might be comfortably housed for the season?

Did Claire ever hold sweet converse with from fifty to one hundred house agents, in order that Julie might have three windows to her drawing-room and a pretty *portière*? You see I am determined not to be done out of my full meed of gratitude.

Well, my friend, I had no idea till yesterday how closely we were packed in this great smoky beehive, as tightly as herrings in a barrel. Don't be frightened, however. By dint of squeezing and crowding, we have managed to make room for two more herrings in our barrel, and those two are yourself and your other self, *i.e.* your husband.

Let me begin at the beginning. After having looked over, I verily believe, every undesirable residence in West London; after having seen nothing intermediate between what was suited to the means of a duke, and what was suited to the needs of a chimney-sweep; after having felt bed-ticking, and explored kitchen-ranges till my brain reeled under my accumulated experience, I arrived at about half-past five yesterday afternoon at 32, —— Street, May Fair.

'Failure No. 253, I don't doubt,' I said to myself, as I toiled up the steps with my soul athirst for afternoon tea, and feeling as ill-tempered as you please. So much for my spirit of prophecy. Fate, I have noticed, is often fond of contradicting us flat, and giving the lie to our little predictions. Once inside, I thought I had got into a small compartment of Heaven by mistake. Fresh as a daisy, clean as a cherry, bright as a *seraph's* face, it is all these, and a hundred more, only that my limited stock of similes is exhausted.

Two drawing-rooms as pretty as ever woman crammed with people she did not care two straws about; white curtains with rose-coloured ones underneath, festooned in the sweetest way; marvellously, *immorally* becoming, my dear, as I ascertained entirely for your benefit, in the mirrors, of which there are about a dozen and a half; Persian mats, easy chairs, and lounges suited to every possible physical conformation, from the Apollo Belvedere to Miss Biffin; and a thousand of the important little trivialities that make up the sum of a woman's life: peacock fans, Japanese screens, naked boys and *décolleté* shepherdesses; not to speak of a family of china pugs, with blue ribbons round their necks, which ought of themselves to have added fifty pounds a year to the rent. *Apropos*, I asked, in fear and trembling, what the rent might be—'Three hundred pounds a year.' A feather would have knocked me down. I could hardly believe my ears, and made the woman repeat it several times, that there might be no mistake. To this hour it is a mystery to me.

With that suspiciousness which is so characteristic of you, you will immediately begin to hint that there must be some terrible unaccountable smell, or some odious inexplicable noise haunting the reception-rooms. Nothing of the kind, the woman assured me, and she did not look as if she were telling stories. You will next suggest—remembering the rose-coloured curtains—that its last occupant was a member of the demimonde. Wrong again. Its last occupant was an elderly and unexceptionable Indian officer, without a liver, and with a most lawful wife.

They did not stay long, it is true, but then, as the housekeeper told me, he was a deplorable old hypochondriac, who never could bear to stay a fortnight in any one place. So lay aside that scepticism, which is your besetting sin, and give unfeigned thanks to St Brigitta, or St Gengulpha, or St Catherine of Siena, or whoever is your tutelar saint, for having provided you with a palace at the cost of a hovel, and for having sent you such an invaluable friend as

        Your attached

                        Elizabeth De Wynt.

P.S.—I am so sorry I shall not be in town to witness your first raptures, but dear Artie looks so pale and thin and tall after the whooping-cough, that I am sending him off at once to the sea, and as I cannot bear the child out of my sight, I am going into banishment likewise.

### Mrs Montresor to Mrs De Wynt.

                    32, —— Street, May Fair,

                              May 14th.

Dearest Bessy,

Why did not dear little Artie defer his whooping-cough convalescence till August? It is very odd, to me, the perverse way in which children always fix upon the most inconvenient times and seasons for their diseases. Here we are installed in our Paradise, and have searched high and low, in every hole and corner, for the serpent, without succeeding in catching a glimpse of his spotted tail. Most things in this world are disappointing, but 32, —— Street, May Fair, is not.

The mystery of the rent is still a mystery. I have been for my first ride in the Row this morning; my horse was a little fidgety; I am half afraid that my nerve is not what it was. I saw heaps of people I knew. Do you recollect Florence Watson? What a wealth of red hair she had last year! Well, that same wealth is black as the raven's wing this year!

I wonder how people can make such walking impositions of themselves, don't you? Adela comes to us next week; I am so glad. It is dull driving by oneself of an afternoon; and I always think that one young woman alone in a brougham, or with only a dog beside her, does not look *good*. We sent round our cards a fortnight before we came up, and have been already deluged with callers. Considering that we have been two years exiled from civilised life, and that London memories are not generally of the longest, we shall do pretty well, I think.

Ralph Gordon came to see me on Sunday; he is in the ——th Hussars now. He has grown up such a *dear* fellow, and *so* good-looking! Just my style, large and fair and whiskerless! Most men nowadays make themselves as like monkeys, or Scotch terriers, as they possibly can. I intend to be quite a *mother* to him. Dresses are gored to as *indecent* an extent as ever; short skirts are rampant. I am sorry; I hate them. They make tall women look *lank*, and short ones insignificant. A knock! Peace is a word that might as well be expunged from one's London dictionary.

Yours affectionately,

Cecilia Montresor.

## Mrs De Wynt to Mrs Montresor.

The Lord Warden, Dover,
May 18th.

Dearest Cecilia,

You will perceive that I am about to devote only one small sheet of note-paper to you. This is from no dearth of time, Heaven knows! time is a drug in the market here, but from a total dearth of ideas. Any ideas that I ever have, come to me from without, from external objects; I am not clever enough to generate any within myself. My life here is not an eminently suggestive one. It is spent digging with a wooden spade, and eating prawns.

Those are my employments at least; my relaxation is going down to the Pier, to see the Calais boat come in. When one is miserable oneself, it is decidedly consolatory to see someone more miserable still; and wretched and bored, and reluctant vegetable as I am, I am not *sea-sick*. I always feel my spirits rise after having seen that peevish, draggled procession of blue, green and yellow fellow-Christians file past me.

There is a wind here *always*, in comparison of which the wind that behaved so violently to the corners of Job's house was a mere zephyr. There are heights to climb which require more daring perseverance than ever Wolfe displayed, with his paltry heights of Abraham. There are glaring white houses, glaring white roads, glaring white cliffs. If anyone knew how unpatriotically I detest the chalk-cliffs of Albion! Having grumbled through my two little pages—I have actually been reduced to writing very large in order to fill even them—I will send off my dreary little billet. How I wish I could get into the envelope myself too, and whirl up with it to dear, beautiful, filthy London. Not more heavily could Madame de Staël have sighed for Paris from among the shades of Coppet.

Your disconsolate,

Bessy.

## Mrs Montresor to Mrs De Wynt.

32, —— Street, May Fair,<br>May 27th.

Oh, my dearest Bessy, how I wish we were out of this dreadful, dreadful house! Please don't think me very ungrateful for saying this, after your taking such pains to provide us with a Heaven upon earth, as you thought.

What has happened could, of course, have been neither foretold, nor guarded against, by any human being. About ten days ago, Benson (my maid) came to me with a very long face, and said, 'If you please, 'm, did you know that this house was *haunted*?' I was so startled: you know what a coward I am. I said, 'Good Heavens! No! is it?' 'Well, 'm, I'm pretty nigh sure it is,' she said, and the expression of her countenance was about as lively as an undertaker's; and then she told me that cook had been that morning to order groceries from a shop in the neighbourhood, and on her giving the man the direction where to send the things to, he had said, with a very peculiar smile, 'No. 32, —— Street, eh? h'm? I wonder how long *you'll* stand it; last lot held out just a fortnight.'

He looked so odd that she asked him what he meant, but he only said, 'Oh! nothing! only that parties never *did* stay long at 32. He had known parties go in one day, and out the next, and during the last four years he had never known any remain over the month. Feeling a good deal alarmed by this information, she naturally inquired the reason; but he declined to give it, saying that if she had not found it out for herself, she had much better leave it alone, as it would only frighten her out of her wits; and on her insisting and urging him, she could only extract from him, that the house had such a villainously bad name, that the owners were glad to let it for a mere song.

You know how firmly I believe in apparitions, and what an unutterable fear I have of them: anything material, tangible, that I can lay hold of—anything of the same fibre, blood, and bone as myself, I could, I think, confront bravely enough; but the mere thought of being brought face to face with the 'bodiless dead', makes my brain unsteady. The moment Henry came in, I ran to him, and told him; but he pooh-poohed the whole story, laughed at me, and asked whether we should turn out of the prettiest house in London, at the very height of the season, because a grocer said it had a bad name. Most good things that had ever been in the world had had a bad name in their day; and, moreover, the man had probably a motive for taking away the house's character, some friend for whom he coveted the charming situation and the low rent.

He derided my 'babyish fears', as he called them, to such an extent that I felt half ashamed, and yet not quite comfortable either; and then came the usual rush of London engagements, during which one has no time to think of anything but how to speak, and act, and look for the moment then present. Adela was to arrive yesterday, and in the morning our weekly hamper of flowers, fruit, and vegetables arrived from home. I always dress the flower vases myself, servants are so tasteless; and as I was arranging them, it occurred to me—you know Adela's passion for flowers—to carry up one particular cornucopia of roses and mignonette and set it on her toilet-table, as a pleasant surprise for her.

As I came downstairs, I had seen the housemaid—a fresh, round-faced country girl—go into the room, which was being prepared for Adela, with a pair of sheets that had been airing over her arm. I went upstairs very slowly, as my cornucopia was full of water, and I was afraid of spilling some. I turned the handle of the bedroom-door and entered, keeping my eyes fixed on my flowers, to see how they bore the transit, and whether any of them had fallen out. Suddenly a sort of shiver passed over me; and feeling frightened—I did not know why—I looked up quickly.

The girl was standing by the bed, leaning forward a little with her hands clenched in each other, rigid, every nerve tense; her eyes, wide open, starting out of her head, and a look of unutterable stony horror in them; her cheeks and mouth not pale, but livid as those of one that died a while ago in mortal pain. As I looked at her, her lips moved a little, and an awful hoarse voice, not like hers in the least, said, 'Oh! my God, I have seen it!' and then she fell down suddenly, like a log, with a heavy noise. Hearing the noise, loudly audible all through the thin walls and floors of a London house, Benson came running in, and between us we managed to lift her on to the bed, and tried to bring her to herself by rubbing her feet and hands, and holding strong salts to her nostrils.

And all the while we kept glancing over our shoulders, in a vague cold terror of seeing some awful, shapeless apparition. Two long hours she lay in a state of utter unconsciousness. Meanwhile Harry, who had been down to his club, returned. At the end of two hours, we succeeded in bringing her back to sensation and life, but only to make the awful discovery that she was raving mad. She became so violent that it required all the combined strength of Harry and Phillips (our butler) to hold her down in the bed.

Of course, we sent off instantly for a doctor, who on her growing a little calmer towards evening, removed her in a cab to his own house. He has just been here to tell me that she is now pretty quiet, *not* from any return to sanity, but from sheer exhaustion.

We are, of course, utterly in the dark as to *what* she saw, and her ravings are far too disconnected and unintelligible to afford us the slightest clue. I feel so completely shattered and upset by this awful occurrence, that you will excuse me, dear, I'm sure, if I write incoherently. One thing I need hardly tell you, and that is, that no earthly consideration would induce me to allow Adela to occupy that terrible room. I shudder and run by quickly as I pass the door.

Yours, in great agitation,

Cecilia.

### Mrs De Wynt to Mrs Montresor.

The Lord Warden,
Dover, May 28th.

Dearest Cecilia,

Yours just come; how very dreadful! But I am still unconvinced as to house being in fault. You know I feel a sort of godmother to it, and responsible for its good behaviour. Don't you think that what the girl had might have been a fit? Why not? I myself have a cousin who is subject to seizures of the kind, and immediately on being attacked his whole body becomes rigid, his eyes glassy and staring, his complexion livid, exactly as in the case you describe.

Or, if not a fit, are you sure that she has not been subject to fits of madness? *Please* be sure and ascertain whether there is not insanity in her family. It is so common nowadays, and so much on the increase, that nothing is more likely.

You know my utter disbelief in ghosts. I am convinced that most of them, if run to earth, would turn out about as genuine as the famed Cock Lane one. But even allowing the possibility, nay, the actual unquestioned existence of ghosts in the abstract, is it likely that there should be anything to be seen so horribly fear-inspiring, as to send a perfectly sane person *in one instant* raving mad, which you, after three weeks' residence in the house, have never caught a glimpse of?

According to your hypothesis, your whole household ought, by this time, to be stark staring mad. Let me implore you not to give way to a panic which may, possibly, probably prove utterly groundless. Oh, how I wish I were with you, to make you listen to reason!

Artie ought to be the best prop ever woman's old age was furnished with, to indemnify me for all he and his whooping-cough have made me suffer. Write immediately, please, and tell me how the poor patient progresses. Oh, had I the wings of a dove! I shall be on wires till I hear again.

> Yours,

> Bessy.

### Mrs Montresor to Mrs De Wynt.

> No. 5, Bolton Street, Piccadilly,
> June 12th.

Dearest Bessy,

You will see that we have left that terrible, hateful, fatal house. How I wish we had escaped from it sooner! Oh, my dear Bessy, I shall never be the same woman again if I live to be a hundred. Let me try to be coherent, and to tell you connectedly what has happened. And first, as to the housemaid, she has been removed to a lunatic asylum, where she remains in much the same state. She has had several lucid intervals, and during them has been closely, pressingly questioned as to what it was, she saw; but she has maintained an absolute, hopeless silence, and only shudders, moans, and hides her face in her hands when the subject is broached. Three days ago, I went to see her, and on my return was sitting resting in the drawing-room, before going to dress for dinner, talking to Adela about my visit, when Ralph Gordon walked in.

He has always been walking in the last ten days, and Adela has always flushed up and looked very happy, poor little cat, whenever he made his appearance. He looked very handsome, dear fellow, just come in from the park; seemed in tremendous spirits, and was as sceptical as even you could be, as to the ghostly origin of Sarah's seizure. 'Let me come here tonight and sleep in that room; do, Mrs Montresor,' he said, looking very eager and excited. 'With the gas lit and a poker, I'll engage to exorcise every demon that shows his ugly nose; even if I should find—

*Seven white ghostisses*
*Sifting on seven white postisses.'*

"'You don't mean really?' I asked, incredulously. 'Don't I? that's all,' he answered emphatically. 'I should like nothing better. Well, is it a bargain?'

Adela turned quite pale. 'Oh, don't,' she said, hurriedly, *'please, don't!* why should you run such a risk? How do you know that you might not be sent mad too?' He laughed very heartily, and coloured a little with pleasure at seeing the interest she took in his safety.

'Never fear,' he said, 'it would take more than a whole squadron of departed ones, with the old gentleman at their head, to send me crazy.' He was so eager, so persistent, so thoroughly in earnest, that I yielded at last, though with a certain strong reluctance, to his entreaties. Adela's blue eyes filled with tears, and she walked away hastily to the conservatory, and stood picking bits of heliotrope to hide them. Nevertheless, Ralph got his own way; it was so difficult to refuse him anything. We gave up all our engagements for the evening, and he did the same with his. At about ten o'clock he arrived, accompanied by a friend and brother officer, Captain Burton, who was anxious to see the result of the experiment.

'Let me go up at once, he said, looking very happy and animated. 'I don't know when I have felt in such good tune; a new sensation is a luxury not to be had every day of one's life; turn the gas up as high as it will go; provide a good stout poker, and leave the issue to Providence and me.' We did as he bid. 'It's all ready now,' Henry said, coming downstairs after having obeyed his orders; 'the room is nearly as light as day. Well, good luck to you, old fellow!' 'Goodbye, Miss Bruce,' Ralph said, going over to Adela, and taking her hand with a look, half laughing, half sentimental—

'*Fare thee well, and if for ever*
*then for ever, fare thee well,*

that is my last dying speech and confession. Now mind,' he went on, standing by the table, and addressing us all; 'if I ring once, *don't* come. I may be flurried, and lay hold of the bell without thinking; if I ring twice, *come*.' Then he went, jumping up the stairs three steps at a time, and humming a tune. As for us, we sat in different attitudes of expectation and listening about the drawing-room.

At first, we tried to talk a little, but it would not do; our whole souls seemed to have passed into our ears. The clock's ticking sounded as loud as a great church bell close to one's ear. Addy lay on the sofa, with her dear little white face hidden in the cushions. So, we sat for exactly an hour; but it seemed like two years, and just as the clock began to strike eleven, a sharp *ting, ting, ting,* rang clear and shrill through the house.

'Let us go,' said Addy, starting up and running to the door.

'Let us go,' I cried too, following her.

But Captain Burton stood in the way, and intercepted our progress. 'No,' he said, decisively, 'you must not go; remember Gordon told us distinctly, if he rang once *not* to come. I know the sort of fellow he is, and that nothing would annoy him more than having his directions disregarded.'

'Oh, nonsense!' Addy cried passionately, 'he would never have rung if he had not seen something dreadful; do, *do* let us go!' she ended, clasping her hands. But she was overruled, and we all went back to our seats. Ten minutes more of suspense, next door to unendurable; I felt a lump in my throat, a gasping for breath;—ten minutes on the clock, but a thousand centuries on our hearts. Then again, loud, sudden, violent, the bell rang! We made a simultaneous rush to the door. I don't think we were one second flying upstairs. Addy was first. Almost simultaneously she and I burst into the room.

There he was, standing in the middle of the floor, rigid, petrified, with that same look—that look that is burnt into my heart in letters of fire—of awful, unspeakable, stony fear on his brave young face. For one instant he stood thus; then stretching out his arms stiffly before him, he groaned in a terrible, husky voice, 'Oh, my God! I have seen it!' and fell down *dead*. Yes, *dead*. Not in a swoon or in a fit, but *dead*. Vainly we tried to bring back the life to that strong young heart; it will never come back again till that day when the earth and the sea give up the dead that are therein. I cannot see the page for the tears that are blinding me; he was such a dear fellow! I can't write any more today.

   Your broken-hearted

Cecilia.

  This is a true story.

# Under the Cloak

If there is a thing in the world that my soul hateth, it is a long night journey by rail. In the old coaching days, I do not think that I should have minded it, passing swiftly through a summer night on the top of a speedy coach with the star arch black-blue above one's head, the sweet smell of earth and her numberless flowers and grasses in one's nostrils, and the pleasant *trot, trot, trot, trot,* of the four strong horses in one's ears. But by railway! in a little stuffy compartment, with nothing to amuse you if you keep awake; with a dim lamp hanging above you, tantalizing you with the idea that you can read by its light, and when you try, satisfactorily proving to you that you cannot; and, if you sleep, breaking your neck, or at least stiffening it, by the brutal arrangement of the hard cushions.

These thoughts pass sulkily and rebelliously through my head as I sit in my *salon*, in the Ecu at Geneva, on the afternoon of the fine autumn day on which, in an evil hour, I have settled to take my place in the night train for Paris. I have put off going as long as I can. I like Geneva, and am leaving some pleasant and congenial friends, but now go I must. My husband is to meet me at the station in Paris at six o'clock tomorrow morning. Six o'clock! what a barbarous hour at which to arrive! I am putting on my bonnet and cloak; I look at myself in the glass with an air of anticipative disgust. Yes, I look trim and spruce enough now—a not disagreeable object perhaps—with sleek hair, quick and alert eyes, and pink-tinted cheeks. Alas! at six o'clock tomorrow morning, what a different tale there will be to tell! dishevelled, dusty locks, half-open weary eyes, a disordered dress, and a green-coloured countenance.

I turn away with a pettish gesture, and reflecting that at least there is no wisdom in living my miseries twice over, I go downstairs, and get into the hired open carriage which awaits me. My maid and man follow with the luggage. I give stricter injunctions than ordinary to my maid never for one moment to lose her hold of the dressing-case, which contains, as it happens, a great many more valuable jewels than people are wont to travel in foreign parts with, nor of a certain costly and beautiful Dresden china and gold Louis Quatorze clock, which I am carrying home as a present to my people.

We reach the station, and I straightway betake myself to the first-class *salle d'attente*, there to remain penned up till the officials undo the gates of purgatory and release us; an arrangement whose wisdom I have yet to learn. There are ten minutes to spare, and the *salle* is filling fuller and fuller every moment. Chiefly my countrymen, countrywomen, and country children, beginning to troop home to their partridges. I look curiously round at them, speculating as to which of them will be my companion or companions through the night.

There are not very unusual types: girls in sailor hats and blond hair-fringes; strong-minded old maids in painstakingly ugly water-proofs; baldish fathers; fattish mothers; a German or two, with prominent pale eyes and spectacles. I have just decided on the companions I should prefer: a large young man, who belongs to nobody, and looks as if he spent most of his life in laughing—(alas! he is not likely! he is sure to want to smoke!)—and a handsome and prosperous-looking young couple. They are more likely, as *very probably*, in the man's case, the bride-love will overcome the cigar-love. The porter comes up. The key turns in the lock: the doors open.

At first, I am standing close to them, flattening my nose against the glass, and looking out on the pavement; but as the passengers become more numerous, I withdraw from my prominent position, anticipating a rush for carriages. I hate and dread exceedingly a crowd, and would much prefer at any time to miss my train rather than be squeezed and jostled by one. In consequence, my maid and I are almost the last people to emerge, and have the last and worst choice of seats. We run along the train looking in; the footman, my maid, and I—full—full everywhere!

"*Dames seules?*" asks the guard.

"Certainly not! neither '*Dames seules*,' nor '*fumeurs*,' but if it must be one or the other, certainly '*fumeurs*.'"

I am growing nervous, when I see the footman, who is a little ahead of us, standing with an open carriage-door in his hand, and signing to us to make haste. Ah! it is all right! it always comes right when one does not fuss oneself.

"Plenty of room here, 'm; only two gentlemen!"

I put my foot on the high step and climb in. Rather uncivil of the two gentlemen! neither of them offers to help me, but they are not looking this way, I suppose. "Mind the dressing-case!" I cry nervously, as I stretch out my hand to help the maid Watson up. The man pushes her from behind; in she comes—dressing-case, clock and all; here we are for the night!

I am so busy and amused looking out of the window, seeing the different parties bidding their friends goodbye, and watching with indignation the barbaric and malicious manner in which the porters hurl the luckless luggage about, that we have steamed out of the station, and are fairly off for Paris, before I have the curiosity to glance at my fellow-passengers. Well! when I do take a look at them, I do not make much of it.

Watson and I occupy the two seats by one window, facing one another. Our fellow travellers have not taken the other two window-seats; they occupy the middle ones, next us. They are both reading behind newspapers. Well! we shall not get much amusement out of them. I give them up as a bad job. Ah! if I could have had my wish, and had the laughing young man, and the pretty young couple, for company, the night would not perhaps have seemed so long. However, I should have been mortified for them to have seen how *green* I looked when the dawn came; and, as to these *commis voyageurs*, I do not care if I look as green as grass in their eyes. Thus, all no doubt is for the best; and at all events it is a good trite copy-book maxim to say so.

So, I forget all about them: fix my eyes on the landscape racing by, and fall into a variety of thoughts. "Will my husband really get up in time to come and meet me at the station tomorrow morning? He does so cordially hate getting up. My only chance is his not having gone to bed at all! How will he be looking? I have not seen him for four months. Will he have succeeded in curbing his tendency to fat, during his Norway fishing? Probably not.

Fishing, on the contrary is rather a *fat-making* occupation; sluggish and sedentary. Shall we have a pleasant party at the house we are going to for shooting? To whom in Paris shall I go for my gown? Worth? No, Worth is beyond me." Then I leave the future and go back into past enjoyments; excursions to Lausanne, trips down the lake to Chillon; a hundred and one pleasantnesses. The time slips by: the afternoon is drawing towards evening; a beginning of dusk is coming over the landscape.

I look round. Good Heavens! what can those men find so interesting in the papers? I thought them hideously dull, when I looked over them this morning; and yet they are still persistently reading. What can they have got hold of? I cannot well see what the man beside me has; *vis-à-vis* is buried in an English *Times*. Just as I am thinking about him, he puts down his paper, and I see his face. Nothing very remarkable! a long black beard, and hat tilted somewhat low over his forehead. I turn away my eyes hastily, for fear of being caught inquisitively scanning him; but still, out of their corners I see that he has taken a little bottle out of his travelling bag, has poured some of its contents into a glass, and is putting it to his lips. It appears as if—and, at the time it happens, I have no manner of doubt that he is drinking. Then I feel that he is addressing me. I look up and towards him: he is holding out the phial to me, and saying:—

"May I take the liberty of offering *madame* some?"

"No, thank you, *monsieur!*" I answer, shaking my head hastily and speaking rather abruptly. There is nothing that I dislike more than being offered strange eatables or drinkables in a train, or a strange hymn-book in church.

He smiles politely, and then adds:

"Perhaps the *other* lady might be persuaded to take a little."

"No, thank you, sir, I'm much obliged to you," replies Watson briskly, in almost as ungrateful a tone as mine.

Again, he smiles, bows, and re-buries himself in his newspaper. The thread of my thoughts is broken; I feel an odd curiosity as to the nature of the contents of that bottle. Certainly, it is not sherry or spirit of any kind, for it has diffused no odour through the carriage. All this time the man beside me has said and done nothing. I wish he would move or speak, or do something. I peep covertly at him. Well! at all events, he is well defended against the night chill. What a voluminous cloak he is wrapped in; how entirely it shrouds his figure; trimmed with *fur* too! why, it might be January instead of September.

I do not know why, but that cloak makes me feel rather uncomfortable. I wish they would both move to the window, instead of sitting next to us. Bah! am I setting up to be a timid dove? I, who rather pique myself on my bravery—on my indifference to tramps, bulls, ghosts? The clock has been deposited with the umbrellas, parasols, spare shawls, rugs, etc., in the netting above Watson's head. The dressing-case—a very large and heavy one—is sitting on her lap. I lean forwards and say to her:—

"That box must rest very heavily on your knee, and I want a footstool—I should be more comfortable if I had one—let me put my feet on it."

I have an idea that, somehow, that my sapphires will be safer if I have them where I can always feel that they are *there*. We make the desired change in our arrangements. Yes! both my feet are on it.

The landscape outside is darkening quickly now; our dim lamp is beginning to assert its importance. Still the men read. I feel a sensation of irritation. What can they mean by it? it is utterly impossible that they can decipher the small print of the *Times* by this feeble, shaky glimmer.

As I am so thinking, the one who had before spoken lays down his paper, folds it up and deposits it on the seat beside him. Then, drawing his little bottle out of his bag a second time, drinks, or seems to drink, from it. Then he again turns to me:—

"*Madame* will pardon me, but if *madame could* be induced to try a little of this; it is a cordial of a most refreshing and invigorating description; and if she will have the amiability to allow me to say so, *madame* looks faint."

(What *can* he mean by his urgency? *Is* it pure politeness? I wish it were not growing so dark.) These thoughts run through my head as I hesitate for an instant what answer to make. Then an idea occurs to me, and I manufacture a civil smile and say, "Thank you very much, *monsieur!* I am a little faint, as you observe. I think I will avail myself of your obliging offer." So, saying, I take the glass, and touch it with my lips. I give you my word of honour that I do not think I did more; I did not mean to swallow a drop, but I suppose I must have done. He smiles with a gratified air.

"The other lady will now, perhaps, follow your example?"

By this time, I am beginning to feel thoroughly uncomfortable. *Why*, I should be puzzled to explain. What is this cordial that he is so eager to urge upon us? Though determined not to subject *myself* to its influence, I must see its effect upon another person. Rather brutal of me, perhaps; rather in the spirit of the anatomist, who, in the interest of science, tortures live dogs and cats; but I am telling you *facts*—not what I ought to have done, but what I *did*. I make a sign to Watson to drink some. She obeys, nothing loath. She has been working hard all day; packing and getting under weigh, and she is tired. There is no feigning about her! She has emptied the glass.

Now to see what comes of it—what happens to my live dog! The bottle is replaced in the bag; still, we are racing, racing on, past the hills and fields and villages. How indistinct they are all growing! I turn back from the contemplation of the outside view to the inside one. Why, the woman is asleep already! her chin buried in her chest; her mouth half open; looking exceedingly imbecile and very plain, as most people, when asleep out of bed, do look. A nice invigorating potion, indeed! I wish to Heaven that I had gone in *fumeurs,* or even with that cavalcade of nursery-maids and unwholesome-looking babies in *dames seules,* next door.

At all events, I am not at all sleepy myself: that is a blessing. I shall see what happens. Yes, by-the-by, I must see what he meant to happen: I must affect to fall asleep too. I close my eyes, and, gradually sinking my chin on my chest, try to droop my jaws and hang my cheeks, with a semblance of *bona-fide* slumber. Apparently, I succeed pretty well. After the lapse of some minutes, I distinctly feel two hands very cautiously and carefully lifting and removing my feet from the dressing-box.

A cold chill creeps over me, and then the blood rushes to my head and ears. What am I to do? what am I to do? I have always thought the better of myself ever since for it; but, strange to say, I keep my presence of mind. Still affecting to sleep, I give a sort of kick, and instantly the hands are withdrawn, and all is perfectly quiet again. I now feign to wake gradually, with a yawn and a stretch; and, on moving about my feet a little, find that, despite my kick, they have been too clever for me, and have dexterously removed my box and substituted another.

The way in which I make this pleasant discovery is that whereas mine was perfectly flat at the top, on the surface of the object that is now beneath my feet there is some sort of excrescence—a handle of some sort or other. There is no denying it—brave I *may* be—I may laugh at people for running from bulls; for disliking to sleep in a room by themselves, for fear of ghosts; for hurrying past tramps: but now I am most thoroughly frightened. I look cautiously, in a sideways manner, at the man beside me. How very still he is! Were they *his* hands, or the hands of the man opposite him?

I take a fuller look than I have yet ventured to do; turning slightly round for the purpose. He is still reading, or at least still holding the paper, for the reading must be a farce. I look at his hands: they are in precisely the same position as they were when I affected to go to sleep, although the pose of the rest of his body is slightly altered. Suddenly, I turn extremely cold, for it has dawned on me that they are not real hands—they are certainly false ones. Yes, though the carriage is shaking very much with our rapid motion, and the light is shaking, too, yet there is no mistake.

I look indeed more closely, so as to be quite sure. The one nearest me is ungloved; the other gloved. I look at the nearest one. Yes, it is of an opaque waxen whiteness. I can plainly see the rouge put under the finger-nails to represent the colouring of life. I try to give one glance at his face. The paper still partially hides it; and, as he is leaning his head back against the cushion, where the light hardly penetrates, I am completely baffled in my efforts.

Great Heavens! what is going to happen to me? what shall I do? how much of him is *real*? where are his *real* hands? what is going on under that awful cloak? The fur border touches me as I sit by him. I draw convulsively and shrinkingly away, and try to squeeze myself up as close as possible to the window. But alas! to what good? how absolutely and utterly powerless I am! how entirely at their mercy!

And there is Watson still sleeping swinishly! breathing heavily opposite me. Shall I try to wake her? But to what end? She, being under the influence of that vile drug, my efforts will certainly be useless, and will probably arouse the man to employ violence against me. Sooner or later, in the course of the night, I suppose they are pretty sure to murder me, but I had rather that it should be later than sooner.

While I think these things, I am lying back quite still, for, as I philosophically reflect, not all the screaming in the world will help me: if I had twenty-lung power I could not drown the rush of an express-train. Oh, if my dear boy were but here—my husband I mean—fat or lean, how thankful I should be to see him! Oh, that cloak, and those horrid waxy hands! Of course I see it now! They remained stuck out, while the man's real ones were fumbling about my feet. In the midst of my agony of fright, a thought of Madame Tussaud flashes ludicrously across me. Then they begin to talk of me. It is plain that they are not taken in by my feint of sleep: they speak in a clear, loud voice, evidently for my benefit.

One of them begins by saying, "What a good-looking woman she is—evidently in her *première jeunesse* too"—(Reader, I struck thirty last May)—"and also there can be no doubt as to her being of exalted rank—a duchess probably." ("A dead duchess by morning," think I grimly). They go on to say how odd it is that people in my class of life never travel with their own jewels, but always with paste ones, the real ones being meanwhile deposited at the bankers. My poor, poor sapphires! goodbye—a long goodbye to you. But, indeed, I will willingly compound for the loss of you and the rest of my ornaments—will go bare-necked, and bare-armed, or clad in Salviati beads for the rest of my life, so that I do but attain the next stopping place alive.

As I am so thinking, one of the men looks, or I imagine that he looks, rather curiously towards me. In a paroxysm of fear lest they should read on my face the signs of the agony of terror I am enduring, I throw my pocket-handkerchief—a very fine cambric one—over my face.

And now, O reader, I am going to tell you *something* which I am sure you will not believe; I can hardly believe it myself, but, as I so lie, despite the tumult of my mind—-despite the chilly terror which seems to be numbing my feelings—in the midst of it all a drowsiness keeps stealing over me. I am now convinced either that vile potion must have been of extraordinary strength, or that I, through the shaking of the carriage, or the unsteadiness of my hand, carried more to my mouth, and swallowed more—I did not *mean* to swallow any—than I intended, for—you will hardly credit it, but—I *fell asleep!*

★★★★★★★★★★★★★★★★

When I awake—awake with a bewildered mixed sense of having been a long time asleep—of not knowing where I am—and of having some great dread and horror on my mind—awake and look round, the dawn is breaking. I shiver, with the chilly sensation that the coming of even a warm day brings, and look round, still half-unconsciously, in a misty way. But what has happened? how empty the carriage is! the dressing-case is gone! the clock is gone! the man who sat nearly opposite me is gone. *Watson is gone!* but the man in the cloak and the wax hands still sits beside me! Still the hands are holding the paper; still the fur is touching me! Good God! I am *tête-à-tête* with him! A feeling of the most appalling desolation and despair comes over me—vanquishes me utterly.

I clasp my hands together frantically, and, still looking at the dim form beside me, groan out—"Well! I did not think that Watson would have forsaken me!" Instantly, a sort of movement and shiver runs through the figure: the newspaper drops from the hands, which, however continue to be still held out in the same position as if still grasping it; and behind the newspaper, I see by the dim morning light and the dim lamp-gleams that there is no real face, but a mask. A sort of choked sound is coming from behind the mask. Shivers of cold fear are running over me.

Never to this day shall I know what gave me the despairing courage to do it, but, before I know what I am doing, I find myself tearing at the cloak—tearing away the mask—tearing away the hands. It would be better to find *anything* underneath—Satan himself—a horrible dead body—anything—sooner than submit any longer to this hideous mystery. And I am rewarded. When the cloak lies at the bottom of the carriage—when the mask, and the false hands and false feet—(there are false *feet* too)—are also cast away in different directions, what do you think I find underneath?

Watson! Yes: it appears that while I slept—I feel sure that they must have rubbed some more of the drug on my lips while I was unconscious, or I never could have slept so heavily or so long—they dressed up Watson in the mask, feet, hands, and cloak, set the hat on her head, gagged her, and placed her beside me in the attitude occupied by the man. They had then, at the next station, got out, taking with them dressing-case and clock, and had made off in all security. When I arrive in Paris, you will not be surprised to hear that it does not once occur to me whether I am looking green or no.

And this is the true history of my night journey to Paris! You will be glad, I dare say, to learn that I ultimately recovered my sapphires, and a good many of my other ornaments. The police being promptly set on, the robbers were, after much trouble and time, at length secured; and it turned out that the man in the cloak was an ex-valet of my husband's who was acquainted with my bad habit of travelling in company with my trinkets—a bad habit which I have since seen fit to abandon.

# Was She Mad?

## CHAPTER 1

"Now, if it had been another man! We are already two women over! We are always two women over! Why are there so many women in the world?"

The question might not perhaps issue with any peculiar grace or fitness from the lips of Miss Monro, since she was herself one of the superfluous women whom she reprobated: one of the great and apparently indefinitely multiplying number of the unpaired. But perhaps the circumstances under which she uttered her plaint might in some degree palliate it.

"'I have a young lady staying with me for a few days; may I bring her to your luncheon party?'" read Miss Monro from a note held open in her hand, read in a tone which showed beyond possibility of mistake how extremely unpalatable to her was the request.

"I wonder"—in a voice of rising indignation—"how many score of times since I began to give luncheon parties have people asked whether they may bring a young lady? No one"—her tone swelling to the diapason of tragedy—"has ever asked whether they may bring a young man!"

"Perhaps he would not have consented to come if they had, so we may have been saved from some poignant disappointment," replied the person addressed, a rather ugly young woman with a soft voice.

"I hate to be asked to do things," continued Miss Monro, tearing the note that contained the offensive demand sharply across and across; "it is a very different thing if one volunteers; had I wished for Mrs. Wimpole's friend I should have invited her."

"But you did not know of her existence," said Miss Monro's niece.

This was indisputable, and for the moment reduced the aunt to silence. Only for the moment, however.

"The table is already laid," said she, in an annoyed key; "it will have to be all disarranged—another leaf added."

"I do not think so; we can put two at the top, and as she is young—Mrs. Wimpole says a young lady, does not she?—she is probably not very big; girls are not apt to be bulky."

"I do not know that"—shortly—"it is the men who are pygmies now-a-days; the women are giantesses!"

At the determined pessimism of this last speech Miss Sally Monro smiled slightly, but as she was several removes from a giantess herself, she could not take it personally.

"Now we shall be three women over," said the aunt, sighing.

"I do not think it will matter much if you dispose our few men judiciously," returned the niece, consolingly. "I will sit between the two Robertsons—they do not care about men."

"Vey unnatural of them!" (snappishly). "I cannot think why they are both coming; I only asked one."

"The fame of our parties has spread," rejoined Sally, pleasantly. "People come to us from the east and the west."

Mrs. Wimpole does not say where this creature comes from; no doubt she is some odd and end relation. Mrs. Wimpole has a knack of collecting odds and ends of humanity round her."

"Well, at all events, she is young," said Sally, cheerfully: "and very likely pretty. We are not"—running over with her eyes a list of the expected guests that she held in her hand—"quite so well off for good looks as we sometimes are. I am quite resolved that she shall be pretty."

Cheerfulness, we all know, is infectious, though perhaps—since the good things of this world are scarcely ever of such potency as their opposite evils—not so much so as gloominess. So, though not sharing her niece's conviction with the absolute faith of its original owner, the aunt was enough influenced by it to go with some alacrity upon the necessary errand of seeing to the alteration of her luncheon table.

To outsiders it would seem a matter of very small importance whether a dull luncheon party in a solitary East Yorkshire country house was or was not swelled by the addition of one more guest. But the avenues to pleasure possessed by the elder Miss Monro were few, and consequently pursued with an eagerness difficult to understand by those who had more roads to the common goal at their disposal. Her mind was but indifferently furnished, she having come into the world too early to have caught the fever of the higher culture. Her servants, to whom she went in life-long thrall, being old, fat, lazy and bed-loving, forbade her to give dinner parties.

Having a bronchial tendency, and being only less afraid of her carriage horses than of her butler and cook, she was unable to drive out. So it came to pass that, with the least possible appetite for solitude, her opportunities for cultivating the society of her kind were, in a scattered East Riding district, limited in the extreme, and among those opportunities her luncheon parties ranked in her own mind as the highest and most prized.

To see a certain number of persons—agreeable ones, if possible, but if dull, how far better than none—sitting round her old mahogany dining-table eating heartily of her dishes (she had no toleration of a weak appetite) was one of the choicest joys that poor Miss Monro, old, plain, never having learned much and having long ago forgotten that little, knew.

To give a luncheon party, with an equal number of men and women was Miss Monro's Blue Rose; but as yet that flower had not even budded in her garden. Whether her aunt's luncheon parties caused as much poignant a pleasure to Miss Sally Monro as to her senior is not known. It was always difficult to ascertain her likes and dislikes. She was supposed to enjoy so many tiresome things; nor did she ever deny doing so.

On the present occasion she had been on her feet all morning, arranging flowers, running errands for her aunt to and from the neighbouring vicarage, and lastly in placing, altering, and again replacing the names of the expected guests on the dining-room table cloth. For Miss Monro's luncheon parties were no slight collation. They were rather the aspect of tremendous early dinners, to which people were marched arm in arm, and where they found their places mapped out beforehand.

All was at length arranged to the hostess's mind, ten sparse men disposed where they might be expected to radiate most lustre, and Miss Sally bracketed between the two girls who did not care for men.

The clock's hands pointed to two; and the wheels of the first carriage-full of visitors were heard grinding the gravel of the drive. After that they came thick and fast. Mothers, daughters—plenty of daughters—minor clergy, a Girton young lady in spectacles, a widowed rector; another mother, Mrs. Robinson.

But, instead of the expected brace of daughters, there stepped behind this latter matron—oh! Sight almost too good to be true—a couple of young men! One was, indeed, only a hobble-de-hoy cub of a son, evidently dragged there *a son corps défendant*: but the other was an indisputably full-grown man. He could not be a person of much

115

importance, indeed, judging by the pains with which his introducer explained and apologised for him.

"I thought you would not mind. Both the girls had influenza—so unlucky. He is a sort of holiday tutor. My boy runs so wild when he is left to his own devices. I am told he is a profound scholar—Mr. Ayrton, I mean—not my boy, alas!—not much chance of that; so, I thought you would not mind."

Everyone had now arrived with the exception of Mrs. Wimpole and her strange young lady; and irate thoughts were beginning to seethe in the hostess's mind as to the complicated ill manners of foisting upon you an unwelcome visitor, and then keeping you waiting to receive them, when they too, were ushered in.

Luncheon being then summoned with that instantaneousness which is in itself the most pointed reproof to any loiterer, the task of sending in her guests occupied Miss Monro too fully to allow of her bestowing more than a cursory glance upon the stranger whose name she had been unable to catch. But, five minutes later, the feat of pairing the company according to her own and Sally's dispositions had been accomplished, and they had all fallen into their allotted places, she was at leisure to examine the intruder; the young lady whom Mrs. Wimpole had imposed upon her, and about whose possible charms Sally had been so sanguine.

A young lady! Young! It is true that in the vocabulary of some people young is synonymous with unmarried, and in that sense alone could it be true of Mrs. Wimpole's *protégé*. And yet, though her want of youth was obvious it would have been difficult to conjecture her real years, she being one of those ageless, colourless, indicationless persons who baffle observation. She might be 35, and she might be 100. Her figure was thin, without being slight; and her whole structure gave an impression of parsimony having been used in its materials. Her hair was meagre; and in her face there was an evident economy in lips, eyelashes, and eyebrows.

One wished that the same economy had been extended to her eyes as there was on the contrary plenty of them. They were large, glassy, and apparently quite devoid of expression. It was not often that anyone had an opportunity of examining them, as she kept them for the most part obstinately bent upon her plate, though she was obviously quite unaware of what she was eating. Neither did she make the smallest effort to converse with her neighbour on either hand.

At this sight the wrath swelled hotly in Miss Monro's breast, so

116

hotly, indeed, that she looked quickly away, lest it should master her; and her eyes wandered round the table in search of some pleasanter spectacle. There was nothing else to disturb her equanimity. Talk was brisk; appetites good.

As her eyes rested upon her niece a transient regret flitted across her brain that the two unexpected youths—the uncovenanted mercies—should have been wasted upon Sally, who like the Robertsons, "did not care for men."

But, after all, the arrangement seemed to be working very well. Sally was talking more than usual, and setting both the awkward schoolboy on her right, and the agonisedly shy student on her left, completely at their ease. Perhaps it was the only opportunity that she had ever lacked. She was looking almost pretty, too; almost a pretty young woman.

The words reminded Miss Monro irefully of the interloper, who had so shamefully balked her expectations in the matter of youth and fairness, and she glared involuntarily back at her. The glance was unintentional, as all glances at displeasing objects are, and would have been momentary had it not been rivetted by what it fell upon.

The stranger's eyes were no longer cast down upon her plate. On the contrary, they were fastened upon Sally's face. No longer expressionless, they had a sort of terrified stare in them. Perhaps some uneasy movement on the girl's part made the gazer conscious of the pertinacity of her own observation. At all events, she once more dropped her eyes to her plate, and Miss Monro found herself heaving an involuntarily sigh of relief.

In a moment, however, those strange white eyes were raised again. Apparently, they did not dare to return at once to the object of their original scrutiny, but skirted stealthily about it. They stole down the side of the table at which Sally was sitting, they glided over Mrs. Robertson, the Vicar of the Parish, the Girton girl. Miss Monro held her breath. They were within one of Sally. They had reached the shy young tutor. But as they alighted upon him the same look of awful terror came into them as had marked their expression when resting upon the young girl.

With a violent start the strange lady dropped the spoon she was holding, and sliding through her fingers it fell rattling on her plate. Everybody looked round, but seeing nothing particular, returned to their interrupted talk.

"She is evidently let out of bedlam for the day!" said Mrs. Wimpole to herself indignantly. "I shall let Mrs. Wimpole know what I think of her conduct."

## Chapter 2

Perhaps it was the desire to lose no time in telling Mrs. Wimpole her opinion of her friend, that made Miss Monro give the signal to leave the luncheon table sooner than was her wont. Usually that signal was, in the opinion of Miss Monro's visitors, unwisely and unkindly delayed. It was therefore, with surprise as much as pleasure that the company rose to follow her.

Almost everyone was glad to change the hot and flush-begetting air of the dining-room for a cooler one. Mrs. Wimpole was glad to go, because she had her back to the fire, and the deaf old servants could not hear her when she asked for a screen. The gawky boy was glad to go, because he saw no further chance of ravage among the peaches and nectarines, and his spirit whispered to him of possible filberts in the orchard.

Gladdest of all to go were the two neighbours of Mrs. Wimpole's singular charge. They had not been able to extract a word, good or bad, from her, and there was something in her contact that made them vaguely uncomfortable. The only person who was distinctly and obviously not glad was the shy young tutor.

He had enjoyed the last hour wildly; had been absolutely free form mental suffering for the first time since he left his distant Dorsetshire home three weeks ago. Too well he knew that once removed from Sally's gentle aegis, his misery, his dumbness, his hideous consciousness of having more arms and legs than ever man wore before, would return on him with tenfold force.

Arrived in the drawing-room, the party broke up into groups. It was a fine, late September day, and a window was open. Through it some of the younger women passed into the garden, which with its geraniums and dahlias as yet unbitten by the frost's tooth, flamed gaudily below; and at their heels attendant curates trod.

The only man who, with the exception of the two lads, was not a cleric lit a cigar. The tutor turned his agonised eyes round in search of his protectress; but to trip out on sunny terraces with fellow-girls was no part of Sally's portion in life either literally or metaphorically. At the present moment she was straining her soft voice, shouting in a corner to the widowed rector. A sense of fierce jealousy shot across the poor young man's heart. After all what a pull the deaf man had! How close to his ears she had to put her lips!

He turned and stepped awkwardly out of the window, having just become aware that he had lost sight of his pupil; and knocking his clumsy head against the sash, disappeared.

Miss Monro was not fond of open windows, and had no sooner discovered where came the draught of which she had been conscious ever since she had entered the room than she walked quickly towards the current to shut it.

As she got up to it, she started a little. She had not seen that anyone was left in that part of the room, and was already close upon her before she discovered that the figure sitting on a low chair, almost hidden by the droop of the window curtain, was that of Mrs. Wimpole's friend.

"I—I had no idea that you were here. I had no idea that anyone was here." Said Miss Monro in a tone of nervous irritation.

The stranger made no answer beyond rising from her seat with an air of scared deprecation.

"Were you looking at the view?" continued the hostess, conscious that the tone of her last remark had not erred on the side of over courtesy, and with an effort to make amends. "I am afraid we have not much to boast of in that way; this district of Yorkshire is extremely flat."

"Yes." She made no effort to add anything to this monosyllable; and Miss Monro felt herself obliged by courtesy to go on.

"You know this part of the country?"

"Not at all."

"This is your first visit to Yorkshire?"

"Yes." She gave those brief answers in an uncertain and rather breathless voice, that confirmed Miss Munro in her former suspicion of her visitor's sanity.

She drew away from her with an involuntary movement of apprehension. Who could tell whether this bedlamite might not have a carving-knife concealed about her; and the thought of ending her blameless life by having one of her own carving-knives plunged into her breast did not smile upon Miss Monro.

A moment later, politeness having again got the upper hand of fear, and in some dread lest the other should have perceived her shrinking movement, she rushed afresh into conversation.

"You come from the south, perhaps."

"No; not from the south."

As she did not add to this denial any information as to the point of the compass from which she did arrive, Miss Monro had to begin again.

"We are all strangers to you today, I am afraid."

"Oh, yes; all."

"And yet," pursued the other, driven on by an uneasy impulse she herself could not have defined. "I fancied you were, perhaps, acquainted with one or two members of our party."

"Oh, no; oh, dear no." the nervous tone in her voice growing more accentuated.

"How stupid of me; but yet I thought I saw at luncheon that you suddenly recognised the young man sat opposite to you."

The look of awful dread, which the questioner had noticed in them at the moment to which she alluded, had sprung back into the stranger's eyes.

"I," she said, articulating with difficulty. "I? You are mistaken. What made you think so?"

"Oh. I do not know," answered Miss Monro, with a forced laugh, and again increasing the distance between herself and the person whose insanity appeared to her to be so patent.

"I thought I saw a look of recognition in your face. No doubt I was mistaken it was very silly of me. I even imagined that you recognised my niece, too."

"Your niece?" speaking with a great effort, "I do not even know which was your niece."

"She was sitting beside the young man I speak of, a small fair-haired girl."

Foe a moment the stranger did not answer. Her hand clutched the window curtain by which she was standing, and her colourless face had grown livid.

"I never saw her before; I never saw either of them before; I give you my word of honour that I never saw either of them before."

At the unnecessary and excited emphasis with which this assertion was made, Miss Monro glanced involuntarily over her own shoulder. Was she within reach of help if this excitement rose into violence.

"I do not even know their names," resumed the stranger, hoarsely, as if afraid that her passionate disclaimer had not carried conviction with it. "Would you—would you mind telling me what their names are!

"Their names!" repeated Miss Monro, who was by this time so fully convinced of the other's unsoundness of mind that the most rational and innocent remark would have excited her suspicions, and to whom this question appeared to carry confirmation of her worst fears. "Of course"—again laughing, still more uncomfortably than before—"of course I can tell you my niece's name. She is called Sally—Sally Monro. As to the young man, I am not sure. Like you I never saw him until today. I think I heard someone say at luncheon that his name was Ayrton; but I am not sure I will ask."

With this somewhat flimsy excuse for retreating, she escaped with a good deal of precipitation from the Bedlamite, as she now always called her in her own mind.

Seeing that Bedlamite's introducer, Mrs. Wimpole, was sitting on a sofa at the further end of the long room, and well out of earshot of the object of her proposed remark, the hostess made her way to and sat down beside her.

"What a very extraordinary person your friend is!" she said, abruptly opening the conversation.

"Extraordinary!" repeated the other in surprise. "Do you mean Miss Younghusband? Extraordinary is the last word I should have applied to her. We think her painfully ordinary."

"You and I evidently attach a different meaning to the word," replied Miss Monro stiffly. "In my opinion she is one of the most extraordinary persons I ever came across; may I ask have you known her long? Do you know anything of her antecedents? What part of the country does she belong to?"

Miss Wimpole shrugged her large good-natured shoulders. "I am afraid I do not. I only know that her name is Younghusband—ridiculous name, is it not?—ha! ha!—and that we picked her up abroad. She was at the same hotel at Royat with us; and she seemed so lonely, never speaking or being spoken to by anyone, that I took compassion on her; and when I left I asked her, in the vague way one does, to look in upon us if she ever happened to be in our part of the country; and the other day—to tell you the truth, I had quite forgotten her existence—I received a note from her offering herself for the week, and here she is!"

"Hem," replied Miss Monro, by no means reassured by this extremely indistinct biography: "has it ever struck you that she is—a—a little———." She tapped her own forehead meaningly with her forefinger.

"What do you mean?—mad?" cried Mrs. Wimpole in a startled voice. "Good heavens, no; what a dreadful idea! I wish you had not put it into my head."

"There is something so very strange about her eyes," continued Miss Monro. "Is it possible that you have not noticed it?"

"Now you mention it, there is something odd about them (in an alarmed way). "However," (in a more reassured tone), "she is to leave us tomorrow morning. If what you say is true I shall of course, never ask her again; but, indeed, I should not have done that in any case, we all think her so very uninteresting."

The words were scarcely out of Mrs. Wimpole's mouth before both ladies were aware that the subject of their discussion was at their elbow.

She had crossed the room so noiselessly as not to have been heard, and it was only some slight rustling of her dress that betrayed her close neighbourhood. Both looked round with a start, and a guilty flush rose to their mature cheeks.

There is nothing that for the moment robs one so completely of one's presence of mind as the discovery that someone upon whom one has been passing unfavourable comments has infallibly overheard these comments.

It seemed that by nothing but a miracle could Miss Younghusband have been prevented from hearing that she was considered not only uninteresting but insane. Her face, however, betrayed no consciousness of having done so. It had returned to its normal condition of dark pallor; and her eyes, though they still had a scared expression, had lost the look of awful dread that Miss Monro had seen so unaccountably revisit them five minutes before at the mention of Sally and of the young tutor.

In the confusion of the moment both Mrs. Wimpole and her hostess rushed into simultaneous speech.

"Are you thinking that it is about time for us to be setting off home?" asked Mrs. Wimpole, with a hastily forced smile, and a bright red colour; and at the same instant Miss Monro inquired whether the stranger would not like to see the garden.

She disregarded both queries. She was evidently too preoccupied even to have heard them.

"I beg your pardon for interrupting you," she said, speaking with more composure and less hesitation than before, "but I have a request to make to you."

"A request!" repeated Miss Monro, again stepping back a pace or two—both she and her friend had risen in the excitement of the moment—of—of course; I shall be delighted; but what sort of a request?"

Both listened breathlessly for the answer. Would it contain patent evidence that the latent insanity had forced its way to the front?

"I should be much obliged if you can tell me where I can find writing materials. I wish to write something!"

"To write something!" repeated Miss Monro, involuntarily drawing a breath of relief at the simplicity and apparent rationalness of the petition. Her imagination had carried her so far as to expect some monstrously impossible demand, the necessary refusal of which would have been followed by an outburst of rage.

"Of course," replied she, civilly; "nothing easier; you wish to write a note—a letter"

"I wish to write," replied the other, not replying directly as to the nature of her proposed composition.

Without further words she followed her hostess to a knee-hole writing-table in a distant window, where, having provided her with what she required, Miss Monro prepared to leave her.

"I think you will find all that you need," she said, politely. "Envelopes here; stamps there."

"Thank you; I shall not require a stamp."

This last remark gave Miss Monro fresh food for thought as she returned to her friend."

"She says she does not require a stamp," she said, in a sort of whisper, "so it cannot be a letter that she is writing."

"Perhaps she is a poet," returned Mrs Wimpole, in the same tone and with an uneasy laugh. "That would account for her odd eyes. Perhaps she is penning an ode to you."

But Miss Monro did not join in her companion's rather spurious merriment. Her eyes were fixed upon the figure at the distant writing-table, who, with her left hand shading her face was bending over a sheet of paper.

"She has finished already," said Miss Monro, "it could not have been even a note."

But whatever she might have written, it was clear that the stranger was solicitous for its preservation. The two watchers saw her carefully fold and enclose it in an envelope, then light a taper, and holding a stick of sealing wax to the flame, she now carefully pressed one of a bunch of seals lying on the table upon the hot wax. This done, she rose.

"She is coming back," cried Miss Monro, in a hasty aside, "let us be saying something! Do not let her think that we have been watching her!"

But conversating thus suddenly commanded never comes, and the returning writer found the two ladies perfectly silent. She held the letter in her hand.

"You have finished your note," said the hostess, smiling rather stiffly, "the letterbox is on the hall table. Shall I put it in for you or would you prefer to put it in yourself?"

"Thank you, it is not to go by post."

"By hand, then?" with an unavoidable intonation of surprise.

"By neither."

"You will see"—in a tone that was evidently only with difficulty kept calm and steady—"that it is addressed to you."

As she spoke, she held up the envelope, upon which, indeed, Miss Monro read her own name legibly, if, perhaps, rather tremulously written. She put her hand out to receive it, but the stranger still kept it back.

"I must extract a promise from you," said she in a low but distinct voice, while the pallor of her features seemed to grow more marked, "that you will not open it until I give you leave!"

"Not open it!" repeated the other, her eyes dilating with new surprise and suspicion at this singular condition: "not open it until you give me leave? But I—I—thought—I understood that you intend to leave the neighbourhood tomorrow."

"I have that intention; but you will receive permission from me by letter when the time comes."

"Would it not be simpler if I were to open it now?" asked Miss Monro, her curiosity getting the better of her alarm. "If there is anything in it that needs an answer I might give it on the spot; surely it would be better that I should answer it now."

At this proposition the composure which she had clearly been maintaining with a great effort forsook the stranger's manner.

"Oh, no, no!" she cried excitedly; "not now—not now—not for worlds," and as she spoke the look of miserable fear and horror with which her hostess was by this time familiar, reappeared in her prominent pale eyes.

The alarm which female inquisitiveness had for the moment displaced regained its ascendancy in Miss Monro's breast.

"Promise," countered the other, with rising excitement, and in her eagerness stepping nearer to her now thoroughly frightened auditor;

"promise that under no circumstances—in no case will you open it until I give you permission."

"I promise," faltered Miss Monro, backing away in genuine fear from her companion; "of course, I promise, I promise."

## CHAPTER 3

"Thank God!" said Miss Monro, piously, throwing herself into her accustomed armchair with a large sigh of relief, as the last carriage rolled away. "Thank God that the Bedlamite is safe out of the house."

"What Bedlamite?" repeated Miss Sally, surprised.

She had witnessed nothing of her aunt's experiences, since most of her afternoon had been passed out of doors. After having thoroughly done her duty by the deaf widower, and seen that all the other elders were happily disposed of, she had given herself leave to seek a little pleasure among the young ones, and judging by the unusual brightness of her gentle eyes, she had apparently found it.

"What Bedlamite?" echoed Miss Monro, with an indignant accent, "is it possible that you never discovered that the person whom Mrs. Wimpole had the effrontery to bring with her was a raging lunatic."

"Good heavens, no!" cried the niece startled. "I—I did not think I noticed her much. I—I did not happen to be near her."

"Why, she sat exactly opposite you at luncheon," returned Miss Monro, sharply, "and never ceased staring like a maniac at you, except to glance at that poor creature the Robertson's tutor, who was sat beside you."

The colour that Miss Sally's cheek already wore at this speech deepened obviously, and she turned her head half away.

"I do not think that we were either of us conscious of it," she murmured.

"And now," pursued Miss Monro, far too much occupied with her own theme to have any eyes for her niece's complexion, "she has left me with this thing," distrustfully eyeing the mysterious document which she still held, "upon my hands; she charged me in the most solemn way not to open it until she gave me leave. She looked so wild as she did so that I really thought of calling for help. And now what am I to do with it? I have a great mind to throw it at the back of the fire."

"Oh, do not," cried Miss Sally; "that might hurt her feelings, poor thing, if she came to hear of it."

"How should she hear of it?" asked Miss Monro, shortly; "she leaves the neighbourhood tomorrow, thank God, and returns to her strait waistcoat, I should hope."

But she still hesitated.

"I will tell you what to do with it," said Sally, smiling; "put it in the secret drawer of your new bureau. You know you were wondering the other day what you should use it for."

The aunt paused a moment

"It is not a bad idea," she said, and so saying she moved towards the piece of furniture in question, opened it, and, touching the spring of the secret drawer, laid the sealed envelope within it.

Being thus satisfactorily rid of it, she returned with a sigh of relief to her place by the fire.

"Let us think no more of her and her ravings," said she, holding her hand to the blaze; "but I shall not forgive her in a hurry for having spoiled my luncheon party."

"Did you think it was spoilt?" asked Sally in a somewhat low voice. "I thought it was the pleasantest you had ever given."

"Did you really?" returned the aunt, this unaffected tribute making the entertainment instantly assume a brighter aspect in her own eyes. "We certainly had a man over. In all the years I have lived in this neighbourhood, I never remember the occurrence of such a circumstance before; yes, we really had a man over."

Two days later the post brought a letter to Miss Monro from Mrs. Wimpole. She wrote:

> I must really send you a line to relieve your mind as to Miss Younghusband, who left us yesterday morning; and also, to tell you that we have all come round to your opinion about her. We all think her undoubtedly insane; until your luncheon party, indeed, we had seen nothing that could be called even eccentric; but her conduct then, and her behaviour on that evening after we got home have quite persuaded us that you are right. She sat the whole time after dinner in a corner with her hands shading her eyes, speaking to no one, and Wimpole declares that she was crying. However, '*all is not well that ends well*,' and I trust we have now seen the last of the poor creature. I thought you would be glad to hear that she was safely gone, which must be my excuse for troubling you.—I am, yours very truly,
>
> S. Wimpole.

"And a good thing, too!" said Miss Munro as she folded up the note. "I hope it will be a lesson to that good woman not to go fishing up odds and ends of acquaintances at *table d'hôtes* again."

As the days went by the memory of Miss Younghusband and her *lunes* faded gradually away from the memories of that small Yorkshire neighbourhood. Other luncheon parties effaced the memory of the one at which she had figured. Even upon Miss Monro's mind the recollection of her eccentricities assumed fainter colour (though she could always be aroused to indignation by the thought of Mrs. Wimpole's unwarrantable conduct in introducing such a guest), and the sealed envelope lay half forgotten in the secret drawer. The autumn was a fine and dry one; and during it Miss Monro's health was better than she could usually boast, and neither her bronchitis nor her domestic tyrant hindered her from sharing in various neighbouring hospitalities of a daylight character.

Coachman and footman agreed in not having much objection to her going out to luncheon and tea; so, at several luncheons and several teas she and her niece appeared.

At almost all of them appeared likewise, strange as it may seem, Mrs. Robertson's gawky son and his tutor. Some half imaginary delicacy had induced the doting parents of the former to keep him from school for a couple of terms, and as not, even from their eyes could his boorishness and ill-manners be wholly concealed, his mother, with a view to humanising and softening him, dragged the reluctant youth in her wake wherever she went. His tutor, of course, accompanied him.

Miss Sally did not by any means always have the chance of soothing the latter's shyness by sitting beside him at luncheon, or strolling in trim gardens with him afterwards, but yet it was surprising how often both these contingencies did occur.

Perhaps no one else was particularly eager to engross either of them; perhaps people saw their natural suitability and helped them. Perhaps it was only that being both dependent, kind, and not very happy, they gravitated inevitably to one another.

It was lucky, at all events, for poor Mr. Ayrton that he had a little pleasure to look forward to outside the walls of his temporary home; for inside those walls his position was certainly not an enviable one.

"Did you ever see anything so ridiculous as his clothes?" asked one of the Miss Robertsons of Sally, as she and her sister hung heavily one on each arm of that young lady, on the moccasin of Miss Monro and her niece having driven over to the Robertson's house.

Sally had known perfectly well beforehand that they would hang on each arm. They always did it, and she had never hitherto minded it much. But now, as she saw the object of their sarcasm hovering in hopeless envy near, she felt an inclination, such as never before had assailed her mild breast to shake off the two solid arms; to stop her ears against the loud giggles, and run away—run away—but whither or to whom she did not exactly formulate to herself.

"Do you know," continued the other of Sally's admiring female friends who had just spoken, "that when first he came he had not even a dress coat; he came down to dinner in a frock coat; and the one that he has now we are sure that he must have hired, it is such an absurd misfit! Bobby is so funny about him. I wish you could hear Bobby about hm!"

But Miss Sally expressed no wish to hear Bobby's *facetiae* upon the subject of his tutor's wardrobe.

"One can't dislike him either," said the other girl, with a sort of compunction in her tone, "he must have seen us laughing at him times out of his mind; but yet he never bears malice; he is ready to do anything, tiresome or disagreeable, for any of us the moment after."

"He is a duffer all round," returned the other, contemptuously; "did you ever see such a guy as he looked when Bobby put him on the chestnut; and he does not know the barrel of a gun from the stock. Bobby says that he is a duffer all round."

"I thought he was a great scholar," suggested Sally, indifferently.

"Oh, so he may be; I dare say he is, most smugs are; but for all that he is a duffer all round; Bobby says so."

"I fancy he is very good to his people," said the gentler sister; "sending them all his money; he is always at the post office getting postal orders."

Female friendship is undoubtedly a beautiful thing, and until today Sally would have never thought of questioning it, when, by reason of the Misses Robertsons's obstinate affection in clinging to her till the last moment, all other persons were successfully prevented from approaching her. It would certainly never have occurred to the minds of either of these young ladies as possible that society of their butt could by any rational person be preferred to their own.

But the Misses Robertson could not always be hanging upon Sally's arms; there must be moments when those long-suffering members were free from their too fond burden; and as time wore on, as the leaves fell off the trees, and as autumn leapt into winter—the seasons worsen so much more quickly than they mend—those moments became more frequent. For the Misses Robertson, being young and of a manly turn, would have thought their time in winter wasted upon a female dalliance. When they were not hunting, they were tobogganing, and when they were not tobogganing, they were out with their guns. Both were fair shots, so that from November to April the unmanly Sally was comparatively unmolested by their tenderness.

Naturally, though, nobody offered to mount the tutor. He would have liked it well enough had they done so, though he cherished no more illusions about himself than did those around him as to the certainty of his parting company with his horse at the first fence.

Since his pupil was an even more enraged sportsman than the youth's sisters, Mr. Ayrton had, in open weather, many leisure hours in which to march about the leafy woods, with the brown boughs crackling overhead, and the brown leaves rustling underfoot. And Miss Sally had always loved to walk in the woods, leafy or leafless.

Bye-and-bye Christmas came, with the inevitable bedizened fir tees groaning under their unnatural loads; its conjurors; its carpet dances. And of all those things Miss Monro's neighbourhood had to share, though to none of them did she contribute anything. Winter weather generally made her feel ill and cross, and it was not often that she could make up her mind to spare her niece's company in the evenings. Doubtless she would have done so had the girl asked her, for she was not an ill-natured woman, only lightly touched by the selfishness of age.

But Sally had a foolish habit of never asking for things for herself. However, without asking, to one or two merrymakings she was permitted to go. The last of these was one given at the very end of the Christmas holidays by the Robertsons, as a sort of banquet and finale to the gaieties of the time. It was large and rowdy; a boisterous mixture of young and old. The Robertsons had announced beforehand that there should be plenty of "go" in it; and plenty of "go" there was.

It was perhaps, specially conspicuous towards the end of the evening in young Robertson, who, as the hypercritical noticed under the genial influence of his father's vintages, had exchanged his wonted awkward bashfulness for a still more awkward fluency. It is an ugly word, but young Robertson was drunk; and where was his tutor? The only answer is that his tutor was drunk, too, though certainly not with wine, since in that intoxication Miss Sally, in the usual sense of the word a rooted teetotaller, largely shared.

They had no right to tell each other how kindly they loved. It was a passion that was death-marked from its birth; but for that one evening it sat them, heavily handicapped by fate as they were, on a level with the gods. They came down from that level fast enough. Perhaps they would never have climbed to it; perhaps they would have gone to their graves only suspecting that they had exchanged their foolish hearts., had not their parting been so near.

In two days, they were to bid goodbye. In two days, young Robertson, escorted by his bear leader, was to be sent by his mamma, who still laboured under the unaccountable delusion of his delicacy, to one of the health resorts on our southern coast, in order to enable his hypothetically weak chest the better to bar the brunt of the cold season. It was in vain that in his polished accents he lisped that it was "beastly rot". But he was to go in two days.

In two days, Ayrton and Sally were to bid goodbye. In fact, they never did bid it, for just as Sally was about to slip out to keep her first and last tryst, she was arrested by her aunt, who being labouring under an influenza, requested her niece to keep her company for the whole of the afternoon, assuring her that it would do her no manner of harm to forego the fresh air for a day.

After one faint effort—she was always but a poor hand at speaking up for herself—Sally acquiesced. Goodbyes are painful things, and one is lucky who escapes pain in any form; and yet it cut sally to the heart to lose hers.

Thay said no goodbye, and he went, and Miss Monro, unconscious of the woe she had wrought, cursed her influenza complaint, and called upon Sally for pity and sympathy.

Once or twice, it struck her that the girl was a little slacker than usual in the expression of both. However, the difference was hardly noticeable, and no one could say that she was not a most attentive, dutiful nurse. And for a few days Miss Monro was certainly rather ill, with a touch of fever, a daily visit from the doctor, and a diet of slops.

About the end of the week that followed the departure of young Robertson and his instructor, the invalid mended rapidly, and one evening was so far recovered as to reappear, shawl-muffled, in her usual chimney corner armchair in the well-warmed drawing-room.

"It is pleasant to be up again," said she, heaving a sigh of satisfaction. "How shaky even two days of staying in bed makes one feel!"

"Yes, do not they" answered Sally, absently staring at the fire.

She did not originate any topic, and after a minute or two her aunt remarked in a rather peevish tone:

"I wish there was a chance of someone dropping in. I fear it is quite too late for that; how one needs a change of idea after being three days in a sick room."

"Shall I read the paper to you?" asked Sally rousing herself from her reverie.

"Hem! I dare say there is nothing in them," captiously.

"There has been an appalling fire at Trueminster Theatre," said Sally, rising and fetching the day's journals from a distant table, where, after he had quite done with them, the cross old butler was sometimes obliging enough to deposit them. "A hundred and fifty lives lost!"

"A hundred and fifty lives lost! Dear me, how shocking!" cried Miss Monro, in a livelier tone than the invalid one she had hitherto employed. "How did it happen?"

"It broke out behind the scenes," replied Sally, returning to the fire with a handful of newspapers, "in the middle of the first act; and then somebody in the pit cried 'Fire,' and there was the usual horrible panic and rush."

"Read me the whole account," said the elder woman with animation. "Which paper gives it most fully? *Times? Standard? Morning Post?*"

It was undoubtedly an extremely shocking event that Trueminster Theatre should have been destroyed by fire, and should have involved in its destruction that of a hundred and fifty of her fellow-creatures; but since it was to happen, it was not altogether unlucky that the tidings of it should arrive at a moment when her own life was so singularly in need of fresh interest.

"Come nearer the lamp, child; you will burn your eyes out by the fire."

Sally obeyed, and, placing herself as her aunt directed, began to read. She read the whole terrific story; a story alas, too common in these latter days. The whole story; mirthful opening; the roars of laughter at the farcical humours of the piece; the sudden fall of the curtain; the cry of "Fire"; the scare; the rush; the closed doors; blocked exits; the extinguished lights; the trampling; the suffocation; the mad terror, before which all natural humanity went down; all the inexpressible horrors of that fearfullest valley of the shadow of death.

Then followed a score of heartrending stories of individual loss and sorrow; of parents robbed by that fiery furnace of every child; of wives seeking to identify the bodies of dead husbands; of husbands gone mad with grief over the charred bodies of dead wives. Sickening details of unrecognisable bodies, hideous hurts, gorged hospitals, and at length Sally paused.

"It is one of the most awful things I ever heard of in my life," said Miss Monro, in a shocked tone; "worse, if possible than the Ring Theatre at Vienna or the Opera Comique. I hope to goodness"—in a key of quickened interest—"that young Robertson and his tutor, that awkward young man, what was his name?—did not happen to be there!"

"Why on earth should they be?" asked Sally, almost rudely. "What a ridiculous idea. Trueminster is thirty miles from Ilfracombe, and the papers say" (turning feverishly to them again) "that the sufferers were entirely of the poorer classes."

Miss Monro looked at her niece with unfeigned surprise. Never before had gentle Sally permitted herself to address her before in such a way.

"You need not bite my nose off about it, my dear," she said, with dignity; and at that moment the butler entered.

"If you please'm," said he laying another newspaper on the table beside her, "the vicar has sent you an evening paper, with his compliments. He thought you might like to see the latest details of the fire at Trueminster."

"I am sure I am greatly obliged to him," replied the old lady, eagerly taking up the *York Herald* thus alluded to; and too eager in her pursuit of more horrors even to avail herself of Sally's aid, she put on her spectacles, and thrust her head between the columns.

Sally was glad of the respite. Her voice was tired and her heart sick. She sat staring with wide eyes at the fire, for how long she did not know; there was a vague discomfort in her mind apart from her own private sadness, and apart too from the melancholy engendered by the catalogue of agonies that she had been reading.

Her aunt's voice startled her back into the present again; her aunt's voice, but with an intonation in it that before she knew what she was doing or why, made her leap to her feet.

"Good heavens!" the elder woman was saying, half under her breath; "I was right then. I never thought it, really!"

In a second Sally had torn the paper out of her aunt's hand, and the paragraph on which her eyes had been fixed was burning through the girl's eyes into her brain.

We regret to add another victim to the long list already given, in the person of a young gentleman who had arrived at the George Inn only on the evening of the catastrophe. It appears that; after having partaken of dinner, he and a companion, somewhat his junior, attended the performance at the theatre. When the cry of 'Fire' was raised he succeeded without difficulty in effecting his escape from the stalls, under the impression that he was being closely followed by his friend. On reaching the outer air, however, he found that such was not the case, the younger gentleman having in the crowd and confusion become separated from him.

On becoming aware of this fact, he at once re-entered the burning pile, and having with infinite difficulty fought his way back into the now blazing edifice, he succeeded by nothing short of a miracle, in rescuing his friend, and with the aid of a fireman conveyed him in safety to the outer air. In so doing, however, he himself sustained injuries so severe a nature as to render necessary his immediate conveyance to the hospital; where we regret to learn that he has succumbed to them.

We have ascertained that the name of the young gentleman, who thus gallantly rescued the life of a fellow-creature at the expense of his own, is Ayrton, eldest son of the Rev. William Ayrton, curate at Titherington, Dorset. He had only lately completed his 22nd year. The companion whose life he preserved is Mr. Robertson, son of George Robertson, Esq., of Cannock Court, Yorkshire."

"I never was so shocked in my life," said Miss Monro, looking rather white, "but what a mercy that it was not young Robertson!"

Sally did not answer, but she and the *York Herald* suddenly fell in a heap on the hearthrug together.

CHAPTER 4

Summer had come round again, come later, indeed, to East Yorkshire than to other places, because it is an ungenial climate; but even thither it had come at last; firmly established summer, with all the pleasant splendour of its adjuncts. Ordinarily, in summer both Miss Monro's health and her servants allowed of her sharing more largely than at other seasons in her neighbour's gaieties, and her old landau and fat horses might be seen trotting up most of the neighbouring drives about tea and tennis time.

This year, however, though the season was unusually fine, Miss Monro was scarcely ever seen beyond her park palings. She was not ill, and her servants' tyranny had not made any very perceptible strides in the last six months. But Miss Monro's ideas were old-fashioned, and it would have seemed to her a sort of sacrilegious dissipation even to drive about the quiet lanes in the first months of deep mourning. She had not many relations, and she had lost one of them, for her niece, Miss Sally Monro, was dead.

Sally had not died of grief at her lover's death, but of the scarlet fever. Perhaps that great and sudden sorrow had rendered her less able to make a good fight for her life; but then Sally, as I have said, had never been much of a hand at fighting for herself; and after all, many persons who had had no great grief, and who were bitterly reluctant to part with their lives, had yet lost them by the same disease.

Sally had lived long enough to hear young Robertson, with his face beblubbered with tears, and his hard voice all broken, tell her every detail of the martyrdom of him whom he had once made his butt.

Then life had gone on as before, and by-and-bye Sally had caught the scarlet fever—no one exactly knew how, but it had been crawling about since early springtime—and had quickly died of it.

Sally had not been very lively in her life, you will allow; but in her death she was fortunate, since she died in her sleep. They had thought she was getting better—perhaps she was—and had given her a sleeping draught, and she had gone comfortably to sleep and never reawakened.

Thus, it was that on a certain hot June evening of that year Miss Monro sat alone by one of the open windows of her drawing-room. Her crape gown was oppressive, and she was fanning herself irritably, when the butler, whose entry she had not heard—how deaf she was growing—came up to her with a letter in his hand.

"The vicar's complements, m'm, and he is very sorry, but the letter went to the vicarage by mistake, and they forgot to send it up until now."

The frequency with which notes and parcels went by mistake to the vicarage was a chronic grievance to Miss Monro, but this time she took no notice of it. Her mind had flown back to that January evening six months ago, when the vicar had sent his complements and the *York Herald*.

"Shall I light the candle m'm?"

"No, thank you," indifferently; "I will wait until you bring the lamp."

It could not be a letter from the other side of the grave, and none from this side could have much interest for her. She sat with the letter carefully on her lap until the lights were brought. Even then she did not immediately open it. Her seat by the window was cooler than the one more in the interior of the room; and how sultry it was.

At length, however, she rose; and seating herself by the lamp, looked with lack-lustre eyes through her spectacles at the address. It was quite unfamiliar to her. What strange handwriting! How uncertain, tremulous, and indistinct! No wonder that the letter had gone to the vicarage. She turned the envelope over in irritational way that people do on seeing an unfamiliar hand. The postmark, by some accident, was half effaced, so that from it she learned nothing.

After examining it fruitlessly for some time, she at length opened the cover and unfolded the letter. The first look told her no more than had the outside. The handwriting still seemed unfamiliar, though for an instant a vague idea crossed her that she had seen it somewhere at some previous time. But there was neither address nor monogram, and it began with that formal "Madam", which promises so little.

"A begging letter, I suppose," said Miss Monro, to herself, her faint little flicker of interest dying out. She turned to the signature, with no expectation, however, of being enlightened by it.

"Hannah Younghusband." "*Younghusband!*" In an instant there had rushed back to her on a tide of memories the recollection of that luncheon party of the previous autumn, to which Mrs. Wimpole had asked to bring a friend. "Younghusband." That was her name. She remembered it perfectly, and that Mrs. Wimpole had remarked upon its ludicrousness. With a rush of memory came back, too, the uninvited guest's strange behaviour, her mad eyes, the woman's whole lunatic-seeming personality, her own indignant lament afterwards over the blight she had thrown upon the party, and Sally's kind reassurances.

With a fresh contraction of the heart—she had many of them every day—Miss Monro turned, with an interest quickened almost to painfulness, back to her letter's first page, and holding it close to the lamp, so that the full light might fall on the faint and undecided characters she began to read eagerly as follow:—

Madam—I must begin by apologising for this intrusion upon you at a time which I know must be one of sorrow for you. You have probably entirely forgotten the existence of the writer of this letter, but I may perhaps be able to recall it to you by reminding you of a luncheon party given by you in the month of

September last, to which your neighbour, Mrs. Wimpole, asked permission to bring me. You may perhaps remember the circumstance of my having put into your hands before leaving a letter which I earnestly begged you not to open until you received permission to do so from me. The object of my writing today is to tell you that I now give you permission. If, as I fully believe, you have preserved the paper I then put into your hands, I request you without delay to open and examine its contents. I should be grateful to you if you would do so before proceeding further with this letter.

Miss Monro was growing an old woman, and perhaps that was why she was trembling so much, as she took her way across the large room to her bureau.; perhaps that was why she fumbled so with the spring of the secret drawer. Perhaps, however, it was because her eyes were blurred with tears; Sally's voice suggesting to her that drawer as the depository of the supposes lunatic's paper rang so clear and alive in her ears.

The spring had yielded now, the drawer was open, and there, sure enough, lay the half-forgotten envelope. In a moment the old lady had seized it, torn it open—too impatient to wait even to return to the lamp's neighbourhood, and and read the contents. It did not take her long to do so.

Mr. Ayrton,
Miss Sally Monro.

That was all. Those two names written with unmistakeable clearness—indistinct as was the writer's hand elsewhere, on the otherwise blank page. Miss Monro rubbed her eyes. Is it that her mind is so full of those two dead ones—before Sally's death she had learned all her short story—that she sees their names written everywhere?

She looked again. No there could be no mistake or delusion about it.

Mr. Ayrton,
Miss Sally Monro.

But why these two names? Why out of the whole large and to her equally unknown party should this strange being have picked out just these two names? And what had been her meaning in writing them down with some emphasis and mystery?

In the hope of finding some light thrown upon this apparently answerless question, the old lady hastened tremulously back to where she had left her half-read letter; and, catching it up, resumed her interrupted reading of it.

I was perfectly aware that my manner had impressed you with the idea that I was of unsound mind, and I saw that the pertinacity with which during luncheon I was unable to keep my eyes from fastening upon two of your guests gave you good reason for this supposition. If you remember our positions at the luncheon table you will recall that I was placed exactly opposite the young lady and gentleman whom I afterwards learned to be your niece and Mr. Ayrton. As I am always of an absent disposition and so little used to society that I suffer extremely from shyness on the rare occasions when I enter it, I did not notice them more particularly than others among your guests until towards the middle of the luncheon, when I happened to look directly across the table, full at them.

From that moment until we left the dining-room I was unable to avert my eyes for more than an instant from them, though I was perfectly aware of the surprise and alarm which my conduct and my, I suppose, strange looks excited in your mind. I was not at that time able to explain my behaviour. I am at liberty to do so now. I must tell you, then, that no sooner had my eye fallen upon Mr. Ayrton and your niece than I became aware that I was looking at them through a thin film, as if a very fine grey gauze veil had been drawn over each of their faces. You will, no doubt, suggest that I am subject to optical delusions, but such is not the case; that the appearance saw, or imagined I saw, took its origin from some derangement in my own health or overwrought condition of my nerves.

At the same time the same idea, the same hope, I may say, suggested itself to me; and I looked eagerly round the table to ascertain whether I could observe the same appearance in the case of any other person. But no; it was only over the two face immediately opposite to me that the grey veil was drawn. It remained—that filmy, yet distinctly seen, substance—until the end of the luncheon. As often as I looked back at them—and you will bear witness what an irresistible yet unwilling fascination drew my eyes perpetually to them—I saw it; saw it as plainly as I even see the paper on which I am writing.

Since that day I have not set eyes upon Mr. Ayrton or your niece. You will object, even granting that the appearance which I describe did exist really, and not only in my disordered vision, that there was indeed in it cause for surprise, and for that degree of alarm which anything verging, however remote, upon the supernatural is calculated to produce, but not for the intensity of dismay and horror which I feel sure you were aware that that appearance produced in me. The cause, you will say, was growing disproportioned to the effect. And so, indeed, as far as I have as yet stated the case, it would have been.

I must therefore, go on to explain that on two or three previous occasions, at widely separated periods of my life, I had observed this phenomenon, and that in every case, without exception, it had been followed by the death within the year of the person in connection with whom I had seen it. The interval between the last occasion on which it had been presented to me and the date of my visit to your house had not been a long one, and I had time to persuade myself that the deaths in each case had been merely the result of a coincidence. Long, however, as had been the interval since the last case, my nerves had not yet wholly recovered from the shock of it, and on suddenly seeing the appearance I so infinitely dreaded presented to my eyes in the case of two persons at once, I was wholly unable to conceal my agitation.

It mastered me during the remainder of my stay in your house; and conscious as I was of having completely lost my self-command, I was absolutely incapable of making even an effort to recover it. You will remember the, to you, inexplicable emotion with which I inquired of you the name of your niece; and the incoherence of my apparently meaningless request for writing materials. Both were dictated by a wish to justify myself absolutely from the suspicion of insanity, which I saw you entertained of me.

By writing down these two names in black and white, by committing the paper to your care—so that you might be sure of its being untampered with by me, I put you in a position to judge whether or not I was the victim of a hallucination. When, after having in January last read the account in the papers of Mr. Ayrton's tragic end, I saw the other day also an announcement of your niece's death, I felt that the time had come to give you this explanation. With expressions of regret and sympathy for your loss, I am, madam,

Your faithfully,

Hannah Younghusband.

Miss Monro is still alive, but she never has had the heart to give any more luncheon parties.

# What it Meant

I had the last look. I shall always maintain that. Alice thought that she had got the better of me by going round to the other side of the cab and teasing him to kiss her through the window, though she was all smouched with tears—a thing he never liked, and he was hunting for his flask which he had mislaid; but I was even with her. I jumped in at the last moment and drove down with him to the gate. We did not say anything at all, but he let me hold his hand all the way, and at the very last, when I was actually on the step getting out, he said, "God bless you!"

Alice will not believe it, but he did. He, so undemonstrative, who never in his life be-dear-ed or be-darling-ed us, he said, "God bless you!"

I am so glad that I did not annoy him with tears. I think that that was his way of paying me. I told Alice so, which made her very angry, as she had cried like a pump; but after all, perhaps it distracted us a little to brawl over it, as we did intermittently for the rest of the day. If we had not quarrelled, I cannot think how we should have got through the day at all. It was at least an occupation, and the only one which was not rendered intolerable by being inextricably entangled with his memory. Ever since he came home on sick leave, five months earlier, our life had been so built upon him and his convenience, that now that the keystone was withdrawn, our bridge seemed to collapse. For five months our every action had had some reference to him. Now that he was gone, all action seemed useless.

This parting was, as we both agreed, worse, far worse, than any former one. They had all been bad enough, but when he was at school there were at least the long Midsummer and the short Christmas to look to; there was jam to send him, and the penny post to bring letters only twelve hours old. Even when he first went out to join his regiment in India, his own buoyant gladness in the prospect, his confidence that the climate would suit him—(did not hot weather here always suit him? the hotter the better)—had imparted to us, too, some faint ray of courage. But now that we knew certainly that that young confidence had been misplaced, now that there was burnt in upon our memories the look of him sent back to us as he had been last autumn—faint, deathly, bleached and emaciated almost past recognition-is it any wonder that our pulses beat low as we gave him back trembling to that feverish soil that is ever being new-paved with British graves?

And though he would not for a moment have suffered us to indulge, nor indeed would we have plagued him with, any morbid forebodings, yet we agreed, Alice and I, that his own dear heart seemed to grow heavy as the time for parting drew nigh. Not so heavy though as ours which he left behind. On that black first day, house and garden were equally bitter to us; the house where in the hall still stood the invalid couch on which, for weeks after his return, he languidly lay stretched; the garden where in his later better time, during the two or three days of premature summer that had thrust themselves among February's harsh cold troop, he had swung a hammock for us.

There it still hung between the ilex that the hard winter had pinched, and the cedar that no stress of frost or storm could change from its unaltered green. I stood with my hand on the hammock ropes. "Only sons should not be sent on foreign service!" I said with sententious sadness; my eyes absently fixed on the solid red brick Georgian house that seemed to share the sullenness of the low slate-coloured sky.

"Only sons' sisters should be sent on foreign service with them!" answered Alice, bettering my sentiment; "oh, if" (with a profound sigh) "we were all three steaming down to Folkestone together!"

"How pleased the regiment would be to see us!" rejoined I drily, and we both laughed. We were surprised and shocked the moment that we had done it, but we did laugh. Yes, he had not been gone three hours when we laughed! At luncheon we were quite upset again by Figaro the black poodle going unasked through all the tricks that Dick had taught him. Usually it required entreaties, threats, and unlimited Albert biscuits to induce him to execute one; but today, just when he knew they would be too much for us, he volunteered them all! In the evening—the evening latterly dedicated to our rubber-that happy muff-rubber which in its qualities of levity and clamour much more nearly resembled a round game—in the evening, I say, we all lay strewn about, limp and tearful in our armchairs, leaving sacredly empty his, and gazing at it wistfully till the clock struck ten, and the day was mercifully at an end.

The next day was a shade better; we cried less and ate more; the next a shade better again; and the next a shade better again than that. In fine, by the end of the week we had plucked up our spirits so far as to teach Figaro half a new trick, and our armchairs being limited—and our dear boy's empty one patently far the most comfortable one—we had, reluctantly at first, but with ever-growing callousness, abandoned the idea of its consecration to emptiness and memory. Indeed, Alice and I had wrangled a good deal over our respective claims to its possession.

By-and-by came his letters, the first from Paris, to say that he had had a rough passage, and that everybody on board, except himself, had been sick, but that he had walked about and enjoyed it; that he was going to the play at the *Variétés*; and that he hoped we would not forget to send him the sporting papers. The next letter was from Brindisi; the third from Aden, and so on. Very soon father and mother began to drop into their old way of showing his letters about taking them with them to exhibit when they paid visits, and bringing them forth to read, in whole or in part, when anyone called. It was a plan that Alice and I had always deprecated, and that no one would have disliked more than Dick himself, could he have known it.

Alice and I had often noticed the stifled yawns of indifferent guests during these readings, and had still oftener observed the hurried excuses and regrets for being unable to stay longer as soon as there was any talk of the Indian letters being produced. And so, in time, he reached India, and was welcomed back as one from the dead by his fellow-soldiers, who hardly knew him again, so hale, and brown, and strong on his legs. And as to us, we fell into our old tame and tranquil ways—our main events, the Indian mail days; our twin bugbears, cholera and war. We had returned to our evening rubber; mother, who never could tell one card from another, and hated them all, being mercilessly compelled by us to take a hand.

As the season advanced, and the air warmed, and the buds swelled, we spent more and more of our time lying in his hammock in the garden, where the cedar let fall its uncapricious dark shade on us, and even the shrivelled ilex put out some new leaves. When May came, there was scarce a moment of the day when it was not occupied by one or other of us, and we quarrelled over the right to occupy it as sharply as we had quarrelled over the possession of his armchair, and of the old torn gloves too worthless to take with him, that he had left lying—petulantly pulled off and rejected—on the hall table.

May had now just gone, and June's first splendid days were holding high holiday in earth and sky. The lilacs were over; they had been exceptionally profuse this year; even the thorns were on the wane, and the hot sun gave them the *coup de grâce*; and though the pink horse-chestnut still held up its stiff and stately spikes, yet a little tell-tale flushed carpet at its foot betrayed that it too was departing. But to make up to us for what we lost, the white pinks spread their spicy mats everywhere about the borders; the roses were only waiting for one lightest shower, to rush forth, one and all, and the cloying syringa made the air languid. It was not only the syringa, however.

The day had been weighted with excess of unwonted heat, and even oncoming night had brought but little freshness. We had strayed on the parched lawn and under the unstirred trees in vain search of a reviving breath, listening to the owl and the harsh but summer-voiced corncrake. We strayed till bedtime had come and passed—since our dear lad went, the day had seemed long enough, yes over-long by ten—and the clocks with one consent were telling the hour of eleven. So, we turned homewards, and limply climbed the stairs to bed. My room was in the roof, and on that roof, all through the immense June day, the sun had been mightily striking, so that, though all my three windows were set open to their fullest extent, the atmosphere was as of an engine-room.

I undressed dejectedly and lay down beneath the one sheet, which on that night seemed to have the weight and consistency of five good blankets. With small hope of sleep, I lay down; my eyes, widely open, staring out at the tennis-ground and the hammock, and the pink horse-chestnut tree, not pink any longer now, but (all distinctions of colour lost in one grave gloom) of the same hue as the cedar and the idex and the elm. I had small hope of sleep; and yet, by-and-by, sleep came. It must have come rather soon too, as I have no recollection of having heard the clocks strike again. I was awaked or, at least I seemed to be awaked, not with a start, but gradually by a voice. I found myself sitting up in bed and listening. I have no recollection of any panic fear, of any loud heart-beating, or paralysing of tongue or limbs, of any cold sweat of terror at this unexplained sound that was breaking the intense stillness of the night.

I was only sitting up and listening. I could not tell whence the voice came, not even from what direction it seemed to issue. I had no slightest clue as to whom or what it could belong to. It was accompanied by no rustling of any earthly garment, by no most cautious stirring of any human foot. It was only a voice. I caught myself pondering as to whose voice it could be. To what voice that I knew had it any likeness? I could find none. Yet there was nothing dreadful, nothing threatening or fear-inspiring in its quality. It was simply a voice, and it was saying most slowly, most solemnly and most sadly, with a light pause between each two words, "Your brother!—your brother!—your brother!"

Then there was silence again. I listened intensely, poignantly, still unaccountably without fear; but there was nothing more. There was no sound of any one breathing near me, and no form intervened between me and the casement square. I do not know for how long I listened; it might have been minutes, or only half a minute. Then I spoke. I can hardly believe now that I dared to do it; were such a voice to come to me again—which God avert! —I am very sure that I should have no power to unclose my lips or utter intelligible speech. But then I did. I said, still sitting up in bed, and staring strainingly out into the dim but not dark room, and I can still recall the odd sound of my own voice as it broke upon the dumbness round me: "My brother! what about my brother?"

There was another pause, during which you might, perhaps, have counted ten rather slowly; and then the voice came again, exactly the same as before; as slow, as solemn, as profoundly sad, and as impossible to trace whence it came—"Go into the garden and you will find a yellow lily striped with brown, and then you will know!" That was all. I listened, listened, listened, but there was nothing more. The words that I had heard kept ringing and echoing in my head, without my attaching any meaning to them at first; but then all at once they grew clear. "Go into the garden and you will find a yellow lily striped with brown, and then you will know!" How could I go into the garden now—the clocks were just striking one—alone—(for the idea of waking anybody never occurred to me)? The doors would be locked and bolted.

I doubted if I should be able to draw the heavy bolts. Go into the garden in dressing-gown and bare feet at one o'clock in the morning! I had never done such a thing in my life! And a yellow lily striped with brown?—there was no such lily in the garden, I was sure. It was not so large in extent that I could not have an intimate acquaintance with each blossom; and I recollected no such flower. In what border could

145

it be? I ran over in my head our lilies. There were turncap lilies, but they were some red and some yellow. There were Mary lilies; but they were white, and as yet only in green bud. There were irises indeed so curiously and whimsically painted and streaked that there might be among them a yellow one striped with brown, but then irises are not lilies.

Seized by a hot and biting curiosity, I slipped out of bed and—still inexplicably free from fear—walked barefoot to the window. There lay the garden—not precisely dark, for I could still see the tennis nets and the hammock, but overspread with so dusky a veil, that a hundred strange lilies might be hiding in its beds without my being able to distinguish or detect them. There was nothing for it but to go down and search. I could not resist the apparently senseless impulse. Go I must. I put on dressing-gown and slippers, and not lighting any candle, trusting to the lenity of the summer night and the bright planets, I opened my door and ran along the passages and down the stairs, whose every step I knew so well as to be able safely to race blindfold down them.

I had recollected that the garden door locked less stiffly than the others, and had no bolts. In effect, I opened it without more noise than the slight unavoidable click that any key makes in turning, and stood on the sward outside. How strangely strange the familiar garden looked! Could this really be the tennis-ground, worn bare by our feet—this solemn silent space? Could this be the pink horse-chestnut at whose rosy foot I had left my book lying last evening—this towering mass of darkness?

How in this universal gloom that spread one colourless shade over all, could I distinguish the tint of one flower from another? I walked alongside the borders, stooping as I went to peer at the faces of the blossoms, both those that thriftily close at advancing night, nor waste their beauty on the unperceiving darkness, and those that still hold up their chalices to the stars.

It was perfectly useless. I was stepping hopelessly across the grass, to a large oval bed of mixed shrubs and herbaceous plants which occupied the space immediately in front of the drawing-room windows, and of which I well knew, as I thought, every inmate, and was convinced that among them grew no such flower as I sought, when suddenly the moon, who tonight rose late, looked over the belt of girdling forest trees that hedged us in. At once, directly before me, as plainly as if it were in the very eye of noon, I saw—I can see it now—a large tall yellow lily, with lines of brown streaking its petals. That there had been no such lily there, when last—late on the previous evening—I had visited the parterre (by which old-fashioned name we always called this part of the pleasure grounds) I was thoroughly convinced.

Growing there straight and stately, unlike also any of our lilies, it was absolutely impossible that I could have overlooked it. It was still more absolutely impossible that it could have sprung up in its strength and beauty in the course of the night. Was it an optical delusion? Could I be suffering from some strange hallucination? I bent down low and touched it; put my fingers about its vigorous stem, and peered into the great orange-stamened vase of its expanded flower. For, like other lilies, it was as widely open as if it were the noon of day, instead of the noon of night. Into their pure cups the constellations look as freely as does the sun. It was certainly real, and as I stood in complete bewilderment, the words that the voice had uttered echoed back on my mind: "Go into the garden, and you will find a yellow lily striped with brown, and then you will know! But I had gone into the garden and found the lily, and I knew no more than before.

No ray of enlightenment pierced my darkness. The moon had sailed up above our elms, and was raining down her white and dreamful radiance. I gazed long and earnestly at the mystic blossom, eagerly trying to wile its secret from it, but it was in vain. The answer to the riddle, the key of the puzzle, escaped me.

After long or what seemed long and hopeless waiting, I had to turn away baffled, and retrace my steps across the ghostly white open spaces, and through the ghostly black shadows to the house. Up the dark stairs I climbed to my room. It was exactly as I had left it, only lighter, silent and empty. The shadow of the window-frames lay in a crossbar pattern, black and white upon the floor. There was even a patch of wan radiance upon the bed-quilt. I looked out of the window, trying if at this distance and by the aid of the now powerful moon, I could distinguish the strange new lily, but it was too far off.

So, at last, I unwillingly threw off my dressing-gown, and again lay down, meaning to await in bewildered wakefulness the coming of the morning, when I could correct by the help of daylight the errors and delusions of the night. But strange to say, almost before my head was well laid on the pillow, I was asleep again. For how long, who shall say? There is nothing more difficult to measure than the periods of sleep.

I had been too preoccupied to ascertain at what hour I had returned to the house, nor at my waking did it even occur to me to think of the length of my slumber. For I awoke again, precisely as I had done before, without start or jump or heart-throbbing; woke to find myself once more sitting up in bed and listening, listening to the same voice, monotonously mournful, that had spoken to me before, and that was now a second time addressing me in precisely the same words: "Your brother!—your brother!—your brother!"

The room, which before had not been really dark, was now almost quite light. Besides the moon, which still sailed high, the dawn was breaking—in June, there is virtually no night—and had there been any person, any form or apparition of any kind in the room, I must have perceived it. But in this case hearing drew no aid from sight. It was quite as impossible as before for me to decide whence the sound came. It was neither from above nor below, nor did it seem to proceed from any one point of the compass more than another. It was a voice, that was all. It was neither loud nor low, it was neither soft nor harsh. It was a voice and it was sorrowful. That was all you could certainly say of it. It repeated the words as before, three times: "Your brother!—your brother!—your brother!"

And I as before, still strangely stout-hearted, but in a passion of haste and eagerness, answered without any such interval as I had let elapse on the former occasion, staring out the while vaguely, for I did not know in which direction to look into the still and vacant chamber, where the two lights—the one that must wax and the one that must wane—were contending: "My brother! what about my brother?" Again, there was a little pause, as there had been before, and then the voice sounded again, vague and sad through the room: "Go to your wardrobe, and you will find a yellow ribbon striped with brown, and then you will know!"

I am not sure that I had not expected a repetition of the former words—to be again bidden to go and seek the lily; but at this new injunction, I remained for a few moments awed and still, waiting perhaps for something more to follow. But nothing came. A yellow ribbon striped with brown!" It flashed upon me that I had no such ribbon in my possession. I ran over in my head my simple and limited stock of personal adornments. I could remember among them none such. I was perfectly convinced that I owned no such ribbon. But then, on the other hand, I had been as firmly convinced that there was no such lily in the garden as the one that I had not only seen with my own eyes, but also touched and smelt there.

I sprang out of bed and ran to my wardrobe. It was composed of a hanging press for gowns on one side, and drawers on the other. With feverish haste I pulled out every drawer, beginning at the bottom. To reach the higher ones I had to mount upon a chair. I had pulled them all out except one, and had eagerly turned over and rummaged their contents, without finding anything that I did not already know to be there. Only one more drawer remained to be examined!

The probabilities were twenty to one that it also would be found to be empty of what I sought, or rather of what I anxiously sought not to find. I drew a heavy breath of relief at the thought that this time the voice had spoken falsely, and that therefore even if I heard it again and yet again repeat its melancholy message, I might dismiss it from my thoughts as some curious form of aural delusion.

I hurriedly drew out the top drawer, and the first thing that met my eye, lying above everything else, and unrolled so as to stretch across almost the whole width of the drawer, lay a ribbon—a yellow ribbon striped with brown, a ribbon that I had assuredly never been possessed of, or even seen before! There could be no mistake as to its colours. Momently the morning was broadening across the world, and the two tints were so distinct, the stripes so clearly marked, that error was impossible. I took it out and let it fall across my fingers. No! I had never seen it before.

As to how it came there, or whence it came, I could hazard no conjecture. "Go to your wardrobe, and you will find a yellow ribbon striped with brown, and then you will know!" But I had gone to my wardrobe; I held the ribbon in my hand, and still I knew not. The message of the ribbon was as dark to me as had been that of the flower.

As I so stood, in even more hopeless bewilderment than I had stood in the garden, painfully striving to find the moral of this twice-repeated enigma, a bird—some little finch—struck up the first few notes of his sleepy dawn song. I listened eagerly to him, thinking that perhaps he might give me the key to the riddle. But in his little song there was nothing but joy—joy at the coming of another day; joy at being alive; joy at being a little garden finch. He could not help me. Neither could the widening morning red, nor the awakening flowers. None of them could help me.

By-and-by I laid down the ribbon in despair, carefully replacing it exactly as I had found it. I closed the drawer, got down from the chair, shut the wardrobe, and went back to bed. This time I was resolved that sleep should not again overtake nor expose me to the possibility of being again aroused by that tormenting riddle-speaking voice. And indeed, so vividly, agitatedly wakeful was I, that it seemed most un-likely that I should again lapse into slumber. And yet as before, scarce had my head touched the pillow, before I was sound asleep again.

Next time that I woke, the June sun was blazing aloft; for the one sleepy finch, a score of blackbirds and thrushes and linnets were mak-ing their heavenly din, and my maid was offering me my morning tea. I took it drowsily, but before I had tasted it—the act of sitting up having fully aroused me—the incidents of the night rushed back on my mind. Hastily thrusting aside the tray, I jumped out of bed, and running to the wardrobe, opened it, climbed up on a chair, and pulled out the top drawer, in which I had so plainly seen the ribbon lying; not only seen but touched and handled it. There was no brown-and-yellow ribbon there. Then I pulled out hastily all the others. Neither in any of them was there such a ribbon; nor, although I clearly recol-lected having overturned and displaced their contents, was there any least trace of such overturning and displacing.

Everything lay neat and orderly as was its wont. I was feverishly ex-ploring the bottom drawer, when my maid in a voice, through which her astonishment at my unwonted procedure plainly pierced, asked me "What I was looking for." I answered. "Nothing", or at least, re-closing the wardrobe as I spoke, "nothing that I was likely to find." I dressed in feverish haste—usually I was of a lazy habit; lay long and was hard to rouse—and in half an hour from the time at which I was called, I was racing across the sward to the bed that had held the mystic flower. What a different garden it was to the midnight one! holding no secrets in its frank and sunny breast, and sung to by what sweet and practised minstrels! I reached the bed, but I could see no lily. In the night, as I remembered, it was the very first object that had struck my sight.

It was impossible to overlook it, even in that comparatively faint light; but now, even with strong daylight helping me, I could find no trace of it. I searched through the whole large bed, pushing even be-tween the Gueldres rose and mock-orange bushes, but it was not there. There were peonies—huge red ones, pale pink ones—that seemed as if they were trying to be mistaken for great roses; there was weigelia, delicate as apple-blossom; there were irises; there were Canterbury-bells; there were lupins—but there was no yellow lily striped with brown. As I still—though now convinced that it was in vain—peered and pushed aside leaves and blossoms, the voice of Alice, who had come suddenly up behind, startled me:

"What are you looking for?"

"Nothing," I answered hurriedly, stepping back on to the grass again.

"Have you lost a ring or a glove?" inquired she, looking at me with some attention, for I suppose I appeared flurried and disordered.

"No," I replied, "I have lost nothing; at least"—casting one more fruitless glance around—"nothing that I am likely to find."

Neither flower nor ribbon! Must it then have been only a dream? At first, I rejected scornfully this explanation. Had ever dream such consistency? Did ever dream move with such apparent coherence from its beginning to its close? In it had been none of the strange starts and freaks that are always occurring in the dream-world. In it there had been nothing *décousu*; no leaps from the probable to the entirely impossible; no metamorphosis of myself into someone else; no unexplained transition from here to there, from now to then, such as have abounded in every dream—even the most vivid and lifelike ones—that I have ever previously had. And yet, as the day wore on, the suspicion deepened, changed at last into a conviction, that it was a dream. I had never awakened really. I had never trodden the midnight garden, or opened my wardrobe doors.

All the time that I imagined I had been so doing, I had been in point of fact resting quietly on my bed; possibly some awkward way of lying, some uneasiness of posture, had produced the phenomena that I have described. I spoke of my dream, if it was a dream, to no one, not even to Alice. Some strange reluctance tied my tongue. But I went heavily and ill at ease all through the day. It was never out of my head. I puzzled over its enigma from early morning until night again fell, and bedtime returned.

The heat had moderated and the air was fresher. Tired and yet excited, I lay down. I closed my eyes, dreading a repetition of the vision (though, indeed, that is a misnomer as there was nothing to be seen), and yet nervously hoping for some continuation of it that might give me the clue to guide me through its labyrinth—that might give me a reassuring solution of its riddle. But none such came.

I had difficulty in falling asleep at all at first, so hopelessly alert and at work seemed my brain; but gradually lassitude got the better of my excitement, and I slept. But no trace of any dream disturbed or varied my deep slumber. Nor on any of the succeeding nights did I hear any repetition of that strange and melancholy voice. It seemed to have had leave to speak but that once. And as the days and hours passed by, time's influence, invariably numbing, deadened the impression that at first had been so keen. After a while I tried to avoid thinking of it, as of something painful, unnerving, and yet meaningless, nor did I mention it to any living soul. To relate it would have seemed to give it added importance.

And so, a week of our placid and uniform life slipped away. The weather was cool again, and we played tennis from morning to night. At first the same sentiment which had made us leave Dick's chair vacant, prevented us from supplying his place in the game; but as this principle could not be carried out through life, that whatever he had done must henceforth, until his return, be left undone, we by-and-by associated to ourselves, as occasion offered, a neighbouring curate, or squire, and so, all day long, the balls flew, and the grass waxed ever barer, balder, and more worn, where our persevering feet continually trampled it.

But still, of course, the Indian mail remained the event of our lives. We were so much behind the time and lived so deep-sunk in the country, that we had no second post, nor would my father take any steps to obtain one, as he said that once a day was quite enough to be pestered with letters, and that, for his part, if it were once a week instead, he could very well put up with it.

But it was by the second post that the Indian letters came to our post town, and on the mail day it was an invariable custom that some of us should drive in to fetch them. To send a servant for them would have balked our impatience and would besides have seemed a disrespect to them. So, whether it shone or rained, Alice and I, as surely as the post day came, might be seen whipping up our old pony into unwonted and unwilling speed along the road to ———.

On that day it shone; shone so strongly that Alice, who drove, asked me for a share of my large sunshade; and beneath it we trotted along in happy expectancy. The air blew heavily sweet from the bean field (until that day I loved the smell of a blossoming bean field), and the birds sang—oh, *how* they sang!

"*For there was none of them that feigned*
*To sing, for each of them him pained*
*To find out merry crafty notes,*
*They ne spared not their throats.*"

When we reached the post office, the letters were still being sorted, so we had to wait a few moments. But we were rewarded for our waiting. A letter in the beloved handwriting, and with the usual postmark, was soon put into our eager hands. We waited to open it till we were out of the little town, and off the cobble stones, so that we might comfortably enjoy it, the one who read without raising her voice, and the one who listened without straining her ears. It was addressed to Alice, though of course, like all his letters, meant for the benefit of the whole family. We were always glad when the letters were to either of us, as they were usually of a lighter and more conversational type than those directed to our parents—less about the customs and habits of the natives, the resources of the country, &c., and more about the gossip of the station, the picnics, the quarrels of the regimental ladies, the flirtations.

This was a particularly good specimen of our favourite kind, and as we passed along, the old pony dropped unrebuked into a leisurely rolling amble, the reins fell loose on his back while Alice and I together stooped our heads over the page in the vain effort to decipher an illegible but obviously important word on which the point of a whole sentence turned.

We were so absorbed that we did not perceive a telegraph boy who was marching along the dusty road in the same direction as ourselves, until recognising our pony chaise, he made signs to us to stop, holding out, as he did so, one of those familiar orange missives that alternately order dinners and announce deaths. I took it, though with no particular misgiving: people employ the telegraph wires for such harmless trifles nowadays. It was addressed—not to any of us—but to

Mrs. Grainger,
Housekeeper at Hall.

Mrs. Grainger was one of those servants who—rail, and justly rail as one may at the class of domestic servants in general—are yet so numerous that one can scarcely ever take up a *Times* without reading the lamented death of one of these chronicled in its obituary. She had nursed us all three lovingly: Dick first, and most lovingly, and was now almost as well known to our friends—to some even of Dick's friends, notably to his *alter ego*, Major ——, who not long before our boy's departure had been paying us a visit—as we ourselves.

"It is for Na Na!" I said (we still called her by that infantile name). "I hope that it is no bad news for her; she was rather frightened by the last accounts of her consumptive niece."

"You had better open it, at all events," answered Alice; "it may require an answer."

So, I opened it, she looking over my shoulder.

From Major ——,     to Mrs. Grainger,
India.     Housekeeper at ——Hall,
                 ——shire.

Mr. —— attacked by tiger, out shooting. Killed on the spot.
Break it to his family. Have written.

I read it through at first without any comprehension, so totally
unexpectant was I, so prepossessed with the idea that the telegram
did not concern us at all, but contained ill news for Na Na; and when
comprehension did come, there came with it utter incredulity. It was
nonsense! Why, it was not two minutes since we had been reading his
letter; laughing over his account of the misadventures that had happened at the picnic he had been at; puzzling over the ill-written word!
How *could* he write letters and be dead?

I snatched up the letter, and frantically turned back to the date on
the first page. It was a month ago! The telegram was not twenty-four
hours old!

Then I believe I gave a dreadful yelling laugh, and then God had
pity on me—indeed I needed it—and I remember no more.

But that was what my dream meant, I suppose. The yellow lily
striped with brown; the yellow ribbon striped with brown. They were
figures and foreshadowings of the cruel striped beast that tore our boy.

★★★★★★★★★★★★★★★★

The singular dream and its solution related above are true. Only
the dressing-up is fictitious.

154

# Betty's Visions

### Her First Vision

I can see nothing *unnatural* about her!" says the mother, with an aggrieved accent on the adjective. "She is a remarkably nice child, if that is unnatural. Everyone says she is a remarkably nice child, everyone but you."

"Did I say that she was not a remarkably nice child?" retorts he, nettled; "should I be likely to say that my own child was not a nice child?"

"You said that she was *unnatural*, what more could you have said of her if she had had two heads?"

"How you harp upon a mere word!" replies he, crossly, "if I said *unnatural*, I only meant that she was not like other children!"

"If, as I incline to think, since Rachel's arrival, to be like other children means to be voracious, idle, and uncivil, I am not sorry she is unlike other children."

Perhaps because he feels that he is getting the worst of it, Mr. Brewster declines into silence, and walking to the window, stands there, whistling subduedly, and watching the object of dispute and her cousin Rachel, both at present visible upon the lawn. But though they are both in the same place, their occupations are dissimilar. Rachel, seated in the fork of the mulberry tree, to which she had hoydenishly climbed, is gnawing an unripe apple, rudely snatched, half-eaten, from one of the boys; while little Betty, the daughter of the house, is soberly walking over the sward beside a stout, middle-aged gentleman, one of whose hands she is quietly caressing with both hers.

"Uncommonly fond little Miss of her uncle!" resumed Mr. Brewster, presently, in a not very complacent tone; "I never heard of any child being so fond of an uncle. I am sure I was not when I was a boy. I remember one of mine giving me a precious good licking because I filled his top-boots with cold water!"

"And richly you deserved it!" retorts his wife.

"But as to Miss Betty," continued he.

"*Miss Betty* is a very amiable child," interrupts Mrs. Brewster, with a not altogether amiable accent on her daughter's name.

"I never said she was not," rejoins he, with a testiness born of the implied slur upon the amiability of his own infancy. "All I say is that there is something un——"

"Natural," he is going to add; but, bethinking himself in time how gravely displeasing the expression is to his wife, he pulls himself up. Perhaps she is grateful to him for his self-control. Perhaps the various little shafts she has winged at him have eased her spleen, for she says presently, in a far better humoured voice—

"She *is* uncommonly fond of him; of course he is a very good fellow, being your brother" (with a little malicious laugh); "how could he help being? But I confess I cannot see his attraction. I really do not know," she adds, thoughtfully, "how I shall break to the child that he is going on Tuesday."

"Whatever you do, do not put it off till the last moment," says he, hastily, "or we shall be having a scene."

"She never makes scenes," replies Mrs. Brewster, coldly.

"I wish she did; she would not feel things so deeply if she made scenes."

"Well, as he is only going for a fortnight to Maidenhead," returns Betty's father, with a short laugh, "in my humble opinion it will be rather a waste of deep feeling in this case; it is like the parson who preached from the text '*Knowing well that they should see his face no more,*' and took an affecting farewell of his congregation when he was only going by penny boat down to Margate."

"You must remember that to a child a fortnight is as long as two years would be to old people like you and me," replies his wife, passing by with grave contempt the dubious facetiousness of her husband's illustration; and as she speaks, she leaves the room.

The dreaded Tuesday has come. The carriage that bears away the beloved Uncle John has driven from the door. The whole family—gathered to bid him God speed on the doorstep—have again dispersed to their various avocations. Rachel, having pumped up a few noisy and unnecessary tears—tears speedily dried by half a dozen cobnuts thrust into her hand by the warmest-hearted of the boys—has gone off rabbiting with the latter, forgetful and elate; a bag of ferrets in her lily hand. Betty, who, on the contrary, has not cried at all, remains rooted to the doorstep, silent and still; her eyes fastened to the spot where the departing vehicle had last blessed her sight.

"Why, in Heaven's name, if she is so cut up, cannot she cry?" says Mr. Brewster to his wife, as they saunter away together towards the garden. "If Rachel or the boys are in trouble, one cannot hear oneself speak for the noise of their sorrow; I do not care what you say, there is something unna———"

The forbidden word dies half spoken on his lips.

"She will get over it," replies the mother, throwing back a compassionate look at the disconsolate little figure still rooted to the doorstep; "she will outgrow it. I believe that I was a very odd child, and you must own"—(laughing)—"that there is nothing very odd about me now."

Five days have passed. "*July*," as Horace Walpole said, "*has set in with its usual severity.*" After a brief spell of tantalising sunshine, just to show what weather can and ought to be, ———shire has relapsed into its normal state of drip, drip. It has poured all day. All day the rooms have rung with the din of the bored and house-bound children. From the schoolroom have issued noisesome smells of amateur cooking; squeals as of a pinched Rachel; yells, as of retaliated upon boys; yelps of trodden-on dogs; Bob's voice; Bill's voice; Geoffrey's voice; highest, shrillest of all, Rachel's voice.

But among all the voices, there is not to be detected one tone of little Betty's. She is not even with them; is not even playing her usual part of meek *souffre douleur*. All through the rainy day she has sat alone in a disused attic, often haunted by her, sat among old trunks and family pictures that have had their day, and now live with their pale faces to the wall; has sat watching those cunning mathematicians, the spiders, spin their nice webs; and the little nervous mice dart noiselessly In and out of their wainscot homes. It has grown dark now; too dark, one would think, even for the spiders to see to weave their webs, but perhaps they do not need sight.

Perhaps they go on weaving, weaving all through the night. Mrs. Brewster is sitting in her *boudoir*. Her husband is dining out, and she is alone. It is not an evening on which one would choose to be alone; an evening on which the wet tree boughs slap the window, and the rain comes sometimes even down the chimney; making the fire spit and fizz. It is the sort of evening on which, looking out into the straining dusk, one might expect to see a Banshee's weird face pressed against the pane. Some such nervous thought as this has prompted Mrs. Brewster to stretch out her hand to the bell, to ring for the servant to draw the curtains, when the door noiselessly opens, and her little daughter enters.

"Betty!" cries the mother, in a cross tone, for there is something ghostly and that harmonises with her vague fears, in the child's soundless mode of entry, "not in bed yet? It is nine o'clock! What do you mean?"

Betty makes no answer. She has silently advanced out of the shadows that enwrap the further end of the room, into the little radius of red light diffused by the wood fire.

"What is the matter with you? Why do you not speak?" cries Mrs. Brewster, irritably. The child is beside her now, and her eyes are lifted to her mother's; and yet the latter feels that they are somehow not looking at her, but, as it were, at some object beyond her.

"What is the matter with you?" repeats she, with growing nervous ill-humour, shaking the little girl by the shoulder.

Then Betty speaks. "Uncle John is dead!" she says, in a level, dreaming voice. "I know it; he touched me on the shoulder as he passed by."

"What nonsense are you talking cries Mrs. Brewster, angrily. "How can Uncle John have touched you when he is a hundred and twenty miles away? What do you mean by telling such a silly falsehood?"

The child does not answer. She neither retracts nor re-asserts her statement. She only stands perfectly still, with that odd, unseeing look in her eyes.

"If you do not know how to behave more rationally you had better go to bed," says the mother, displeased and frightened—she scarcely knows at what—and noiselessly and still, as if in a dream, Betty obeys.

The morning has come, and it and the sunshine it has brought with it, have dispersed and routed the eerie terrors of the night.

Sitting in her light and cheerful *boudoir*, Mrs. Brewster has forgotten with how creepy a feeling she had looked into its dark corner overnight. She has forgotten also Betty's strange speech, and her own ire at it. She is smiling to herself at the recollection of some little whimsical incident of his dinner party, retailed to her by her husband, when that husband enters.

"A telegram?" says she, seeing a flimsy pink paper in his hand. "From whom? No bad news, I hope?" She says it without violent emotion, all that the world holds of great importance to her being safely housed within the same walls as she.

Mr. Brewster does not answer.

"From John, I suppose?" suggests she, calmly. He is coming back sooner than he intended."

158

Then, surprised at his silence and looking up for the first time into his face—

"Good heavens, what is it?"

For all answer he puts the paper into her hand, and her eye in an instant has drunk Its contents.

'From Mr. Smith, Skindle's Hotel, Maidenhead. To Mr. Brewster, Taplington Grange, ——shire. Accident on the river last night. Col. Brewster drowned. Body just recovered. Come at once.

Mrs. Brewster has turned very pale; but at such news a change of colour is not surprising.

"Last night!" she says, Betty's speech flashing suddenly back upon her mind.

"What time last night? It does not say what time."

"What does the exact time matter?" replies he, gruffly; turning away his head with an Englishman's unconquerable aversion from being seen, even by a wife, under the influence of any emotion. He had liked his brother; and is thinking of the time when they were little boys together.

"It does matter!" she cries, excitedly, "It does! it does!"

But he has left the room to give hasty directions relative to his departure, which immediately follows. On the next day he returns, bringing with him his brother's body, and such details of the catastrophe that had caused that brother's death, as are ever likely to be arrived at. Upon that ill-starred evening, the weather at Maidenhead, unlike that in ——shire, had been fine, and Colonel Brewster had, according to his frequent habit after dinner, taken a boat and sculled himself on the river.

He had not returned at his usual hour, which excited some slight surprise at the hotel, but not much alarm was felt until early on the ensuing morning, when his hat was brought in by a countryman, who had found it near the bank of the river, and had also seen a skiff floating, keel uppermost, further out in the stream.

Drags were immediately procured, and after half an hour's search the body was discovered half a mile lower down the river in a bed of rushes. By what accident the boat had capsized, and its occupant, an excellent swimmer, lost his life, will probably never be known. Only the fact remains, that on the evening of his death his niece, at the distance of one hundred and twenty miles away, had become aware of its having taken place. She expressed no surprise at the news, nor ever revealed, further than by that one sentence, how she had become apprised of it This was her First Vision.

## Her Second Vision

Time has been galloping away. It has begun to gallop even with Betty; for she is grown up. At eighteen, time gallops, though not violently; at thirty-eight, it outstrips an express train; and at fifty-eight it leaves the electric telegraph behind it. Betty is eighteen, and full grown. No longer is she measured, with heels together and chin tucked in, against the school-room door; since, for the last year, she has continued stationary at that final inch in the paint; which proclaims that her height is to remain at five feet five inches until, that is, the epoch, which arrives sooner than we expect it, when she will begin to grow down again. She has developed into a demure, pale comeliness; and no one any longer thinks her odd.

Her father no longer considers her as unnatural; and his altercations with her mother on the subject of her (Betty's) eccentricities have long died into silence. At eighteen, there is nothing eccentric in being indifferent to dolls, and averse from ferrets; in speaking with a soft voice, and liking rather to walk than to run, in seeking solitude, and being able to look at a loaded apple tree without any desire to swarm up it.

With the good word of many, and the ill word of few, Betty takes her still course along life's path; a little thrown into the shade, perhaps, by her cousin Rachel, who has shot up into a very fine young woman—a splendid young female athlete, whose achievements in hunting field, or on frozen river, in ballroom, or on tennis-ground, are admired by all the country side, and in the wake of whose glories Betty follows with distant, unenvying humility.

It is a winter evening, crisp and stilly cold, and in the once school-room now elevated and transmogrified by the aid of a clean paper and a few girlish gimcracks into a grown-up sitting room, are the cousins. They are standing side by side at the window, having pulled back the curtain, and are looking out, as well as the hard frost-flowers on the pane will let them, at the moon-ennobled snow.

"You will have a moon!" says Betty.

"At this time tomorrow, as nearly as possible, I shall be getting there," rejoins Rachel, with a sort of dance in her voice. "I wish they had asked you too."

"I do not think that I do," says Betty, reflectively; letting her finger travel slowly down the window, in the effort—a vain one, since they are on the other side of the glass—to reach the airy frost traceries. "I do not think that I enjoy things much at first hand. When you come back and describe them, they sound entrancing!"

"I do not see how this visit can help being entrancing!" cries Rachel, pursuing her own joyous anticipations

"And yet visits do help it," answers Betty, with gentle cynicism.

"Two balls and a play! Skating if it freezes; hunting if it thaws!" continues Rachel, triumphantly; checking off on her fingers her promised pleasures. I cannot think why they did not ask you!"

"I can," replies Betty, with a grave smile, "since they could get the plums without the dough, they were quite wise to do so; but," (with a change of tone to a wistful intonation) "however delightful they may be, you will come home for Christmas?"

"By the number of times you have asked me that question it is evident that you think I shall not," answers Rachel, with a good-humoured impatience.

"There is nobody cheers up mother in the way you do," pursues Betty, leaning her elbow on the sill and looking pensively out at the steely December stars. "If one wanted a proof, which one does not, of what a melancholy world this is, one would have it in the fact of the extreme gratitude that people feel for mere animal spirits in anyone."

"Mere animal spirits!" repeats Rachel, laughing lightly, "thank you for the compliment."

"I really do not know how I shall break it to the boys if you do not come back for the Workhouse tea and the servants ball," says Betty, gravely.

"But I shall! I shall! I shall!" cries the other, resolutely; "dead or alive you will see me back on Christmas Eve!" She repeats the assertion emphatically at her departure next day, leaning a radiant face out of the brougham window to blow kisses to the three grave persons assembled on the doorstep, and to bid her God speed, as they and she had assembled to bid Uncle John Godspeed some seven years ago.

"She will have a moon," says Betty, following with her serious, youthful eyes the carriage as it rolls briskly away.

"She ought to be there in a couple of hours. It is not more than eighteen miles, and the roads are good. Gad! it is cold!" says Mr. Brewster, rubbing his hands and turning to re-enter the house, whither his wife has already preceded him, and resumed her occupation of that sofa where, from some real or imagined sickness, she now spends the major part of her life. There, some good while later, her husband finds her stretched, discomposed and fretful. Her work is disarranged; her silks are mixed; she cannot sort the colours by candlelight; Rachel always managed them for her.

"She must be nearly at Hinton now," says Mr. Brewster, intermitting for a moment his back-warming process to glance at the clock on the chimney-piece behind him, and glad of a topic by which to divert the current of his wife's plaints, "the roads are good, and there is a moon as big as a cart wheel. I am glad I did not let her have the young horses, as she wanted," pursues he, in a self-congratulatory tone; "they take a great deal of driving."

"I cannot think what I am to do without her for a whole week," sighs Mrs. Brewster, pettishly. "Who is to tell whether this is blue or green?" sitting up and helplessly comparing two skeins of filosel by the light of the shaded lamp that stands beside her couch. "Where is Betty? She would be better than nobody. I do not know how it is," with a distinct access of fractiousness, "but that girl always manages to be out of the way whenever one wants her."

"Talk of the devil," cries her father, cheerfully; "here she is."

And in effect, as he speaks, his daughter enters, and moves slowly to the fire.

"Your eyes are better than mine, Betty," says the mother, holding out her dubious silks for her child's inspection; then suddenly, as she lifts her look to the girl's face, changing her tone, "what is the matter with you?" she asks, abruptly; "how odd you look!"

Betty has paused beside her mother's sofa; and her eyes, wide open, yet unseeing as those of a somnambulist, are fixed unthinkingly upon her.

"Rachel is dead," she says, in a distinct, level, passionless voice, as of one speaking in a dream. "I know it! She touched me on the knee as she went by."

Mr. Brewster has dropped his coat tails, and Mrs. Brewster her silks, and both are staring open-mouthed, aghast, and dumb at their daughter. Mr. Brewster Is the first to recover his speech.

"What gibberish are you talking?" cries he, roughly; putting his hand on the girl's wrist. "Are you walking in your sleep Wake up!"

But Betty makes no answer. She turns slowly, as one who has accomplished her errand, and walks as dreamily out of the room as she had entered it.

Mrs. Brewster has tottered up from her sofa, trembling like a leaf, and crying copiously.

How can you pay any heed to such rubbish?" asks her husband, angrily. "The girl is hysterical. She would be all the better for having a bucket of cold water thrown over her. We have always let her have her own way too much, that is it."

But Mrs. Brewster is sobbing violently.

"Do you not remember?" she cries. "It was just the same, she said just the same years ago, when she was a child, when John died."

"Fiddlesticks," says he, in a fury. "Who would have expected a woman of your sense to be so puerilely superstitious? A mere coincidence. Rachel dead! Ha! ha! She must have been pretty quick about it. Come now, think"—(laying his hand friendly and reasonably upon her trembling shoulder)—"what is likely to have happened to her in less than two hours? If she had had the young horses, I grant you, it would have been a different thing, but as it is—there, that is better. Let me get you some salvolatile, and when next I see Miss Betty, I will give her a piece of my mind for upsetting you in this way."

Mr. Brewster's eloquence, though not of a very lofty order, is yet of sufficient force gradually to soothe his wife into comparative composure, and, when to his reasonings he has added the promise, given with a good-humoured shrug, that a servant on horseback shall be sent off first thing in the morning to inquire after Rachel's welfare, the poor lady is so far restored to her normal state of faint and intermittent cheerfulness, that she is able to sit down to dinner with tolerable appetite. Betty does not appear; which, though neither of her parents confess it, is a relief to both.

Mr. Brewster is not generally much given to table-talk, Being of a hungry and slightly epicure turn, he is of opinion that it is impossible to do two things well at once, but today he puts forth his powers magnanimously to amuse his wife; and the ball of talk is flying briskly from one to the other, when the butler, approaching his master, and even so far breaking through the traditions of his trade as to interrupt him in the middle of a speech, informs him in an undertone "that there is a person in the hall who wishes to speak to him."

"Let him wish!" says Mr. Brewster, somewhat surly at having the thread of his eloquence untimely snapped. "Did not you tell him I was at dinner? He may wait."

"If you please, sir, he says he must see you," rejoins the butler, with respectful persistence. "I beg your pardon, sir," (lowering his voice still further, and looking meaningly towards Mrs. Brewster, whose attention is at the moment wholly occupied by the feeding of a couple of eats) "but I think you had better see him."

There is something so odd and emphatic in the servant's manner, that, without offering any further objection, Mr. Brewster jumps up and hastens into the adjoining hall. There seem to be several persons in it; maid-servants whimpering with their aprons to their eyes; but the centre of interest is obviously a young man, leaning with shaking limbs and a sheet-white face, against the oak table in the middle of the hall. Instantly, Mr. Brewster has recognised him as one of the sons of the house to which his niece had gone. In a moment he is beside him.

"What is it?" he says, hoarsely. Then, as the young fellow struggles in vain for utterance, "What is it he repeats, shaking him by the shoulder. "In God's name, speak out!"

Perhaps there is a bracing power in the harshness of his adjuration, for the stranger speaks.

"There—there has been an accident," he says, indistinctly. "Your—your niece——"

"Yes?"

"She—she."

Again, he stops, looking as if he were about to faint.

"For God's sake, go on!" says Mr. Brewster, hoarsely. "Harris, give him some brandy."

It is not until he has swallowed it that the young man is able to proceed.

"At the corner of Hampton Lane, in a field, there was a rick on fire. The horses took fright, bolted, and upset the carriage into the ditch. Miss Brewster was thrown off."

"*Thrown off!* What do you mean Why, she was inside!"

"She was driving. She had put the men servants inside. She and her maid were on the box. She was thrown violently against some spiked iron railings, and when she was taken up she was——"

"Dead?" asks Mr. Brewster, gripping the young man's arm and speaking in a husky whisper. "Dead?"

The attention of everyone in the room has been so wholly riveted upon the speakers, that no one has perceived the opening of the dining-room door and the appearance of a figure on the threshold, until a terrible loud hysteric laugh breaks upon their ears.

"Dead?" shrieks Mrs. Brewster. "Dead? Then it was true; then Betty was right." And so, falls heavily to the floor in a dead swoon.

# Her Third Vision.

The blow does not kill Mrs. Brewster. Her acquaintances are all agreed that it must, since for years past their and her doctor has gone about the neighbourhood proclaiming the unparalleled weakness of her heart. But apparently it is not so weak as he had imagined, since, after such a shock, it still goes on pulsing, however feebly. Weakly people, with one leg habitually planted in the grave, take a great deal of killing; but the catastrophe turns her at once into a hopeless invalid. After that day she never resumes the habits of health. But as time goes on, her valetudinarian ways assume a permanence and stability with which those about her as little connect the idea of change and death as with their own robuster modes of life.

Never to appear till one o'clock in the afternoon, never to join her family at dinner, never to be seen except in a recumbent posture, never to be told anything disagreeable. These are the features of her case; features which may probably remain long after many of the healthy persons who come to visit her, and who insensibly sink and soften their voices on entering her dim and shaded room, have been carried, feet foremost, to the churchyard.

It need hardly be said that no allusion either to her niece's violent death, or her daughter's strange prevision of it, is ever allowed in Mrs. Brewster's presence. And though no doctor has prohibited the communicating of any number of disagreeable truths to Mr. Brewster, yet neither does he ever allude to the facts above referred to.

To whom should he, indeed? To Betty, then? But as to Betty, both her lips are shut in a silence as close as that of death. On being told of her cousin's tragic end, she had expressed no more surprise than she had manifested seven years before, on hearing of the death by drowning, of her Uncle John. Not the slightest hint as to the mode in which the catastrophe had been communicated to her has ever fallen from her. It is even a matter of doubt to her father whether any consciousness or remembrance of it remains with her. Sometimes, as he sees her seated tranquilly working or quietly reading, with as humdrum and everyday an air as it is possible for any human being to be dressed in, a poignant desire assails him to question her as to those strange and supernatural intimations, of which she has twice been the recipient.

But always a sort of reluctant awe restrains him. And meanwhile, life flows dully by in the old house. The boys are out in the world, and return but seldom to the house whence their bright playfellow has been borne to the grave. There is nothing to amuse them when they do return, since the state of Mrs. Brewster's health precludes (or she thinks so, which comes to the same thing,) the possibility of society. Betty has quietly abandoned the world at eighteen, in order to devote herself more completely to her parents.

To speak more exactly, to her parent; for Mr. Brewster is of a social turn, and would fain take his daughter into the world with him, making her an excuse for his own presence at festivities abroad and merrymakings at home. But how can he have the inhumanity to set up his coarse and brutal claims against those far more sacred ones of his moribund wife. He is fond of music; but, since Rachel's fingers were stiffened in death, no one has dared to open the piano; the least hint of such an intention would re-plunge the sickly wife and mother into those terrible hysterics, from which it is the main end of life with her nearest kin to keep her and themselves.

And so, poor, convivial Mr. Brewster, except when someone charitably asks him out to dinner, nods through the dull evenings over his newspaper, or tries to feign an interest he is far from feeling in the game of patience which is the one excitement of his good lady's life. In complete unconsciousness, that good lady pursues her gentle way, quietly and simply accepting the sacrifice of the two lives daily offered on her invalid altar, and, with equal simplicity, the owners of those two lives unite in the cult of sanctified selfishness embodied in the charmingly dressed, diaphanous, prostrate being who has succeeded in delicately snuffing out all the mirth of their existence.

It is three years since Rachel died, or, to speak more exactly, three years and a quarter, for it was in the deepest, blackest depth of winter that she went, and now the long-stretching light, the bold crocus rows, the courting thrushes, all tell that spring has come.

Betty is twenty-one years old, for it was in the spring that she came, a spring gift blown in by the bustling March winds.

"Twenty-one! Twenty-one!" she says over to herself. It seems to her a great age. She wonders whether it strikes other people in the same light.

"Father!" she says, putting her arms about his neck as he sits running his eye rather disconsolately over the theatrical announcements in *The Times*, "Do you know what an elderly daughter you have got? I am twenty-one today!"

"Twenty-one?" repeats he, with a jump. "You do not say so. God bless my soul!"

He sighs heavily, but trying to turn it off into a cough, cries cheerfully,

"Well, I am to give you a present, I suppose. Is that what it means? Well, what is it to be? A new gown—a necklace—what?"

But Betty shakes her head.

"I never wear out my old gowns, and who would see my necklace?"

"What do you say to a little outing?" asks he.

He says it in a low voice, as if he knew that it was a proposition of a contraband nature, and nervously glances over his shoulder as he makes it.

"A little jaunt—quite a little one. It is so long since you and I have had a jaunt together, Betty."

But again, Betty shakes her head.

"Impossible!" she says, reproachfully; and yet a little regretfully, too. "How could mother spare us?"

"Not for long, of course," rejoins he, hastily, "but just a run up to London for a couple of nights. We might be there and back almost before she had time to miss us; just a run up to see a play."

"It is a long time" (rather ruefully) "since I have seen a play," says Betty.

She is leaning over his chair, her arms round his neck, and is reading the theatrical announcements with him.

"Lyceum, Strand, Vaudeville," she says, with a little sigh, that shows that she, too, is nibbling at the temptation. "How nice they all look!"

"We will do a couple of plays, Betty!" cries her father, audaciously, and in a higher key than he has yet spoken in. "I see that they are giving that old piece, *The First Night*, at the Court. It was the first play I ever saw. My father took me to it when I was quite a little chap. Horace Wigan played in it. You do not remember Horace Wigan No! Why should we not go tomorrow, eh?"

His daughter has put up her hand apprehensively to check him:

"Hush!" she says, hurriedly; "here is mother!" And in effect, as she speaks, the folding-doors have been thrown open; and, as always happens at this hour of the day, Mrs. Brewster is wheeled slowly in on a couch out of her bedroom; Mrs. Brewster, prostrate, transparent, suffering, as usual. In a moment the husband's voice has sunk to a subdued invalid pitch:

"How are you today, dear?" he asks, hastening to his wife's side, and kindly taking her languid hand, "any better?"

"I shall never be better in this world," replies she, exhilaratingly;

"but," (her sick eyes wandering suspiciously from one to the other of her two companions) "what is it that I am not to hear, Betty? Why did you say 'hush'?"

There is a moment of confused silence, uneasily broken by Mr. Brewster. "Betty has been telling me that she is twenty-one today."

"She could hardly object to my hearing that," replies her mother, drily. "Come, Betty, what was it?"

"It was only that father was talking nonsense; you know that he does sometimes," replies the girl, with a little constrained laugh, kneeling down beside her mother's sofa, and raising her thin fingers.

"I am not at all sure that it was such nonsense, after all!" says he, speaking in a rather blustering voice, which his daughter knows to conceal much inward misgiving.

"I—I—was only proposing to—to—take her for a little outing, you see," (after a pause, as his proposition is received in entire silence) "you see," (growing nervous) "she—she has not a very lively time of it—for a girl mewed up with us two old people."

Still silence. At last, "I am sorry that you are so dull, Betty," says the invalid, in a wounded voice, withdrawing her hand. "Why did you not tell me so before?" But at this, poor Betty collapses into sobs.

"Good God!" cries Mr. Brewster, starting up and stamping about the room for a moment, forgetful of the sanctity of the spot. "I mean, bless me, Maria, my dear, what has the poor girl done?" Maria's answer is what the answer of any invalid who respects herself must inevitably be, a sinking flat back on her pillows, with hands and feet grown suddenly rigid, in a faint, so admirably counterfeited, as to take in even herself. Mr. Brewster is quietly, and perhaps a little compassionately, hustled out of the room by his daughter, and thus in disastrous ignominy his bold project ends.

And yet—such are the tides in the affairs of men—on that very day week he is buying *Worlds* and *Truths*, and *Queens*, for Betty at the station, to beguile their joint journey up to London, for that very outing upon which Mrs. Brewster would seem to have put so complete an extinguisher. And, stranger still, it is Mrs. Brewster herself who sends them. Whether it is the sight of her patient daughter, or of her clumsy, yet most genuinely remorseful husband, or some pinch of her own not dead but only slumbering conscience that effects the change, is of little moment. Certain it is that it is effected.

"What day do you set off?" she asks, suddenly; one evening, as she lies with her eyes fixed on her daughter's face; that unjoyous young face, which is bent with untiring gentleness over that piece of work of her mother's which is eternally needing to be set right.

"Set off?" repeats Betty, lifting her head, and looking apprehensive and a little guilty. "Where to?"

"That is what you can tell me better than I can tell you," replies the mother, drily, with a faint shade of resentment still lingering against her will in her tone. "Your father was anything but explicit; he spoke of 'an outing;' that might mean Kamschatka or Kew."

"He—he was talking nonsense!" replies Betty, red and stammering.

"No, he was not," rejoins the mother, calmly; "but I was taken so ill—if you remember, it was on the day that I was taken so ill—that he had not time to explain."

This sincere attempt to displace her husband's unlucky suggestion and her own seizure from their natural relation as cause and effect, an attempt which, as she knows in her own heart, takes in neither herself nor her daughter, brings a weak pink flush into the sick woman's cheek.

"He was talking nonsense!" repeats Betty, murmuringly; "men often do," she adds, with an audacious and illiberal generality.

"What he said was quite true," rejoins Mrs. Brewster, reflectively; "it is a cruelly dull life for a young thing like you."

"But I am not young!" cries Betty, eagerly; "I am old, old! If you only knew how old I feel inside."

"Well, if you do, I do not!" says Mrs. Brewster, with a sort of tremulous playfulness. "To tell you the truth, I think we have been mewing ourselves up a great deal too much of late; that we should be all the better for having a little air from the outer world let in upon us; in short," (laughing nervously) "I have half a mind to join in your outing myself."

"Oh, if you could!" cries the girl, kneeling down by her mother, and laying her head caressingly on the pillow beside the invalid; "but since you cannot——"

"Since I cannot," interrupts the other with decision; "you must go instead of me, and come back and tell me all about it. There, say no more. That is settled."

And settled, despite Betty's many tearful and compunctious remonstrances, it is. The day has come. Betty has, as nearly as possible, lost the train through her inability, at the last moment, to tear herself away from that shaded room and that, couch that of late have been all her world.

"Are you sure that you can do without us? Are you sure that you will not miss us?" she reiterates, with her eyes full of tears; and half-a-dozen of Mr. Brewster's impatient "Bettys" are turned a deaf ear to by his daughter. But at last, he gets her away; at last, he gets her to the station and into the train. She had set off in a most unenjoying mood—apprehensive, half remorseful—but she has not gone five miles before nature and youth resume their inevitable sway. Did ever express train rush with so smooth a speed? and how pleasant once again to see the flying hedges, browsing sheep, smoky towns galloping away together. Gallop as they may, they are yet stationary, and she is tearing onwards. What a feeling of superiority it gives one!

And then, when London is reached, what can be more exhilarating and amusing than the streets? They seem to present a broad farce, got up and acted expressly for her entertainment. And the real farce to which they go in the evening? It is not very funny, but they laugh till they cry over it. Their mirth is so uncontrollable, indeed, that one or two persons in the stalls near them turn their heads to look in astonishment at them. But then, perhaps, these persons laugh every night. Mr. Brewster and his daughter are still laughing over the threadbare jests in their sitting-room at the hotel on their return. They are still laughing when Mr. Brewster leaves the room to give some directions to the servant for the next day. He is not absent more than ten minutes.

On his return, he finds Betty standing in the middle of the room. Her face is turned towards him, but, as he sees at the first glance, it is not the same face as that with which he had left her. There is no smile upon it, nor any expression of recognition. It wears the look which he has once before seen upon it—the sightless stare of a somnambulist. An indefinable terror seizes him as he goes up to her.

"What is the matter with you he asks, unsteadily. "Why do you look so odd

"We must go home," she says, speaking in a mechanical, immodulated voice, as one in a trance, to whom the words are dictated by some resistless alien power. "Mother is dead! She touched me on the foot as she went by."

They are nearly the same words as those which Mr. Brewster had heard his daughter employ on the occasion of her cousin's death; but this time he can meet them with no derisive incredulity. A sudden trembling has seized him, such as had seized upon his sick wife on that former occasion.

"What do you mean?" he asks, almost in a whisper—"did you—

did you *see* her?"

She makes no answer; only moves slowly towards the door of the adjoining bedroom.

"Betty!" cries the father, in an agony of apprehension, following her, "you *must* speak! You have no right to say such things! What did you see? In God's name tell me what *did you* see?"

But she is as if she heard him not. Without making any answer she passes out of sight. Something tells him that it would be vain to make any further appeals to her. It is even extremely doubtful whether she was aware of his presence. He throws himself into an arm chair, and then, rising, begins to walk fast and feverishly up and down the room, in the vain endeavour to shake off the panic that is mastering him.

"The girl is of an exceptionally nervous organisation. She has been upset by this sudden change from the long gloom of her past life; it is a form of hysteria."

But even as he says to himself these reassuring phrases, a cold reminiscence checks them. He had called her hysterical on the occasion of that former warning. His eyes fall accidentally on the clock. The hand points to half-past twelve. The thought crosses his mind with a sort of relief that all the telegraph offices must be shut. The only sensible course to pursue is to dismiss the matter as quickly as possible from his mind, go to bed and dream, if he can compass it, of the farce, whose merriment seems now to be parted from him by a chasm. But to go to bed is one thing; to go to sleep another.

Mr. Brewster finds the one as difficult as the other was easy. Reason as he may with himself, chide, ridicule his own folly, there is not one hour of the night or early morning that he does not hear told by all the church and hotel clocks. From the short, tired doze, into which he falls at last, he is awakened by the opening of the door, and springs back to consciousness with a frightened jump. Pooh! it is only his man with his hot water! And so, it is.

But, beside the hot water, what is it that his valet is carrying in his hand? Is it not an envelope, the first glimpse of whose colour turns the master sick? In a second, he has snatched it, torn it open, mastered its short contents, which, after all, he had already known.

Come home at once. Mrs. Brewster died suddenly at twelve last night.

★★★★★★★★★★★★★★★★

Mr. Brewster and his daughter have returned to the so lately left home. It is the day before the funeral, and they are sitting together in that heavy idleness which characterises such dread days. It is a dark afternoon, and the gloom is so greatly deepened by the lowered blinds that occupation would be difficult. They are holding each other's hands, as if that helped them a little. For nearly an hour neither has spoken, but suddenly Mr. Brewster breaks the leaden silence.

"Betty," he says, in a low voice, "how did you know? Did you see her? I asked you at the time, but you did not answer me. You did not seem to hear."

She hears him now at all events, for her hand first trembles violently in his clasp, and is then withdrawn from it. But neither now does she answer.

"Tell me," repeats the father with imploring urgency, "Betty, tell me, did you see her?"

Betty has put up her hand to her forehead, and into her face has come an expression of dazed, bewildered misery.

"I don't know," she answers, uncertainly.

"You do not know?" repeats he, with gathering excitement; "you *must* know! Think, child, think! You cannot have forgotten; did you really *see* her?"

The look of puzzled wretchedness grows intenser.

"Oh, do not ask me," she cries, loudly, in a voice of acute pain. I would tell you if I could, but—I—I—do not know."

Her voice dies slowly away at the last word into a wail of misery, and on her forehead the intense look as of one agonising to overtake a gone memory, grows more painfully evident. It would be inhumanity to urge her further, so the problem has to be left as unsolved as ever.

### HER FOURTH VISION.

Another year has slipped by. Poor Mrs. Brewster's sudden death has long been superseded as a topic of conversation in the neighbourhood by less threadbare ones. To tell the truth, it had never been a subject of universal lamentation. Even into the very earliest expressions of pity and regret have crept hopes, that, when the days of mourning for the poor lady are ended, the house may be once more open for social purposes. And now that the year of conventional seclusion is running to its last sands, faint signs of such an impending re-opening are not altogether wanting, to gladden the hearts of the dancing boys and girls in the vicinage. Mr. Brewster is far from being an old man.

At fifty-five, under healthy conditions, there is still a great deal of enjoying power left in a man, and Betty is undeniably a young woman. At twenty-two, in fact, she is, and looks, a younger woman than she was and did at twenty-one. Betty and her father would account it blasphemy were you to hint such a thing to them, but in point of fact they are a great deal happier than they were while their suffering Maria yet blessed them with her presence and her sofa. The sofa had been reverently wheeled into a corner, the rooms are again full of light and air. Mr. Brewster need no longer tone down his hearty voice lest it should break into some doze, snatched fitfully at unexpected moments of the day.

Betty need no longer cut short her stroll in the garden, or her rides in the lanes, in the fear that a faint, complaining voice may be summoning her, and she out of hearing. They have both, to do them justice, honestly tried to check the first weak germs of cheerfulness in themselves and each other, but in vain. Little innovations, for which neither knew whom to blame, have crept in somehow. The tennis ground, long disused, has been new-mown, rolled, and marked out; occasionally, a young man or a girl, driving over to call, has lured Betty, reluctant at first, half-shocked and yet hankering, into a game.

Occasionally, too, one such young guest, a man, has stayed so late that it would be a breach of the first elements of hospitality not to invite him to stay to dinner. And somehow, after dinner—if one has a guest, one must do what one can to amuse him. All three have strayed into the billiard room, and knocked the balls about till the stable clock has tolled midnight. This one guest, after a while, becomes singled out from the other chance comers, by the frequency and regularity of his appearances. Without any but a tacit invitation, he has fallen into the habit of coming, first on all Mondays; next on all Mondays and Fridays; then on all Mondays, Wednesdays and Fridays; by-and-bye he occasionally throws in a Sunday too; and sometimes a Saturday, if he has anything particular to say.

Perhaps, being a moderately well-to-do-squire, with an agent whom he has no reason for distrusting, and a house which, though of comfortable dimensions for two, is over roomy for one, he is thankful to find a complaisant small family on whom he can bestow his too abundant leisure. It is a Thursday evening, and Mr. Brewster and his daughter are sitting *tête-à-tête* after dinner; he turning over the sheets of the just-arrived *Globe*, she placidly stitching opposite him, when a ring at the hall door bell is heard through the house. Rings at the front door are, in the depth of the country, not common occurrences at nine o'clock in the evening, and are wont to excite surprise if not alarm.

Such, however, is not the emotion provoked in the master of the house on this occasion. He looks over the top of his *Globe* at his daughter, who shows no great eagerness to meet his eye, and says, lifting his brows, with an expression half reproachful, half humorous, "Again, Betty? Why, I thought this was our free day, did not you?"

"Free day!" repeats Betty, stammering. "Free from what? I—I—don't know what you mean!"

"I am sure you do not; of course not; you cannot give a guess," replies her father, drily.

There is a smile on his lips, but his eyes are vexed. He has just begun to enjoy his life again, good, easy man, and in that enjoyment Betty's presence is a main factor. She hears, and is stung by the annoyance in his tone. Running impulsively over to him, she sits down on the floor at his knee.

"Do you think he comes too often?" she asks, trembling. "Do you mind?"

"It is to be hoped for my sake that I do not," rejoins he, still more drily than before; then, lifting by force the girl's face, which she has buried on the arm of his chair, "Why, Betty, you are as red as a turkey cock. You traitor, you knew he was coming. Might I ask—with an ungovernable intonation of bitterness and alarm—whether he has anything particular to say?"

Steps are heard in the hall. The servants, who have not hurried themselves, are going to the door. She must make haste to answer.

"Do you mind?" she repeats, agitatedly. "If you do, he shall go away; he shall say nothing."

For a moment Mr. Brewster struggles, and it would be, perhaps, rash to say that no malediction against his future son-in-law formulates itself in his heart. Then, his natural unselfishness, which was kept in high training through many years by his sainted Maria, conquers, and he says cheerfully, "Mind? Why should I mind? Do you think that I want to have a cranky old maid on my hands?" Then, as the door opens and the guest is announced, "How are you, Carrington? Very glad to see you."

★★★★★★★★★★★★★★★★

Two months later, Carrington and Betty are made one. Mr. Brewster has been the life of the wedding party, has made a better speech and more jokes, and has thrown more shoes and rice than any other member of the company. When the last guest has gone, he shuts himself into his study and cries like a child. Then he has his portmanteau packed, and takes the night mail for London and Paris. His empty house, void now both of his poor, peevish Maria and his consoling Betty, is more than he can bear. He is absent above a year, his travels being extended beyond the familiar bounds of Europe to China and Japan. What is there to bring him back? But at the end of the year there is something.

Does not obligation lie upon him to go home and see Betty's baby? The thought of Betty with a baby makes him laugh, albeit tenderly. And then, at the close of a lone summer day's travelling, comes the re-union with Betty herself Betty, who cannot hang long enough about his neck, or reproach him fondly enough with his protracted absence, or tell him often enough how she has wearied for a sight of his face. And yet, he thinks to himself, with a sort of semi-bitterness, "Can anyone so blooming have wearied much really?"

His Betty was a pale, shut bud, this Betty is an expanded flower, that has opened its petals wide to the sun of happiness—that sun which he had never been able to make shine upon her. But, in time, honestly struggled against, this bitterness goes. His daughter's unfeigned delight in his company, the ruthless way in which she makes everyone's convenience—even adored husband's and worshipped baby's—curtsey to his, could not fail to soothe a self-love more susceptible than Mr. Brewster's.

His visit prolongs itself from days to weeks, from weeks to months. His daughter is always pressing upon him her loving importunities that he should live with them. "Why should you ever go?" she asks, for the hundredth time, on the evening preceding the day he has at length finally fixed upon for his departure. "Jack says he does not know what he shall do without you."

"Perhaps time and the consolations of religion may reconcile him to the blow," replies Mr. Brewster, with a little mild satire.

"He says he cannot account for my not being nicer than I am, having such a father," pursues Betty, wheedlingly; "come, you have not answered me; why should not you stay with us always?"

"I must not make myself too common, Betty," says he, jestingly; "if I lived with you, you could not make such a fuss with me as you have been doing for the last three months. I like to be made a fuss with."

And this is all the answer she gets out of him, and so she has to let him go, but not without plenteous tears and strenuous adjurations to return, before the month is out, for good. He has now been gone a week. For the first day or two after losing him, his daughter's spirits drooped extremely; but before long, her youth, the happy conditions of her life, her husband's good humour, and the baby's allurements restore her equanimity. It is an August evening, hot and fair, and Betty has stepped out of the dining-room window, according to her wont on such evenings, to bid the sleepy flowers goodnight, and hail the moon, the great, red, harvest moon wheeling up above the beech-wood, and waited on by her silver handmaid, stars.

Mr. Carrington remains at the dining-table, sipping his claret, and looking out contentedly at the flitting white figure that now and then stops to throw in an affectionate glance at him, and an enthusiastic ejaculation as to the loveliness of the night, to which latter he re-sponds with all a Briton's unexpansive brevity. For a moment or two the figure has disappeared—gone, no doubt, to visit its Night Stocks, and Mr. Carrington has fallen into a placid reverie on beeves and farming implements, when he is startled by the sound of a sharp cry from the direction of the garden.

To jump up and fly through the window is with him the work of a moment. He has, after all, not far to go. At a hundred paces from him on the terrace, he sees his wife standing, and, as he nears her, perceives that she is gazing before her in a blank, unseeing way. Surprised and frightened, he takes her by the arm, crying "What is it?"

"Father is dead," she says, in a voice of acute agony; not as if an-swering him, nor even being aware of his presence. "I know it; he touched me on the head as he went by."

"Betty," cries the young man, puzzled and frightened, "what is the matter? What are you talking about?"

He knows nothing of her visions. It is not a subject, which, since her father's last appeal to her for explanation, on the occasion of her mother's death, has been mentioned between him and her. Much less has any breath of them ever reached an outsider. She does not an-swer." She only gazes stonily straight before her in the moonlight. A cold terror seizes on Carrington. Has she gone mad? In an instant the thought has flashed through his mind. Is there madness in her family? Can he ever formerly have heard a whisper of, and forgotten it? If not, is this the beginning of some frightful illness, some hideous catalepsy? He catches her hand. It is cold and rigid.

"Betty! Betty! why do you frighten me so? What is it? For God's sake, speak!"

But she turns away from him, and begins to walk dumbly towards the house. He overtakes her, and now, thoroughly alarmed, catches her in his arms, "Betty, what have I done to you? Will not you speak to me You must speak."

Still, she is silent, nor can any adjuration, however solemn, or entreaty, however tender, succeed in drawing one further word from her. Before he knows it, she has slipped out of his arms and made her way indoors, Mr. Carrington passes a dreadful night, entirely sleepless, and crowded with hideous fears. Before his eyes, whether shut or open, the spectre madness does not cease to dance. On what other hypothesis can he explain his wife's sudden seizure? Is it the first of the kind, or has she previously been subject to such? This is one of the problems that torment him, and that he has no means of solving.

There is no old nurse or other faithful family servant, whom he can consult upon the point. His wife's maid came to her only at her marriage. He has not had the heart to go to bed, but has seen from his dressing-room window, with the tired eyes of one that has all night watched the stars go out, and the new day that in August still comes early, unfolding one after another, and putting on its many-coloured robes of splendour. Will this new day solve his riddle for him? His head aches, and his eyeballs burn. Perhaps the morning wind may make him feel less stupefied.

Having listened at Betty's door and heard no sound—perhaps she may be in a wholesome sleep, from which she may wake cured and sane—he goes downstairs and out of doors. As he is walking towards the stable, drawing in long breaths of the exquisite summer air, he sees a telegraph boy approaching him. "For me?" he asks, indifferently, as the messenger holds out his missive to him, and so absently opens it, his thoughts full of his own trouble—so full that for the first moment they do not grasp the meaning of the words presented to his eye:

Mr. Brewster seized with apoplexy last night at nine o'clock; dead in ten minutes; come or send directions.

For a moment, he reels as if he were drunk, Betty's words rushing back in ghastly letters of fire before his mind's eye. She knew it at the very time it had happened! Great God! how did she know it?

## Her Fifth and Last Vision.

It is no great wonder that after such a shock Betty falls dangerously ill. For weeks she lies between life and death, and months elapse before she is restored to her former strength. Her husband nurses her with devoted and untiring tenderness; sits by her through long night after long night, listening to her wanderings—(for she is often delirious)—wanderings about the long-departed playfellow of her childhood, Rachel; about dear, dead dogs and birds; about her sick mother; nay, most of all, about her father too.

And yet, listen as closely as he may, not once does he catch any least word as to the mysterious seizure and the unexplained forewarning which had preceded that father's death. Not even in highest delirium, when the bonds of reason are loosened, and the thoughts and feelings deepest buried, come to the surface, does she make any most distant allusion to it.

It must be gone from her mind as completely as if it had never found a resting-place there. After a long time, she creeps slowly back to convalescence, an uncertain, precarious convalescence, at first, but which gradually gains in solidity and dependableness as the languid days go by. Days passed, in lying for the most part, silent and pale in her great armchair, pressing occasionally her husband's hand, as he sits fondly at her feet, or stroking his hair, and occasionally breaking into faint smiles at the antics of the baby, who has taken the opportunity of her mother's illness to double herself in size, and has adopted a mode of progressing along the floor from chair leg to chair leg, which Betty, not having much acquaintance with other babies, thinks original, and admires with proportionate ecstasy.

After a while, the hand that had feebly patted Carrington's head rests on his arm, as he leads her, warmly wrapped up, to the nearest of her garden haunts. The first day she does not get further than the terrace. The last time that she had visited it, was the evening on which he had found her cold and struck in the moonlight. His memory is full of this circumstance, as he leads her slowly along; but it seems to have no place in hers.

Perhaps it is the entirely changed aspect of the scene, from summer moonlight to winter sunshine that keeps recollection at bay. She makes little, interested comments upon the rimy grass, the frost-bound flower borders, upon the removal of some remembered shrub, but no ripple seems to stir the waters of any deeper memory.

Seeing her so insensible, he cannot resist experimentalising upon her, so far as to pause at the exact spot upon which, on that fatal night, he had found her standing. But she only looks up at him, smiling out of her furs, her thin face a little tinted by the sharp wind, and asks:

"What are you stopping for? You need not think that I am tired yet." He looks earnestly into her eyes, but they are obviously entirely unconscious, as is the brain behind them, of the remembrances of which his are full. It is clear that he must defer any probing of memory until she is fully restored to health. And when at length—it is indeed at length—this comes to pass, his mind has taken such a habit of anxiety for his fragile treasure, that he shrinks from imperilling the hardly-won good by presenting to her mind any images but those that are smiling and cheerful.

From day to day, he defers the putting of that question which is so often at the end of his tongue, and so it comes to pass that it is never asked at all. Time, as he goes by, brings many good things to the Carringtons, and so far—and now the baby is three years old—no bad ones. If there are any drawbacks to the fact of possessing an only child, even they will shortly be removed, for Betty hopes, ere long, to embrace a son. She is looking forward with strong longings, and without any fear, to the expected blessing.

No dreams or visions, or eerie warnings of any kind have disturbed her placid prosperity. The season is as prosperous as she, and now, in late June, the farmers are garnering their heavy hay crops without a drop of rain, and life is one long fragrant feast with the strawberry beds for board. Mr. Carrington has set off upon a long day's trout fishing—an elastic sort of little excursion, which may end tonight, may be prolonged till tomorrow.

"Do not hurry back," says Betty, bidding her husband goodbye; "enjoy yourself, old man! I am only afraid"—glancing from the absolutely unclouded sky to the rather parched grass—"that you will find the river a little low." And so, in the early morning, she waves him a smiling farewell, leaning in her cool white gown against the porch, and crying cheerfully, "Bring me home plenty of trout!"

The day turns out a very hot one, but what matter to one who can sit under a great beech's shade all day, with a cabbage leaf full of strawberries beside her, and engaged in no severer exertion than to watch little Betty tumbling in the hay, and occasionally set her dislocated hat straight again upon her yellow curls. There seems a slight want of imagination in having christened the child Betty, too, and so the elder Betty pointed out to her husband.

"Will not it make a great confusion having two Bettys.?" she asks. But he, in all the hot and foolish ardour of young husbandhood, asseverates that there cannot be too much of a good thing; there cannot be too many Bettys. She lifts her eyebrows with a languid smile.

"Then if we have six daughters they will all be Bettys!" But this extravagant supposition he refuses to face. And now little Betty's bed-time has come. It is hard work to tear her away, kicking and screaming, from the sympathetic hay-makers. It is hard work to get her into her bath, and it is harder still to get her out again. Far and wide the water splashes, and the soap suds fly under the excited plunges of her fat legs. The delights of the day have almost turned her little brain. Laughing, crying, wildly hilarious; finally, very tired and outrageously cross, she is at length laid in bed, and almost before her naughty gold head has touched the pillow, is asleep.

"Fast as a rock," says the nurse, bending admiringly over her. So fast that neither nurse nor mother need lower their voices as they discuss with the grave interest that befits so momentous a theme, what frock little Betty is to wear at a strawberry-eating and hay-making party in the neighbourhood to which she is to be taken on the morrow.

"Of course, she looks best in white," says the nurse, thoughtfully reviewing the little garments spread out for inspection; "it shows up her skin best. I never saw such a skin, if you will believe me, ma'am. I really cannot tell sometimes where the child's frock ends and her neck begins."

"She is as fair as a lily," asserts the mother, proudly.

"She has got shockingly tanned today," pursues the nurse, regret-fully. "I could not get her to keep her hat on. As fast as I put it on, she tore it off again. She was like a mad thing, and I did want her to look her best tomorrow."

"But she will," rejoins the mother, fondly. "She is a most satisfac-tory child; she always looks her best when one wants her. Bring out some more of her frocks. I do not quite like any of these."

The nurse complies, and walking to a high press, sacred to little Betty's voluminous wardrobe, begins to pull out drawers and choose the daintiest of the many little changes of raiment lying there in lav-ender. Her mistress does not interrupt her by any comment or sugges-tion. When her selection is at length made, the nurse returns towards her mistress with a heap of little clothes thrown over her arm. She is so occupied in turning them over, that she does not look up until she is quite close to Mrs. Carrington, when, lifting her eyes, she becomes aware that the latter, with an ash-white face and a terrible blank look, is putting up both her hands, as if keeping off from herself something unspeakably feared and terrible.

"I must die tomorrow!" she says, in a voice so changed, so full of awe and horror, as to be almost unrecognisable. "I know. *It* touched me on the heart as it went by."

"Good God, ma'am, what is the matter? What ails you? What touched you?" shrieks the nurse, beside herself with vague fear.

But her mistress makes no answer, and only falls from her chair on the floor in a dead, dead swoon.

★★★★★★★★★★★★★★★★

The river has not been so low as Mr. Carrington feared, the sky too, has clouded over opportunely, and he has had better sport than he hoped for. He has fished on and on and on; down and down the river, until it was too late to return home that night; so, he puts up at a little, riverside ale house, well known to him of old; dines hungrily on some of his own trout, and, sleeping sweetly, dreams of May flies and Ginger hackles. All next day he fishes again; and it is not till evening that he at length sees his own house rise before him against the rose red sunset. He has walked from the station. Since he had not sent word at what hour he was to be expected, no vehicle awaits him.

But the distance is short, and he enjoys the walk, with the prospect of Betty's smile and some more trout at the end of it. "How early they have shut up the house," he says to himself as he comes within sight of the building, and becomes aware that all the blinds are drawn, down. "What is the meaning of that, I wonder."

A little puzzled, but not alarmed, he walks in, and, entering the house by the garden door, looks into his wife's *boudoir*. She is not there. Into the drawing-room, she is not there; the library, not there; the smoking-room, not there. He passes out upon the terrace and calls "Betty, Betty," but there is no answer. "Pooh! how stupid; of course she has gone up to dress for dinner." He runs lightly upstairs and turns the handle of his wife's bedroom door.

It is locked. What does this mean? He calls "Betty, Betty, open the door." But she does not answer. The idea strikes him that he can enter by his dressing room. Yes, it's door is not locked. In one moment, he has passed through it and is in the bedroom. Why are his legs beginning to shake under him? The light is dim, the blinds pulled down to the bottom, and no candles lit. Betty cannot be here; surely, she is not here. Involuntarily his eye falls on the bed. *What is this?* There is a great white sheet drawn over it, and beneath that sheet an outline. In a second (how he gets there he never knows) he is at the bedside, the sheet is turned down, and he has learned what lies beneath it. His

Betty dead and rigid, with a dead baby beside her! For *it*, whatever the mysterious messenger was, has kept its word.

# Mrs. Smith of Longmains

## 1

It was a bitter January morning, a morning that obviously was not going to mend into a tolerable day, but had every intention of increasing into an intolerable one. The state of the weather was, perhaps, enough to account for that of my appearance, as to the unfavourable condition of which, the chorus of comments from three over-truthful daughters could not and did not leave in doubt for a moment after my entering the breakfast room.

"How wretched you look!" said Alice, the eldest.

"You are in for one of your bad colds," said Ruth, the second.

"You have been writing upstairs in a room without a fire, as we forbid you to do," said Susan, the youngest and most tyrannous,

I made no sort of answer to these compliments, but walking up to the fire stood holding my hands to the blaze.

"Do not play us the same trick that you did last year," said Alice, setting a chair close to the fender for me, "and fall ill on the eve of the bachelors' ball!"

"No," added Ruth, laughing; we bore it once in a way, but we draw the line at a second time!"

"You would not palm us off again upon Lady Brown, would you?" asked Susan, coaxingly, kneeling down on the rug beside me, and beginning to rub one of my cold hands between her two warm ones. "You would not entrust your little ones to an old monster who eats supper until she cannot see, and then snatches them away just as the real fun is beginning."

"It is very odd," said I, with a somewhat sarcastic crossness; "how solicitous you girls always grow about my health at this time of year. I might be moribund all through Lent without any of you perceiving it."

"I think we are very kind to you all the year round," returned Sue, giving my hand, which she still chafed in her own, a rather rebuking pat, "It is very carping of you to notice it if we are a little more attentive one month than another."

"Well, don't be nervous," said I, trying to laugh. "When the day comes, you will not find me absent from my bench of torment." But at that they all burst upon me in full cry. "Your bench of torment! Well, I do call that hypocrisy, mammy! We always say that nobody enjoys a ball so much as you; it is invariably we that have to drag you away, not you us."

I had not spirits to disclaim,

"'If I were you,' said Alice authoritatively; "I should just go straight back to bed and have some salvolatile and water."

"Or some white wine-whey," suggested Ruth.

"Yes, do," said Susan, "and I will come and read you to sleep. You always say that my reading puts you to sleep faster than anyone's."

"That is a left-handed compliment, Sue," said Alice, laughing,

"I know it is," replied Sue, composedly, "but she does say so, don't you, mammy?"

"Will not you come now—at once?" asked Alice, taking my other hand. "It would be far the wisest plan if you could get into a good perspiration——"

But at that I found voice to interrupt her, rising suddenly from my chair, and flinging away the caresses of my too officious children.

"I do not know what you would be at," said I, indignantly. "*Quelle mouche vous pique?* What possesses you all with the idea that I am ill. Have I made any complaint? though indeed, to have six gimlet eyes fastened upon your face, and three croaking voices in your ears, is enough to make you ill if anything is. For heaven's sake disabuse your mind of this extraordinary fancy, and let us come to breakfast!"

There was such unmistakeable exasperation in my tone, that my children saw I was not to be trifled with, so, acquiescing in my proposition, they and I sat down to breakfast. But I caught them several times casting surreptitious glances at me to see whether I ate as usual, and whether or not I shivered aguishly in the chill with which they were so determined to credit me. To baulk them, I dodged behind the tea kettle, and tried to eat more heartily than my wont, in which, however, I was not very successful.

Conversation was slack, which, to do us justice, it was not apt to be at our breakfast-table. Its present flagging condition was attributable, I imagine, partly to my supposed ill health (my appearance must have been, very much more deplorable than I had had any idea of), partly and chiefly to the absence of the master, always, when at home;

the originator or fosterer of every joke, and who last night set off for Ireland, in which country he, for the punishment of his sins, possessed some landed estates.

"Poor daddy!" said Alice, looking towards his vacant place. "He must have had a cold crossing last night. I woke at four this morning, when he must have been just halfway over, and thought, 'Poor daddy! rather you than I.'"

"I dreamed of him," said Ruth—"such an absurd dream. I dreamed we were giving a large party on the sly in his absence, and that he came back unexpectedly in the middle of it, like Sir Thomas Bertram in *Mansfield Park*, and that we were all in such a fright. I woke just as I was trying to hide one of my partners between the legs of the billiard-room table—such a likely place to escape detection!"

They all laughed.

"And I," said Sue, "slept so soundly that I never once thought or dreamt of him at all—rather brutal of me!"

"It is fortunate that one is not answerable for one's dream-self," said Ruth, recurring to the thought of her own dream; "one is sometimes such a rogue and sometimes such a booby in one's dreams."

"And you, mammy?" said Sue, amiably trying to draw me into the conversation, from which, since the beginning of breakfast, I had almost entirely excluded myself, "what sort of a night had you? The drunkard's heavy slumbers" (laughing) "like mine? Or pleasant and probable visions like Ruth's? Which?"

But I was prevented from replying to this question by the entrance of the butler, who came in to ask whether there were any orders for the coachman.

"Surely not," said Alice," answering for me. "We shall be skating all the day, and you—you will not be so insane as to stir from the fireside!"

I have always disliked being answered for. I have always known perfectly what my own opinions and wishes were, and have been fully able to express them. My eldest daughter's growing tendency to reply for me had already on several previous occasions fidgeted me. After a moment's hesitation, I turned to the butler saying, "There are no orders for him this morning; if there are any for the afternoon, I will let the coachman know at luncheon time."

Having thus established my authority I rose and left the room rather disagreeably conscious that the girls were whispering behind me. However, I suppose they saw that I was not in a humour to be trifled with, and wisely forbore from offering me any more of their extremely ill-received advice. By and bye I saw them all three setting gleefully off with their skates over their arms to the frozen mere, of which I could catch a glimpse—stiff among its stiffened sedges—between the brown limbs of the January trees. I watched them till their light figures, their tailor gowns and tight jackets, were quite out of sight, and then returned to the oak drawing-room in which I always spent my mornings.

Here I at once found traces of that solicitous care for me on the part of my girls, which my ferocity had hindered them from expressing in words. My favourite chair was drawn close up to the hearth; every chink of window carefully closed—usually we were a madly open-air family. On a little table at my elbow stood a bottle of salvolatile, one of camphor, a small jug of hot water, and several lumps of sugar. I rang at once and had them all taken away. Then I sat down by the fire, and sat staring into it for the best part of an hour in entire idleness.

I was not apt to be such a drone. Occupation I had always in plenty. What mother of a family and mistress of a house has not? And, to do myself justice, I had ordinarily no inclination to slight my duties. But, on this particular morning, I neither turned nor attempted to turn my hand to any one thing. I sat over the fire; not even shivering or sneezing (for my children were on a wrong scent when they made up their obstinate young minds that I was threatened with influenza), occasionally conscious that I was muttering to myself under my breath. At last, "this will really not do," said I, aloud; pushing back my chair from the fire. "I do not know what has come to me. I hope that I am not going off my head."

So saying, I put my hand to my forehead, in which there was a disagreeable pulse beating, and walked to the window, An ugly, grinding, black frost, long, iron bound bare borders, through which it seemed impossible that crocuses could ever push their gracious golden heads; a sad robin, a chaffinch, and three sparrows, all hungry, and naturally silent, seeking on the gravel walk the poor remains of the crumbs thrown out at breakfast. There was nothing assuredly in the face of the outer world to put me in better spirits. But none the less did I continue aimlessly to gape at it.

"Shall I?" said I, under my breath; "anyone would say I was mad if I did, it would be the *ne plus ultra* of folly and irrationality; if the girls heard of it, and of my reason, they would think I was ripe for Bedlam; but—but it would be a relief! After all, I am mistress in my own house, why should not I? I will." I almost ran to the bell, and rang it sharply. But, in the interval between my having pulled it and the appearance of the servant who answered it, there was time for another change to come over my spirit.

"It is twelve miles if it is a step," said I, internally; "the days are dark at four; if I give way to these imaginings, I shall gradually become unfit for all the ordinary duties of life: it may be an insidious form of hysteria."

The footman entered.

"Some coals, please," said I.

I resumed my place by the fire, and took up some knitting. Turning the heel of a stocking requires some attention. It might absorb mine. In vain. My heel, or rather Ruth's—I had rashly embarked upon hers—entirely failed to follow, even approximately, the outline of the human foot, and I dropped it back into the work-basket. I picked up a novel. Alice had described it as breathlessly interesting, and, indeed, had sat up late over night to finish it, unable to tear herself away from its pages. I could not chain my mind even so far as to make acquaintance with its characters. I laid it, too, down.

"I believe the girls are right," I said. "I must be ill; this restlessness must be the forerunner of some serious sickness."

I walked uneasily out of the room into the adjoining one, which, as we never sat in it except of an evening, looked unfriendly and formal by daylight; then out into the hall, down a passage into the billiard-room. I had no motive for going there or anywhere else, only I could not keep still. As my eye fell on the billiard-table, I remembered Ruth's silly dream of having hid her admirer between its legs. What an absurd dream! All dreams are absurd! I strayed back into the hall, and again looked through the window.

The drive stretched away before me, dark-coloured between the whitened winter grass. "It would take an hour and three-quarters, driving at a good pace," said I; "if I set off at two, I should be there by a quarter-past three. I need not stay more than half-an-hour, and should be back here by half-past five. Pooh! In the country that is a mere nothing. I will decide to go."

A second time I pulled the bell; but a second time, before it was answered, half-a-dozen adverse reasons rushed into my mind and made me repent my resolution. The road, as far as I remembered it—for part of it I had travelled only once or twice in my life—was not a good one. The stables might be cold, and give the horses influenza, a pleasant piece of news with which to greet the master of the house on his return from Ireland. That last thought was conclusive, I would abandon the idea definitively. And meanwhile the footman had come in, and was looking expectantly at me. What could I be supposed to have rung for? My fancy supplied no suggestion.

"Never mind," said I, stupidly; "it was a mistake; it was nothing."

At the same moment the back door opened, and in came the three girls, bringing a whiff of frost, and buxom health and jollity with them, and still—as I was not long in discovering—that baneful idea of my ill-health.

"Mammy, what are you thinking of? Out in the draught, away from the fire. Back, back, this instant!"

"Did you take the salvolatile asked the first, anxiously.

"Did you try the camphor?" inquired the second.

"Did you see that we had put the sugar handy for you?" asked the third.

I saw all your kind remedies," replied I, drily, "and I had them all at once removed. I see no reason why a perfectly healthy woman's drawing-room should be littered with physic bottles."

While I was speaking the gong sounded—for some reason, I forget what, we were lunching earlier than usual that day—at one. The girls scampered off to get ready. During our repast I do not think that I was much more loquacious than I had been at breakfast, but my children made up for my silence by the volume of their chatter.

Once or twice, they asked me why I was looking out of the window, and what I expected to see there? In point of fact, I was repenting of my repentance, but I need not say that I did not tell them so. Towards the middle of luncheon the butler again enquired, "whether there were any orders for the coachman?"

"Surely not," said Alice, answering for me, "the roads are like looking glass, and it is beginning to snow even if you were well."

"Tell the coachman," said I interrupting her with some tartness "that I will have the brougham at *two*."

There was a moment of silent consternation among my little flock

"Then, if it is only into Leighton that you want to go for any shopping,' said Ruth, in a conciliatory voice, "could not you let us do it for you?"

"I am not going into Leighton," replied I, shortly.

Another moment's silence.

"Come, now, where are you going?" cried Sue, getting up, coming over to, and kneeling down beside me, in order to try, as I knew, what personal wheedling—usually a very effective weapon in her hands—could do with me.

"Why are you so mysterious?"

"I am not aware," replied I, pompously, "that I am answerable to my children for my goings out and comings in," then, sinking into a less majestic tone, "I have no objection to telling you where I am going," This was not quite true. "I am going to call on Mrs. Smith."

"Mrs. Smith!"

"Mrs. *Smith!*"

"*What* Mrs. Smith

In three different keys of disapproving astonishment.

"Mrs. Smith of Longmains."

"Why, you do not know her."

"Why, it is twelve miles off."

"Why, daddy and Mr. Smith are not on speaking terms."

"I beg your pardon," replied I, gaining in firmness as I perceived the weight of opposition brought to bear upon me, "I *do* know Mrs. Smith. I have no dislike to a long drive, and if the men of two families come to loggerheads, it is the more reason why the women should try to keep the peace."

The girls gaped at me.

"But why today, in Heaven's name?"

"Why *not* today?"

It seemed as if the butler had taken upon himself to answer my question, for he had again entered the room and was speaking.

"If you please, the coachman is very sorry, but the roads are like ice, and he has not had the horses roughed."

I hesitated,

"That settles the question," cries my eldest girl, triumphantly.

"Does it?" said I, toniced back into instantaneous decision. "Let him send for the blacksmith at once to rough the carriage horses as quickly as he can. I must have the brougham as soon as it can be got ready, whatever the weather."

Servants never look surprised, and the girls were too angry with me, and I suppose thought me too great a fool to be worth spending any more breath upon, so I had no further remonstrances from them to battle with.

It was past three o'clock, instead of two, before I started, but I did set off at last, I got my way!

I got my way, always a pleasant thing to do. But I think in this case the pleasantness inseparable from making one's will override the wills of other people was reduced as low as it well could be. I was setting off on a raw winter afternoon, with a rising wind, falling barometer, and thickening snow, upon a twelve miles' drive along a rutty road, to visit a woman whom—despite the stoutness of my assertions to the contrary to my children—I scarcely knew; against whose husband mine had a rooted prejudice, and for bringing her into more intimate relations with whom I was well aware that he would be less than moderately grateful to me. Why, then, was I doing it? This is the question that I am about to answer; and when it is answered, you will probably think me an even greater fool than did my girls, who were ignorant that I had any reasons beyond native pig-headedness.

It would be putting the amount of thought that I was apt to devote to Mrs. Smith far too high to say that I thought of her once a year. She had certainly never crossed my mind on the previous day. Why then, was it that no sooner was I asleep last night than I was with her? It would have seemed natural that I, who, during all my waking hours, had been occupied with my husband, his plans, his departure, his absence, his return, should, if I dreamed at all, have dreamed of him. He never once crossed my brain.

I had other absorbing subjects of interest; an attachment of Sue's, that I disapproved of, and over which I worried head and heart through many an anxious hour; a budding taste for play in my eldest boy; debts of his to be hidden from his father; a wearing fear lest my excellent younger son should break down under the strain of his examination for the Indian Civil Service.

Yes, I had a choice of nightmares in my stable, a row of skeletons in my closet, any one of which would, one might think, have furnished the stuff for my sleeping thoughts as they did unceasingly for my waking ones. Not at all! I passed them all by, to dream wholly, connectedly, and with an astonishing vividness, of Mrs. Smith.

I was with her in a room—a room I had never, to my knowledge, been in before; presumably at Longmains, whose doors I had never entered. It was a room simply. No feature of it impressed itself with any distinctness on my memory, as I have heard has often been the case in other vivid dreams. On reflection, I was not sure that I should know it again. Of one only fact in connection with it was I quite certain, and that was—that as we sat together at the fire, the door, the only door the room possessed, was on our left hand.

We were sitting, as I say, together by the fire. There was a clock on the mantel-piece, what kind of clock it was was dim to me; but there was a clock, for I remembered hearing it tick. Mrs. Smith was sitting opposite to me, her back towards the door, facing which I was. I could see her features as plainly as I had done Sue's when she knelt beside me at luncheon, asking why I was so mysterious. I could not have believed that I knew Mrs. Smith's face so well; her unimportant nose, her slightly indicated eyes, lustreless hair, and characterless figure. But out of some lumber-room of memory they must have started, conjured up by the strong spells of sleep.

It was a perfectly connected, rational dream. I was I, and she was Mrs. Smith. She was not half Mrs. Smith and half somebody else. She did not suddenly, and without exciting any surprise in my mind—so eccentric are the laws of dreamland—become metamorphosed into another person. She was, and continued to be, Mrs. Smith of Long-mains.

The one thing that clashed with probability was the fact of my being sitting *tête-à-tête* with Mrs. Smith in any room late at night, for somehow, I knew that it *was* late at night. I do not remember looking at the clock, but I was by some means aware that such was the case. We were both working, and one of us had said something about its being twelve o'clock. This was followed by Mrs. Smith making an observation which I had forgotten. I was sure that I had heard it perfectly at the time, for immediately on waking I had re-called it, but afterwards it had escaped me, and make what efforts I might, I was unable to recapture it. After all, it was of no great consequence whether I remembered it or not.

What I did remember with a startling distinctness was, that no sooner had she ceased speaking than there came a knock at the door. I remember thinking that it was an odd time of the night for any-one to knock at the door, but Mrs. Smith showed no surprise. She said, phlegmatically, "Come in;" and the door opened at once and in walked the butler. For some strange dream-reason I could not see his face. It was all mist and blur to me. On waking, I felt sure that I should not be able to recognise him again. I was only conscious that he was a young man. He had a coal-box in his hand, and the next thing of which I was aware about him was that he was kneeling at the hearth making up the fire.

Again, it struck me that it was an odd time to choose to make up the fire. I had, as I tell you, for some reasonless reason, not seen his face, though it must have been turned towards me as he entered the room, but as he knelt at the fire, I saw his back saw it so clearly that I felt that, stooping in the same attitude over the flame, I should recognise it among ten thousand. I saw it far more distinctly than, as I drove along, I saw the frozen pastures and the shivering sheep.

Mrs. Smith had risen from her chair, and walked to the other side of the small room where she stood doing something—I did not know what—at a piece of furniture with drawers in it. I was not looking at her but at the man, and suddenly I found myself wondering what that was that I saw sticking up dimly visible out of his coat-tail pocket.

As I wondered, I became aware that he was stealthily rising to his feet, and that his hand was cautiously travelling to his pocket in search of that very object which had arrested my attention. In another second, he had drawn it out—it was a revolver; had cocked it, aimed it at his mistress's head and fired!

There was a thud, a horrible thud that I heard plainly even now as I drove along in my safe brougham, and I woke screaming so loudly that if anyone had been occupying a room near mine, they must have been awoke by the sound; but as it happened, nobody was. The girls were separated from me by a long passage, and the servants were in an entirely different region.

The dream had been so much more real than reality, that it must have been some minutes—it seemed to be hours—before my reason could assert itself enough to tell me which was which. I do not know how long it was before I at length summoned up resolution to strike a light, and, shaking with terror, so that I could hardly hold the candle to get out of bed and examine the room for some indication of what could have been the cause of that dread, dull noise, which I could by no possibility believe to have existed only in my imagination.

I searched in vain. The windows were all securely fastened; the door bolted, as I had left it overnight. The pictures hung on the walls; there was no brick fallen from the chimney on the hearth; not even a handful of soot or a starling's nest. Nothing, nothing anywhere.

I crept back to bed, still quivering in every nerve. I must make up my mind that the whole thing had been the work of my own fancy, preternaturally alive in sleep. Good Heavens! Could the power of any imagination be adequate to presenting to me with the astounding vividness mine had done the figure of that man, kneeling with his back to me by the fire and stealing a covert hand to that coat pocket.

I shut my eyes. Still, I saw him, and with such distinctness, I felt that if I put out my hand, I must touch him. I lit another candle, the more light the better.

Still, I saw him. I hid my head under the clothes. Still, I saw him. The cold sweat stood on my forehead. I lay in an agony till daybreak; and, when the reassuring light began to creep in, I became a little more able to summon to my aid such reason as I was master of, to correct the hitherto overwhelming influence of that grisly vision.

Several circumstances of improbability in the dream presented themselves with some reassurance to my mind. The murderer, as seen by me, had been a young man. Now, I happened accidentally to have learnt only lately that the Smiths possessed as butler an old family servant, who had lived with them over thirty years, and whom they were most unlikely to have parted with. Also, throughout the dream, I was conscious that but for servants, Mrs. Smith and I were alone in the house. Now, only yesterday, one of the girls had casually mentioned meeting Mr. Smith in Leighton. As the light broadened, I dwelt with more and more confidence on these discrepancies, and was able to go down to breakfast presenting such a distant resemblance to my usual self as I have described.

But when left to myself after breakfast, with nothing to distract my thoughts and no appearances of equanimity to keep up, the vision returned upon me with almost its first force.

Again, I saw that kneeling figure, that stealthy rising, that travelling of the hand to the coat pocket. I heard the click of that cocked revolver! I could not bear it. It *must* mean something! I *must* go to her. Must warn her. As you know, I rang the bell to order the carriage. But in the interval before it was answered, the vision passed; reason, or what I supposed to be reason, reasserted its sway, telling me how shadowy was the pretext upon which I was going to intrude upon this stranger; and how little my husband would thank me.

This same thing was repeated more than once; it was only Alice's triumphant "That settles it!" which gave me the final impetus that enabled me to decide which of the two courses to adopt. Though, indeed, I thought I must have gone in any case, I *could* not get that man's kneeling back from before my eyes. I *could* not have faced another night alone in the dark with it.

So now, reader, you know my reason for setting off at past three o'clock on a January afternoon, upon a twelve-mile drive along a rutty road, with rising wind and thickening snow, to visit an almost entire stranger, whom my husband did not wish me to hold any communication with. Probably you think me as great a fool as the girls would have done, I was too much occupied with my own thoughts to notice the weather or the landscape much. I was worried with the stupid effort (which yet I could not help making) to recall that remark of Mrs. Smith's which had immediately preceded the knock at the door in my dream. In vain; no glimmering of it would recur to me.

I was still cudgelling on my restive memory for it, when my attention was awakened by the carriage stopping and the footman appearing at the window.

"If you please, the coachman is afraid he is not sure which of these roads he ought to take."

I put my head out. We were at three crossroads.

"Why, there is a signpost!" said I, tartly. "Why do not you look at it?"

"If you please, the names are all rubbed out."

Here the coachman leaned from his box to join in the conversation.

"The snow is coming on very thick, ma'am; I doubt our getting to Longmains tonight."

"At all events we will try," replied I, with decision. "Go slowly along whichever road you think looks most likely, until you pass a cottage, or some inn at which you can ask."

I was obeyed. We moved slowly in a dismal uncertainty for some way; in the waning light the figures of the two men, with their whitened hats and great-coats, grew indistinct. Then we stopped again. Praise Heaven, we had met someone! I let down the glass to look and listen. Yes, there was a whitened countryman standing in the snow, being questioned. He was deaf, apparently; and it was some time before he could be got to understand the drift of the interrogatory addressed to him.

When at length he did, I gathered from his words and gestures, as well as the wind would let me, the reassuring information that we had come wrong. And, as ill-luck would have it, the road had narrowed so much that we had to go on for some distance before finding a place wide enough to enable us to turn. So that it must have been fully half-an-hour from the time of our first passing it, before we found ourselves once again at the finger-post: that blind leader of the blind. The dark had fully fallen before we found ourselves rolling noiselessly as snow could make us, over the cobble-stoned streets of a little country town.

"This must be Salcote," said I to myself, "I know that Salcote is their town. Courage! We can't be very far off now."

Let no one holloa before they are out of the wood!

This thought had scarcely passed through my mind before I was conscious of a jolt, severer than any that the snow wrapped pavement of Salcote could inflict; the carriage gave a sort of dip on one side; In an instant the horses were pulled up on their haunches; the footman off the box and holding the carriage door open.

"If you please, ma'am, you will have to get out, one of the wheels has come off."

I did not need a second bidding. In an instant I was out, standing in the snow, and peering with the help of Salcote's dim street gas at one of the hind wheels, in order to verify my servant's words. They were but too true. It had come off. Fortunately, in so doing, it had fallen, inwards, instead of outwards, in which latter case the carriage must, of course, have been overturned. I stared stupidly at it. Was this a judgment on me for my pigheadedness What was to be done?

"Which is the best inn in the town?" asked I, addressing generally a group of gapers, which, snowball-like, had gathered round me and my broken wheel Half-a-dozen voices instantly cried "White Hart"—as many dirty fingers pointed up the street, to where, about a hundred yards off, I could faintly see an old-fashioned sign hanging out.

"I suppose," said I, disconsolately to the coachman, who was already beginning to unfasten the traces, "that you will have to stay here for the night, I must go home in a fly."

As I spoke, I set off to walk to the White Hart, which I reached in about two minutes.

"My carriage has broken down," said I as I entered, addressing the civil woman—landlady, I suppose—who came to meet me. "I want a fly at once, please, as soon as it can be got ready. Have you one in; a good fly? I want a good fly at once, please," repeating the words with an emphasis which I though must impress them upon my hearer. She assured me that she had, though, from the length of time that had elapsed before it appeared, I have since felt certain that she had not spoken the truth, but had to wait in hope of the return of some vehicle now conveying another fare, and of some poor tired horse, destined through me to be baulked of his hard-earned feed.

And as I sat waiting in the little inn parlour, my thoughts were not of the most complacent. Perhaps I had had enough of having my own will now! After all, I had better henceforth submit tamely to Alice's rule. I was clearly not fit to rule myself. Into what a stupid quandary had I brought myself, guided only by the Will-o'-th'-Wisp of a senseless dream. Well, the only rational course now left me to adopt was to return home as quickly as possible, acknowledge my folly, submit, with what good humour I could muster, to the just laughter that folly would provoke, and resolve never to make such a fool of myself again. As I so resolved, a girl entered to poke the fire, and asked if I would like to take anything. I refused, and inquired how far they called it to Longmains.

"To Longmains, ma'am? About three miles, ma'am; not quite three miles, but it is not a good road."

She left the room again. Only three miles! To have come so near, and then turn back! Should I not turn back? Should I go on? As I hesitated, again I saw that kneeling figure stealthily rising, with its backward travelling hand. I looked round with a shiver. I wished the girl would come in again; I wished that I was not alone in the room. I shut my eyes, and still before them was that kneeling figure.

I must go on! I would go on! At the same moment the landlady entered to tell me that a fly was at the door, and I followed her out. There it stood, with the horse's head—it was a dispirited, disappointed head, poor beast—turned towards my own home, and the footman holding the door open. I got in.

"Home, ma'am?" asked he, touching his hat, and evidently in no doubt as to the answer.

"No," said I, desperately; "to Longmains."

For an instant he looked staggered, as if doubting his own ears, then prepared to get on the box.

"Stay," said I, "you must not come with me; you must find your own way home and tell the young ladies not to be alarmed however late it may be before I return. And tell him to go on and drive as quick as he can."

I was off; we clattered with a spurious briskness until we had left behind us the streets of the little town. Then we dropped into a tired crawl in which we continued. The horse was evidently all but done. Ah! but for me, he might have had his poor nose in his manger!

They certainly had not erred on the side of exaggeration who had told me that the road was not a good one. It was abominable. I was tossed up in the air and caught again a hundred times, like a cup and ball, by the monstrous ruts; the fly smelt rampantly of straw, and fust, and worm-eaten cloth; the piercing winds blew through it. If anyone in after time ever asked me what was the distance between Salcote and Longmains, I always answered thirty miles. And I really believed it.

At last, however, we stopped at a gate, the driver got down, there was no lodge, and after interminable fumbling he opened it, and we passed through. There were three more gates, at all of which he fumbled, so that when at last we drew up at a hall door I had the pleasure of hearing the hour of six told distinctly by several clocks within and without the house.

What an hour at which to call, with a twelve miles drive home afterwards! If a white-headed *seneschal*—obviously the confidential family servant of whom I had heard—appeared in answer to my ring, I would thrust in my card, and return whence I came, without asking to be admitted. I waited breathlessly. It was some time before anyone appeared.

Who, indeed, would be expected to arrive at such an hour? At length there was a sound of steps, and of a turning handle. The door opened, and in the aperture appeared a man. Was he an old or a young one? I craned my head out feverishly to ascertain. Young, obviously young. But perhaps he was a footman. Again, I stared feverishly out. No, he was not in livery. He was a butler and he was a *young man*.

### 3

Mrs. Smith's was not a face upon which I imagine as a rule any emotion painted itself with much vividness. It was a dull, flat, masklike face; but there was one feeling that upon my entry it showed itself at all events fully capable of portraying, and that was *astonishment*. I shall never forget the way in which her eyes and mouth opened as I sheepishly followed my own name into her drawing-room. She rose from a work-table at which she was sitting and advanced to meet me civilly enough, but all over her face was written such an obvious expectation of hearing from my lips some immediate explanation of this surprising visit, that not all the shock of the discovery that, in its first particular—that of the changed butler—my dream was fulfilled, could prevent my feeling covered with confusion at my own apparent intrusiveness.

"I am afraid this is rather a late hour at which to call," said I, constrainedly—she tried to put in a faint disclaimer—"but the fact is I met with an accident on my way. My carriage broke down in Salcote—-something went wrong with the axletree."

"Indeed! I am very sorry." Perfectly politely, but still with that undisguisable look of astonishment and expected explanation. It must be remembered that she had been living twelve years in the neighbourhood, and that I had made no slightest attempt to visit her before.

"And so, I had to wait till a fly could be got ready, which threw me later still," continued I, boldly.

She again repeated. "Indeed!" and that she was very sorry, adding that the Salcote flies were very bad ones. But I saw the puzzled look grow acuter, and I could follow the chain of thought that was running through her mind as plainly as if it had been written on a piece of paper before me. That my carriage should have broken down, and, that yet I should have been so determinedly resolved to visit her as to push on in the teeth of circumstances in a mouldy fly at six o'clock at night, and on such a night, was the problem, her total inability to solve which she was perfectly unable to disguise, nor could I help her.

It was utterly impossible that I could tell her what motive had brought me. Had she been another kind of woman I might possibly have confessed myself to her; but being such as she was, I felt that I had sooner be torn in pieces by wild horses. As we were toilsomely trying to keep up a conversation, rendered almost impossible by our relative positions, the butler entered, bringing tea. As he set down the tray on the tea table, I could not help stealing a sidelong glance at his face. It told me nothing. I had never, to my knowledge, seen it before, nor was it one that I should ever have noticed. But, then, neither had I seen the dream-face. It had been unaccountably hidden from me. As soon as he had left the room, I said abruptly,

"So, you have lost your old butler."

A fresh access of surprise overtook her, as I saw. How did I know that they had an old butler?

"Yes," she answered, slowly; "we kept him as long as we could, poor old man, because we were so fond of him, but he grew so infirm at last that he had to go."

"And your present one?"

"Our present one?" Repeating my words with a puzzled air.

"Yes; do you like him? Had you a very good character with him?"

Her eyes opened wide at my extraordinary curiosity.

"Well, I am afraid that we were a little imprudent in his case. I am sure it is very good of you to take an interest in the matter." ("For good, read *impertinent*," commented I, internally.) "But the fact is, that there seems to be a little mystery about the reason why he left his last place. However, Mr. Smith took a fancy to his appearance, and so we engaged him. But I do not know"—formally—"why I should trouble you with our domestic affairs."

I did not answer for a moment I was thinking with a sort of stupefaction. They have taken him without a character! Who knows what his antecedents were? When I did speak it was with an apparently brusque change of subject. I myself knew the link that bound the two topics together in my mind.

"Mr. Smith is well, I hope; at home?"

"He was quite well when he left home this morning, thanks."

"Left home!" interrupted I, breathlessly; "he has left home

"He was summoned away unexpectedly," answered she, tranquilly; "but I expect him back tomorrow, or the day after, at latest."

"But not tonight?" hurriedly.

"No, not tonight, certainly," with her usual phlegm.

At that moment the butler again entered, bringing coals—apparently Longmain's did not boast a footman—and knelt down before the fire to put them on.

For a moment my eye fell on him; then I turned suddenly sick. Surely that was the very back, the very kneeling figure altogether that I had seen in my dreams! I suppose I looked very odd, pale and faint; for I found Mrs. Smith's white eyes fixed upon me, and her voice asking me, "Did I feel the fire too much? I stammered out a negative, and for some moments could do no more. At last, the object that had excited my emotion being no longer in the room, I rose, driven by some inward power stronger than myself, and went towards Mrs. Smith. She, thinking that I meant to take leave, rose too.

"I do not know whether your fly is at the door," said she, "you had better let me ring and ask."

Her hand was on its way to the bell, but I arrested it. She had misunderstood my action in rising. I had not meant to go yet. But now she was virtually dismissing me. I must leave her. What pretext had I for further intrusion? I had come twelve miles in the teeth of circumstances; I had seen and spoken with her, and now I was to leave her. What object had I then served by my wild freak? I had not warned her; I had given her no slightest hint of the peril that to my excited imagination seemed to hang imminently over her. I had been of no least service to her; and now I was leaving her—leaving her to her fate.

It was impossible! It was equally impossible that I should expose myself to her more than probable ridicule by telling her what had brought me! I embraced a desperate resolution. I still held her hand, which I had seized to prevent her ringing the bell. I was so agitated that I was hardly aware that it was in my clasp, until her face of profound astonishment, almost alarm, betrayed the fact to me.

"I do not know what you will think of me," said I, in a shaking voice; "but I'm going to make what I am afraid you will think a very extraordinary request to you."

"Indeed!" said she, with a perceptible accent of distrust and a decided drawing away of the hand so convulsively clasped by me.

"Yes," said I, going on with feverish haste, now that the ice was once broken, "you see it has happened so unfortunately, the distance was greater than I expected, and then the axletree breaking, and the poor fly-horse is so done that I am sure he could not crawl another mile; in short, I am afraid I must throw myself upon your hospitality, and ask you to give me shelter; to let me stay here for the night."

Out it had come, and now it only remained to be seen bow she would take my proposition. At first, she was too dumb-foundered to utter. I saw at once that the idea of my being deranged crossed her mind; for she looked hard at, and at the same time backed away from me. Then her civility revived.

"Of course!" she said, "of course, I shall be only too delighted!" and then she stopped again.

I saw that, having gained my point, my next task was to convince her of my sanity. I, therefore, with profuse thanks and apologies, and as composed a voice as I could master, asked leave to send my orders by the flyman back to my coachman at Salcote. I took care that she should hear me give them myself to the man, so that she might know that the broken axle-tree and disabled brougham were not figments of my own diseased imagination. But I do not think that this measure had much effect in removing the suspicion of my insanity from my hostess's mind. I had gone out to the hall door to speak to the flyman, whence we both returned to the drawing room to begin our sixteen or eighteen hours *tête-à-tête*.

I think that both our hearts sank to our boots at the prospect. I am sure that mine did. In order, perhaps, to abridge it as much as possible, Mrs. Smith soon left me, with some murmured sentence about seeing that my room was comfortable, which it certainly was not. It was, on the contrary, as I found on being led to it, as uncomfortable as a hastily got-ready bedroom, with a just-lit fire, and a sensation of not having been occupied for some indefinite time past, would naturally be on a biting January night.

Having taken off my bonnet, and made myself as tidy as I could with the aid of Mrs. Smith's brush and comb, and told myself repeatedly that the world had never seen such a fool as me, and that neither the girls nor my husband would ever forgive me, I went downstairs, and we presently betook ourselves to dinner. There we sat opposite to each other in *tête-à-tête*. I had faintly hoped that some female friend, old governess, or cousin might crop up to make a third with us. But no; there we were, we two! We were waited on by the butler, and by him alone.

By questions, whose impertinence Mrs. Smith must have thought only palliated by the unsound state of my mind, I ascertained that the Smith establishment in its normal state consisted of butler and footman, but that the footman had, two days ago, been suddenly taken ill and sent home. The butler was therefore now, in his master's absence, the only man in the house. I also ascertained, during one of his absences from the room, that the stables were at an inconveniently long distance from the house, and that there was no cottage nearer than a quarter of a mile off.

Altogether, as lonely a spot as you would wish to see. My eyes travelled uncomfortably and furtively after the man on his return into the room, but I could see nothing in his appearance to justify my terrors. His face had no specially sinister cast It was almost as insignificant as his mistress's. And his figure! Could it be possible that the startling resemblance I had traced in it to my dream-figure was only the figment of my horrified fancy?

But no! no! a hundred times no! As I watched the butler, in precisely the same furtively apprehensive way, I was conscious that Mrs. Smith was watching me. Her slow brain had adopted and clung fast to the belief that I was mad; nor, indeed, was that conviction devoid of a good deal of justification. I think that she would not have been at all surprised if I had at any moment risen, and playfully buried the carving-knife in her breast. I have often thought since what a pleasant dinner she must have had. It was over at last, it had seemed enormously long, and yet on our return to the drawing-room it proved to have been disastrously short; short as women's dinners always are. We had dined at eight, and it was only five-and-twenty minutes to nine. Three hours and five-and-twenty minutes until the period indicated in my dream.

We sat down dejectedly on each side of the fire. I noticed, almost

201

with a smile, that Mrs. Smith took care not to place herself too near me. We had long exhausted our few poor topics of common talk. I had not even any more impertinent questions to ask. It is true that after having run, as we both thought, quite dry already, we had had the good fortune to happen upon a common acquaintance. Very slightly as she was known to either of us, with what tenacity did we cleave to that poor woman! How we dissected her character; anatomised her clothes; criticised her actions; enumerated her vices; speculated on her motives; about none or all of which we either of us knew or cared a button.

But at last, she was picked to the bone, and bare-naked silence stared us in the face. What a dreadful evening it was; saved, to me at least, from the simplicity of bottomless tedium by alternate rushes of burning shame and icy apprehension. At ten o'clock Mrs. Smith could bear it no longer. She rose and rang for candles.

"I daresay that you will not be sorry to go to bed," she said, a sort of relief coming into her tone.

I believe she nourished a secret intention of locking me into my room when once she had got me there.

"After your long drive you will be glad of rest."

"And will you too?" asked I, stupidly, for she had had no long drive. "I mean are you also going to bed?" She hesitated.

"It would not be much use my going to bed so early; I am a bad sleeper."

"You are not going to bed, then?"

"Not just yet."

"You are going to stay here—in this room, I mean?

"No, I am going to my *boudoir*."

A cold shiver ran down me. Her *boudoir*! That was the room we were sitting in in my dream. There was a moment's pause.

"I wonder," said I, with a nervous laugh, and in a voice whose agitation I could but partially control, "whether you would let me come with you. I—I—am not at all sleepy, after all; it—it is so very early, is not it? I—I—should like to see your *boudoir*, may I?"

Polite woman as Mrs. Smith was, and had proved herself to be tonight, she could not prevent a flash of acute annoyance, mixed, as I saw, with fear, from crossing her face.

"It really is not at all worth seeing," replied she, stiffly; "and I cannot help thinking that you look tired."

"But I am not, at all," rejoined I, obstinately. "I should like to come with you, if you would let me."

"Of course, if you wish it," said she, grudgingly.

Before finally succumbing, she made one or two more efforts to shake me off in vain! I was quite immovable. I heard her give an irrepressible sigh of impatience and apprehension at my unaccountable and offensive pertinacity as she preceded me upstairs. We reached her *boudoir*. It was a common-place room, common-placely arranged. I had seen hundreds like it, but never to my knowledge, either in waking or sleeping, had my eyes made acquaintance with it before.

I looked at once upon entering to see whether the relative position of door and fire-place were the same as those seen in my dream, and also whether there was a clock on the chimney-piece. In both particulars my vision had told me correctly. But, after all, there was nothing very remarkable in this. Most rooms boast a clock, and in many the door is on the left hand of the fire-place. But, to me, it seemed confirmation strong as Holy Writ.

"I told you that there was nothing to see here," said my hostess, noting my eye wandering round, and speaking in a tone out of which she could not keep all the resentment she felt.

"But it—it is very—very comfortable!" rejoined I, hastily fearing that this was the prelude to a curt dismissal of me. "I should like to stay here a bit with you, if I might."

She made some sort of murmured sound, which might mean acquiescence, and we sat down. This time we did not even attempt any conversation. She occupied herself with some work that apparently required a great deal of counting; and I—I had no other occupation but my thoughts. I could not well have had a worse one.

As I sat there, in silence, listening with ears continually strained to catch some sound that was not swallowed up in the shutter-shaking of the storm-wind, with eyes perpetually travelling to the clockface, I asked myself over and over again what purpose I hoped to serve, by this apparently so insane procedure of mine?

Were the dream to prove a fallacy, I had made as great a fool of myself as the world—fertile in that product—had ever seen. If, on the other hand, the dream, hitherto proved curiously true in some slight particulars, were to be carried out in its terrible main features, of what avail could I suppose my presence to be in averting the catastrophe with which it concluded. All I had done was to involve myself in Mrs. Smith's fate, which there could be no doubt about my sharing. Again, that cold shudder ran over me. I could not help breaking the silence to ask my companion whether she never felt it a little eerie, sitting up here all alone so late at night?"

She answered briefly, "I am not nervous."

Do you never even take the precaution of locking the door?" asked I, glancing nervously towards it.

She smiled rather contemptuously.

"Never; and even if I wished I should be unable, as I see, what I never noticed before, that the lock is broken."

The clock struck eleven. One hour more! It passed, too, that last hour. It was endless, an eternity, yet it rushed. As it drew towards its last sands I hardly breathed. If Mrs. Smith had once looked up from the stitching at which she was so tranquilly pegging away, she must have seen the agitation under which I was labouring, and would of course have at once assigned it to her old count of insanity. I wondered that she did not hear the thundering of my heart, pulsing so loudly as to impede that intensity of listening into which all my powers seemed to have passed.

How near it was growing! Five minutes, four minutes, three minutes. two minutes, one minute. I held my breath. I clenched my hands till the nails dug into the palms. Twelve! The clock struck! With that ringing in my head, with that hammering heart, should I hear the knock, even if it came? Mrs. Smith made some slight movement, and I almost shrieked, but I bit in the scream, and listened again. One minute past; two minutes past; three; four; up to twelve! The clock said twelve minutes past twelve. As each minute went by, I drew a longer breath, and my tense nerves slackened. At the twelve minutes past Mrs. Smith looked up—

"Do you feel inclined to go to bed yet she enquired. "I am afraid (looking more attentively at me) "that you are more tired than you will allow."

"I think I will go," said I, rising and drawing a long breath; "it is ten minutes past twelve."

"Not quite that," rejoined she; "that clock is ten minutes fast. I must have it regulated tomorrow."

"'*I must have it regulated tomorrow!*' Like lightning it flashed upon me that that was the speech Mrs. Smith had made in my dream immediately before the knock came. The speech I had made such vain efforts to recall. And, as panic-struck, this dawned upon me, someone knocked. A mist swam before my eyes. I tried to speak, but no words would come, and Mrs. Smith apparently did not see the agonised hand

I stretched out towards her."

"Come in, she said, phlegmatically. The door opened, and in the aperture appeared the figure of the butler, with a coal-box in his hand. My horror-struck eyes were rivetted on him, but I could not stir hand or foot. To what purpose if I had? Were not we alone in the house with him—we two wretched, defenceless women?

Mrs. Smith had, as in my dream, moved to the other side of the room, to the piece of furniture with drawers at which I had seen her standing. Then she looked over her shoulder and said, composedly, "Thank you, Harris; we do not want any more coal tonight." Then, as he seemed, or seemed to me, to hesitate, she added quietly, "I shall not require anything more tonight; you may go to bed."

Could I believe my eyes? Was he really retreating; shutting the door after him? Were those his footsteps, whose lessening sound I heard along the passage? For a moment everything grew dark before me. I clutched the arms of my chair, to assure myself that this was reality and no dream. Then I staggered to my feet, and towards Mrs. Smith.

"Is he gone?" asked I, in a hoarse whisper.

"Gone!" repeated she, in astonishment, all her old doubts as to my soundness of mind rushing back in flood. "Yes, of course he is gone! Why not?"

"And he will not come back?" still in that husky whisper.

"Of course not. I told him I needed nothing more tonight. I think"—eyeing me distressfully—"that you really had better go to bed; you seem a little—a little—feverish!"

"Yes," said I, making an effort to recover some decent amount of composure, "perhaps I am; I will go to bed if you are quite—quite sure—"

She looked so really alarmed at my manner and words that I did not finish my sentence. I followed her, still shaking in every limb, to my bedroom, when she left me; and into which, I am almost certain, though she tried to do it as noiselessly as possible, that she locked me. For hours after she left me, I remained, sunk in the armchair by the fire, into which I had almost fallen on entering. I still shook as if ague-struck, and every now and again I held my breath to listen—to listen for that stealthy step which even now I felt must come;—for the noise of that awful thud which still sounded so loudly in the ears of my imagination that I could not even yet believe that it neither had, nor ever would have, any echo in a real sound.

At length I dropped into an uneasy doze, from which I was awoke by a sensation of extreme cold, to find the fire black out and the temperature of the room at or below freezing point. I rose and threw myself, dressed, upon the bed, and, wrapping myself in a fur cloak, fell into a heavy sleep, from which I was only roused by the eight o'clock entry of the housemaid.

On first opening my bewildered eyes I could not recollect where I was, but stared round wonderingly at the unfamiliar room. Then recollection came upon me with a rush, and I buried my face in the pillow. Oh, why had I ever woke again? Why had day ever had the inhumanity to dawn again upon such a candidate for Earls Wood? As the details of the previous day's incidents came back upon me with brutal vividness, I called to the rocks to fall upon me and the mountains to cover me!

Had anyone since the world first began, ever written themselves down so egregious an ass? Befooled by an idiotic dream; misled by a fancied resemblance of trivial circumstances, floundering deeper and deeper into the quagmire of unreason, which had landed me at last, fully dressed, on this strange bed, and with the appalling prospect before me of having to go down and meet Mrs. Smith at breakfast.

She would probably and wisely meet me with a lunatic asylum-keeper and a strait waistcoat. And my children, my servants, my husband, how should I ever look any one of them in the face again? I writhed. But writhing did not help me. I had seen the housemaid's astonished glance at my full-dressed condition, a fresh proof of my insanity, which would, no doubt, be conveyed to Mrs. Smith.

I must get up. I must go down and appear as soon as I could. That was all that was now left me. And that much I did. With what inward grovelling, mentally though not apparently on all fours, I entered that dining-room will never be known save only to myself. She came to meet me, civil, dull, unemotional; though I thought I caught a look of lurking apprehension still in her eye.

Stupid woman! Why could not she have been shot through the head, and fallen with that thud I had expected of her? I felt a sort of anger against her for standing there so stolid and sound after having wrought me such irremediable woe.

Oh, that breakfast! Shall I ever forget it? How did I live through it; through it and the moments that followed it, and the leave-taking? At the latter I do not think that I said anything. My tongue clave to the roof of my mouth. I had just sense left to give her my hand stupidly, and to notice the look of scarcely subdued joy and relief on her face at seeing the last of me.

She sent me in her carriage as far as Salcote, which I thought she looked upon as the surest method of being rid of me. At Salcote I got into my own brougham, and returned home a sadder, if not a wiser, woman. Reader, will you despise me very much if I tell you that I cried the whole way, and that on reaching my own fireside I gathered my children about me and made a clear breast of my folly to them? They took my confession characteristically.

Alice said that if I had taken her advice I should have been spared a great annoyance.

Ruth said that all dreams were nonsense, and reverted to her own puerile one, which even at that moment of humiliation I felt wounded at having paralleled with mine.

And Sue, dear Sue, held both my hands fast in hers, and said she should have done precisely the same in my case.

But I refused to be comforted, the more so as it turned out that the most valuable of the carriage horses had caught in the cold White Hart stables an influenza which was rapidly developing into inflammation of the lungs. But even without that final straw I had sunk hopelessly in my own esteem.

### POSTSCRIPT

Just a year later the public was shocked by the account of a murder which, in its circumstances, exceeded the measure of brutality usually connected with such crimes.

It was the murder of a lonely old maiden lady by her butler—a butler to whom, as it appeared, she had been in the habit of showing exceptional kindness.

I read the account with about the same degree of shuddering disgust, I suppose, as my neighbours; but without any feeling of a personal character until it transpired, in the course of the evidence, that the murderer's name was Harris—a name by which I had once, and once only, heard Mrs. Smith of Longmains address her butler.

I dismissed the thought at once as far as I was able. Had not I had enough of giving the reins to my imagination? Was not Harris an extremely common name, almost as common as Smith? But when the trial came on, which, as the crime had been committed shortly before the Assizes, it did very soon after the committal to prison, I, perhaps, unknown almost to myself, followed it with a keener interest than, but for this trifling circumstance, I should have done.

The trial was a short one; the evidence overwhelming; the man found guilty, condemned and executed, without any sentimentalist being found to petition the Home Secretary in his favour.

On the evening before his execution, he made to the Gaol Chaplain a full confession of his crime; and not only of that one which brought him to the gallows, but of a previous one which he had been prevented from carrying beyond the stage of intention by a curious accident. What that curious accident was you shall hear, and judge of my feelings on reading the following extract from the murderer's confession:—

In January of last year, I was living in the service of Mr. Smith of Longmains. I was at very low water at the time, over head and ears in debt, and did not know where to turn for money which I wanted desperately and felt that I must obtain by fair means or foul. My chief inducement for entering Mr. Smith's service had been that I had accidentally heard that he was in the habit of keeping considerable sums of money in the house, for the purpose of paying the weekly wages of the workmen employed upon some extensive drainage works which he had undertaken. I thought, on reaching Longmains, that I had never seen a house better adapted to my purpose. It was as lonely a spot as I have ever seen; the stables at an unusual distance from the hall, and no dwelling-house within less than a quarter of a mile. The establishment consisted, as to men, of myself and one footman; but about a week after my arrival the footman fell ill, and had to be sent home.

I had not yet matured my plans, though I had ascertained that Mr. Smith kept his money in a strong box in his business room, and that in the case of his absence, Mrs. Smith had charge of the key, when one morning my master was unexpectedly summoned from home, leaving me alone with my mistress and the female servants in the house.

Such an opportunity, which, very probably, might not soon occur again, was, I felt, not to be lost. Mrs. Smith's habits were such as to favour my project. She usually sat in her *boudoir*, situated in a rather isolated part of the house, until late at night. I made up my mind to wait until the rest of the household had retired, and then to go to Mrs. Smith's *boudoir* on the pretext of taking coals for the fire, obtain from her the key of the strong box, by fair means if possible; but if she resisted—and she was a resolute woman—I had determined to shoot her through the head, having provided myself with a revolver for the purpose; furnish myself with as much money as I could get hold of, and make tracks for America. I was prevented from carrying out this intention by a very unlooked for accident.

Late in the afternoon of that day—the weather was extremely bad, snowing hard, with a high wind and bitter cold—a lady arrived in a fly to call on my mistress. I could see that my mistress was greatly surprised when I took in the lady's card; for, as far as I could make out, she was very slightly acquainted with her and lived a matter of twenty miles off.

I have never to this day made out why she came. We all thought she was off her head, and I believe she was. My mistress certainly thought so, all the more when she asked leave to stay the night. I could see that my mistress was very much annoyed, and rather alarmed, but as the lady would not go, there was no help for it; stay she must.

I was a good deal upset at first, as I was afraid her being there would knock my plan on the head, but afterwards I comforted myself with the thought that she would be sure to go to bed early, tired with her long drive, and I should find Mrs. Smith alone in her *boudoir*.

I lit them their bedroom candles in the drawing room at ten, and then went off to wait. I would not risk it till twelve. By that time everyone would be sure to be in bed and asleep. I thought I never had known time go so slowly, but at last the clock pointed to five minutes to twelve. I put my revolver in my pocket, took up the coal-box, went upstairs, and knocked. Mrs. Smith's voice said "Come in," and I opened the door.

What was my horror to find the strange lady still sitting there with my mistress? The sight of her took me so aback that I did not know whether to come in or not, and as I was hesitating, Mrs. Smith said, 'We do not want any more coals; you may go to bed, Harris,' or something like that. And all the while the strange lady was staring at me so oddly, as white as a ghost, that I began to think she must have somehow found out what I was after. Her being there and her looking at me like that, altogether made me feel so queer that I actually shut the door and went away again. I thought I would put it off till next night.

But on the following day Mr. Smith returned, and I never had another chance!

I had no sooner reached this last word than I rose to my feet. I was certainly a yard taller than when I sat down.

"Girls!" said I, calling to them in a voice of solemn authority, and as they gathered round. "Be so good as to read those paragraphs," pointing to them with my finger. I watched their faces as they did so, and when they had finished, I said, turning to Alice, in a voice of more than mortal dignity, "You see that wisdom is justified of her child!"

I was interrupted by the door opening and a lady rushing past the footman to precipitate herself into my arms. It was Mrs. Smith of Longmains come to thank me for having saved her life, and to apologise with tears for having ever thought me ripe for Bedlam.

# Rent Day

Two men were riding slowly along a muddy country lane on a mild February afternoon. The younger was in pink, and a large stain on one shoulder, an irretrievably damaged hat, and a lame horse proved that he had not escaped some of the casualties incident to the chiefest among the *"plaisirs étranges"* of the Anglo-Saxon male. The question which he was putting as to the number of miles still left for him to traverse before reaching a railway station, which he named—to traverse at the foot-pace rendered necessary by the condition of his horse—proved him to be a stranger in the neighbourhood. The other, a hardy old man, to whom one would not have given the nigh eighty years of which he had just been boasting to his chance-met companion, was jogging along on a fat cob nearly as old—with relation to the smaller dole of life allotted to horses than to men—as himself.

"I can show you a short cut that will save you a good three miles. Turn in at this gate to the left, and cross that pasture as far as the copse, then into the Denbury Road, which you must follow for a few hundred yards; then take the second—no, the third, turn to the right. But stay, I had better come with you and show you the way myself—it will be safer. Oh, no apologies—time is no great object to me!"

The person addressed, conscious of an ominous feeling that, left to his own unaided instincts, the short cut was destined to have but an ironical sound for him and his poor limping animal, which was not even his own, but a friendly mount, felt too heartily grateful for the old man's offer to make any but a very slender protest against the trouble it entailed upon him. They crossed the pasture to the copse; entered the highroad; left it; and after many devious turns and twists through by-lanes and bridlepaths, farmyards and spinneys, found themselves once again in a highroad, and faced by the gates and stone-dolphin topped pillars of what was evidently a place of some importance.

The old squire rode up to the gates, through whose elegant wrought-ironwork peeps of an Elizabethan house standing at a little distance were visible; and the other followed him, protesting somewhat, and asking —

"But is not this private property? Shall not we be trespassing?"

"I think you will find that we are not taken to task," answered the other, drily, stooping from his cob, and trying with fingers and whip handle to pull up the bolt that secured the two leaves of the portal. But it was so stiff that the younger man had to dismount and come to his aid. The bolt yielded at last and they passed through, the stranger wondering a little at the evidence of long disuse in the rusty fastening, and still more so in the high, white last year's grasses that had grown up, and now limply waved right across the entrance. Similar grasses—nay, more, what amounted to grass—covered the approach, along which it was evident that no wheeled vehicle, nor apparently any human foot, had for many months passed.

"Is the place uninhabited?" asked the stranger, in surprise, and looking with a startled admiration at the noble old dwellinghouse, which, gabled and black framed, stood at the end of the approach, within two hundred yards of the king's highway, as so many houses of that date did; causing one to wonder whether in those happy days of elbow-room and leisure there were few passers-by to stare in upon their privacy, or that privacy itself was a gift less prized in that simpler period.

He had no sooner put the question than he felt it to have been a superfluous one.

Uninhabited? Well, it was hardly likely that any dweller, save the bat, the owl, and the hawk, would care to inhabit a house where scarce a whole pane of glass survived in the diamonded casements; when through the vacancies thus made could be seen fragments of the beautiful Tudor ceilings lying on the uneven boards of the bare oak floors; when the wind could be heard sighing dolorously through the lady's bower, and the flutter of owls' wings, disturbed by the sound of the horses' feet, from the banqueting hall. And yet it was evident that it was not because it had become unsafe for human habitation that the house had been abandoned.

The walls still stood stout and firm, as when the Tudor roses in the great-nailed hall door had been copied—with a difference—from blooming ones; the roof still showed a compact array of slim red tiles, though the vivid moss and the ingenious lichen had made them their own; the graceful cluster of slender chimneys was still ready to transmit the fumes of baked meats to the thin bluish air above them. But it was evidently long since they had been used, except as nesting-places for jackdaws. The problem of the desertion of a house, at once so beautiful and, despite the neglect to which it had been subjected, so easily to be again fitted for human habitation, seemed insoluble; and the younger man, forgetting his lame horse and his train, looked with interested inquiry at his companion for *le mot de l'énigme.*

"I do not understand," he said. "What does it mean? Why is such a fine specimen of early Tudor architecture given over to the bats and owls?"

His companion gave vent to a sound between a laugh and a sigh.

"A good many people beside you have asked that question," he said; "it has puzzled the countryside for some years, and it was only the other day that the cause of it transpired. But it is a long story," he added, without attempting to enter upon it; either really shirking a relation which he must have so often been called upon to make; or with that wish to be pressed for his reminiscences which is an old man's coquetry. "You will not have too much time if you wish to get to Holmhurst Station by daylight."

"Could not you give me a short abstract of it before our roads part?" asked the younger man; but his companion for the moment did not seem to hear. He was sitting with the reins on his cob's neck, staring up at one particular window on the second-floor, above which a row of swallows' nests showed under the eaves and between the grotesquely carved oak heads that ornamented the spouts.

"That was the old lady's bedroom," he said; "the old lady—the late man's mother, you know. She was a good-plucked one if ever there was. I have known that old woman live for a whole winter quite alone in this old barrack—that winter of '-6, when, for some reason or other, she had to retrench, and had reduced her establishment to three or four maid-servants and a little page boy, a poor little chap who was so frightened of the bogies that he had to get the maids to put him to bed."

The narrator stopped to chuckle at this recollection, and then went on:—

"It is a lonely sort of place, and in that particular winter there were a great number of burglaries committed in the neighbourhood, and the police had entirely failed to get hold of the burglars. One morning, the maids and Alfred—Alfred was the page's name—I do not know why I remember it—were frightened out of their wits by finding the footmarks of a man in the snow, going all round the house.

Probably he was only someone who had taken a drop too much to keep out the cold, and lost his way on his road home from Market Brigton; but nothing would have persuaded them of that, and they begged the old lady, with tears in their eyes, to get at least one of the bailiff's men—she had put down her stables too—to sleep in the house. Not a bit of it! She took a revolver to bed with her, and told the frightened women and boy, if the thieves came, to direct them to her room, and if the sight of her in her nightcap did not scare away the boldest burglar that ever handled a 'jemmy,' her name was not Jane Winstanley! Oh, she was a fine old lady!"

"Then it was not in her lifetime that the place was deserted?" asked the other, endeavouring by this question to recall the old gentleman to a topic that interested him more than the valour of any previous owner of the Manor House.

"Oh, bless your heart, no, she lived and died here."

As he spoke, he picked up the reins off his cob's neck, and saying, "We really ought to be going," put his horse in motion again; then, shaking his head several times as he took a final look at the solitary pile, standing almost pathetical in its desolation against the evening heaven—

"I was very fond of her, dear old lady, and though you would not think it to look at it now, I have spent some of the jolliest days of my life under that roof-tree; but I said then, I say now, and I shall say to my dying day, that it was one of the worst cases."

"That! What was one of the worst cases?" asked the other, extremely *intrigué*—a word for which I find no precise English equivalent, or I would not employ it—by this enigmatic utterance.

They were riding by this time slowly down another grass-grown drive.

"Oddly enough I was in the house at the time when it happened."

"When what happened? You forget," with a faint tinge of impatience, "that I am quite in the dark as to what you are alluding to."

The narrator waved his hand slightly, with a deprecating gesture:

"I am coming to it, I am coming to it! You must not hurry me, and you will have plenty of time between here and Holmhurst —for though I cannot promise to go quite as far as the town itself with you, I will set you well on your way—to hear a longer story than mine."

He paused for a moment, then began—

"It must be nine-and-twenty years ago—no, thirty—no, I am wrong, twenty-nine—it will be twenty-nine years ago, the end of

September, since I was staying there for a shooting party. The old lady had some very pretty shooting—it is all let now, to a button-maker from Birmingham, who brings down a pack of commercial gents every year—and we assembled on the 28th of September, because Mrs. Winstanley liked to have a jolly gathering round her on her rent day. She had been left a widow very young, had complete control over the estate—she was an heiress—and the children—of whom there were four, two of each sex—and I suppose what had begun in being a necessity, ended in choice—I mean her high-handed way of ordering and managing everything about the place, including the boys, even after they had left school.

"They had been so used to it that they did not seem to feel it, and I suppose to them she had always appeared father and mother in one. I always told her that she was much more like a man than a woman, and she took it as a compliment, and dressed to the part. Often and often, when I have met her driving her dogcart in a billycock hat and a frieze coat, I have really thought she was one of the farmers, until I got quite close up to her. You could not please her better than by telling her so, and indeed she had a great deal more practical knowledge of land than the majority of them. She never would have an agent, but managed her property—it was not very large and was very compact—with the help of a bailiff, a rough fellow enough—she had a horror of what she called a fine gentleman—whom she ruled with a rod of iron. It was one of her favourite sayings that Mr. Briggs's axiom was hers, '*If you want a thing done, do it yourself.*'

"Among the things which she always insisted on applying her rule to was the collection of her own rents. Nothing would have induced her to depute it to her bailiff, though she had a faith, which sometimes appeared to her friends exaggerated, in his honesty. It was before these pleasant days, when almost every poor devil of a landowner has to return 20 or 30 *per cent.* to his tenants every rent day, and look as if he liked it.

"She was a good landlord; you scarcely ever saw a farm-building out of repair, or a cottage that was not tight and weather-proof, on her property. She generally, in consequence, succeeded in getting a good class of tenants, and they mostly paid up to a penny; so that, unlike what she would have done had she been alive now, she herself enjoyed her rent day, and had always some stock job on-hand with three or four of the principal tenants, to show the pleasant feeling that subsisted on both sides.

215

"For years she had made it a habit to have a houseful for Michaelmas; a houseful which was expected to stay on well into the week of the 1st. And the neighbourhood had grown to regard the dance with which the party concluded in the light of as fixed an event as the recurrence of Michaelmas itself. Thirty years ago, we were less sophisticated and more stay-at-home than in the present day, and, at least in this neighbourhood, people did not go to Scotland nearly so much, nor stay there nearly so late as they do now, so that by the end of September most of the houses had refilled for the winter.

"On the occasion I speak of the old lady was in great spirits—she was a most sociable soul, and at that time not really old—because she had succeeded in collecting an even larger number than usual of gay young people: college friends of the elder son, brother officers of the younger one—he had just joined the ——th Hussars—young lady friends of the girls; the old house where the bats and the jackdaws have had it all their own way for ten years was crammed from attic to cellar. Sprinkled among the boys and girls were a few cronies of her own, that she 'might have a little age and ugliness to keep me in countenance among so much youth and beauty,' as she told me in her blunt way; and it was on that footing that I happened to be there.

"Among the Oxford friends of Frederic, the elder boy, there was one of the name of Armitage, whom Mrs. Winstanley always said she never could make out, nor what was the attraction that bound him to her boy. He was not much of a sportsman, nor did he ever contribute any jokes or any accomplishments to the general fund of entertainment; he had no personal beauty to make his silence forgivable, and nobody seemed to know anything of his origin or social status. But yet he was treated by Frederic with a deference, and obviously exercised over him an influence, quite out of proportion to his apparent merits, and which provoked surprised comments from his other and less made-much-of, while conscious of being more attractive, friends.

"What made it odder was that if Armitage was a man unlikely to inspire enthusiasm, Frederic was the last person one would have expected to manifest it. He was a quiet, humdrum, rather negative fellow, who so far had gone through his Oxford career quite without *éclat*, but also quite without scandal. The younger son, Randal, though less colourless than his brother, was of a rather neutral-tinted character too, and I remember their mother saying to me once, *apropos* of both, 'I used always to be told that two negatives make an affirmative; but in the case of the boys' father and me, two affirmatives have succeeded in making two negatives.' Still, though she had this little fling at them, she was a most tender doting mother, and quite wrapped up in her children.

"It was the day before the rent day—glorious weather—the old lady always piqued herself upon her weather, real Queen's weather. The young ones, that is to say the men, were all going off to a cricket match, and we were most of us in the hall, where you saw just now through the window the ceiling lying in patches on the floor, waiting for the brake, which was to take the cricketers, to come round. We were looking over the morning papers, when one of the men said from between the sheets of the journal he held, 'I see that Mademoiselle Vel Vel has come to grief at last.'

"I had no particular interest in Mademoiselle Vel Vel, who was a trapeze performer of great note in those days, and had awoke notoriety still more marked; but as the man spoke I just lifted my eyes from my own paper. Armitage happened to be leaning against the chimney-piece opposite to me, so that my eyes could not help lighting on him, and I was struck by seeing him give a sort of involuntary start, and by noticing a wave of—I could not tell what sort of emotion, but it was a strong one—rush over his face, which was usually as expressionless as a mask.

"It was gone in a second, and I noticed that he looked hastily round the room, as I supposed, to discover whether anyone had observed his change of countenance. The next moment the youth who had first given the piece of information lifted up his voice again: 'Oh, I see that it was not much of an accident after all: it was not one of her high performances, in fact it was one of the lowest ones; so she fell into the net and was only a little shaken, so little that she was able to resume her feats later in the evening.' I could not resist the impulse of curiosity which prompted me to glance again at Armitage to see how this news, so reassuring to the admirers of Mademoiselle Vel Vel, affected him. But he had baulked me by moving away out of sight.

"'Vel Vel!' cried one of the daughters of the house, who had just entered the room to speed the departing cricketers. 'Is that the lady who walks along the ceiling like a fly? Oh, *how* I should like to see her! Frederic! Randal! one of you must take me to see her when next we go to London.'

"'Have you seen her diamonds?' asked the young man who had first introduced the subject. 'They really are a sight! I believe she has a couple of policemen told off on purpose to protect her when she wears them; she has had her portrait painted, with them all on, on purpose to show them. You can't put a pin's point between them! You never saw such a spectacle in your life!'

"Oh, *how* I should like to see them!' rejoined the same girl who had spoken before. 'And is she beautiful too?'

"But Mrs. Winstanley broke in rather severely, 'Come, come, I think we have had quite enough of her, and you ought to be setting off.'

"I was not much surprised, as I knew that our hostess very much disliked the practice—not so common then as now—of discussing the doings and triumphs of women of dubious reputation in the presence of ladies. Not that the word *dubious* applied to Mademoiselle Vel Vel. There was nothing dubious about her. The theme was of course dropped like a hot potato, and the cricketers got into their brake and started. They were late in returning, as the match was played at a distance of twenty or thirty miles away, and entailed a railway journey, so that we did not sit down to dinner till near nine. I do not know why I remember the circumstance, as it had no bearing on after events.

"The party had come back in high feather, as their eleven had carried off the honours of the day; and for the first half of dinner the talk ran wholly on runs, and scores, and catches. But towards the middle of the meal, the topic—rather to the relief of the non-cricketing part of the company—changed. I had taken our hostess into dinner, but at the moment her attention and her talk were given to her other neighbour—one of Randal's brother officers. Poor fellow, he was killed at Rorke's Drift long afterwards. I was not speaking at the moment, so overheard what they were saying. It was about the rent day, which, as I have said, was the next one. It was the young soldier's first visit, so that he was ignorant of Mrs. Winstanley's habit of collecting her own rents, and she was narrating her mode of procedure.

"'*If you want a thing done, do it yourself*, as Mr. Briggs says.' I heard her uttering this to me very familiar formula, with a jolly laugh. 'And I have no opinion of middlemen! I wish to be brought as often as possible into personal relation with my people. Agents, like all go-betweens, are very apt to misrepresent, either intentionally or unintentionally; and misunderstandings are far less likely when the dealings between landlord and tenant are direct.'

"'And you have the rents paid here in this house?'

"'Yes, in my business room. I shall be sitting there from eleven o'clock tomorrow. I assure you I quite enjoy it; several of the largest farmers are old friends, and have been from father to son, and I like having my joke with them for old sakes' sake.'

"'But when the rents are paid in, what do you do with the money? You surely do not keep it in the house?'

"'Just for the night I do; and the next morning I take it myself to the bank.'

"'But is it not rather risky keeping so large a sum for even one night?'

"'Oh, I do not think so; at least not more so than any of the ordinary actions of one's life. Of course there is a certain risk in doing anything. While one is walking along a lane a pitchfork may fall out of a hay-wain and kill one; as happened to a man in the neighbourhood last year; but that is scarcely a reason for never walking along a lane again.'"

"Mrs. Winstanley said this rather impatiently, so nobody liked for the moment to pursue the subject, though on the other hand I think that no one was convinced by such a line of argument.

"She herself resumed: 'I keep it in a safe in my own bedroom, and I always put the key under my pillow, so any burglar will have to wake me out of my beauty sleep, and hear a few plain words from me and my revolver, before he gets hold of it!'

"We all listened in a silence not untinged with respect for this valiant utterance. The servants had been in the room during the whole of the conversation; but at this point the requirements of service had taken them all for a moment or two out of the room in the interval between two courses. The conversation, or rather the interest in it, had ceased to be confined to our hostess's immediate neighbours, and had spread lower down the table. Armitage, who was sitting about midway, here put in his oar.

"'Are not you rather rash,' he asked, leaning forward and lowering his voice a little, 'to talk so openly of where you keep the money and all the details you gave us before the servants?'

"Mrs. Winstanley broke into an almost derisive laugh. 'I should quite as soon think of suspecting myself as old Britton the butler; as to the two footmen, I have known them both from infancy; John's mother was my maid for years when she and I were girls. William's family have lived on the estate since George the II.'s reign, and Frederic's man——' But here she broke off, interrupted by the re-entrance of the persons of whom she was speaking; and whether she had had enough of the topic, or that she simply forgot all about it, neither she nor any of the. rest of us took it up again. We all went to bed rather early that night, as the cricketers after their long day did not seem inclined for the usual dancing and games.

"The rent day, I remember, dawned rather wet, but improved as it went on—that is to say as regards weather, for in other respects it needed no improvement, having been perfectly satisfactory from the beginning, as at that halcyon epoch rent days not uncommonly were. It ended up with an influx of country neighbours to dinner, and an evening of *tableaux*, Dumb Crambo, and general boisterous fun. They were prolonged so late that it must have been two o'clock before the whole household was in bed; and the consequence was the natural one, that we were later than usual next morning in coming down to breakfast."

"What!" cried the listener in a disappointed tone, "then there was no burglar after all?"

The narrator did not answer directly this interpellation, but went on.

"Late as we were, and very much contrary to her usual practice, our hostess was later still, and the laziest of us was half way through his breakfast before she appeared. We all got up of course to greet her; and the man who had sat by her at dinner the night before—Browne was his name, and he was rather a favourite of hers—made her a facetious sort of bow, and said—

"'I congratulate you.'

"She gave a start—I remembered long, long afterwards, when the whole thing came out, that I had noticed it at the time—and said in a queer voice—

"'Upon what?'

"'Why, upon having bested the burglar once again. I mean, having got through another rent night without his help,' replied Browne, still jocose. He was a rather thick-skinned fellow. She gave a laugh which sounded even queerer than her question, and almost pushed past him to her place at the top of the table. I was surprised for the moment, but in the course of the next few minutes forgot the circumstance entirely; and nothing occurred till many years afterwards to recall it to my mind. The shooting was that year exceptionally good; but for some reason which we could not fathom, the party went off less brilliantly than it had promised to do.

"There seemed a languor about it, and a want of go, which we all felt without being able to explain. And I remember, when the day for breaking up came, my surprise at my own most unwonted feeling of relief at turning my back on a house which I had never before quitted without unfeigned regret. The feeling seemed shared by Mrs. Winstanley herself, for on my taking leave of her she uttered none of her usual hearty hopes that I would come again; and I felt concerned at the idea that I might have unwittingly forfeited her good graces, until on comparing notes with my fellow guests I found that all, without exception, had left her with the same impression."

"But the explanation?—the *mot de l'énigme?*" cried the other still more impatiently than before, judging by the flight of time and the sinking of the sun that his goal would be reached before anything but the preliminaries of the story thus unnecessarily drawn out had been arrived at.

"I am coming to it! I am coming to it!" replied the old gentleman in a pacifying tone; then, turning in his saddle, so as to look full at his companion, he asked in an impressive voice—

"Shall I tell you what really happened on that night, while we were all comfortably asleep in our beds?"

"But do, pray do!"

"The old lady—I keep calling her the old lady, though at that time she could not have been much past fifty—went up to her room with the rest of the ladies; but as she dawdled a good deal over her undressing, she heard the men come up from the smoking-room before she got into bed. The money from the rent had been deposited in the safe as soon as the last payment had been made; and she was just going to put the key under her pillow as usual, when she suddenly altered her mind. A fragment of the conversation at dinner recurred to her, *viz.*, Armitage's remark as to the rashness of her being so communicative in the presence of the servants.

"'After all, I do not really know much about Frederic's man,' she said to herself. 'Perhaps it is best to be on the safe side!'

"So, for the first time in her life, instead of putting the key in its usual place, she hid it in a little japanned box, which she deposited under a heap of handkerchiefs and gloves in a drawer of her wardrobe. 'He will never dream of looking for it there!' was her thought; and then she got into bed, and fell asleep almost at once, her last waking impression being one of self-derision at her needless precaution. She had no fire in her bedroom, but as she actually disliked darkness, always slept with her blinds drawn up and her curtains pulled back.

"In addition, she always had one of the old-fashioned rushlights burning in a green tin shade like a tower, with round holes like windows, through which the light played extraordinary tricks. Perhaps you are too young to remember them, but in my boyhood, they were very general, and left an impression upon my childish memory more terrifying than the most Egyptian darkness could have produced.

"On the night of which I speak there was no moon, and the stars were obscured by clouds, so Mrs. Winstanley had only her rushlight to depend on. She was dreaming a tiresome plaguing sort of dream that she was doing up her household accounts at the bureau in her *boudoir*, and that she was prevented from getting her entries added up right by the fact of someone—she was not clear who—distracting her attention by walking up and down the room, when she suddenly found that she was wide awake, and that though she was neither in her *boudoir*, nor yet doing her accounts, yet that somebody was undoubtedly moving about the room. At first, she could not even be sure that it was somebody—it might be something, a dog or cat.

"As it kept out of the region where the rushlight had sway, she could at first be certain of nothing, save that some live thing was stirring near her, creeping about with a species of caution which soon convinced her that her visitor was human. No sooner had she become assured of this than she stretched out her hand—taking excessive care to make not the least noise in doing it—for the loaded revolver which she always kept, with matches and candlestick, on the table at the side of her bed. The box of matches and the candlestick were still there, but—there was no mistake about it—the revolver was gone! In an instant the thought flashed through her mind—this stealthy unknown thing must have known that it was there, and had removed it while she slept.

"How could he have been acquainted with her habits, unless—— The image of Frederic's man darted before her mind's eye, and with it a lightning-quick recollection of someone a day or two ago having remarked that he had a bad countenance. The thought that it was one of the inmates of her own house, at whose absolute mercy she now lay, coupled with the discovery that she was in far worse case than being merely disarmed, since her own murderous weapon would certainly be used against her, almost paralysed her, plucky as she undoubtedly was. How he had got into the room without sooner awaking her, since she distinctly remembered having drawn the night bolt before retiring to bed, struck her in the midst of her terror with wonder.

"She was quite incapable of uttering a sound which would be

audible to any of the no doubt profoundly sleeping household, and the bell-rope hung by the fireplace on the opposite side of the room. When she realised this last fact the very extremity of her danger restored to her some part of that presence of mind on which she was wont to be complimented by her friends. She recollected stories she had heard of persons who, under similar circumstances, had saved their lives by feigning sleep, and determined to imitate them, and not by the slightest movement to betray herself. She even shut her eyes all but the tiniest chink.

"The object of her alarm had by this time moved within the radius of the rushlight's influence, and she could make out that he had the shape of a man, though whether her suspicions of his being her son's servant were correct she was unable to judge, as where the face ought to have been there was only a blackness, and with a cold shudder she said to herself that it represented the, to many people, most terrifying feature of a burglary—the crape mask in which it is committed. Through the little slit in her eyes, she saw this blackness turned towards her.

"The man was obviously looking at her, was her first terrified thought, and had discovered that she was not asleep; but next moment she drew a grain of reassurance from the knowledge that since the rushlight was so placed that the light should not fall on the bed, and that it was mercifully a dark night, it was impossible that he could see her. And yet he acted as if he did, for after turning his veiled face to her for a moment or two, she saw him begin to move towards the bed with the same stealthy caution as had characterised the movements which had first aroused her.

"The room was a large one, and it seemed to her as if he took a quarter of an hour in stepping round the various obstacles in his way, and drawing one foot after another before he reached the bedside. When he did so, he stopped for a moment and listened. The whole powers of her mind were at that alarming moment, as she related many, many years afterwards, concentrated on the difficult problem of mastering her body, making her breath come evenly, and her heart not jump through her side. She actually tried to recall how sleeping persons draw in and send out their breath, and to mimic them.

"Her powers of self-command were put to their severest test when, having stooped over her so closely that his breath swept her cheek—even at that moment she perceived how hot and panting it was—he slowly and tentatively stole a hand beneath her pillow. There could be no doubt as to what that hand was seeking—the key. This midnight visitor evidently knew her habit of placing it there, a habit which her own insane garrulity had betrayed; and once again the idea of Frederic's man flashed with the almost certainty of its being he before her mind.

"The darkness that enveloped the bed prevented her—even had her wits been sufficiently collected to do so—from ascertaining whether in figure and height he resembled the rather lately engaged valet. And, indeed, her whole senses were so occupied by the apprehension lest that groping hand should discover the madly wakeful thumpings of her heart, as to leave small room for any other emotion. To her strained faculties it seemed as if those greedy searching fingers were full half-an-hour in prying beneath the bolster; first very carefully and gently, as if the fear of rousing the supposed sleeper were the guiding motive. Then as the unsuccess of the quest became obvious, with fewer precautions, as though the balked aim had made all else forgotten.

"When once assured of this, and apparently still quite unsuspecting the feigned character of his intended victim's sleep, the burglar moved away from the bed, and towards the dressing-table, when she half saw in the capricious light, half heard him searching among the toilet objects, and in the silver boxes, evidently for the same key which her change of plan had baffled him in finding. After he had in vain turned them all over, he began to pull out the little drawers in the old-fashioned Chippendale looking-glass, where Mrs. Winstanley kept some of the slighter trinkets that she daily wore, and, once again balked, stood for a moment inactive, and evidently irresolute. Then, with a new, and this time correcter impulse, he turned towards the wardrobe. Having reached it—it was too distant to gain any illumination from the rushlight—she heard him feeling about for the handle of the lock.

"It was some moments before he found it, and she was informed of his having done so by the loud squeaking sound of the hinge of the folding door as it opened, a sound which she had herself been annoyed by for two or three days past, though she had always forgotten to speak to her maid about having it oiled. The noise was followed by another and lesser one, whose purport she could at first hardly credit, but which she soon found, with a relief almost too immense to be realised, was caused by the precipitate retreat of her visitor to the door. The noise made by the unoiled hinge had been so sharp that the burglar had apparently jumped to the conclusion that it must have awakened her, and in that belief had abandoned all idea but that of securing his own retreat. He reached the door, passed through it—it must have been left ajar—and disappeared into the darkness of the passage.

"He was gone, that was beyond doubt; though it was more than possible that he had not retreated further than just outside, where it was likely that he was listening, and that not hearing anything stirring, he might regain courage to return and resume his so far unsuccessful quest. Partly deterred by this icy fear, partly that for a short while she was really incapable of conquering the paralysis of terror left by those groping hands and that murderous breath on her face, Mrs. Winstanley lay perfectly motionless, straining her ears to catch the lightest sound which might reveal whether her deliverance was a real and personal one, or only apparent and momentary.

"She was decided by the fact—her ears were almost sure of it—that a door opened or shut—she could not be certain which—at some distance down the long corridor on which her own room opened. There were no doors in the corridor save those of bedrooms, and in the crowded state of the house not one of them but was occupied. If her late intruder had opened a door, it must be that of some sleeping visitor, or perhaps one of her own children, on whom he was creeping to rob and probably, if opposed, to murder them. This thought restored her to the full use of limbs and faculties. She hastily struck a light, jumped out of bed, threw on a dressing-gown, and ran to the bell.

"She would ring it violently, on the chance of its raising some of the distant servants, and then without any distardly fear for her own safety, would fly down the passage to her eldest son's room. A confused recollection of there having been some question of his giving up his bedroom to one of his friends—Armitage was it?—flashed across the mother's mind, but was driven thence by the discovery that the bell rope had been cut. Probably it had already been done—without her discovering it—when she went to bed.

"She flew to the door—a touch revealed to her that the screws of the night bolt had been loosened—and down the passage. As she neared Frederic's room, she saw a thin stream of light issuing from it. The sight filled her with a new terror. The suspicion she had already felt that the burglar was none other than Frederic's man became a conviction. And now, baffled in his prime effort, he had gone to his master's room to rob and, if resisted, almost certainly murder him. That he would be resisted—that her boy would not tamely allow himself to be despoiled, without making a desperate fight, she had not a vestige of doubt.

"Her first impulse was to rush in at once; but a second one— both were instantaneous—corrected it. It was possible that Frederic might really be asleep, as she herself had feigned to be, in which case the robber would perhaps withdraw without harming him, whereas her sudden irruption would hasten if not cause his destruction. Adopting, therefore, a different course, she blew out her candle and stole on tiptoe up to the door, which must have been carelessly closed or left intentionally ajar, as a chink quite wide enough to look through remained open. Holding her breath, she crept up to it and peeped through."

The old gentleman paused, either because he was out of breath, or with a dramatic intention.

"And saw what?" asked the other, eagerly.

"She saw," pursued the old gentleman, with tantalising slowness, "a young man standing with his back half turned towards her, taking off a crape mask!"

"The valet? Frederic's man?"

"No!" shaking his head, "not Frederic's man; her first glance told her that the person was not of the height or build of the unjustly suspected servant. Her second impression was that the change of rooms which had been suggested before the party assembled had been made, and that the burglar was Armitage. But she had scarcely time for the momentary shock caused by this idea, when, reflected in a glass on the other side of the room, she saw with perfect clearness the features—by this time freed from their disguise—of her own eldest son Frederic!"

"Good heavens!"

"She supposed, afterwards, that she must have made some slight movement—she said she was certain that she had uttered no groan or cry—for he gave a great start, and came quickly to the door and opened it wide, and saw her; and she walked in, and they stood looking at each other for what seemed two years. He was whiter than any ashes, and shaking all over as with the rigors of a violent fever; but she was turned into a stone. It was, or seemed, a long while before she was able just to lift her finger and point to the crape mask, which had been thrown down on the table, and to her own revolver which lay beside it. It was a still longer while before she could bring out the four husky words, 'What does this mean?'

'The only answer she got at first was an increase of the awful shaking which already convulsed Frederic's whole body, as he held by the table, evidently scarcely able to stand; then, all in a moment, he had fallen in a heap at her feet, and burying his face in the carpet broke into horrible sobs. The sound had the effect of turning her back from stone into flesh again.

"'Hush!' she said, authoritatively, 'hush! you will rouse the house.'

"He had always been so used to obey her that even at such a moment the habit of a lifetime asserted its power, and he made a convulsive effort to control the violence of his sobs. The exercise of her own familiar authority had given her back the use of her voice,

"'It is true, then?' she said, in a low but distinct tone; 'there is no mistake?—it was you?' She could not have believed a negative, even if one had come; but none did, only a writhing movement of the prostrate creature at her feet—that creature, between whom and her own son she could not even yet realise that there was any relation. There was a pause. Then she pointed once again to the revolver.

"'And this?' she asked, 'did you mean to murder me with it if I resisted?'

"Again, no answer, but that awful grovelling on the floor before her. The poor woman felt as if something in her own brain was giving way, but she made a tremendous effort to keep hold of her faculties.

"'I do—not—understand! Why—did you do it? You must have had some motive! My—own—son!'

"At these last words, spoken, as she afterwards felt they must have been, in a tone of dazed stupefaction, the wretched boy struggled half up from the ground on to his knees, and flung his arms about hers.

"'I went—mad!' he said, incoherently, in a dreadful unnatural voice; 'I had to have the money—it did not matter how I got it—I had to have it!'

"Again, she felt conscious of that something broken inside her heart, and she put up her hand to it.

"'Did—I—ever—refuse—you money?' she asked.

"'No! no!' he answered, gasping; 'I do not say that you ever did, but—it had—to be a large sum—a very large sum—and—if you had known the purpose for which I wanted it, you would not have given me a penny!'

"His words were so broken by breathless gasps that she had great difficulty in catching them.

"'What was the purpose you wanted it for?'

"There was another pause, filled by those terrific sobs; then Frederic lifted his face—such a face—so livid, so wild, that even his own mother, for one instant, scarcely believed it to be his.

"'That—profession of hers,' he said, in words whose wildness seemed to match that of his look; 'that profession of hers! it will be the death of her! Only yesterday that paragraph in the papers about her having been so nearly killed——!'

"A conviction had been growing in Mrs. Winstanley's mind as she listened to these, to her, perfectly meaningless words, that Frederic— save as he had always hitherto appeared—must be labouring under an access of madness, and this new explanation of his conduct deprived her, for the moment, of the power of speech.

"'It will be the death of her,' he rambled on, 'and yet I can't expect her to give it up, unless I can offer her something in exchange; and she is so surrounded—so beautiful—there are so many about her who have far more to offer her than I—that my only chance—my only one—lay in the money!'

"He paused, and his mother, still in the belief that he was under the spell of some hallucination, interposed in the soothing tone one would employ to a person who had lost their wits.

"'You forget that I do not know of whom you are speaking.'

"He lifted his bloodshot eyes to her face.

"'Yes,' he said, 'I forget; she makes me forget everything. I was speaking of Vel Vel.'

"'*Vel Vel!*'

"'Yes, Mademoiselle Vel Vel! You must have heard of her! She is world famous!' (The advertisement adjective coming in with a touch of the ludicrous.)

"'Vel Vel! that infamous mountebank! What has she——'

"'Do not call her names!' cried the miserable boy, flaming up into a momentary fury, then sinking down on the floor again in his first attitude.

"'Yes, yes, call her what you like! she has made a murderer of me! I do not care for anything but her in earth or heaven, or the hell where she is driving me as fast as she can. For the last two days I have not known what I was doing—ever since I got a letter from her telling me that unless I would immediately make some considerable settle-ment on her, she must break with me definitively. Since then, I have not been in my right senses! I have had only one idea, to get out of my misery, to put an end to myself. I had made up mind to blow my brains out, when I heard you telling Armitage about the rents; where you kept the money; where you put the key

"'Armitage!' repeated she, with a flash of something that had almost the complexion of hope. 'It was his idea then? it was he who put it into your head?'

"Her son shook his head.

"'No, no, good God, no! He knew about her! that was why I had him here! He was the one person to whom I could talk about her; but as to this—to this——'

"His voice died off in a groan. There was silence again. He had staggered up to his feet, and, as when she had first come upon him, they stood looking each other in the eyes. She probably at that moment felt nothing at all. The first blow dealt her in the discovery of Frederic's identity with her assailant had been so stunning as to procure her immunity from any after one. She was the first to speak.

"If you have no further need for these tonight,' she said, taking up the revolver and the mask from the table, 'I will, with your permission, carry them away with me.'

"She turned to the door as she spoke, and after relighting her extinguished candle with a hand that did not shake, passed out into the passage, and so back into her bedroom. She must have swooned on getting back there, though not before she had had time to lock the evidence of her son's crime into her bureau, for her maid on coming to call her as usual at seven o'clock, found her stretched insensible on the carpet. The woman—an old servant—knowing her mistress's dislike of any fuss about her own health, lifted her on to the sofa, and without calling in anyone's assistance, restored her to life after a while by the usual methods, methods which in her case had never before been needed.

"Her extreme anxiety on regaining consciousness that no one should be made acquainted with her unwonted seizure, proved to the judicious lady's-maid how right she had been in her estimate of her mistress's wishes, and being gifted with the power of holding her tongue, it was not till many, many years afterwards, when the whole tale had become public property, that she threw her little tribute of light on this dark story.

"Mrs. Winstanley was rather late for breakfast on that particular morning, as I have already said, and did not seem to see much point in her favourite Browne's mild pleasantry about the burglar. Beyond this, no change was perceptible in her. Afterwards, indeed, it was remembered that her correspondence during the succeeding day seemed heavier than usual, that she received and sent a large number of telegrams, and that one day she took a solitary trip to London, of which she gave no explanation. On the day after the party broke up, she sent for Frederic, to whom she had since the night of his attempt addressed just so much conversation as was necessary to avoid exciting the suspicion of the company.

"She was sitting in an armchair in her sanctum as he entered, sitting very upright, and she began to speak at once, as if it were a prepared lesson that she was uttering.

"'I had a nightmare a few nights ago,' she said, 'a nightmare dream. I need not, I think, repeat it to you, and as one's dreams are extremely uninteresting to one's acquaintances, I shall not make it public.'

"He was about to precipitate himself at her feet, when she waved him off with a gesture of repulsion.

"'You will perhaps not be surprised to hear that I do not wish to have that dream repeated. I have taken your passage to Australia in the steamship *Swallow*, which sails from Southampton on the 14th of this month. I have engaged a young man to accompany you as travelling tutor, and I have written to Oxford to the master, to tell him that I wish your name taken off the college books.'

"She had said all this in a perfectly level, unemotional voice, and without looking at him.

"'I have made arrangements with my bankers to pay a certain sum into the hands of an Australian bank, out of which a weekly allowance will be made you for as long as you choose to remain in the colony, but which will cease the instant that you set foot in Europe, leaving you to support yourself by whatever means approve themselves to you. I should, however, hardly recommend you to pursue the trade in which you lately made an essay, as you promise to be but a bungler. Your travelling companion is to arrive tonight, and you set off tomorrow morning under his escort. I need not detain you any longer.'

"She motioned him to the door as she spoke, and he, too cowed and conscience-stricken to get out even one prayer for forgiveness, slunk out like a whipped hound. They never saw each other again.

"We were all rather surprised when we heard that Frederic Winstanley had cut short by one half his Oxford career in order to make a trip round the world—such jaunts being a good deal less common thirty years ago than now. We had almost forgotten to notice how much that trip had prolonged itself—he was, as I have said, a colourless fellow, as we thought—when our memory of him was revived with a vengeance by an announcement in the papers of the marriage at Sydney, New South Wales, of Mr. Frederic Winstanley, son and heir of Mrs. Winstanley of —— Hall, ——shire, to Miss Araminta B. Perkins (better known as Mademoiselle Vel Vel, the world-famous trapeze *artiste*). The whole neighbourhood was thunderstruck—marriages of the adventurous type were less numerous than now. And some among us—I was not one—hastened to call on Mrs. Winstanley, to see how she took it.

"But they did not get much 'change' out of her, as the phrase goes. She had by that time married both her daughters well, and Randal was in India, so that it was natural she should live a more retired life than while she had her children round her. But she still gave shooting parties, even up to the end of her life; only it was noticed that she discontinued her rent day festivities, though she still collected her own rents. She kept up very friendly relations with her neighbours, and there was never a word spoken or heard against her until after her death, when the contents of her will became known, and there was one cry of indignation at its injustice.

"She lived to be an old woman, and only on her deathbed revealed to her younger son the tragedy of her life, a revelation made necessary by his brotherly remonstrance with her upon her intended disposition of her estate."

"Then how did it come to light? Surely, he—Frederic——"

"I am getting to that. Her property was entirely in her own power with one exception, which I will mention; and at her death it was found that after making a handsome provision for her daughters, she had left the whole of it to her younger son Randal. The name of Frederic was no more mentioned than if he had never existed. The one exception to her power of disposal was the house you have seen with an acre or two of garden, which, by some singular legal accident, had been omitted when the entail was cut off. And into possession of it—and it only—Frederic came at his mother's death.

"It was, of course, absolutely useless to him. Being entailed, he could not sell it, and who would take a place of that stamp without a foot of land or a head of game? Randal, as I told you, lets the shooting every year. There was, on this fact being made known, a very strong revulsion of feeling in favour of the excluded son. People forgave him even his disgraceful marriage. After all it was honourable of him in a way to marry his acrobat. He might have done much worse, and escaped quite unpunished. If he had returned to England and this county at that time he would have received quite an ovation, but he never came."

"Then how did the story leak out?"

"It appeared after his death, which occurred in Australia three years ago, that during all the years of his colonial life he had been steadily going from bad to worse. Both he and his Vel Vel took to drinking. He was never in actual want, because since he adhered to the letter of the agreement and did not return to Europe, his mother was too honour-able to discontinue his weekly allowance, even upon his marriage. But he fell into the hands of low associates, to one of whom, in a fit of maudlin penitence not long before his death, he confided the story.

"The scoundrel wrote it down in all its details, made him sign it, and no sooner was the breath out of his body than he flew over here with it in his valise, in the hope of extorting hush-money from Frederic's relatives. But Randal, very sensibly, I think, refused to pay him a penny; so, to vent his spite he had the narrative typewritten, and circulated it among the servants and tradesmen, and so it reached the masters; and that is how the whole thing got out."

"And so that fine old lady's reticence went for nothing?"

"For absolutely nothing. Well, at all events, the tale has beguiled a tedious hour. There is your railway-station straight ahead; you can't possibly miss it. I wish you a good evening."

LEONAUR

# ALSO FROM LEONAUR
## AVAILABLE IN SOFTCOVER OR HARDCOVER WITH DUST JACKET

**MR MUKERJI'S GHOSTS** *by S. Mukerji*—Supernatural tales from the British Raj period by India's Ghost story collector.

**KIPLINGS GHOSTS** *by Rudyard Kipling*—Twelve stories of Ghosts, Hauntings, Curses, Werewolves & Magic.

**THE COLLECTED SUPERNATURAL AND WEIRD FICTION OF WASHINGTON IRVING: VOLUME 1** *by Washington Irving*—Including one novel 'A History of New York', and nine short stories of the Strange and Unusual.

**THE COLLECTED SUPERNATURAL AND WEIRD FICTION OF WASHINGTON IRVING: VOLUME 2** *by Washington Irving*—Including three novelettes 'The Legend of the Sleepy Hollow', 'Dolph Heyliger', 'The Adventure of the Black Fisherman' and thirty-two short stories of the Strange and Unusual.

**THE COLLECTED SUPERNATURAL AND WEIRD FICTION OF JOHN KENDRICK BANGS: VOLUME 1** *by John Kendrick Bangs*—Including one novel 'Toppleton's Client or A Spirit in Exile', and ten short stories of the Strange and Unusual.

**THE COLLECTED SUPERNATURAL AND WEIRD FICTION OF JOHN KENDRICK BANGS: VOLUME 2** *by John Kendrick Bangs*—Including four novellas 'A House-Boat on the Styx', 'The Pursuit of the House-Boat', 'The Enchanted Typewriter' and 'Mr. Munchausen' of the Strange and Unusual.

**THE COLLECTED SUPERNATURAL AND WEIRD FICTION OF JOHN KENDRICK BANGS: VOLUME 3** *by John Kendrick Bangs*—Including twor novellas 'Olympian Nights', 'Roger Camerden: A Strange Story', and ten short stories of the Strange and Unusual.

**THE COLLECTED SUPERNATURAL AND WEIRD FICTION OF MARY SHELLEY: VOLUME 1** *by Mary Shelley*—Including one novel 'Frankenstein or the Modern Prometheus', and fourteen short stories of the Strange and Unusual.

**THE COLLECTED SUPERNATURAL AND WEIRD FICTION OF MARY SHELLEY: VOLUME 2** *by Mary Shelley*—Including one novel 'The Last Man', and three short stories of the Strange and Unusual.

**THE COLLECTED SUPERNATURAL AND WEIRD FICTION OF AMELIA B. EDWARDS** *by Amelia B. Edwards*—Contains two novelettes 'Monsieur Maurice', and 'The Discovery of the Treasure Isles', one ballad 'A Legend of Boisguilbert' and seventeen short stories to cill the blood.